The *Unexpected Heir*

By

L.L. Diamond

The Unexpected Heir
By L.L. Diamond
Published by L.L. Diamond
Copyright ©2025 L.L. Diamond

Cover and internal design © 2025 L.L. Diamond
Cover design by L.L. Diamond/Diamondback Covers
Cover art: Regency Woman wearing evening dress and holding fan courtesy of Servian Stock Images
Magical Lights Sparkling in Mysterious Forest at Night by Muamal3f courtesy of Shutterstock
A Graceful White Reindeer walking in the wild by Wirestock Creators courtesy of Shutterstock

ISBN: 978-1-960057-16-7

Facebook: https://www.facebook.com/LLDiamond
Instagram: @l.l.diamond
Bluesky: https://bsky.app/profile/lldiamond.bsky.social
Blog: http://lldiamondwrites.com/
Austen Variations: https://austenvariations.com/

To Brandon:

*Release day for this book marks 27 years
of marriage.
We've survived 3 children and 7 duty stations.
Now we just need to survive retirement!*

I love you!

Author's Note

In writing this book, we learn early on that Elizabeth is the heir, however, even though she is female, she is never referred to as an "heiress." This was a conscious decision on my part. Yes, she is a lady and an heir, and of course, the word heiress did exist at the time, but in the book, she is the first female to inherit magical power. As far as her father and those in the magical world know, she will be the only lady to be an heir. For that reason, she is called an heir as any male would be. Perhaps in time, if another female heir exists, then the terminology might change, but that is why I opted to call Elizabeth an heir instead of an heiress. The decision seemed right and also a way to separate the magical world from the non-magical that exists in the book. I hope you understand and happy reading!

Prologue

21ˢᵗ of December 1791

"I can see the head! Keep pushing, Frances. He is almost here, and he has a full head of thick auburn hair."

Anne's hand smarted as her friend bore down with an ear-splitting scream, the babe slipping into the waiting grasp of the midwife as though the entire process had been the product of minutes and not the long interminable hours that had actually occurred. The woman began to vigorously rub the babe, bringing forth a cry that was, no doubt, heard throughout the house.

"Is it the heir?" asked Frances, her tone urgent. Her grip on Anne's hand just as firm.

The midwife smiled. "You have a beautiful daughter."

Frances's face crumpled. "What? No! This child was supposed to be the heir! What am I going to do with another girl?" Anne's heart sank. She would have been grateful for any child, but Frances had always been fickle. Still, how could anyone not cherish an innocent babe?

The midwife caught Anne's eye and pointed to a distinct mark on the inside of the child's arm. Anne gasped. "I shall clean her up and bring her to her father." Without another word, she took the babe to a table near the fire where she wiped away the remnants of the birth. She turned the child's arm to run a finger over the mark. How was this possible? By all that was known, this was impossible. She shook her head. All she could do was take the little girl to her father and hear his opinion on the matter, so she swaddled her in clean warm blankets. Anne could not help but give a tiny laugh. The wide-eyed little one watched her so intently. She almost seemed to be taking her measure while Anne cared for the infant. She had never seen such an alert newborn.

Once the babe was presentable, Anne gathered her up but paused on the way to the door. "She is truly beautiful. Would you care to hold her?" When Frances turned the opposite direction without uttering so much as a "no," Anne's heart split and bled. She looked down upon the small child in her arms. The poor dear! She had done nothing—except being born a girl.

As Anne departed and made her way down the narrow stairs, the babe's eyes were still open and alert. She brushed her finger down the child's soft cheek. How could anyone not love a baby? Anne had to shove the stirring in her stomach back down where it belonged. She and Frances had been friends for years now, but at this moment, Anne had to forcibly resist the urge to return to the bedchamber and shake the woman. Why was Frances so recalcitrant?

When Anne reached the library, she knocked and was bid enter.

Henry Bennet and Anne's husband, George, jumped to their feet as soon as she stepped inside. "Well?"

She smiled. "You have a beautiful daughter." She held her breath in her lungs while she awaited Bennet's response.

He did no more than frown. "But I saw—"

"She bears the birthmark," said Anne.

Both gentlemen gasped. "Are you certain?" asked Bennet, who hurried forward.

She handed the child to the father and with great care, showed him the four-point star on the inside of the babe's left arm.

"A female has never borne the mark in any family." Bennet's voice was low, as though he whispered to himself.

"She will require protection," said George. "A lady with the abilities of a man will be sought after—will be in great danger from those who would wish to use her for their own purposes." A pang ripped through Anne. Her husband was correct of course. This child would not have an easy time of it. Those who understood the meaning of the mark would do anything to marry her into their families by whatever means necessary.

Bennet dropped back into his chair and stared at his new daughter. "My God. What am I going to do?"

George wagged a finger and took the chair across from his friend. "Do not despair just yet. I think I may have a solution."

Chapter 1

14th of September 1811

The warmth of the sun bathed Elizabeth's face as she wound through the stones, her fingers trailing along the varied textures of the weathered rock. The stone circle was her favourite place to idle away a morning. Here, in the middle of Oakham Forest, she was surrounded by the trees and the gentle caress of the breeze. Few ventured into this wood without reason, and it was a rarity for someone not magical. Most outside of their circles had forgotten this place existed. Over the centuries, the Bennet family had ensured that those other than the people of Meryton had ceased to come here. Outsiders now believed this wood to be haunted. The enchantments and charms she had spent so many hours learning as a child had been successful. Now, she spent countless hours here. Why would she not? This place brought her a solace nowhere else could.

A gentle breeze wound through the forest surrounding her, tickling her flesh while it whispered its secrets into her ear. Here and there, she closed her eyes and listened more diligently in the hopes of catching every nuance. The trees added their own voices with the rustling of the turning and falling leaves, which contributed further to the discourse.

While she meandered, the huge white stag she called Herne stood in the centre watching her. Several sizeable hares also bounded about the clearing. They enjoyed the soft, verdant grass that grew near the edges. Now that autumn approached, their favourite meal was not as abundant as during the warmth of the summer, but that did not deter their search. During some early mornings, she was joined by the local pheasants, but this morning, they seemed to be elsewhere.

When she neared the middle, she pressed her hands on the largest of the stones that appeared to be lying on its side. The enormous rectangular altar hummed under her fingers, which made her flesh prickle. Her eyes fluttered closed, and she allowed the sensation to wash over her.

The stone, whose source of power deep inside the earth ran along the same vein as that at Stonehenge and Avebury, only hummed unless the equinox or the solstice were near. The surrounding rocks here were not as grand as the other stone circles; they barely protruded from the earth, though their magic was no less powerful. The Autumn Equinox was in three days, so the altar should be readying itself. So why was the vibration stronger than she could ever remember?

She straightened and faced Herne. "Time to return."

The stag threw his head up and down with a snort before he followed her from the ring. Every time she left for one of her solitary rambles in the forest, he was her most faithful companion. He met her at the first of the trees where she entered the wood and followed her back when she departed for the day. She was never alone, and at times, he almost appeared to watch more of their surroundings than he did her, but deer often kept an eye out for danger, did they not?

Her bare fingers trailed along the bark of the great oaks as she wound through the trees, her ear still trained on what the earth was willing to reveal. Soon, she met the brook that trickled towards Longbourn and the willow where she spent many hours hiding from the world and reading. How she loved this place! The boughs provided a respite when her home and her four sisters became overbearing. The stone circle did as well, but it did not provide the sense of solitude and security the trailing leaves of the willow provided so generously.

When she reached the edge of the wood, she held up her hand and closed her eyes to whisper the incantation she had recited every time she left Herne. He did not blend into his surroundings like others of his type, and his size and almost silver-white fur made him an obvious target for those brave enough to disregard the tales of ghosts and spectres and seek to kill their dinner within. Since she first found Herne, she had shielded him from the sight of others for his protection. Those who were magical would see him as a messenger from heaven and leave him unharmed. To anyone else, he was easy prey.

Herne touched her hand with his nose and allowed her to stroke his head. He was the most stunning creature she had ever beheld. They had both been young when they first met fourteen years ago, but he had become old while she had merely grown to adulthood. She did not want to consider the day when she came to the forest and he was gone. Her eyes burned at the thought. He was her best friend. What would she do when that day finally arrived?

"If weather permits, I shall return on the morrow."

He nudged back against her palm, then she turned to begin the walk through the field. While she made her way down the well-worn path that led to Longbourn, sheep grazed on what was left of last year's wheat planting, which had been threshed a month prior.

Once she had slipped through the break in the hedgerow, the sounds of her family became discernible. Elizabeth meandered through the herb gardens towards the door to the kitchens. Her mother's high-pitched tone was the most prominent. As soon as she entered Longbourn, Mrs. Hill shook her head.

"Your mother is in a right dudgeon this morning. She has already broken two teacups and sent a muffin flying at your father's head. The teacups I can repair, but unfortunately, I can do naught about your father's pride. Jane has been making every attempt to calm Mrs. Bennet, but your mother is volatile today. If Jane continues to exert herself as she has, she will be worn out before noon."

Elizabeth smiled. Mrs. Hill had been housekeeper at Longbourn since before Elizabeth had been born and had been more of a mother to her than her own. "Papa has not attempted to soothe her?"

"No, he sent for a potion from the apothecary. You know how wearing he finds it to temper your mother's moods. He is not as young as he once was, and I am willing to vow that her fits take more out of him than some of the more powerful magic." Mama had been losing her wits since she had carried Elizabeth, though her father's weariness at tending to his wife's capricious behaviour had stemmed more from his inability to hide himself from the strife rather than to temper the disturbance in the first place.

"I shall see what I can do," said Elizabeth as she made her way to the door.

"Your father will not be pleased if you interfere. Without him in the room to mask your magic, your mother will sense who is inhibiting her, and he will be forced to manipulate her memory once again. You know that only makes her condition worse."

Elizabeth sighed and scrubbed her forehead. "I shall speak to him first then."

The servants' passages of Longbourn were narrow and dark, but she had memorised the way long ago. As soon as she opened the door to the breakfast room, the light from a nearby window blinded her for a moment before she could continue into the parlour.

"Where have you been?" screeched her mother as she entered. The tone was ear-splitting and made Elizabeth wince. Mary took her stack of books and made her escape while Kitty and Lydia giggled as they skipped from the room and out of the front door with titters about the new groom at the inn. Once again, Mama was letting them venture to Meryton alone. Why would Papa not exert himself to stop them?

"I took a walk, Mama," said Elizabeth. "I hope you are well this morning."

A fork from the tea tray rattled then flew at her face. Elizabeth shifted to the side, the fork missing its target and embedding into the wall. Mrs. Hill would need to repair that later as well.

Jane, Elizabeth's elder sister, placed a hand on her mother's arm. "Lizzy walks every morning unless the weather is poor; do you not remember?"

Mama's countenance made a gradual change before she blinked and nodded. "Yes, I suppose." Her forehead furrowed as she turned to Jane. "Why is my mind so muddled?"

Her sister's hand squeezed ever so slightly. "You must not have slept well last night. Perhaps a nap would do you good."

Before her mother could utter a word a maid, hurried over and helped Mama stand. "Come, Mrs. Bennet. I am certain Mrs. Hill can send up one of her nice draughts for you to drink. That should help you sleep."

As soon as Mama departed, Elizabeth sat beside her sister. "You cannot keep exerting yourself on her so. She cannot be dependent upon you to subdue her rages. One day, you will meet a gentleman, fall in love, and wish to marry, and if you continue as you are, you will feel compelled to remain at Longbourn to care for Mama instead of following your heart."

Jane exhaled. "She is losing control more and more. The effort it takes to soothe her agitation has become exhausting. I fear cannot calm her wrath for long anymore. What will become of her if Papa is left to care for her alone?"

"Maybe if I had been a boy. . ." said Elizabeth. "This all began when Papa told her I was to be the heir. Perhaps her lack of control before my birth had been more like excitement, then when she learnt I was a girl, that anticipation became anger."

Her sister's hand landed on her forearm, and she took a quick glance behind her. "Do not even think such a thing. Mama cares for you in her own way. How was she to know you would be the first female heir? Can you imagine? Centuries upon centuries of powerful male magicians, then you shock what everyone has believed for all that time. She was bound to dismiss you at first glance. 'Tis unfortunate she cannot be trusted with the information now."

Elizabeth removed her hand from Jane's. "I can feel the magic trickling through my skin, sister. I do not require your talents to soothe me."

Her sister's shoulders slumped a little. "Forgive me. I had not intended . . ."

"I know. Between Mama and Lydia, you use it too often, so you do not always realise you are influencing our behaviour. Papa sent for a potion from Mr. Jones. Let him and Mrs. Hill manage Mama's moods as much as possible. I understand she will require your taming touch from time to time, but your ability should not be the sole means to maintain her balance. 'Tis not fair to you."

Jane nodded. "Have you seen something of my future I should know?"

With a smile, Elizabeth shrugged a shoulder. "Even if I had, you are well aware I would not tell you. Papa has warned me of the dangers of altering the course of what is to come. That which seems a simple and benign disclosure could have devastating consequences."

"At times, I wish I could see what will happen." Jane sighed.

Elizabeth grasped Jane's hands in hers. "Believe me when I say visions are not as exciting or straightforward as they sound. Many times, I see bits and pieces of the future or even the past. The meaning is rarely clear. I have all these fragments that do not always fit together as a whole."

"I had not considered it being as such. Papa has never spoken of his, but little surprises him."

"My sex shocked him," she said with a laugh. "And when he was first told I was a girl, he considered that he could have foreseen the birth of a subsequent child—then he saw my birthmark." Jane had known for years of the four-point star on the inside of Elizabeth's arm. Concealment bore no purpose with Jane, who would guard the knowledge with her life. Her dearest sister would never reveal her identity until the right time. Her other sisters, however, remained ignorant to this day. Elizabeth's stomach churned at the idea of them discovering what she was. They would tell all and sundry with no regard for the consequences.

They still believed as most did: that the Bennets had no magical heir, that all of the girls had no more than similar talents to most women and those males who were not the heir. Why would they not? It was how magic had passed through families for longer than Elizabeth's lifetime or even her father's and grandfather's lifetimes. The last all-powerful woman to exist had been the Lady of the Lake, although most outside magical circles considered her a legend or tale to be told. Niniane[1] had also been a water fairy, thus, she had not been human.

"I suppose you are correct," said Jane. "Speaking of Papa, he wishes to talk with you."

Elizabeth shrugged. "When does he not?"

"How much more do you have to learn before Papa is satisfied?"

---

[1] Niniane was believed to be the name of the Lady of the Lake in medieval texts. *Paton, Lucy Allen* (1903). <u>*Studies in the Fairy Mythology of Arthurian Romance*</u>. *Boston, Ginn & Co.*

She paused after rising. "No limit exists to the magical arts. Papa is constantly learning, and I shall, no doubt, do the same." Papa would likely continue to teach her until she departed for her own household or he died, whichever came first.

Longbourn was now oddly quiet as she went to the library. No sooner had she knocked than Papa's warm voice called for her to come. Her father lowered his book, his green eyes studying her over his half-moon glasses. He never took anything at a moment's glance.

"How was your ramble?"

"The wind is restless. Change is coming."

He gave a dip of his chin. "I have heard the whispers too."

"I have endured so many visions of late—the past and the future—that I can hardly make sense of them all." Her sleep was not restful when foresight came to her in dreams. Last night, she had once again witnessed her birth. She had never been able to see all of what had occurred that morning. This time, she had woken up not long after her father had taken her in his arms. She had awakened with her head pounding and her heart racing. Her walk had helped put her to rights. That said, a slight thrum still echoed within.

Her father set his book upon the desk. "I believe some shift has already occurred. An imbalance has begun, but I am unsure of where it arises. Visions become more frequent during times of change."

"Is that also why the altar stone is humming stronger than it has in the past?"

Papa sat straighter and furrowed his brow. "The altar is a conduit for magical power as we approach the solstice and the equinox. A steady stream comes from the vein in the earth, but if the vibration has increased, then the magical presence in the area has altered or will soon, and the stone is anticipating the new power. Only a handful of families could cause the altar to make so noticeable a change." He said the last in a mumble, almost to himself.

Families had varying degrees of magic, and he was correct that at this time in England, only a small number held the most substantial power. The non-magical had come to be commonplace while the belief of magic became more of a superstition. Their abilities faded with their denial—the power reverted back to the earth and the channels that flowed through it.

"Lizzy, I. . .I must admit that I have kept something from you all of these years. You have seen, in visions, the morning of your birth, but we have not spoken of it often. I have also avoided telling you everything."

"I have seen some. I know a lady was in the room with Mama and the midwife. After Mama rejected me, I was brought here to you. You have explained why she never told Mama of the birthmark, but I know little else."

Papa cleared his throat. "The lady in the bed chamber with your mother was Lady Anne Darcy. The Darcys and the Bennets have been friends for generations. Lady Anne's husband, George Darcy, was a gifted mage, and Lady Anne's family, the Fitzwilliams, have a legacy of magical talent as well. Since I had foreseen the birth of the heir, George and his wife offered to come to your birth and to welcome the next of the Bennets to carry the mantle.

"When you were born and we knew you to be a girl, we spent the next day going over and over how to protect you once you came of age. As you know, we have delayed your announcement in our circles, which was never questioned since we had no boy child. Our most pressing concern was those who would seek you out and manipulate you once you became of marriageable age. We have delayed to protect you."

Her spine stiffened. "I can protect myself, Papa."

"Yet, the ways to harm you—to bend you to the will of others—are not all known to you. I have taught you of our ancestors—of Niniane's seduction of Merlin so he would teach her his magic. How, knowing what Niniane was as well as her plans, Merlin removed any memory of their babe from her so she would not manipulate the child to further her own means as she did with Lancelot. Merlin loved Niniane, even though he knew she would be the one to bring his end."

Elizabeth had heard this story how many times? The family history was known to her; her father had ensured it. "Yes, and King Arthur saw the child hidden and gifted him Longbourn—or the land on which our home now resides. You have told me the story countless times. But I must say that I have no intention of falling in love with a water fairy." One side of her lips quirked.

Her father gave a slight growl. "This is no time to jest. We have enjoyed a pocket of peace these last hundred or so years. We have had some suspicious occurrences but nothing to indicate a true evil—yet that does not mean those who would commit such atrocities are not lurking in the shadows. Those who will seek to harm you will assume you are not as strong as a man—"

"Is that what you believe?" How many times had they practiced, and how much had she learnt? Years and years of education were to prepare her for when her father announced who she was to the world. Could he truly believe she was weaker than a man?

His bushy eyebrows drew down. "No, of course not. The magic that flows through you is potent, quite potent. I believe you will surpass my abilities, but you must understand that others will underestimate you."

"Is that not more a detriment to themselves?" After all, she could elude them more easily if they believed her weaker than she was.

"It can also be a detriment to you, my dear. George posed a solution at the time, and as much as I was not fond of the idea, his suggestion had merit."

"I am afraid to ask," said Elizabeth. Her hands had clasped in her lap, her knuckles almost white with the sudden tenacity of their grip. "Am I to be locked in a tower? Or will you place an enchantment upon me? I wish to face whatever danger would come instead of hiding away like a coward."

He held up a palm. "And you will, but you will have another by your side."

Her chin hitched back. "Another? Who and what are you suggesting?" None of her sisters possessed a talent that would be of great aid in a confrontation. Jane's nature was to calm those she touched, Mary could press her hand to a book and instantly know its contents, even though she preferred to read, Kitty could make a plant grow or bloom, which did prove useful with potion-making and for food but little else, and Lydia. . .well, Lydia was a siren of sorts. She could charm a man with a certain lilt of her voice, an ability that could be quite dangerous for a fifteen-year-old young lady if she was proficient. The effect of Lydia's charm was not long-lived, however. Within a good half-hour, most were free of her magic and soon exhausted of her vapid behaviour.

Papa stood and rounded his desk. He took her hands and exhaled. "Lizzy, we planned your marriage."

"My marriage?" Surely she had heard him wrong! He would not take away her ability to marry for love, would he?

He squeezed her hands. "Forgive me, but before the night of the winter solstice, you will be joined with the only person besides myself I would entrust with your life."

Her heart began to pound in her ears, and she shook her head. "I do not need to wed anyone to be protected. I will not do it!"

"Lizzy," he said in a gentle tone as he placed a palm to her cheek. "I must consider your safety above all else. You have no choice."

Chapter 2

21st of September 1811

The crisp evening air greeted Fitzwilliam Darcy as he slipped from the door at the back of Netherfield and with a quick step, started in the direction of Oakham Forest. When he reached the fields, the remnants of this autumn's wheat harvest crunched beneath his feet. He took in a bracing inhalation. His soul rejoiced at being out of doors and out of Netherfield. Since his arrival, Miss Caroline Bingley had been following him like a dog in heat, and he had been at his wit's end to escape her clutches. Much to his relief, the Bingleys and the Hursts had departed the day before for Stonehenge, which had given him a reprieve, but today, leaving the house provided him the additional respite he required.

He had spent a prodigious amount of time riding the fields atop his stallion Hengroen[2] during the past two days. This morning, after racing through the fields, he had skimmed the wood along the edge of Netherfield's lands. The magic from within the forest was strong, the pull it created similar to that of Nine Ladies on his own lands in Derbyshire. Of course, the stones were emanating more power due to the equinox; the strength of the draw would fade after a week or so.

As he rode, he had passed villagers who had come to make their offerings of libations to the trees, pouring cider, mead, or water upon the ground around their trunks. Some harvested from a cluster of apple trees along the south side of the forest.

Since the earth was nearing its time of rest, all and sundry prepared for winter by drying and storing from the harvest. Those in Meryton were doing the same as what occurred in Lambton this

---

[2] The name of one of King Arthur's warhorses.

time of year. He had never missed an equinox at Pemberley before, but he had an obligation to fulfil in Hertfordshire this year, and while he could have delayed this until closer to the winter solstice, something in him itched to satisfy a certain curiosity.

Little contact had occurred between Mr. Bennet and him in the years since Fitzwilliam's father had died. Of course, their lack of correspondence had been part of the plan to help protect Elizabeth. Their betrothal had been arranged while she was in her cradle, but while it had been known that his marriage had been arranged long ago, the identity of his bride was a well-guarded secret to most. Mr. Bennet had not wanted Elizabeth to be forced to wed at too young an age. Fitzwilliam, however, was more than ready to marry. His sister required the steady presence of an older sister, and he required an heir. The time had finally come.

He lifted the hood of his cloak while he continued towards Oakham Forest. He had never visited the stone circle here, though he had read of the site in his father's journals. The pull of the power in its midst steered him as he wound through the trees at the periphery of Netherfield's fields. As he walked, voices could be heard in the distance; villagers who were also going to the circle to celebrate. Bingley and his sisters had chosen Stonehenge since the "fashionable" people were to gather there. Miss Bingley had been put out that Fitzwilliam had chosen to remain behind. Her presence, and that of the *ton*, were all the more reason to do so as far as he was concerned!

As he drew close, a creature bounded before him, making him jump back. His jaw gaped at the sight. A white stag? Those were exceedingly rare. When he stepped further into the trees, the creature took one step closer, then another. Fitzwilliam extended his hand, and a prickling shot up his arm as he drew closer. Someone had levelled a protective spell upon the animal, and a powerful one at that.

The stag eyed him in a way that unnerved him before it closed the distance between them and sniffed Fitzwilliam's outstretched fingers. The air glimmered as they drew close to each other. The great beast had been shielded as well. Why was it he was able to see the animal?

"I shall not harm you. I can only assume Elizabeth cast the spell to protect you, but do you protect her as well?" He spoke in low, soothing tones. He had no desire to frighten the beast.

The magnificent animal snorted and threw his head up and down before he crept a bit closer. He nuzzled Fitzwilliam's hand for a moment, but soon, his head lifted with a start before he bounded back into the trees.

"I wonder if Elizabeth has entered the wood," he said softly.

He allowed his hand to fall before he walked towards the centre of the forest. He had just crossed a small brook when he came to an abrupt halt. "Blast, I forgot a log for the fire."

His eyes darted to take in everything around him as he continued. After a couple of minutes, his gaze landed upon a fallen limb off to the side. The large branch appeared to have broken upon its impact with the ground and several pieces were suitable for his purpose. He noted one thicker piece about three feet long. That piece would do nicely. After all, he could not appear at an Autumn equinox celebration without an offering for the fire. He would be considered rude indeed.

He removed his gloves and shoved them in his cloak pocket before picking up the sizeable log and returning to the path.

After about four minutes more, a clearing became visible through the trees. People had already gathered, and a bonfire was being set up in the middle while offerings of leaves, nuts, apples, and candles had been set upon the altar.

"Mr. Darcy," exclaimed Sir William Lucas, a portly gentleman who stood near the logs as they were being arranged. "I see you have come to join us for our Mabon[3] celebration. You are quite welcome, of course! The Bennets have yet to arrive, but I believe most of the village has come for the festivities. Have you met Mr. Bennet yet? I should be pleased to introduce you when he arrives."

"I thank you for your kind offer, but my family has been acquainted with the Bennets for generations. I am certain that when the time is right, Mr. Bennet and I shall speak."

Sir William pressed his palms to his broad waist with a booming laugh. "Yes, yes, I am sure you will."

All around them quieted as an unusual warmth filled Fitzwilliam's chest and gooseflesh covered his neck. As he glanced around, those in attendance had all turned to greet a gentleman and his wife who had just entered the clearing. They were followed by five young ladies of varying age from a tall blonde who appeared to be the eldest, to a shorter, stout young lady near the back who could be no more than sixteen. The man was older and wore half-moon spectacles that were perched on the mid-point of his nose. On his arm was an attractive lady whose red curls framed her face well and who also seemed to enjoy being the spectacle of the moment. She nodded to her neighbours as she entered the circle.

"Ah, there is Bennet now. Good, we can proceed."

While Sir William shuffled away, Fitzwilliam's gaze flitted over the tall blonde who stood directly behind her mother, but he did not spare her a second glance. His gaze was drawn to the smaller lady to her side. Everything in him locked onto her. He could not look away.

She seemed petite to him, but he was six foot three. Most ladies were small when compared to his stature. Despite that the hood of her pristine white cape was up, her auburn curls could be discerned

---

[3] A feast held around the equinox by the Druids. Pronounced Mah-bon in British English.

as they framed the edges of her face, and her eyes sparkled in the dim light of the setting sun.

Her head lifted a hair, and she frowned. As she turned in his direction, he remained rooted to the spot when their gazes collided. The warmth inside him burned a bit brighter, and gooseflesh now covered him from head to toe. He had never experienced anything similar to this. Did she feel that too, or was he alone in his response to her presence?

Their gazes held while her family shifted to the front of the group, Mr. Bennet taking his place behind the altar.

"Good evening. . ."

If Fitzwilliam had been asked later to repeat the ceremony and the words Mr. Bennet must have said before and after, the task would have been impossible. Oh, he turned to face north, south, east, and west with the rest of the group when the time came, but otherwise, he was completely distracted by the lady standing four feet ahead of him and slightly to his right.

Two or three times she turned and glanced at him, but never for long before she returned her attention to her father. As soon as the bonfire was lit to complete the ceremony, the families all set themselves on blankets to enjoy the feast, each family adding a dish for all to consume.

Fitzwilliam stood near the edge of the celebration until Elizabeth rose, her white cape making her easily identifiable as she entered the woods. He followed behind her at a slight distance while she wove through the trees until the white stag from earlier stood before her.

She approached the great beast without hesitation and stroked his head. "I know you are behind me. Why have you followed?" Despite her obviously speaking to Fitzwilliam, she remained petting the stag's head, her back facing him.

"I thought perhaps you had cast his protection spell. Now I am certain of it."

"What makes you believe I am capable of such magic?"

He stepped closer, so he could speak more freely. "Because I know you bear the mark of the Bennet heir on the inside of your arm, Elizabeth."

She pivoted in place and quirked one eyebrow. "What makes you believe that?" Her voice was softer this time.

"Do you not know?"

Hesitant steps brought her to stand even closer. "If I indeed bear the birthmark you speak of, would my father not have declared it to the world by now?"

"Not if he wished to protect you for as long as possible." She had not answered his question. Did she not feel in her bones who he was? He had been aware of her in an instant.

"And now you are meant to protect me as well, are you not?" So, she did know who he was.

"If you will allow it."

"Do you mean I have a say? According to my father, I have no choice." She crossed her arms over her chest. "Does he know you are here?"

"He has not come to Netherfield to greet my friend Bingley yet, so I do not believe so. We are not faithful correspondents. We had no wish for the betrothal to be discovered as it could compromise your identity as the heir. You know as well as anyone that there are always those watching who would wish harm on those who wield their power for good. We could not be too careful.

"I confess I came in the hopes of catching a glimpse of you. My parents told me of you, but what they knew was mostly from your birth or tales your father and mine exchanged when you were young." He often had dreams of her: when she felt strongly about something. A number of times, he had seen bits of their future.

Visions of what was to come could change, so as much as he had come to anticipate those sights, he did his best to tame his heart—to tame his expectations and not become attached to her or what he saw. He refused to be heartbroken if she decided against him.

"Pray, do know that I believe this marriage would be what is best for the both of us, but I would not have you marry me for no more than obligation."

She scraped her teeth along her bottom lip. "You are giving me a choice about whether I marry you?"

"Yes. And I assure you, I shall abide by your decision. You will always have any support and protection the Darcy family can provide. The bond of our families demands no less."

She removed her glove and held out her hand, palm facing him. He nodded and stepped forward, so they were almost toe to toe. He removed one glove and drew back one side of his cloak. When she placed her hand over his heart, he covered it with his own.

Her gaze held his, though his body trembled at the surge of magic that accompanied her palm against his clothing as well as their ungloved hands. While she was now determining the truth of his heart, would this sensation occur every time they touched?

After a few minutes, she drew back. "I should like some time to consider what I shall do."

With a nod, he put on his glove. "Am I allowed to do what I must to convince you of my suit?"

One side of her lips curved. "You hope to court me when you hardly know me?"

He shrugged. "Is it not the standard practice—to court a lady with the intention of coming to know her? You must be aware that I have my own reasons." He would not speak to her of the visions he had seen—at least not yet.

"You will not disclose those reasons to me?" Her arms were again crossed over her chest while she spoke, but the barely there smile and the tilt of her head indicated more of a playfulness to her stance rather than a true challenge. His own lips quirked at her manner.

"No, I believe your continuing curiosity will be to my benefit."

She bestowed a full smile upon him, and the effect was similar to the sun emerging from the clouds on a dreary day. "Very well. I suppose I shall allow you your secrets—for now."

Without another word, she turned and began her return to the stone circle. His heart and soul pulled for him to follow, but he had done what he had intended—more, really. He had never meant to speak to her tonight, but fate had intervened. Now he must decide how to woo the fair Elizabeth Bennet.

Elizabeth returned to her family and attempted to behave as though naught had happened when she entered the woods. Her father knew well that she would venture into the trees to seek out Herne, but meeting that gentleman was not what she had anticipated before departing Longbourn this evening.

Her insides had been tumbling and fluttering more and more as she approached the stone circle, and when they had entered the clearing, her entire body had erupted in gooseflesh. Had he experienced the same response to her proximity? She had never heard of the like happening before. What had caused such a response this evening?

The Darcy family held a history of powerful magic. Could her body have sensed the additional power? She never had such a reaction to her father's presence, but she had been with him since birth. They were accustomed to the magic that radiated from each other.

The oddest part of the encounter had been that, even from the moment she set eyes on him, she had been acutely aware of who he was. No explanation existed for how, yet every tiny part of her screamed out that he was Fitzwilliam Darcy, the man she was supposed to wed. One thing was certain: he had not lowered the cape, but what she could discern of his face was pleasing. He was handsome and tall. Was it strange that she now longed to know what he looked like without the cape? He appeared as though he was broad shouldered and likely muscular. Why did that make her chest flutter more than it already had been?

Her father, who had been speaking to Sir William Lucas, glanced over at her and lifted one of his eyebrows. Did he know she would be approached tonight? Thank God he could not read the direction of her thoughts!

"Miss Elizabeth, your father was telling me you have made a study of your family history. 'Tis fascinating, is it not? It is no wonder the non-magical have been creating tales of Merlin and the Lady of the Lake for centuries."

She smiled and shrugged as she joined the two gentlemen. "If only they had all of the particulars. I believe the truth to be more fascinating than anything that has been written thus far. Of course, my ancestor did not want a few of the specifics immortalised, lest the lady herself know of our existence before her demise."

Sir William's head jolted a bit to the side. "Forgive me, but I see Mr. Goulding. We need to discuss the matter of the spring that runs along the border of our properties."

"No good will come of arguing over the matter, Lucas," said her father. "I suggest the two of you agree to get along and share the magic. That spring is given freely by the earth for all to use. Its bounty is not meant to be owned and hoarded by one man. Those who share without reserve reap the benefits in the long run."

The portly gentleman nodded in a twitchy manner. "Yes, I am sure you are correct. I shall attempt to smooth matters over with Goulding."

As soon as the man was across the clearing, her father leaned in a hair. "Do you believe him?"

"Not in the slightest."

Her father groaned and wiped his hand over his face. "The people of Meryton have used that spring for potions for centuries."

"It would be a tragedy to have to hide it." Magical springs often disappeared. No sooner had the Fountain of Youth been discovered in the Americas than it had been hidden because all and sundry sought it out as word spread of its existence.

He nodded while he glanced around them. "The hour is becoming late, and many are beginning to depart. We should as well." He looked at her over his spectacles. "I do expect you to tell me what occurred with that young man who followed you from the stones."

She arched her one brow at him. "Do you not know who he is?"

He offered her his arm. "I am certain I do, but I should prefer to hear it from you."

Of course, he would, and he would not relent until she told him all.

Chapter 3

1st of October 1811

"Oh, Mr. Bennet! Do you not see that this would be a marvellous thing for our girls?"

Her mother's cries carried out of the library and into the hall. Elizabeth paused and breathed deeply for a moment. She had once again returned from her walk to one of her mother's fits. They occurred more and more often these days. She could not escape them it seemed.

After steeling herself, she stepped inside her father's sanctuary, and her mother sneered. Whatever words were to come would not be good. Elizabeth's body tightened.

"And what are you doing about finding a husband? When your father dies and we are cast out, do not think I can keep you. If *you* had been a boy—"

Papa held up a hand. "Do not say it, Mrs. Bennet! As for my visiting Netherfield, we know little of the gentleman who has leased the property. He and his family may not be magical. We must tread with care. I shall speak to Sir William. I heard he has called on them."

"What do I care if they are magic or not?" Her mother's voice had become shrill. "I shall not have the funds to keep your daughters when something happens to you. They must be wed. I shall not have it any other way. I insist you go and go now!"

Elizabeth crept around her mother to sit in her preferred chair. If she said nothing, her mother might forget her presence for the time being.

"I have your tea, Mrs. Bennet," said Hill as she entered quickly with a tray.

"When did I say I wished for tea?" The housekeeper remained so patient with Mama when she was like this. Such a skill was one

Elizabeth desired. Her equanimity was difficult to maintain when her mother's ire was so often directed at her.

Papa stood and moved a book so Hill could place the tea tray on the desk. "I ordered it. Now, sit and take a cup, my dear."

With a flounce and a huff, her mother sat then accepted the tea from the housekeeper. After her first sip, she opened her mouth to continue her vitriol, paused, and rested her hand with the cup in her lap, a frown marring her pretty face.

"What was I to say? My mind is so foggy all of a sudden." Mama blinked and looked down into her tea.

"Do not worry yourself over such triflings," said Mrs. Hill. "I believe you were about to remove to the parlour to attend to your needlework. Miss Bennet is sewing clothing for the Smith's new baby. You could join her. Would that not be lovely?"

"I *am* embroidering a tablecloth for the dining room, with five-petaled lilacs. Those are for good fortune, you know."

"You showed me your progress two days ago if you recall. The piece shall be beautiful when it is finished." Mrs. Hill aided Mama to stand and placed a hand upon her back as she helped her from the room. "If you would like, I can bring the tea for you to drink while you work."

"Yes, thank you, Hill," said Mama as they departed. Hill closed the door after returning briefly for the tray.

"I am pleased you did not employ Jane to calm her. Jane exerts herself too much to care for Mama."

Her father dropped back into his chair and leaned forward against the desk, rubbing his temples. "I agree. I am attempting to do better. Jane will not be with us forever, and we must learn to do for ourselves."

"So you have had the same visions?" She was not prepared for Jane to leave, but the day was coming if the glimpses Elizabeth had seen were correct. How she would miss her dear sister when she was married and gone!

"I have seen a little. I only know she is to marry a fair-haired gentleman."

Elizabeth leaned against the arm of her chair. "Mr. Bingley I have heard him called in mine. He is a very happy fellow from what I have seen." He never failed to wear a wide grin in her visions.

"He does seem to be that," said Papa. "Mr. Bingley is also the name your mother just used for the gentleman leasing Netherfield. I suppose there may be something to her rantings."

"And it is also likely they are from a magical family." The assumption was one that could be made. Her father would not sanction a marriage between someone without magic and one of his daughters. He could not take the risk that someone would inadvertently notice one of their talents and accuse them of witchcraft. Such an unequal match was dangerous.

Papa dipped his chin to look at her over his glasses. "Have you seen Fitzwilliam since the equinox?"

She shook her head. "No, but I have reason to believe he will find me out walking at some point."

"Will you allow him to get to know you? Lady Anne and Darcy were excellent people. I cannot imagine they raised their son to be anything less. I could never part from you for someone unworthy."

Through the window, the leaves falling from the trees caught her eye. The last thing she wished for was an arranged engagement, but what if this Mr. Darcy was indeed well-suited for her? She might regret rejecting him without giving him an opportunity to prove himself. "I feel I should see if we are a good match first."

"I fear there are few who would challenge your quick mind. Fitzwilliam was intelligent and talented, even at a young age. While we awaited your birth, Darcy and I both worked with him. He exceeded all of my expectations at that time. From what I heard from his father in the years following, the young Darcy continued to impress his father with his skill."

Elizabeth could not help but fidget. She had withheld a few details when she had told her father of their meeting. Could he provide insight into the questions she had from that night?

"What are you holding back, my dear?"

She almost laughed at his perception. He always knew when she kept secrets.

"Well, as we approached the stones on the equinox, the vibrations from the altar greeted me at the edge of the wood, but so did other sensations—strong ones—and they strengthened when I spoke to him. Could I be sensing his power?"

He sat back, his gaze penetrating. Could he see through her? "You are accustomed to sensing magic. The hum is what one characteristically feels, and the strength can vary based on the other's talent. I would venture this is more than the usual, but what, I only have suspicions. You and Fitzwilliam will need to discern that meaning between the two of you. Since the sensations greeted you when you entered the forest, I am sure it must be more than mere attraction."

Her cheeks heated. "I would rather not discuss any attraction with you, Papa."

With a laugh, he picked up a book near the edge of the desk. "I feel the same, Lizzy. I feel the same. Come, I believe we were to review a few more advanced protective charms today. If we are to make any progress, we should begin."

2nd of October 1811

"Sir," said the butler. "Mr. Bennet of Longbourn." The servant shifted against the door as the gentleman being announced stepped into the drawing room.

Fitzwilliam had to hold his breath for a second not to chuckle. Since he had little recollection of the gentleman from his youth, his father had oft times described Mr. Bennet to him as resembling the illustrations they had once seen of Merlin, without the long robes, of course. Mr. Bennet wore a suit that appeared at least five seasons old, and his hair was cropped closer to his head, just as Fitzwilliam would have expected. He even had a longish sort of beard.

Bingley stepped forward with his usual jovial countenance. "Mr. Bennet, I am pleased to welcome you to Netherfield. May I present my good friend Mr. Fitzwilliam Darcy of Pemberley, my brother-in-law, Mr. Reginald Hurst, his wife Mrs. Hurst, and my sister Miss Caroline Bingley." Bingley gestured to each as he introduced them then he motioned to the couch. "Please do sit. I have been eager to get to know all of my neighbours."

As Mr. Bennet took the offered place on the couch, their guest tilted his head for a moment while he glanced about the room, his lip curved ever-so-slightly on one side. The expression was not so dissimilar to the one Elizabeth wore from time to time on the evening of the equinox. If he had to guess, Mr. Bennet was amused by them all. How much could the gentleman perceive from the brief time in their proximity? His father once said Mr. Bennet was rarely fooled by people. Fitzwilliam could not wait to ask for Mr. Bennet's opinions of his friends.

"It is a pleasure to make your acquaintances," said Mr. Bennet. "I hope you are enjoying the neighbourhood. Meryton is small, but we are an amiable lot."

Bingley nodded with his hands clasped together in his lap. "The few I have met thus far have been quite agreeable. I have heard from more than one person that Longbourn borders the Netherfield lands. Is that true?"

"Longbourn is approximately a two mile walk south through the fields. Netherfield's lands stop at Oakham Forest as you near the west side of the property."

Fitzwilliam cleared his throat. "The forest is part of Longbourn, is it not?"

"Yes," said Mr. Bennet. "The Bennets have owned Oakham Forest for centuries."

Miss Bingley tittered. "I confess to knowing little of property, but would not the land be more profitable if you were to clear it and use it for farming or livestock?" Mrs. Hurst gave a slight cackle. The lady said little and usually followed her younger sister's lead, and Miss Bingley would never see the value in trees. She possessed a weak talent and placed more emphasis on status and money.

"Caroline, you know very well that trees are valued in our circles." Bingley leaned forward and glared at his sister. He could attempt to exert her to behave, but whether she responded was unlikely. Miss Bingley listened to no one.

Mr. Bennet watched the exchange, his eyes bright and darting from one person to the next. "I have heard the owners are seeking to sell Netherfield. May I enquire if such was mentioned to you, sir? I know the neighbourhood is concerned of who might purchase the property."

"With good reason," said Bingley. "None of us wishes to be accused of witchcraft. Meryton is one of the few magical hamlets remaining near London. I find the town enchanting, and it would be a shame if the neighbourhood did not remain as it is. Do you know how long it has existed?"

Mr. Bennet relaxed into his seat and crossed his ankle over his knee. "Meryton is recorded as having existed in the Domesday Book. I have documents stating the Bennets were gifted their land in the 6th century. I assume the town came into existence not long after."

Miss Bingley's nose crinkled as though she smelt something foul and looked at Mr. Hurst who mirrored her sister's expression. They would never see the value of such a place.

"'Tis that old?" asked Hurst. He was already in his cups, so thankfully, he had not said anything more thus far.

"How fascinating!" Bingley grinned from ear to ear. A surge of what could only be described as joy filled Fitzwilliam, and he steeled himself to force his friend's emotion from his body. Bingley needed to control himself. The elder Bingley son had been the heir, but he had died five years ago. Bingley was, as a result, head of his family, but with no more than the mere talent of being able to project his happiness onto those around him. The magic suited him. Bingley was so pleased with everything and everyone, it was almost contagious.

A chuckle came from Mr. Bennet. "'Tis an interesting gift you have, sir."

Bingley reddened. "Forgive me. I had not intended—"

Mr. Bennet held up a hand. "I am not offended. Spreading happiness to others is harmless. I would wager a little joy could do many a great deal of good."

"Well, Darcy is helping me learn to control my outbursts. They occur less often than they once did."

"Bingley was often exhausted and drained from the power he was exuding," said Fitzwilliam. He could recall Bingley's eyes being red-rimmed and lined with dark circles. Holding in his emotions had been difficult at first, but Bingley had practiced and become more proficient.

"Forgive me, Mr. Bennet, but I must ask," said Bingley. Fitzwilliam had to keep from laughing. Bingley wore an expression that made him appear almost like an eager puppy. "But I have heard mentioned that you have five daughters—all reputed to be rather pretty."

Bennet's eyebrows shot up. "I do have five daughters, and I believe they are all beautiful in their own way, but I am hardly impartial. My eldest is Jane, then comes Elizabeth, Mary, Kitty, and Lydia."

"I heard they are *all* out?" asked Miss Bingley.

"Their mother insisted upon it, so yes, but I would not approve of an engagement for Kitty or Lydia as yet. They are still too silly to understand a lifelong commitment."

The clock in the hall chimed and Mr. Bennet stood. "Well, I should be returning to Longbourn. Will we see you at the next assembly? I believe it is in a little over a fortnight."

"Yes," said Bingley, beaming. "I should be pleased to go."

"Good." Bennet stepped forward and offered his hand.

After Bingley shook it, he held out his arm towards the door. "Let me walk you out."

Fitzwilliam stood. This was the opportunity he required. "I shall join you."

His friend shook Bennet's hand one more time at the front door, but Fitzwilliam stepped outside with Mr. Bennet and walked with the gentleman to his carriage.

"You look just like your father did at this age," said Mr. Bennet. "I would have recognised you instantly in a crowd. You do have your mother's eyes and nose, however."

Fitzwilliam laughed. "Yes, Mrs. Reynolds tells me the same quite often. Has Elizabeth told you of our meeting?"

"She did, but should you not call her Miss Elizabeth?"

"Yes, I should, yet the glimpses I've had over the years of her have been frequent enough to make me feel as though I know her. I assure you; I shall address her properly when we are in company."

The older gentleman dipped his chin with a slight smile. "From what Elizabeth has told me, you intend to court her instead of relying upon the arrangement. Well done, young man. My daughter can be wilful, and she was not best pleased at the idea of marrying a stranger."

"I dreamt of your conversation of our engagement."

"A fortuitous foresight I would say," said Mr. Bennet.

"Yes, I have known of this most of my life while she has not. I am uncertain whether she has had visions of me, so she may not have any attachment. I shall not know more until I can talk to her."

"She speaks little of what she sees. I have impressed upon her the importance of allowing the future to unfold as it will."

Fitzwilliam nodded. "Yes, I would not have spoken of the matter unless I was assured it had already happened."

Mr. Bennet clapped him on the shoulder. "Knowing your father as I did, I am sure you would not. Since I would prefer you to wed my daughter over anyone else, I shall tell you she takes walks every morning, usually in Oakham Forest. She likes the stones and visits them often. There is also a willow near the brook where she seeks solace on occasion."

"Will she not object to you revealing her sanctuaries?"

He grinned with a slight chuckle. "Most certainly." He wagged a finger. "But ensure you win over that beast of hers. Herne is quite protective of her."

Fitzwilliam allowed a quirk of his lips. "She named him Herne?" Herne was said to be a ghost with antlers who haunted Windsor Forest in Berkshire. The name was appropriate.

"She thought it fitting."

"Well, he did not take issue with me speaking to Elizabeth the night of the equinox festival, but I shall be prepared nonetheless." An apple or carrot would be appreciated by the stag, would it not?

He had never left treats for the deer on Pemberley grounds, but his horses appreciated those particular foods.

"You could see him?"

"Yes; I could also sense the protection spell, but I could not miss him when I approached the forest."

Mr. Bennet looked at him over his half-moon spectacles. "How fascinating! If I may ask: your friend, Mr. Bingley—I have sensed that he is a good sort of gentleman?"

With a frown, Fitzwilliam shrugged one shoulder. "He can be capricious, but he is not one to do evil. His brother was the heir, but he died five years ago. He was thrown from his horse."

"How tragic," said Mr. Bennet.

"Yes, and Bingley was left to take up the mantle. He may have difficulty finding a wife who is willing to settle for a talent, but he is a good fellow. Why do you ask?"

Mr. Bennet waved a hand. "No reason, really. Just wanted to ensure my sense of others is still working properly. But I should go. My wife was in an ill temper when I departed, so I should return."

"Of course. I hope Mrs. Bennet is feeling better."

"Thank you, Fitz. . ." He laughed and shook his head. "I should call you Darcy now, though it is strange to do so."

When Mr. Bennet climbed inside his carriage, Fitzwilliam stepped forward to close the door. "I shall see you soon, sir. Good day."

Chapter 4

4th of October 1811

Elizabeth took in a great inhalation of the brisk morning air. After being cooped up inside Longbourn for two days of rain, the freedom of walking through the fields was welcome. As volatile and capricious as her mother's moods had become, they were worse when Elizabeth had no opportunity to escape the house and her mother's presence. Perhaps her powers fed her mother's instability? More than likely, Elizabeth reminded her mother of the disappointment that her second born was not the heir—as far as Mama knew anyway. When Elizabeth would visit her aunt and uncle in London, Jane would report in her letters that her mother was much improved during Elizabeth's absence, which was why she believed it to be so. Her stomach twisted. Despite living with her mother's disdain for so many years, the rejection still smarted.

The fields were still damp from yesterday's light misting rain as well as this morning's dew, but not so sodden that she sank into the mud. She had worn her older boots lest she ruin the new ones her aunt had sent from town a month ago. Regardless of Mama's feelings towards her, she had no desire to increase her mother's agitation, which ruining her boots would surely do.

The thudding of hoofbeats made her stop and glance about her, and as they grew louder, she whirled around as a great black steed came to a halt about five yards away from her. He was a beautiful horse, his bright white blaze and socks a stark contrast to the darkness of the rest of his body. Nevertheless, she took a step back. Her heart fluttered madly against her ribs. The beast's proximity was unnerving.

The gentleman atop the horse dismounted and drew the reins from the horse's head as he stepped before her. "Good morning, Miss Elizabeth."

It was him—the gentleman from the forest. His proud bearing and tall stature helped make him recognisable, even without the cloak he wore on the equinox. The penetrating gaze of his crystal blue eyes caused a frisson within her that accompanied the sensation emanating from him that she could not identify. She could not describe it, either. It was most unusual.

"Good morning, Mr. Darcy." She had not required an introduction that night in the forest, and she had no need of one now.

One side of his mouth curved. "Good morning, Miss Elizabeth."

"You already wished me well, or have you forgotten so quickly?"

He smiled wider. "I have not forgotten." He cleared his throat. "As the fields are not terribly muddy from the rain yesterday, I had thought to find some peace before my hosts demand my presence for the rest of the day, but I would enjoy your company if you are inclined to join me."

She started and stepped back once again. "You wish me to ride with you?" Her heartbeat quickened. She liked to give the horses of Longbourn treats of apples and carrots and to brush them, but she had never taken to riding. Her own two legs were sturdy. They could take her anywhere around Meryton and Longbourn she wished to go, and if the distance was too great, a carriage was not objectionable, but she preferred the breeze to caress her cheeks and whisper in her ear. Some of her most meaningful moments were spent rambling.

"No, I thought we would walk together. I have given Hen a good run. He will be pleased with a reprieve before we return to Netherfield."

"His name is Hen?" He named his horse for a chicken?

The gentleman chuckled and gestured towards his stallion. "Miss Elizabeth, may I present Hengroen."

"Do you also have a mare named Llamrei?" If he had one mount named for a warhorse of King Arthur, would he also have one named for King Arthur's own steed?

"I do, but she remains at Pemberley. She will soon birth a foal by Hen, and I would not cause her strain by bringing her so far from home when in such a delicate condition."

While he spoke, Elizabeth tilted her head and made a study of the gentleman before her. As she had discerned on the equinox, he was quite tall and handsome. His well-tailored greatcoat fit snug across his broad shoulders and even with it on, little doubt existed that he was an active sort by the snug fit of his topcoat.

Once he had finished his explanation, she glanced in the direction of the forest. "I usually walk in Oakham Forest. Would your horse object to the woods?"

"No, I do not believe he would."

When she turned to continue forward, he fell into step beside her. "Will we meet your white stag today?"

She lifted one shoulder. "He joins me whenever I enter the forest, and if I sit to read, he always hovers nearby until I am ready to depart." She frowned and stopped to face him. "I do not understand why you can see him."

"I believe your father was dumbfounded as well. I could sense the protective charms on him, but I was able to see him and let him sniff my hand."

She stared at the forest ahead of them for a moment. None of her sisters nor her mother had ever noticed Herne, or they would have commented on his presence when they had entered Oakham Forest for the Mabon celebration.

"I believe your spell is working, even if I cannot explain why he is visible to me."

"But I do not want him to be noticed by hunters. 'Tis why I have protected him since I first found him as a young stag." He had been much smaller and so adorable at that time, but he had grown into a stunning creature.

He dipped his chin to catch her gaze. "He protects you as well I would say."

"I would say we protect each other. However, he has become quite old. I do worry how many rambles we have left together. The hares would remain in Oakham Forest, but they are not my constant companions. They and the pheasants are fickle creatures who worry more about their next meal than roaming through the trees with me. They care naught for the secrets carried on the wind."

He smiled and held out his elbow. "Well, may I offer my services to accompany you then? I vow to protect you with my life and listen with adept ears for the confidences that might be shared along the way."

Elizabeth could not stop the huff from escaping at his vow and whirled to face him. "Why does everyone believe I require protection? First my father, then Herne, and now you. Do you not believe I can keep myself safe? Moreover, who would seek to harm me? No one knows I am the heir but Papa, Jane, our housekeeper, my old governess, and you." That secret had been hidden well after all. The midwife who had delivered her had died a few years ago, so she took the confidence to her grave, and her governess would never tell a soul.

"I am certain you do not require anyone to guard you and keep you from harm," said Mr. Darcy. He pivoted around to face her. "But you must understand there are those who have sensed your growing power over the years, which was why it was imperative to keep your identity hidden. You also cannot control the visions other mages may have of you. You also have to consider how many would believe a lady is the heir to one of the most powerful magical families in the world. Claiming you are the heir without protection might be dangerous enough. We have no way of knowing.

"I have no doubt in my mind that you will one day need to prove yourself—to defend yourself against evil, and if I can be of any aid to you in the endeavour, I would do so without hesitation."

The earnestness of his expression pulled at her heart. "You do not even know me."

His fingers ran from her temple to her jawline. "I have seen glimpses of you since I was a little boy. Your feelings, when strong enough, travelled the miles between us to me. I did not always know what had happened, but I knew if you were happy or sad, and eventually, my visions showed me you. My father then confirmed what I had come to believe: we are connected by more than the magical contract our parents signed when you were born. Have you never felt it?"

Was that the sensation she could not identify? Thus far, she had only experienced that oddity when he was nearby—

She gasped and backed away from him. "When I was five, I shut myself in my room and sobbed for two days. Hill and Papa could not make me eat. I was sad for weeks after, but I could not explain why."

He paused for a moment. "Fifteen years ago," he said in almost a whisper. "That happened in May—May fourteenth—did it not?"

She nodded.

"You were feeling my sadness from my mother's death. She died in childbirth."

Elizabeth swayed in her spot. "What of the child?"

"Georgiana lives. She is at Pemberley."

Her palm pressed to her stomach in an effort to relieve the uneasiness within. "Three years ago, I was angry and sad all at once . . ."

Mr. Darcy swallowed hard, his Adam's apple bobbing. "My father died in a carriage accident."

Her eyes burned. "I am sorry." How had she never known what was happening when he had understood some time ago? Papa had not given any ideas for why she was prone to those fits of emotion. She had been terrified it meant she would one day be like Mama. What could be worse or more tragic than losing her wits?

She frowned and rubbed some gooseflesh that had erupted on her arm. "In August, I was frustrated then I had a surge of anger. I have learnt to temper the mysterious emotions I have from time to time, so I held it in, but the event was no less strange."

He cleared his throat, and his eyes darted away from hers for a moment. "I should prefer to speak of that later—when we are more assured of our privacy. I could cast spells to ensure the confidence, but I prefer to wait if you do not mind."

"Yes, of course. I understand." She did not really. Yet the entire connection of their emotions was a mystery as well. She would have to ask Papa if he had ever heard of the like. If so, why had he never suspected it when those things occurred? He had to know of Mr. and Mrs. Darcy's deaths.

"Where do you wish to go today?" asked Mr. Darcy.

"Oh, I should like to walk to the stones."

He held out his arm once again. "Then allow Hen and me to accompany you."

They walked in silence for a bit until he released her to cross the rocks at the brook ahead of him. He followed close behind but a little slower so his horse could find his footing through the water. The quiet was not unnerving or uncomfortable, but as though they had no need to speak to understand the other, which was unsettling in and of itself.

When they emerged on the opposite side of the stream, they continued through the trees until they reached the sizeable clearing where the stones rested. Elizabeth stepped up to the altar while removing her gloves and after tucking them into the pocket of her redingote, set her bare palms upon the surface. The hum that had built up to the equinox had subsided some but had not yet returned to the gentle pitch she was accustomed to.

"Is something amiss?" asked Mr. Darcy.

"At the equinox, the altar hummed stronger than I had ever felt, and now, the vibration is still stronger than is its wont."

His eyebrows drew down a little in the middle. "That could by influenced by a number of possibilities. Bingley and his family would not bring enough power into the area to alter the balance around the circle."

"What of you? My father has said your family is talented in the magical arts."

He dropped his stallion's reins and removed his own gloves as he approached the altar and set his fingers upon the smooth stone. Much as she had done at times, he closed his eyes then opened them and shook his head.

"Perhaps if we. . ." He gestured to her hand. "May I?"

"What is it you want to do?" Butterflies erupted in her stomach as he stepped up behind her. He was not touching her back, but his chest was so close, his warmth was evident even with the chill.

"Perhaps if we combine our power to read what is amiss with the stone, we can learn more than we would alone."

"I have never tried such magic. Have you?"

"My father and I did so to cast a charm before his death. For this, however, I would place my hand over yours, and we would both channel our energy into the source of the vibration."

She nodded and returned her palm to the altar. When he covered her hand with his own much larger one, she inhaled sharply. Gooseflesh peppered the back of her neck at his proximity. This would not do! She needed to stop being such a silly goose.

Her eyes fluttered closed, and she turned her mind to the source, doing her best to ignore the heat and power coming from Mr. Darcy's hand over hers. She stumbled forward, her other hand landing on the surface as she fell headfirst into darkness.

Visions seemed to float in front of her until she fell headlong into the first but seemed to land on her feet. The difference in position made her dizzy. She shook herself and took in her surroundings, but she had only appeared to move to the centre of the clearing to face the altar.

Elizabeth blinked and gasped. What was before her was not what was happening in the moment. Instead, she gaped at her own figure, who stood behind the altar with Mr. Darcy standing at her right side, her father on her left. Papa stood tall and gazed at her with adoration and pride while she held her hand over the altar. She was wearing her white cloak and what appeared to be a crown of rosemary and sage. What was this ceremony, and why would she require a crown that would harness additional magic?

A hard pull yanked her from that vision and dropped her into a strange room. When she glanced about her, she gasped. Standing near the fire was Mr. Darcy with his arm wrapped around her. His opposite hand was on her rounded stomach, a gentle smile upon his features. "I care not if this is the heir," he said. "One day, he or she will come. I am in no hurry."

Once again, she was forced from what was happening around her and flung into another room. Wait! She stood in the far corner of Longbourn's library. She watched as a version of herself sat with Mr. Darcy in the chairs. From the hall, a blonde gentleman entered wearing a wide grin, and she departed. Elizabeth followed the dream version of herself to the parlour where Jane stood, in front of the other Elizabeth, smiling with tears flooding her eyes. "Oh, Lizzy! I am so happy!"

All of a sudden, she was once again yanked forward to a burst of colour beneath her eyelids. "When I learnt of your existence, I sought to prevent you from claiming your full potential, but you thwarted me. But that has come to naught as you are now nothing to me. Bow before me descendant of Merlin!" The flash that struck Elizabeth in the vision caused pain to permeate her body. Bile rose from her stomach into her throat. She ripped herself away and ran to the edge of the ancient oaks to cast up her accounts.

Mr. Darcy hastened to her side and placed a hand between her shoulder blades until she was finished. He handed her his handkerchief while she remained leaning against the tree. "Are you well?"

"The light at the end was accompanied by pain."

"I do not believe those were in any particular order," he said. "If we start at the beginning, rosemary symbolises love, happiness, and loyalty while sage is a symbol of wisdom and immortality. Together, they can form a magical crown to aid in warding off one's enemies and enhancing one's own magic through their own wisdom. Obviously, we must have believed you required it, or you would not have been wearing it.

"The next seemed to be further into the future. We were in the master's sitting room at Pemberley. What I said was true, by the way. I shall welcome whatever child regardless of ability."

She heaved out a sob. Her mother's vitriol was not necessarily her fault, but if Elizabeth had been a boy maybe—

"Your mother would be the same, even if you had been a boy."

Elizabeth jolted up and stared at him. "How did you know?"

He bent some to catch her gaze. "I made an assumption. Your father shared his suspicions about your mother with my own mother and father. He recognised how her behaviour—"

"Resembled that of my grandmother's. Yes, he has mentioned as much to me."

"He also had some idea of what was happening even before your birth. Your sex would not have altered her future."

Mr. Darcy took her elbow and led her to another tree where he helped her rest against the trunk. "I do not believe the next vision was relevant to the information we seek."

She shook her head. "That was my sister Jane. I do not know how she would fit into how the stone is behaving. As I mentioned before, the final one, however, caused me pain. Whatever or whoever that was—"

"We know danger is coming. If we consider each of the scenes, I believe only the vision with your crown and the last are pertinent to the behaviour of the altar. The others have likely existed in our minds and helped ease us into what we were attempting to see. We need to speak to your father, and we need to speak to him as soon as possible."

Chapter 5

As soon as Fitzwilliam was assured Elizabeth was steady enough on her feet to walk out of the woods, they began to make their way to Longbourn with Herne following a short distance behind them. Fitzwilliam had not been so affected when he and his father had combined their powers, but they had not experienced a vision like Elizabeth's, nor had they experienced the pain their vision had created.

Before the forest gave way to the fields and farms, she rested a hand upon Herne and whispered the protective charms. The spells did not require reinforcement often, but this seemed to be a long-standing habit. It was no wonder the charms were so potent.

When they emerged from the trees, he paused. "Pray, allow me to return you to Longbourn atop Hen. We shall hasten our trip, and you will not be exerting yourself so."

Her vivid green eyes caught his with little effort. "The walk to Longbourn is no trial; I assure you."

"No, but combining our powers appears to have fatigued you. I can only imagine the pain you described is the cause of your lack of energy, yet I shall be more at ease once we can speak to your father. He is the only person who can assure me that what happened has not harmed you." Surely, she would not be so stubborn as to refuse him, would she? Before she could answer, he turned her around by her elbows then lifted her up onto his stallion's back.

"Mr. Darcy! I am perfectly capable—"

"I am certain you are but allow me to be concerned." He tossed Hen's reins over the horse's head then mounted to sit behind the saddle so she would not be pressed against the insides of his thighs. As he cued the horse forward, she grasped the pommel in a white-knuckled grip.

"Have you never been on a horse before?"

She shook her head in a stiff manner. "No, we do not have the horses to spare on the farm. Papa has his gelding, but even he is put to work most days." She gave an awkward lurch. "I do not feel secure at all."

He slipped an arm around her waist and drew her back against his chest. "I vow you will not fall. I shall keep you safe." Her body remained rigid for almost five minutes, then her form began to soften—to almost rest against his a little.

Hen was a trusted mount and would not bolt on a whim, so Fitzwilliam closed his eyes. "Ceilt," he whispered. They were drawing closer to Longbourn, so he had cast the charm so they were not witnessed together in such a position. If someone were to look in their direction, they would see no more than an empty field.

When he opened his eyes, he resisted the urge to press his lips to the top of her head. "Are you well?"

"Yes, sir, but I maintain that walking is superior to riding."

He could not help but smile at her impertinence. "I shall not argue over any pleasure of yours."

"That is far too diplomatic a response," she said with a glance over her shoulder. "You will not defend your horse's ability?"

How was he supposed to respond? "I am in no doubt of my horse's skill, yet I believe I am a reasonable man. If you prefer to walk, why should I argue? Riding and walking are both suitable diversions. Should you wish to travel, a horse or a carriage is superior in my view. I would not wish to walk to Derbyshire."

Her light laughter warmed him. "No, I would not enjoy such a long journey on foot either."

"Then I am glad we can agree on something."

She turned and examined his face. "I am certain we agree on more than whether a carriage is required for a long journey."

He lifted his eyebrows. "Oh?" This should be interesting!

"I enjoy novels and poetry. Perhaps we should compare favourites and see if we share similar preferences. I also take great pleasure in music, though I play the pianoforte very ill indeed and do not take the time to practise as I ought."

"My sister is quite proficient at the pianoforte. I am certain you would greatly enjoy one of her performances."

"Your sister would be fifteen?"

"Yes, she is shy and quiet and is not comfortable with those she does not know well, so I left her where she would be at ease. My housekeeper will take excellent care of her, and should she require aid, my cousin Richard is close by at his father's estate." He should be receiving a letter from his cousin soon. Richard had promised to call on Georgiana to ensure she was well and undisturbed. That visit should have been a couple of days ago.

"Where have you gone, sir?"

He startled. "I beg your pardon?"

"Well, your body was here, but your mind was elsewhere."

"Forgive me. My sister has had a difficult time of it these past few months. She encouraged me to come here, yet I cannot help but worry." He had sent how many letters back to Pemberley since his arrival?

"Is this what you would prefer to speak to me about later?"

She was quite perceptive. "Yes, and I know we seem alone, but..."

"No, I understand. Even in the open, such as we are, people can use magical means to eavesdrop."

He nodded. The subject was also difficult to speak of. "We are approaching Longbourn. We should dismount now so we do not startle the grooms when we arrive."

Once they dismounted, he whispered the reversal of the charm that had shielded them from prying eyes.

"Come, Mr. Darcy," said Elizabeth. "I believe you wished to speak to my father."

A groom took Hen at the stable, and Elizabeth led Fitzwilliam through the gardens to a door on the side of the house. The servant within gasped and straightened at their entrance. "Miss Elizabeth!"

"Forgive me, Mrs. Hill, but Mr. Darcy desired a word with Papa. Since this is not a formal call, I thought we would make our way to his library through the servants' passages."

"Of course, miss. You gave me a fright is all." She nodded at Fitzwilliam. "Good morning, sir."

He dipped his chin. "Good morning."

Mr. Bennet's library was a quick walk down one passage with a right at the end. When they stepped inside, the gentleman himself blinked, and his bushy eyebrows shot up onto his forehead. "If you had asked me at breakfast what the most unexpected part of my day would be, I would have never considered the two of you sneaking into my library together."

After shifting around Elizabeth, Fitzwilliam bowed. "Forgive me, sir. If we did not have important information that could not wait, I would have called in a more traditional manner."

Mr. Bennet looked at Elizabeth and frowned. "Why do you appear so fatigued? What has happened?" Her father had surely noted the same dark circles under her eyes he had. Fitzwilliam had never seen the like. Why would a vision cause such a response?

"I am well," she said in an almost placating tone. "We sought to discover why the altar is still vibrating so strongly, and what we saw was. . .disturbing."

"Disturbing?" Mr. Bennet glanced between them. "Pray, sit and tell me what has happened."

Fitzwilliam looked at the chairs in front of Mr. Bennet's desk. One was well-worn, as though it had been used every day. No doubt existed that particular chair was Elizabeth's preferred seat, so he took the one beside it.

"Sir, Miss Elizabeth mentioned the elevated humming of the stone, and I believe the altar is anticipating what is to come."

Mr. Bennet's forehead furrowed. "A certain amount of that disturbance could be from your entrance into the neighbourhood. The altar would need time to adjust to the influx of magic."

"Yes, sir. I am aware, but the vibration is stronger than I would expect to occur for just my presence. I suggested to Miss Elizabeth that perhaps joining our power in an attempt to discover the origin might reveal what is at the heart of the matter."

The older man shifted in his seat and gestured towards Miss Elizabeth. "Combining your power with my daughter's should not cause such an alteration."

Fitzwilliam glanced at Elizabeth. She appeared more exhausted now than at the forest. He blew out an exhale. "No, I agree."

"I would not say all of what we saw was disturbing, Mr. Darcy," said Elizabeth. "When we placed our hands on the stones together, we both saw a series of visions. Several were future occurrences that I do not believe relevant to the altar; however, we saw one where I wore a crown of rosemary and sage."

Mr. Bennet gave a sharp inhale. "A crown to harness your power." He mumbled the words then ran his hand over his mouth. "What else did you see?"

Elizabeth sat a little taller. "I can tell you little about what I saw in the last since it was a bright light accompanied by a voice. The voice said, 'When I learnt of your existence, I sought to prevent you from claiming your full potential, but you thwarted me. But that has come to naught as you are now nothing to me. Bow before me descendant of Merlin!' A white light flashed, and I was jolted back."

"She hastened to the edge of the clearing where she cast up her accounts. The dark circles have become more prominent since then, even though I insisted she ride my horse for her return to Longbourn."

Mr. Bennet stood and rounded the desk to stand before his daughter. He took her cheeks in his palms and gazed at her a moment. "You convinced her to mount a horse?" He released her and opened a tall cupboard in the corner of the room. When he revealed the contents, a myriad of glass vials and jars filled the small space.

"I did. I felt it prudent to return her to you at once."

Mr. Bennet selected several vials as well as a small glass and returned to his desk.

"He left me little choice in the matter, Papa. Without warning, he lifted me atop the great beast. I objected, but he would not listen."

"Hmm," said the older man. He pulled a small brass cauldron from under a shelf behind his desk and set it upon the surface with the vials and jars. "You are not one to give in so easily." His piercing green eyes set on Fitzwilliam over his half-moon spectacles. "I trust you protected my daughter's reputation on this ride?"

Fitzwilliam cleared his throat. "Yes, sir."

The gentleman nodded while he added bits of certain vials and dabs of other jars. "Thankfully, this potion does not require a fire."

"What is the potion for?" asked Elizabeth.

"I cannot be sure what spell caused the light, but by witnessing the encounter with the altar as the conduit, you were more present in the moment than if this was a normal vision, so you took a glancing blow of the spell. It explains the increasing weakness and your pallor."

"If they sought to force Miss Elizabeth to her knees, they could have used the traochta."

Mr. Bennet nodded while he added a pinch of one last herb and steam appeared over the edge of the cauldron. "I should say it is ready."

"Then you would have made a spreagaim," said Elizabeth, "to return vitality to the drinker."

"Very good, Lizzy. The steam it seems to emit is not from heat, so the potion will not be warm. Try to take it in one swallow if you can. The results will be quicker." He poured the contents of the cauldron into a small glass.

When he handed it to Elizabeth, she sniffed the contents, and her nose wrinkled. "It does not smell appetizing."

Her father chuckled. "Not many potions do. Now drink up. This nature of potion can cure many ills, so even if the curse was not the traochta, this may be of aid."

She took the potion in one swallow as her father had instructed, her face contorting as she swallowed. "It is vile." A shudder wracked her body.

"Give it a moment," said Mr. Bennet. He tugged the bell pull near his desk while watching his daughter.

Meanwhile, she set the glass on the counter and gasped. "How odd!" She squeezed her eyes closed and reopened them a moment later. When she looked at him, her eyes were once again bright, and the circles had vanished from beneath. Her cheeks had regained their rosy colour.

Mr. Bennet chuckled. "Thankfully, we shall not need Mr. Jones." He set the cauldron off to the side. "Now, in either of those visions you mentioned, could you see nothing of use in determining when this will occur?"

"I wore my white cloak in the first one that was mentioned."

Fitzwilliam sat up straighter. "In the last part, my vision was more from my perspective, although I could not see the identity of the individual. A layer of snow covered the hedgerow and the ground."

"Then we have some time," said Mr. Bennet. "I want to review defensive spells and charms with you, Lizzy. Darcy, if you would be willing to join us or even aid us, I would be appreciative. These old bones do not move as quickly as they once did. I fear practicing a duel would not be wise at my age."

"Papa, I do not need to practise in such a way." Elizabeth's tone was firm.

"I would be willing." Fitzwilliam bent towards Elizabeth. "My father and I duelled on occasion. I would cast spells and charms while he attempted to counter them. We would then change places and start again. I have never had the opportunity to use those lessons in a practical sense, but I do feel more prepared should it be required."

Mr. Bennet nodded. "During pleasant weather, we shall have lessons at the stones. Otherwise, we can use the cellar. Hill will not speak of it, but if my wife was privy to what is occurring, she would tell the entirety of the neighbourhood. Like her grandmother, Frances has become a prodigious gossip.

"I assume you will still attend the assembly?"

Fitzwilliam almost startled at suddenly being addressed. "Yes, Bingley and his family are to attend. It would be rude to remain behind without good reason."

The older man sat back in his chair. "I would appreciate you keeping watch over my Lizzy."

"Are you not going?"

"He rarely attends," said Elizabeth.

"I hear about every assembly numerous times from my wife. I have no need to see such a farce only to hear about it in excruciating detail over and over again. I get no respite unless I hide from such frivolities." Mr. Bennet selected a book from the shelf behind him.

"Lizzy, I wish you to read this over the next few days. We shall discuss and practise what is within these pages over the next week or so."

As Elizabeth set the book in her lap, a glance at the cover revealed it to be one Fitzwilliam had brought with him. He read that particular volume now and then to refresh his memory of the skills contained within.

"Have you read this, Darcy?"

"I have studied that book several times, and I actually brought it with me."

"Excellent," said Mr. Bennet. "Then we shall meet at the stones at dawn tomorrow. Should it be raining, come to the door to the kitchens if you would so my wife is not aware of your presence in the house."

"Of course."

Elizabeth rose. "I shall walk you out, Mr. Darcy."

She was quiet as they made their way back through the servants' passage to depart the house through the kitchen. The groom brought Hen, and she stroked his blaze as the boy scurried off.

"Thank you for bringing me home, Hengroen. I hope to see you on the morrow." She dipped her chin to him. "Good day, Mr. Darcy."

Chapter 6

18th of October 1811

The moment she entered the assembly hall, Elizabeth separated from her mother and sisters and strode to the far corner to join Charlotte Lucas, the eldest daughter of Sir William Lucas.

"I am pleased to see you, Charlotte."

Her friend beamed. "I am pleased to see you as well. You have not called on Lucas Lodge since before the equinox. What has kept you so occupied of late?"

"My mother has had a trying time the past few weeks. Jane has required my aid with her." Her mother's trials were not unknown in the neighbourhood. That would be a sufficient excuse, would it not?

"I am sorry to hear your mother has taken a turn for the worse, but she must be doing well to be here this evening." Charlotte motioned towards Elizabeth's mother who, by the waving of her hands, was likely proclaiming some sort of gossip to Aunt Philips.

"My father would not have an easy time of it if he forbade her from coming. Besides, she has had her tonic, and Jane is with us should her calming influence be required."

Charlotte clasped Elizabeth's arm. "I heard your father paid a call at Netherfield. My father speaks highly of the gentlemen there. He also claimed they will attend tonight."

"I heard the same. Papa said Mr. Bingley returned his call about a week ago. He told me Mr. Bingley is quite amiable." She could say little else. Most of what had been said was in front of Mr. Darcy, and those hours spent practicing their magic were not meant to be shared with anyone. As much as she despised deception, she could not tell Charlotte what they were about.

"Yes," said Charlotte, "my father said much the same. He also indicated Mr. Bingley had some family and a friend who were staying with them, but he did not know much of them. None of the others returned the call with the gentleman."

The entire room quieted so the last of Charlotte's statement was heard by a good portion of those around them. They both straightened, and Elizabeth followed the direction of everyone's gazes to the door, where a tall blond gentleman, who could only be Mr. Bingley, had just entered. On his right was Mr. Darcy, who stood a couple of inches taller and appeared every bit the gentleman in his dark suit. To Mr. Bingley's left was a woman almost as tall as he was but with dark hair that she had done in the latest fashion with a ridiculous peacock feather towering over everyone in attendance.

"I am told the lady is Mr. Bingley's younger sister. She is to keep house for him while he is here. The lady behind them is Mr. Bingley's elder sister and her husband, a Mr. Hurst."

Of course, Charlotte would know every bit of the tittle-tattle. After all, Sir William was as proficient a gossip as Elizabeth's own mother. Yet, Charlotte had never betrayed one of Elizabeth's secrets. Not that Elizabeth was aware of anyway, although she had never shared much beyond trivial confidences with her.

As the group passed, Mr. Darcy's eyes flickered to Elizabeth for but a second. Her father had thought it best that the two of them were "introduced" this evening. While some in the neighbourhood may remember the long association of the Darcy family with the Bennets, some would not. Papa and the gentleman believed the deception might protect Elizabeth for a while longer if their connexion seemed new.

As soon as the newcomers found a place near the corner, Sir William bustled over and began speaking while his hands made large gestures. She leaned towards Charlotte, but a sudden grasp of her arm jerked her back.

"What are you doing, child? I said we would seek an introduction. Why are you dawdling?"

"Mama, I do not require—"

"Hush," her mother said in a loud whisper. Before Elizabeth could object further, Mama dug her nails into the underside of Elizabeth's arm and pulled, dragging her forward to stand before Sir William and Mr. Darcy's party. Lydia and Kitty giggled raucously behind her. Mary, no doubt, stood beside them but apart as though they held some illness that might infect her.

"Ah," said Sir William. "Mr. Darcy, Mr. Bingley, these ladies are Miss Jane Bennet, Miss Elizabeth, Miss Mary, Miss Kitty, Miss Lydia and their mother, Mrs. Henry Bennet."

Mr. Bingley bowed. "Mrs. Bennet, I am pleased to make the acquaintance of you and your daughters. May I present my brother, Reginald Hurst, his wife Louisa, and my sister, Miss Caroline Bingley."

Mama gazed at the ladies' gowns, her vision flitting to the expensive lace before she clasped her hands together. "Miss Bingley, your gown is exquisite, as is yours Mrs. Hurst. You must tell me your dressmaker so we can make an appointment the next time we visit my brother in town."

Miss Bingley's eyes widened almost imperceptibly for a second. "Madame Gérard is quite exclusive. She only caters to the wealthiest in London." The lady gave what could only be described as a priggish smile to her sister. "I should be pleased to pen a note to the Madame, but I cannot guarantee she will accept your custom."

Her mother gave a slight flinch. "I see."

"Mrs. Bennet," said Mr. Bingley somewhat louder than necessary. "Might I ask for the pleasure of the first set with Miss Bennet?" He glanced at his sister for a moment while he spoke, and his cheeks held a slight pinkish hue they had not previously possessed. Hopefully, he was embarrassed by his sister's rudeness. Elizabeth would have been if her sister had behaved so.

"Oh!" Mama fanned herself. "I am sure my Jane would be happy to stand up with you." She looked at her eldest. "Jane?"

"I should be pleased to accept your offer, sir." If Mr. Bingley's cheeks had been pink, Jane's now held a healthy blush.

A wide grin overspread Mr. Bingley's features. "Excellent!"

At Mr. Bingley's smile, a surge of joy struck Elizabeth in the chest. She looked towards Mr. Darcy, who winced. He had mentioned Mr. Bingley's lack of control at times. It seemed the prospect of a dance with her sister made him so pleased he could not withhold the emotion. Elizabeth bit her cheek. How sweet!

"Mr. Darcy, I hope you have come eager to dance as well."

The gentleman gaped at her mother, then at Lydia, who guffawed, then her. "I do not dance." Without another word, he strode to where Mr. Goulding stood and began speaking to the other man.

"Well!" Mama crossed her arms over her chest with a huff. "I suppose a rich gentleman can offend where he pleases, but I must say he seems a most disagreeable sort."

"Mama," said Jane in a low tone. Jane placed her palm on her mother's back, and Mama visibly relaxed. "I am certain Mr. Darcy did not mean to offend."

"My friend is uncomfortable in large gatherings, Mrs. Bennet. Pray, do not hold his reticence against him. I assure you he is amiable when in a group of friends he knows well."

Elizabeth could vouch for Mr. Darcy's manner. He had been every bit the gentleman during their time in Oakham Forest.

"Mr. Darcy," said Mrs. Bennet in a mumble. "Mr Darcy. I once—"

"I appreciate your assurances of Mr. Darcy's good temper." Elizabeth spoke a little louder than required in case her mother finished her statement. "Perhaps after a few weeks in our neighbourhood, he may feel more comfortable and more inclined to converse with us."

Mr. Bingley grinned and rubbed his hands together while Mr. Hurst looked everywhere but at them. The sisters wore tight smiles that did not reach their eyes.

The first set was announced, and Mr. Bingley held out his arm to Jane. "Shall we, Miss Bennet?"

Lydia and Kitty were also claimed for the first by the second Lucas boy and young Mr. Goulding respectively, leaving Mary to claim a chair in the corner.

Elizabeth let out a long exhale and remained in her spot. Mama could not be left alone, so it was up to her to keep her mother from mischief. She was the last person who should be responsible for her mother, not that she had any choice in the matter this evening.

After the first set, Mr. Bingley returned Jane. "Miss Elizabeth, would you do me the honour of the second?"

"Yes, thank you." She set her hand on Mr. Bingley's arm, and they made their way to the centre of the room. After they honoured their partners, they waited for a couple to take the first turn of the dance before they took their own.

"I have read of your father, Miss Elizabeth," said Mr. Bingley. "Who has not? I confess I had to rein in my enthusiasm when I met him. If someone had no magic, they might think I was meeting royalty by my excitement."

She laughed. "Royalty? Sir, I believe that is an exaggeration. My father is not—"

"In magical circles, the Bennets are revered. Meeting him made me wish to be the magical heir of my family so I could request he teach me anything—anything at all."

"That is kind of you to say. My father would be flattered, but he does not consider himself more than anyone else."

As Elizabeth passed Mr. Bingley's sisters during the dance, the two ladies spoke quietly and watched the room as though they saw little of worth or beauty. "I hope your sisters are enjoying their time in Hertfordshire."

"They both prefer London, but I do hope to purchase an estate soon, so they accompanied me while I learn what I need to be a good master. Darcy has been invaluable in teaching me what I should know thus far."

She lifted her eyebrows. Mr. Darcy had been busy if he was aiding her and her father in the mornings and spending the remainder of his day with Mr. Bingley.

Due to the movement of the forms, she was separated from Mr. Bingley, and they had little opportunity to converse during most of the second dance. She curtseyed to Mr. Bingley at the end of the set then glanced about them as he walked her to her mother, who was speaking to Aunt Philips.

Mama was calm and enjoying her gossip with her aunt, so Elizabeth sat down for the next set. While she watched the dancers turn with the music, a familiar voice reached her ears.

"You know I am not fond of dancing, Bingley."

"But there are several uncommonly pretty ladies here this evening. I just finished a dance with Miss Elizabeth. She is lovely and the little conversation we had was pleasant. Would you not rather stand up with her than my sister? Caroline *has* been watching if you had not noticed."

Elizabeth chanced a glance over her shoulder. Mr. Darcy stood with Mr. Bingley while Miss Bingley stared at Mr. Darcy's back. She had to choke down a chuckle. If she was Mr. Darcy, she might be frightened by the determination upon that lady's countenance. Miss Bingley was clear in her attempt to will Mr. Darcy to come to her side.

When that particular gentleman started towards Elizabeth, she stood and clasped her hands in front of her.

"Miss Elizabeth," he said with a dip of his chin. "Would you do me the honour of standing up with me for the next?" He held out his arm.

She set her hand near his elbow. "I would be pleased to dance with you, sir."

Those dancing bowed and curtseyed at the end of the set while she and Mr. Darcy waited to take their places. Her palm tingled where it rested on Mr. Darcy's arm and a current that originated at their connexion travelled through her. Was he experiencing the same sensation? He appeared no different than when he arrived, with the exception of his avoidance of Miss Bingley's obvious admiration.

"Are you well this evening, Mr. Darcy?"

"Quite well, I thank you." He did not look at her but kept his gaze on the room in front of them as those who had been dancing cleared the floor. When the next set began to form, he led them to the middle and took his place across from her. "Did you enjoy your dance with Bingley?"

She lifted her one eyebrow. Was he jealous? "Mr. Bingley was agreeable. We did not have the opportunity to speak much, but he expressed his praise of my father and spoke of his desire to purchase an estate. He indicated you have been teaching him what he needs to know about estate management. You must be an exceptionally busy man."

"My morning ride affords me some time to myself, and I spend some time in the forest before Bingley and I speak of the estate." He bowed when the moment came to honour their partners.

She curtseyed and when the music began, stepped forward.

"The time in the forest is hardly a chore," he said. He had not spoken softly, but the music made it difficult to hear the discourse of those around them.

"Truly?" She was often fatigued after they practised. Was he not?

He bent his head closer to her. "Truly, Miss Elizabeth."

She did her best to school her features so she would not give away their familiarity towards each other, but it did not prevent the jolts that shocked her with every single touch. They were both wearing gloves. How was that possible?

"My mother recognised your name earlier. I barely kept her from commenting that our families had a connexion."

"Thus far, no one has enquired of it to me. I must admit I am surprised. My father mentioned Sir William Lucas in his journal. Of course, the man had yet to be knighted then. Your father's assumption that most would not remember the connexion appears to be correct."

She glanced at Sir William. "Almost twenty years have passed as well since the last time your parents journeyed here."

Mr. Darcy nodded. "Yes, that is also true. Even though Sir William was mentioned, I do not believe my father was well acquainted with the gentleman. He even seems to have forgotten that I mentioned our families were acquainted when we met at Mabon." He looked over to where her mother was speaking loudly to Lady Lucas. "Should your mother be without you? What if she tries to speak of it again?"

"Jane is with her. My sister is better at subduing Mama's tempers. If she begins to say something she should not, Jane can calm her to the point of drowsiness."

Papa had felt that until Elizabeth agreed to the betrothal, they would conceal the truth of their acquaintance. If word of their engagement spread, she would be trapped. She could not avoid marrying him without ruining her reputation. The magical contract would be onerous to nullify, but if anyone could do so, it would be her father.

At the end of the set, Mr. Darcy took her arm and guided her back to where she had stood before their dance. "Did you still want to meet in the morning?"

"Yes, if you are amenable."

"Hen and I shall be waiting for you at the forest." After one last bow, he returned to Mr. Bingley.

"It was kind of Mr. Darcy to ask you to dance," said Mary as she stepped beside her.

"Yes, he was an agreeable partner." The neutral response should not raise Mary's suspicions.

"You should know that Mama noticed. She has been crowing that if you managed to tempt a dance from the handsome and wealthy Mr. Darcy, then he should be unable to resist Jane."

Elizabeth groaned and rubbed her forehead. "Mr. Darcy was being kind. Mr. Bingley suggested he dance with me, so he did. He was obliging his host. Otherwise, I do not believe Mr. Darcy intended to stand up with anyone at all." The assumption was a reasonable one. The gentleman had not stood up for the first, and he had returned to where he had been before dancing with her.

"I am sure you are correct, but you know Mama will not listen." Mary spoke the truth. Mama never listened.

"No, you are likely correct."

Over the next couple of hours, Elizabeth had been asked to dance once or twice, but with the dearth of gentlemen, she had sat out a great deal as had several of the ladies. Somehow, Kitty and Lydia had never been without a partner. They had been in high spirits. Their behaviour made her cringe.

After a sigh, she rose and stepped over to the refreshment table for a glass of punch. Mr. Bingley stood up with Jane once more. Her sister wore a reserved smile, but she was obviously happy—Elizabeth could tell.

"Mr. Darcy paid you a great compliment," said Charlotte appearing at Elizabeth's side. "He has danced with none other. Your mother has not ceased crowing of it."

"I am certain the gentleman was being polite. I hope Mama is not making too much out of one set. She will offend him if she does." She sighed. "Excuse me. I should see if I can temper her enthusiasm." Elizabeth took one more sip of punch before she put down her glass and hastened to where her mother sat with Lady Lucas, Mrs. Goulding, and Aunt Philips.

"I cannot say I am surprised Mr. Bingley would choose to stand up with Jane twice. She is so beautiful. Everyone says so. He surely recognises that she will make him an excellent wife."

"Lizzy did well by dancing with Mr. Darcy," said Aunt Philips. "He comes from a prominent family in magical circles, and I have heard he is worth ten thousand a year. Have you not noticed, Frances, that he has danced with no one else?"

"Ten thousand!" Her mother screeched in that tone that never failed to reverberate down Elizabeth's spine.

She hurried forward. "Mama, pray, keep your voice down. He will hear you."

Mama scoffed and waved Elizabeth away. "I do not know why he would wish to dance with you, but you must go over there and persuade him to stand up a second time."

"I shall do no such thing." Had her mother no sense of decorum?

The chandelier rattled, making those around them look up as three candles shot towards Elizabeth. She gave a sharp inhale as everyone gasped. How was she to avoid this? She could not use magic before all of these people—not yet.

Before she could try to shift out of the way, Mr. Darcy stepped in front of her and lifted his hand. "*Gaoth!*" A sudden gust of wind burst through the room, and the candles' flames extinguished, the sticks falling to the floor. Charlotte scrambled forward and picked them up. Not so much as a tiny plume of smoke came from the blackened wicks.

"I thank you, Mr. Darcy," said Elizabeth.

"Are you well, Miss Elizabeth?" He bent forward some to hold her gaze.

"I am."

Jane rushed over and set her hand on Mama's shoulder. "We should depart. I believe Mama is tired."

"I am not—" Jane's lips pressed into a fine line, and her mother's next words became muffled.

While Mary gathered Lydia and Kitty, Jane kept her palm upon her mother.

Elizabeth turned to Sir William. "Pray, forgive us for leaving so early. I am afraid it cannot be helped."

"Do not worry yourself. I understand, Miss Elizabeth."

Lydia and Kitty protested in loud tones as they approached with Mary. After a glance at Mr. Darcy, Elizabeth followed her mother and sisters from the assembly hall. Whether her father liked it or not, he would have to attend the next event. Mama now needed someone around who could control her at all times. After all, had Mr. Darcy not been present, tonight could have been a disaster.

Chapter 7

19th of October 1811

As had become habit every morning, they practiced in the clearing where Elizabeth now stood stiffly across from Mr. Darcy. She was at the ready, her palms itching with the magic she had summoned in preparation for the gentleman's attack. At the moment, they circled each other as though one of them would suddenly launch forward, yet that was not what happened during a magical battle.

Mr. Darcy spun and flung his arms forward as a pink light shot towards her. Her hands pushed forward, ejecting a bright light that engulfed the pink, then disappeared. A mist remained, but the remnant was harmless. It would not injure her or any animal who happened upon the vapour.

The gentleman across from her allowed a curve to his lips. "Your response was much quicker than a fortnight ago."

"I did not consider the best path forward as I did then. My instincts led me."

He stepped forward. "Just as it should be. If you have a firm enough grasp on countercharms and spells, you are better prepared and will respond without a great deal of deliberation over the matter."

She crossed her arms over her chest. Her cloak rested on a tree limb, but without the constant movement, the chill was penetrating the long sleeves of her gown.

"Is that what happened at the assembly? Did you respond without thought?"

"I felt a surge of power within the room and guessed the source to be your mother. Do you not ever feel her surges?"

She blinked. "No, I have become so accustomed to holding back my magic within Longbourn that I rarely experience what comes from my parents. Jane's calming influence is obvious, which is why I recognise the effect on my mind. Mama is more volatile. The fits are usually in bursts."

Mr. Darcy's fingers caressed down her cheek. "Maintaining such regulation must be exhausting."

"Do you find it so, Mr. Darcy?"

He stepped closer but frowned. "I beg your pardon?"

"You were very reserved last night. Do you not find it arduous?"

"Ah," he said. "You mean my discomfort in public."

"Yes."

"I much prefer to be at Pemberley with those I care about. At the moment, I am more reserved than is my wont in order to avoid betraying our connexion. Your father has always intended to announce you as the heir on the solstice. I believe he would prefer to stay to that plan if we can manage."

She lifted her one eyebrow. "You could have waited to come. Then you would not need to conceal your knowledge or our betrothal."

He stepped closer once more and leaned impossibly close. "I thought you might like to know your betrothed before we are wed, or would you have preferred to marry a stranger?"

With a huff, she let her arms drop back to her sides. "Does it matter? You gave me the opportunity to choose, but is it not all a formality? We have seen our future. We are to marry."

"You know as well as I do those visions can change. Are you that set against marrying me?" His eyes darkened, and he appeared forlorn.

"I never said I decided against you—"

He made up the distance between them and pressed his lips to hers before she could finish her sentence. His kiss was soft and tentative. He cupped her bottom lip with his but never pressed for more before pulling back just enough to kiss her forehead.

A snort from the edge of the clearing made them break apart.

Mr. Darcy laughed as he drew back. "I forgot about your chaperon."

She glanced at Herne, who stood in his favourite spot next to the trees. Her father had not come today, but the loyal stag had met them just inside the trees and followed them to the clearing as he always had whenever she walked to the stones. In his own way, Herne was precisely what Mr. Darcy had called him.

"Miss Elizabeth," said Mr. Darcy, "my hope is that you will want to be my wife by the time we wed, whether we marry at the solstice or before."

A gasp tore from her throat, and she pulled herself away.

"What is amiss?" His eyebrows were drawn down in the middle.

There, tucked neatly into the folds of his cravat was a familiar gold pin. "I have seen that moment more than once, but I was unable to see your face in the vision, probably due to how close we stood." She pointed to the pin. "I do not remember what you said just now, but I do remember seeing that. It has the letter 'D' on it, does it not? I cannot believe I never made the connexion before now."

A warmth overspread Fitzwilliam at Elizabeth's confession. He had wondered over the years if she had visions of him as he had of her. Of course, she had already told him of her emotions mirroring his at some of the most trying times of his life. He should not be so surprised by her seeing him as well, but he was. He could not help but allow a grin.

"I cannot pretend I am not pleased. Since I first saw you in my dreams, I have come to have feelings for you that I am certain will become a deep and abiding love between us. I believe the sight we had of you great with our child proves the depth of attachment that will form between us." In the past few years, his visions of her had become more frequent. How could he not have come to hold feelings for the caring yet sometimes impertinent young lady?

He lifted his hand to touch her face once more, but a loud snort made him step back with a chuckle. "It seems I am to receive no quarter from your beast. 'Tis a wonder I managed to sneak in a kiss at all."

She laughed, the musical quality washing over him and relaxing him. "I had no idea Herne possessed such talents. I have underestimated him. All this time, I thought him no more than a trusted companion."

"You have been fortunate to have him. I have only ever heard of white stags in legends. They are elusive, yet you seem to have found him with ease. Does that not make you curious?"

Her lovely face frowned. "I have never considered the matter. He was quite young when I first happened upon him in Oakham Forest, although he was fully formed. I believe I was seven at the time. Papa had just started letting me walk through the forest unaccompanied."

Fitzwilliam glanced over at the beast, who now grazed on some tender green grass. Surely, Mr. Bennet would have mentioned if he had conjured the animal for her protection. Could he have been born of natural means?

"What are you thinking?"

His attention returned to Elizabeth. "Just allowing my thoughts to run away from me. I am certain I am incorrect, so perhaps we should start our return to Longbourn. Your family will worry if you are not home soon."

They had practiced later than they had on most days. Elizabeth's abilities were impressive and came more naturally to her than his ever had. He had worked to perfect his skills, but she wielded new spells as though she was born with the knowledge. After witnessing her magic, he could understand why his father and hers believed she required marriage to another strong magical family. Anyone who witnessed her abilities would know she harnessed great power.

In fact, she was more powerful than most men, in his opinion, yet her sex would be a barrier to being treated as an equal. He had no such qualms. She was a superior creature. He was in no doubt of that!

"I am not certain I believe you. You exercise such an economy of words that if you ask a question, I am sure it is for a reason."

One side of his mouth quirked. "Nothing more than idle curiosity begged me to ask. The uniqueness of Herne's colouring and his demeanour simply made me question his origins. I am probably overthinking matters. I often do."

"You?" She scoffed in a playful manner. "I cannot imagine."

He clenched his hands at his sides. When she was impertinent, everything in him had to resist pulling her into his arms and kissing the smugness from her full lips.

"You should not tease me so when I cannot respond."

That one mischievous eyebrow arched. "Whyever can you not respond?"

"I believe if I do so, your protector will not appreciate my efforts." That was an understatement! He had no wish to meet the ends of those antlers!

"Herne would never harm anyone. I believe you lack sufficient courage."

He gave an incredulous bark. "I beg your pardon?"

"Am I truly so terrifying Mr. Darcy?" While she asked the question, she stepped backwards for three or four paces, then grabbed her cloak from the tree limb and darted into the forest. He did not delay in tearing after her. Her footfalls were easily discernible, and he followed their thudding through the trees until they neared the stream.

When he caught up to her, she was making her way across the stones where she had slowed so she did not fall into the water. He raced forward into the shallow stream, his tall boots protecting his feet from the moisture. He caught her around the waist, and she gave a sharp inhale as he held her over the water.

"Mr. Darcy, what are you about?"

"Not quite the retribution I had in mind, but this will do as well." He dipped her so her head was close to the surface of the chilly water. "You believe me a coward?"

"I did not say that, sir." She breathed quickly, her chest rising and falling in a rapid motion, yet her countenance appeared calm.

"I believe you did."

"Perhaps I should call for Herne, and we shall see whether you are still so bold."

He gripped her to him with one arm while he dug the fingers of his opposite hand into her side. Giggles burst forth from her and she squirmed, so keeping her from falling became more difficult.

"If you continue, I shall not be able to hold on to you."

"Then perhaps. . .you. . .should cease. . .tickling. . .me!" She could barely get the words out, she was laughing so hard.

She lurched, and he made to adjust her in his arms. Yes, he had threatened to drop her in the stream, but he had not intended to actually do it! As he attempted to keep her from falling, the heel of his boot caught something in the water, and he plummeted backwards onto his rear end.

Water splashed around them, and when it settled, he was sitting in the stream, the frigid water rushing by as it travelled to who knows where. Meanwhile, Elizabeth sat in his lap. Her eyes were impossibly wide as she gaped at him. Was she angry? What if she would not forgive him?

She continued to stare for a moment until she burst into peals of laughter. "I believe that did not end up as you had hoped."

"No, I had not planned on either of us becoming wet." He glanced over her and grinned at her amusement. "Are you well?"

"I am. You cushioned my fall quite nicely. I thank you."

Elizabeth lifted from his lap and held out her hand. He took it, and she leaned back as he made to stand, but his foot would not budge, and he tipped sideways, taking her back down into the water with him.

"Are you always so clumsy, Mr. Darcy?"

"No, but I believe my foot is wedged." He dipped his hand down by his boot and, with a push to a couple of rocks, managed to free his boot. When he stood, he helped Elizabeth rise.

"Forgive me. I should not have attempted to tickle you while holding you over the stream."

Her head tilted ever-so-slightly. "You are so serious. I enjoy a good mishap as long as no one is injured. I confess to being cold now, but I was diverted by what occurred. You are so stiff most of the time. I am glad to know you possess the ability to tease as well."

"You are?"

She looked about them. "I need to return to Longbourn, but I have not reinforced Herne's protection spell."

"When was the last time you did so?" Such a charm should last until countered, yet she always ensured the magic was cast anew whenever she visited the forest.

"With the slight rain yesterday, we did not meet, so two days have passed. I know the spell should be indefinite, but I do not leave his safety to chance. I always make certain he is protected before I return home."

He took in her bedraggled gown. "He cannot be far." They should not tarry. While his great coat and buckskin breeches helped keep him dry, her coat had offered no such protection.

She placed her hands on her pelisse and closed her eyes. Water poured from the wool and the muslin peeking from underneath onto the ground below. After the drips became few and far between, she opened her eyes.

"That should keep my gowns from weighing me down."

"You pushed the water from the fabric." Why had he stated the obvious?

"Of course. The elements are always easier to handle than create. Do you not prefer to manage them in the same manner?" While not completely effective, her solution would at least help her gown to dry quicker than it would have otherwise. He admired her cleverness more and more every day.

"Yes, I do. Drawing enough energy from the earth to create fire is more fatiguing as well."

"Exactly. Now, as for Herne, he has followed us more often than not. I am surprised he has not appeared as yet."

She made a valid point. The stag could not be far. "Then we should make our way back to the stones."

At his suggestion, they walked as though returning to the clearing, but about half-way to the stones, Herne snorted and stepped closer as they approached the great beast.

"Forgive me, my friend," said Elizabeth. She placed her hand on the creature's forehead. A glow emanated from where her palm met the stag's fur for a moment before she stroked down to his nose. "We shall see you on the morrow."

Herne tossed his head as though nodding. The animal did not understand, did he?

Elizabeth smiled, and he offered her his elbow. They ambled back out of the forest.

"You did not ride Hen this morning?"

"No, I felt the need to stretch my legs. If he is restless, I shall take him on a good run before the sun sets. When I departed, he was tucking into the oats and hay the groom had given him."

"It sounds as though he is being spoilt."

Fitzwilliam laughed. "He was this morning. I spoke to the groom who fed him earlier than usual, asking him to wait until after my ride tomorrow." He glanced up at the sun, which was higher than he would prefer for his return to Netherfield.

"We should both depart. Papa will worry if I am too late, and your hosts will wonder at your tardiness as well."

"Will your father join us tomorrow?" The gentleman's absence had been a surprise when Elizabeth arrived this morning.

She stepped away from him and put on her gloves. She commonly removed them when they were in Oakham Forest. "I believe he has decided we know what we should, and his presence is not necessary for us to perfect our skills. He has not said as much, but it would be quite like my father. He is, no doubt, sitting in his library reading as is his wont."

"I see. Then I shall meet you here in the morning." He took her hand and kissed her knuckles. "Good day, Elizabeth."

Her eyebrows gave a slight jump at his boldness, but she did not rebuke him for his familiarity. He took two paces backwards before turning and starting for Netherfield. He hazarded a glance over his shoulder, which revealed her travelling towards Longbourn. She peered over her own shoulder at the same time, her cheeks turning pink before she returned her attention to the path ahead of her.

The remainder of the journey to Netherfield was pleasant. The breeze was cool, but the birds chirped as he made his way between the new fields of winter wheat that had been sown last month. The young plants had just peeked through the earth, but they appeared healthy and would grow tall before providing their harvest in late summer or early autumn of next year.

When he entered the house, the peace of the morning was quickly shattered by the strident tones of Miss Bingley. Fitzwilliam grimaced.

"He is your friend! Why do you not know where he has gone? According to the stablemaster, he was on foot. He cannot have walked far."

"Caroline, he is his own master and does not require me to be his mother. He can come and go as he chooses, and he need not tell me nor you where he spends his time."

"How is he to marry me if he does not pass any of his days with me?"

Fitzwilliam paused outside of the drawing room. The cracked door allowed all that was said to be heard with ease from the hall.

Bingley groaned. "I have told you over and over that Darcy's parents arranged a marriage for him. He is intent on following through with that match—"

"He does not need an arranged marriage. He can marry me."

"Caroline," said Bingley on a heavy exhale. "His parents and the parents of this young lady likely made a magical contract—a binding agreement that cannot be broken without the consent of both parties and a counterspell—"

With a steady hand, Fitzwilliam pushed open the door. "Which I have no intention of doing. I have spoken to the young lady and her parents. They are intent on seeing the contract through." His claim was not quite a lie. Besides, Elizabeth had allowed him to kiss her this morning. That had to mean something, did it not? "Pray, find a gentleman who wants you and accept his proposal. You will receive no such attention from me."

Miss Bingley gave a screech and rushed from the room. A crash came from the hall, making them jump.

Bingley peeked through the door. "She shattered a figurine on that table against the wall." He sighed. "I believe that belonged to Louisa. She will not be pleased."

"I thank you for attempting to control your sister's schemes. I am to wed before the solstice, and I shall not allow her to ruin my plans."

His friend clapped him on the shoulder. "I understand. If need be, I shall send her to Scarborough. My aunt will be furious for the inconvenience, but she manages Caroline better than anyone in our family ever has." He clapped his hands together with an expectant look. "Now, enough of my pest of a sister. What part of estate management shall we discuss today?"

Chapter 8

29th *of October 1811*

Fitzwilliam hastened his mount towards Longbourn. The missive Mr. Bennet had sent to him late last night was concerning. Firstly, the gentleman had given no information in his letter. Instead, he had insisted Fitzwilliam call as soon as he was able. So, no morning practice with Elizabeth in Oakham Forest. His chest was heavy. He had come to enjoy those early morning moments sparring with their magic as well as verbally.

At Longbourn, he would surely spend time with Elizabeth, yet with Mr. Bennet's supervision. Even if he had the watchful eyes of Herne in the forest, the stag was a different sort of chaperon than Mr. Bennet. Her father would understand what they were saying— as well as what they were not.

The air was heavy this morning. He had never liked when it pressed on him in this way. The wind was restless, and its agitated whispers carried across the fields. He was not as adept at listening to them as Elizabeth. She understood them with little effort, but her feel of the earth and her ability to wield its power was natural. When he was learning, some spells had required multiple attempts to produce a feeble result. He had learnt to harness the magic and use it as his father had before him. How did a person become almost one with the earth as she seemed to do?

He glanced at the horizon only to find dark clouds looming in the distance. Something was amiss. His gut was too tight, and Mr. Bennet's note was too mysterious for naught.

When he dismounted near the stables, a groom rushed out and took his horse. "Miss Elizabeth is awaiting you by the kitchens, sir."

Elizabeth! They had spent almost every morning together since before the assembly, and he had become accustomed to her presence. She was swiftly becoming necessary. He needed her cheer and humour to face the remainder of his day in the same household as Miss Bingley, Mr. Hurst, and Mrs. Hurst. Of course, that pertained more to Miss Bingley than the others. That woman refused to listen or heed his multiple requests that she desist in her pursuit. Just yesterday, she had attempted to trap him alone in his bedchamber. Thankfully, his valet had entered the room before him and had ensured she was extricated without waking the entire household. What a nightmare that would have been!

He rounded the corner, and at the sight of Elizabeth, his heart immediately lightened. She was lovely, her bright eyes twinkling when she noticed him. Could she be coming to care for him as much as he was for her?

"How long have you been waiting?"

She grinned. "I was sitting in the window of my father's library, so I saw you and Hen approaching through the field."

He nodded and took her hand, rubbing his thumb along her bare knuckles. "I am relieved to hear you have not been in the cold for long." The sun peeked out from the clouds, but the wind was damp and brought a chill with it.

"No, which is why I am not wearing gloves. I made my way through the servants' passages so I would be here when you arrived."

He kissed her hand then held it between both of his. "Do you know what is so urgent? Your father did not give much detail in his letter."

"He has said little, but by his manner, a missive he received yesterday carried some grave news. He has been pensive ever since." She squeezed his hand. "I walked through the gardens just after sunrise. Can you hear the mourning in the wind?"

"Mourning? I could feel an anxiousness about it and perhaps a sadness, but I could not discern anything more." How did she catch those nuances he missed? Could she teach him to listen as well as she could?

"Before you arrived, I sensed change and a similar restlessness," she said. "At first, I believed you were the change, but since we combined our power on the altar, I am convinced the difference is caused by whoever I encountered in the vision. I believe more is afoot than we have believed at a glance."

He cradled her cheeks in his palms. "Whatever comes, I shall stand by your side. You will always have my aid."

She removed his hands and held them to her heart for a moment, then dropped one and tugged on the other. "Come. My father is waiting. Perhaps we shall understand more after he tells us of whatever has disturbed him so."

Her hand did not release his as they entered the kitchen. Mrs. Hill was not present today, so they continued through the back passages until they emerged into Mr. Bennet's library.

"Good morning, Darcy. Mrs. Hill has brought coffee and tea for us as well as some muffins in the event you missed breakfast."

"I shall be pleased to have some coffee, sir."

Elizabeth poured him a cup, with tea for her father. Once she poured some coffee for herself, she sat in her well-worn seat.

He took the chair beside her. "I confess to not sleeping well last night due to the lack of information in your letter. The uneasiness of the wind has not helped my feeling of apprehension."

The older man sighed. "Forgive me my brevity, but I had no wish of this information falling into the wrong hands. The Duke of Ormonde has disappeared."

Darcy sat forward abruptly. He was forced to shift his cup so hot coffee did not spill onto his lap. "Disappeared?" How could this have happened?" Particularly to someone as prominent as Ormonde.

"How have you come upon this news, Papa?"

"It seems Ormonde had some idea he was in danger. He never told his wife by whom or how he knew, but he insisted upon hiring men to protect her at all costs."

"She is carrying his child," said Fitzwilliam. "I would spare no expense under similar circumstances."

Bennet tapped his fist upon the table. "Nor would I. Due to his concerns, he penned a letter and implored her to send it to me should the worst occur. She has had no word of his death, but Her Grace fears the worst has already come to pass."

Elizabeth claimed the wind was mourning. Could this be why?

The gentleman shoved some papers across the desktop. Fitzwilliam set down his coffee and took the missive.

> *30 September 1811*
> *Berwick Abbey, Berkshire*
>
> *My good friend,*
>
> *If you are reading this, my wife has reason to believe I am gravely injured or dead.*
>
> *For the past fortnight, I have been sensing change as I am sure you have heard while walking out of doors and noticed while studying the stars. Soon after, I heard the whispers on the wind and was overcome by a foreboding sensation as well as a vision of what I believe to be my death. I do not know the voice of the creature I heard, but I was forced to drink a purging potion containing rue[4] to rid myself of the evil energy.*

---

[4] Rue is an herb believed to have protective, cleansing, and love-attracting properties. It has been used in magic and rituals for centuries.

I also believe someone is following me. The vision I had was of light and the flashes of spells, so I do not know how I came to be in that predicament or if my wife is well. I have hired men to protect her at all costs. If this child is a girl, I do not believe them to be in danger, but if this child is my heir, I am fearful of what may befall them should something happen to me.

Since you are receiving this, my wife has been instructed to come to you so she can be hidden until the time is right. I trust you to know the best course. My brother is to act as conservator until such time a son can take his place as heir, or until my brother must take over the estate as my successor. I am entrusting you to do what is best for my family. My brother will await word from you on the sex of the child.

I thank you for your aid and your discretion. You have been a faithful friend and correspondent these many years. Forgive me for requesting so much of you, but I know not where else to turn.

Godspeed,

Ormonde

Fitzwilliam handed the letter to Elizabeth, then rubbed his forehead. "His vision is like what Elizabeth described."

"I noticed," said Mr. Bennet. "I do feel the two of you should attempt to persuade the altar to show you more. The rejuvenation potion worked well before, but this time, I could brew a purging potion for you to take with you as well. Since Ormonde found it to be effective, it may be a more appropriate choice as a curative."

"I may see more, but I also may not." Elizabeth dropped the missive into her lap. "I also fear probing further into the matter may filter through to whomever is seeking out power. What if I alert them to my existence? By attempting to learn more, I could be sealing my own fate."

Mr. Bennet held out his hand for the letter. As he glanced over it again, he shook his head. "You are assuming the same as I am, I suppose."

"That this individual is seeking out and perhaps destroying those who possess the greatest magic?" asked Elizabeth.

Her father nodded. "The theory makes sense. There are a large number of magical families, and some have significant power, but at this time, only a handful are capable of the most formidable magic: the Darcys, the Ormonde dukedom, the Fitzwilliams, the Stuarts, and the Bennets."

As those who ceased to believe in magic lost their abilities, the number of truly powerful families had dwindled. Their world was shrinking. How long before it disappeared forever?

"When should we expect the duchess?" asked Elizabeth.

Mr. Bennet made a noise that somewhat resembled a growl. "She cannot come to Longbourn. Your mother's tongue is too loose. She would tell the neighbourhood and beyond that we have a duchess in our home. I also had a missive from my cousin William Collins, who is the heir of Longbourn. He possesses no magic whatsoever—not so much as a talent—and is a vicar at the Hunsford parish in Kent."

"Hunsford is a living that is bestowed by my aunt." Fitzwilliam took his coffee from the desk and took a sip.

Elizabeth frowned. "Your aunt?"

After swallowing, he placed his cup back on the saucer. "Lady Catherine de Bourgh. Sir Lewis possessed significant magic until he died with only a daughter to inherit the estate. My aunt manages

Rosings with an iron fist. If your cousin is unwed, I am certain she will have ordered him to seek a wife. She maintains that anyone who has one of her livings must be wed. She does not believe an unmarried man can tend properly to the needs of the parish without a wife."

"Yes," said Mr. Bennet. "And he indicated in his letter that he must seek a wife from amongst my daughters. I shall allow him to stay for the time he has specified, but I shall not sanction a match between him and any of my girls, even though my wife will be determined to have him marry one."

Elizabeth grimaced and squirmed in her seat. "It will likely be me. She is most disturbed by my presence. Whether he is suitable or not will mean little to her in comparison to the idea of having me removed from her life."

Her father sat forward and propped his forearms on his desk. "That is why I hope to announce your betrothal at Samhain. I confess I have concerns over waiting for you to wed, but I also do not want to rush you, my dear. Darcy has been quite accommodating in allowing you to know him better, but I would prefer your connexion known before your cousin arrives."

With a sizeable gulp, Fitzwilliam bit his cheek. This Mr. Collins could complicate matters! "I am not opposed to announcing our engagement, but I do wish to warn you that my aunt has long planned my marriage to her daughter, Anne. My father told her many times I was not at liberty to wed my cousin, yet he never mentioned Elizabeth for fear of my aunt seeking her out. Mr. Collins learning of our engagement will likely bring her to your door."

Mr. Bennet pinched the bridge of his nose. "Yes, I am aware of Lady Catherine's machinations. Your father mentioned them more than once in our correspondence. Do you know what talent she possesses?"

His forehead bunched. "I do not remember her ever using magic, though she is knowledgeable of the magical community. Hunsford is a larger village and is a mixture of those who still practice and those who no longer have magic. Giving the living to someone who is non-magical makes sense."

The older man stared at him for a moment. "You are not aware of her ability?"

"No. My father assumed it was insignificant, or she was unaware of it, which is why we have never seen nor heard of her using it."

"Curious," said Mr. Bennet. "Nevertheless, I would prefer to announce your engagement so no misunderstandings exist. I shall allow the two of you to discuss the matter for five minutes before I require an answer." Without further comment, Mr. Bennet departed the library.

Elizabeth bent her head to the side and lifted her eyebrow. "Now that you know me some, do you wish to run, Mr. Darcy?"

Run? What was she speaking of? "I do not understand."

"Well, you have mentioned I am impertinent, and I believe I am far too outspoken. Would you be willing to endure such a wife?"

He stood and took her hand, pulling her up to stand before him. "I rather enjoy your impertinence."

She gave a burst of laughter. "You enjoy my impertinence? You are teasing me."

"I assure you; I am in earnest." He tugged her closer. "When you are being clever, the slight curve of your lips begs to be kissed."

"How shocking—and forward. We are not wed. . .yet."

"Then you should put me out of my misery, relieve me of my torment, and consent to be my bride." She was fighting her amusement. That barely-there twitch in her cheek gave her away.

"You exaggerate, sir."

"Do I? I believe I tell the absolute truth. I have come to care for you deeply, and I would be honoured to have you as my bride."

"What of my tongue?"

"What is amiss with your tongue? Open your mouth and let me see. Is it forked or. . ." He feigned as though he was going to peek into her mouth.

"Mr. Darcy! I spoke of my inability to—"

"I am aware of what you speak, but I do not mind your outspokenness. I have been called proud by some, so perhaps your open nature will help to prevent me from being so anxious in company." When they were dancing at the assembly, he had relaxed some due to her presence nearby. It stood to reason she would be of aid in other situations as well.

"Elizabeth, we are not getting married tomorrow. If you are still uneasy at the thought of me being your betrothed, we can delay the announcement until closer to the solstice."

She smoothed his cravat away from the pin and stared at it for a moment. "No, I am well. We shall wed when Papa decrees it should occur."

Fitzwilliam's heart beat quicker than he was accustomed. She had agreed! She would be his! His palms cupped her cheeks. "You have made me exceedingly happy today, Elizabeth."

When her eyes lifted and their gazes met, he leaned down and claimed her lips. He only intended to press his mouth to hers once more, but as soon as she rose on her tiptoes and returned the pressure, he groaned and tugged at her lips, persuading them open. Before he could give in to temptation and taste her, a knock made him step back in haste.

Mr. Bennet entered a second later, his eyes darting between the two of them. "Have you settled matters?"

"Elizabeth said we would marry as you decreed, sir." Fitzwilliam steered Elizabeth to her chair for her to sit, but instead of resuming his place in the chair beside her, he set his hand on her shoulder.

"Good," said the gentleman. "So you will be wed on the full moon before the solstice per the agreement with your father. As you know, marriages on the full moon are blessed with prosperity and good fortune."

"The full moon before should be at the end of November." Elizabeth glanced back at him. "Are we to be publicly wed or will you conceal it until the solstice?"

Her father tapped a finger on his desk. "That is complicated. You see, I intend to hide the duchess in the small house in the forest." Fitzwilliam's head jerked up. House? In the forest? He had not been through the entirety, but he had not found such a place.

Elizabeth's hand covered his. "It is not far from the stream and hidden well with several charms and spells. Most who happen upon the place see the forest in front of them and feel the urge to walk in the opposite direction. It is the perfect place for the duchess."

"Yes," said Mr. Bennet, "but I would have hidden you away there until the solstice if she was not coming. I do have time to repair the dower house. It is small, but we could use the same charms and spells on it as on the house in the woods so those who approach are forced to depart.

"Darcy, you would need to have some excuse for your hosts."

He nodded. "I can easily claim a need to return to London before the wedding."

"I can be visiting Uncle Gardiner in town," said Elizabeth.

Mr. Bennet gave a definitive rap of his knuckles on the wood surface. "I shall speak with the vicar. He is a circumspect man. We have no need for concern that he might reveal our intentions. So, with that, I believe we have everything sorted."

Elizabeth looked at him and bit her lip. She still appeared ill-at-ease about marrying him, but he would ensure she never regretted accepting him as her husband. They would be happy. He would never allow their marriage to be anything less than perfect. After all, his happiness was at stake as well.

Chapter 9

31st of October 1811

During the Samhain celebration, Elizabeth stood beside her father while Papa welcomed the dead to walk among them for the evening. The bonfire behind them had been prepared beforehand and would be lit at the appropriate moment. As soon as her father had concluded the ceremony, he raised both of his hands.

"This evening, neighbours, I am pleased and excited to announce the coming marriage of my daughter Elizabeth to Mr. Fitzwilliam Darcy of Pemberley."

Murmurs erupted amongst the crowd, and Elizabeth's sisters glanced around at each other. Jane, who had been warned by Elizabeth earlier, had a hand on her mother's arm, never breaking her concentration on Mama's capricious mood. Her dearest sister always appeared so serene, but that expression was well known to Elizabeth. Dear Jane was too good!

To be of aid with tonight's revelation, Mrs. Hill had also mixed a substantial dose of calming potion in Mama's tea before they had departed, so between that and Jane's influence, her mother had not spoken a word since their arrival at the top of the hill that overlooked Oakham Forest. They would be fortunate if Jane's control prevented an outburst before they departed for Longbourn.

"Mr. Darcy is the son of my good friend Mr. George Darcy and his wife Lady Anne Darcy. We planned their union after Elizabeth's birth, and I am overjoyed at the prospect of such an esteemed and gifted mage to continue the magical traditions of the Darcy and Bennet families." He waved Mr. Darcy forward.

"My daughter will be joined to Mr. Darcy in a ceremony before the solstice. I will also be making an announcement of great importance during our solstice celebrations."

The whispers of those around them filtered forward while Elizabeth placed her hand on the arm of her betrothed, who had stepped forward to stand beside her.

"It is well known the Bennets have no heir. Is this to somehow make up for that fact?" someone said just loud enough to reach Elizabeth's ears.

Mr. Darcy covered her hand with his. "Do not respond. They will learn the truth soon enough."

While Elizabeth waited for the noise to subside, she glanced to her side in time to catch Miss Bingley glaring at her as though that lady could bore a hole into Elizabeth's head with the heat of her stare. Mr. Darcy had mentioned Mr. Bingley's sister had hopes, and that he had disabused her of any notion that they would ever wed. It seemed the lady had failed to take Mr. Darcy's assurances to heart. Why would Miss Bingley persist in such a futile endeavour?

"Elizabeth, your father is beckoning us to follow."

She was jolted back to what was happening around her. "Forgive me. I was merely distracted by Miss Bingley's countenance. Regardless of all you have said to her, she does not dissuade easily. I hope this will convince her to pursue a gentleman more amenable to her suit."

"I can only pray," he said in low tones.

Papa brought them forward to the light the bonfire, and as the villagers approached with unlit torches, she, Mr. Darcy, and her father set them ablaze on the large fire. All in attendance would take the flame home with them to light their hearths for protection. In the morning, the ash would be saved for its protective and cleansing properties.

Once everyone had their portion of the fire and had departed for their own homes, Papa took Mama from Jane. "Darcy, I assume you will join us for the walk back. Your horse is still in my stable, after all."

Her father glanced at her over his spectacles and led Mama towards home with her sisters following. When they stepped behind her family, Mr. Darcy leant closer to her. "We expected the surprise of the neighbourhood, but otherwise, the announcement went rather well, do you not think?"

What could he mean? Had he expected something more to occur? "The evening went as I had imagined, Mr. Darcy."

"Fitzwilliam," he said in a soft tone. "I would prefer it if you called me Fitzwilliam."

She looked up at him. He still possessed the ability to unsettle her from the inside out. How was he capable of inciting those flutters that could discompose her with nothing more than the volume and pitch of his voice?

"We have not been seen courting in public as yet," said Fitzwilliam, "which is why I expected more of a reaction, I suppose."

"I am certain that is why Papa mentioned the union had been planned. Most of the neighbourhood is surely more concerned with what you are to obtain from our union. It is well known we have no real fortune to offer, and with your wealth and connexions, you could make a far superior match."

He scoffed. "I have never desired to marry for money or for the ability to claim another as my friend or family. My parents loved each other, and I remember them sharing small touches or my father kissing my mother's hand or cheek. I much prefer the notion of having a similar relationship with my wife than one as cold and unfeeling as the one Miss Bingley would expect."

Elizabeth grinned and shook her head. "If that lady had the talent of incinerating one with her glare, I believe I would have been reduced to a pile of ash when Papa made the announcement." Not even Mama had ever levelled such malevolent looks!

A light laugh sent another frisson through her. "If you are curious, her ability is not useful in the slightest. From what Bingley has said, her eyes changed colour when she was a babe, but not the usual change most children have. They would change by the day and sometimes by the hour. Now that she can control it, Bingley has mentioned she will alter their shade depending upon the colour of her gown on a given day. He even told me she once terrified him as a child by turning their shade red one night. I am surprised she did not behave so this evening."

Her palm covered her mouth while she laughed. "Forgive me. The lady does appear to be very taken by her own appearance. At the assembly, I once noticed her primp in a mirror upon the wall." She did not just glance but had taken the time to fluff her gown and touch her face. She was most certainly one of the vainest ladies Elizabeth had ever met.

Fitzwilliam sighed gruffly. "I have witnessed her behave the same at a ball in London. She believes herself to be above most. Do not trust her. If she had any sort of ability that could cause harm, she would use it."

"If only we could match her to my cousin. Papa allowed me to read the letter from Mr. Collins. He is every bit ridiculous. We shall need to keep Mama restrained with potions for the entirety of the man's visit lest he see her hurl an object at me or someone else. I almost wish she had a talent similar to Miss Bingley. Convincing our cousin Mama's eyes were the same as yesterday would be much simpler."

"Your father can remove any recollection of magic if necessary."

"Yes, but as you are well aware, the more you tinker in someone's memory, the more you run the risk of damaging their mind."

"I would trust your father more than most," said Fitzwilliam.

"As would I, but a fortnight can provide many opportunities for Mr. Collins to witness what he should not."

"We have never spoken of your sisters' abilities. Miss Bennet's is not easily discernible. What of the others?"

They had fallen behind the group and spoke in soft tones. Since her betrothed had set their pace, he had likely endeavoured to keep their discourse private. Aside from her confidences with Jane, Elizabeth kept her thoughts and feelings close to her heart. The habit had been long engrained. She could not accidentally reveal herself as the heir, so confiding in others was problematic.

"Mary recalls whatever she reads. She can set her hand on a book and know its contents. The ability would be more useful if she did not restrict her reading to religious texts."

"*She* may consider remembering their teachings useful." One side of his lips ticked upwards. He was teasing her.

"Well, my sisters and I do not, particularly when we are the recipients of her moral platitudes."

His warm chuckle washed over her and made her breath hitch. "What of the others?"

"Kitty can urge a plant to grow, blossom, or produce fruit. She spends a prodigious amount of time in the gardens. We never lack for vegetables or fruit, and Mama's flowers are always bountiful. Kitty enjoys flowers and pretty things, so she walks the gardens whenever the weather is fine and tends to the plants. She can be silly and spends too much of her time with Lydia, but I am pleased she has a productive ability she enjoys. Her dedication to plants gives me hope that she will not always follow my youngest sister's poor influence."

When she looked at him, he watched the path in front of him, his brows drawn down a little. "I understand. My younger sister has not always sought the best of influences. Perhaps as Miss Kitty matures, she will learn to think for herself."

"Then we come to Lydia." Elizabeth returned her attention to her family in front of them. "She adores nothing more than an officer. A red coat makes the gentleman more handsome in her eyes. I am certain you saw her behaviour at the assembly. You must also understand that Lydia can enchant a gentleman with a certain turn of her head and tone of her voice. She discovered the ability two years ago and has been insufferable ever since."

"She is, for all intents and purposes, a siren?"

Elizabeth crinkled her nose. "Not exactly. You see the enchantment is short-lived. As soon as it wears away, the man she has charmed is not only immune to further inducement, but he also is repelled by Lydia's flirtations." Some spells had an aftereffect. Lydia's was just more pronounced and lasted for much longer than most. "Does your sister possess a useful talent?"

"Georgiana has the ability to play any musical instrument without practice. She will read the music for whatever she plans to play, then perform the piece without error. Her preference is the pianoforte, so she rarely practises any other instruments."

"That is impressive and useful in company. I would have welcomed such an ability." With Elizabeth's unwillingness and lack of time to practise, that talent would be welcome. Charlotte always made her play at gatherings. Elizabeth despised performing.

"You would be happy with a mere talent over being the heir?"

She closed her eyes for a moment. The breeze tonight was content, for the most part. An undercurrent of unease remained, but the earth was resting, and the offerings for the equinox and tonight's bonfire had aided in rejuvenating the magic within.

"What do you hear?" asked Fitzwilliam beside her ear.

"All is well, though what is coming is still causing unrest. Tonight's celebrations have shadowed what is to come." She could not describe the effect any other way.

Her eyes opened, and she rested her head against Fitzwilliam's shoulder so she could take in the stars that were bright in the sky. "To answer your earlier question: no, I would not prefer to have a talent over being the heir. I cannot imagine not hearing the restless whisperings of the wind or feel the power coursing through the altar near the equinox and the solstice. Those sensations have been my faithful companions since I was a child. To live without them would be akin to living without my hearing or my sight. They are so ingrained I cannot separate them from my soul."

He shifted his arms to put one around her and lift her for a moment. She gasped.

"I beg your pardon, but I would not have you fall."

She glanced over her shoulder. "Ah, the oak root that lies just behind Longbourn's gardens. I should not have been so inattentive. My thanks for not allowing me to fall on my face." She had done so often enough when not attending where she was walking; however, this time would have been mortifying!

They entered through the front doors with Papa striding to the fireplace to light the newly laid fire with the torch from the bonfire. As was done every Samhain, the fires had been dashed and the remnants of the prior fires removed before the family returned from the celebration. Re-lighting their hearth from the bonfire helped reinforce the bonds of their magical community as well as served to banish the house of any evil.

"Darcy, you are welcome to join us for our family celebration. The girls always enjoyed playing snap-apple. Lizzy has a particular talent for the diversion. She has yet to be burnt by the candle."

She glanced up at him. His eyebrows were raised as he stared at the rod Mr. Hill had hung from the ceiling with a candle on one end and an apple already hanging from the other. "I have never played snap-apple. We had hazelnuts for wisdom, but Mrs.

Reynolds feared burning down Pemberley with the rod and candle required for apples."

"You should try it, Mr. Darcy," said Elizabeth. "You only need master the timing. As the rod spins, it keeps a steady rhythm. 'Tis not difficult to duck and weave so you are not struck by the candle." If he truly wished, he could charm the rod to slow just enough to grab the apple with his teeth. She had never been allowed since her mother or her younger sisters might notice.

Mrs. Hill bustled in and took the torch from Papa. "Sir, my husband will light the remaining fires. Dinner will be served in an hour."

"Thank you, Hill. Mrs. Bennet will require her tea soon."

"Yes, sir. I already have the water ready."

As soon as the housekeeper departed, Mama perched herself into her chair. "What is this about Lizzy marrying Mr. Darcy? No one has ever mentioned this arranged match to me."

Jane's eyes widened, and she hastened to her mother's side and placed a hand to Mama's back. "I am certain Papa has his reasons."

"Since those decisions fall to me as the head of the family, I considered what was best for Lizzy and our family. I have kept the agreement between the Darcys and our family quiet as was planned when our daughter was still in her cradle."

Mama sniffed. "I do not believe she should be the one to wed Mr. Darcy. Jane is more beautiful, and Lydia is much more agreeable."

Elizabeth stiffened when Lydia tilted her head and fluttered her eyelashes towards the man. He visibly recoiled, and a burst of a laugh escaped Elizabeth's lips before she could turn and hide her amusement behind his arm. She could not help it. He almost appeared like an animal about to flee for its life.

"Then 'tis a good thing you never had a say in the matter," said Papa. "As it is, the magical contract is sealed and is irrevocable."

In actuality, if both parties agreed to dissolving the agreement, the proper counterspell could be performed, but Mama never took interest in much beyond her own abilities. The only sister who would know such a fact was Jane. Thank heavens Jane was circumspect!

Fitzwilliam's hand slipped down and wrapped around hers. The slight squeeze that followed managed to settle her a little. Mama was ill. He had possessed knowledge of that fact before they agreed to announce their engagement. He would not hold Mama's ramblings against her.

"Well, it seems our least deserving daughter will make a most advantageous marriage whether I approve or not." A ceramic vase upon the mantel rattled before flying towards Elizabeth's head. Her feet slipped as she was whirled around. When everything around her steadied, she lifted her head to Fitzwilliam's cheek against hers. He was wrapped around her.

"Are you well?" he asked.

"Yes, and I thank you for your quick actions, although I have had years of dodging Mama's anger." Her reflexes had not always been quick enough—not that she needed to tell him that. Once she had even been hit so hard, she had been insensible. Upon awakening, she had been dizzy for a week.

Her betrothed unwrapped himself from her as Kitty giggled in a tittering Lydia's ear. Why did it not surprise her that they would only see the romance of the situation?

At that moment, Mrs. Hill returned with the tray that she placed on the table beside Mama. "Mrs. Bennet, I am sure you have been wanting your tea," said Mrs. Hill. "Forgive me for not having it ready and waiting when you arrived."

Mama took the cup without question, took a sip, swallowed, then opened her mouth.

Elizabeth steeled herself. Whatever Mama had to say would not be good.

Her mother's forehead furrowed, and she snapped her mouth shut. Jane removed her hand from Mama's shoulder but left it to rest on the back of the chair. She was at the ready should Mama recall what was on her mind.

Mama opened her mouth once more, blinked, and shook herself. "What were we speaking of?"

Lydia took in a big gulp of air, but Jane grabbed her arm. Her youngest sister frowned and pulled from Jane's grip. "Do not use your gifts on me. I do not require them."

When Mrs. Hill made to depart, she gave Papa a slight curtsey. Her father's only response was a lifted eyebrow. He was not unaware that the housekeeper had used more than the calming potion in the tea. Mrs. Hill had tended to Mama faithfully for years and knew well Mama's ever-changing moods. Hill had also attended the bonfire, departing while they lit the torches for each household.

"It seems your housekeeper added some chamomile to the tea," said Fitzwilliam in low tones next to her ear.

In a non-magical person, chamomile had the ability to addle the memory, but in an individual with magic, the effect was more pronounced. The herb was a good way to muddle one's mind, and in this instance, would make for a more peaceful evening for everyone.

"Mrs. Hill has always had a good knowledge of herbs and remedies. She can also heal minor wounds." When Elizabeth had been hit in the head by Mama's superiorly aimed crystal figurine, the damage had been more than Mrs. Hill could fix in one attempt. Instead, she had healed Elizabeth a small amount at a time. If she had not, who knew how long she would have suffered the ill-effects of Mama's ire. The housekeeper had a worse time fixing the crystal figurine. Her talent could mend objects back together, but the first attempt did not always put the pieces back in the correct places.

From that moment forward, the rest of the evening was pleasant. Mama's ire subdued, her attention re-directed towards the bonnets Lydia brought out to trim, once again proclaiming over the lace on the Bingley sisters' gowns.

They played snap-apple, and Elizabeth and Fitzwilliam were persuaded to roast two hazelnuts on the fire. The nuts roasted quietly and did not jump away from the heat, which according to lore meant she and her betrothed were an excellent match.

At the end of the night, Elizabeth walked Fitzwilliam outside for him to fetch Hen. "I am sorry for Mama's response to our engagement."

He tipped up her chin with his knuckle. "Pray, do not fret over it. Your mother has little control over what she says and is steadily losing regulation of her ability. You will no longer have to bear her ire when we are at Pemberley. Until then, I promise to do all I can to protect you."

When he bent to kiss her forehead, she lifted up and captured his lips with her own. He did not linger, but they were in front of the house where anyone could see them.

"Will you be well riding at night?"

He smiled. "The moon is full. I should be able to see well enough. Are we to meet in the morning?"

She nodded. "Yes, I shall see you then."

He mounted and before turning his horse towards the road, he dipped his chin. "Good night, Elizabeth."

Chapter 10

1ˢᵗ of November 1811

This morning, Fitzwilliam had awakened earlier than was his wont. Since his eyes opened, he had been pacing, driven by the need to do something—anything. More than any other diversion, he itched to climb atop Hen and gallop through the fields to relieve the restless energy within. His engagement to Elizabeth had been announced and they would be wed on the next full moon. How he wished they had been wed yesterday. His feelings for her had deepened with each glimpse of her over the years, and now that he had held her in his arms and come to know her better, he was losing more and more of his heart with each day he spent in her company.

When he had finally mounted Hen and took to the fields, he allowed the horse his head to gallop with a reckless abandon that soothed Fitzwilliam's agitation. Now, an hour later, he had regained much of his regulation and needed to meet Elizabeth for today's practice.

At the entrance to the forest, he dismounted and took a deep cleansing breath of the crisp morning air. How did Samhain always seem to cleanse the Earth? The breeze was fresher, and the sky this morning was a clear vivid blue. Yes, the breeze held a chill, but when one stood in the sun, the coolness was not as noticeable.

He led his mount through the trees and across the brook. The willow had been a favoured meeting place since they had begun their practices in Oakham Forest. Elizabeth had confessed she enjoyed reading under the long boughs of the old tree, and the soft grass and moss that flourished beneath its branches seemed a comfortable place to rest. Perhaps before they departed Hertfordshire, they could enjoy the solitude the willow afforded together.

A crack of a branch made him whirl around. At the sight of Elizabeth on the opposite side of the stream, he could not help but smile. She was lovely, her bonnet hanging from her arm and her cheeks rosy from the crispness of the morning air.

"Good morning," she said as she crossed on the stones.

He offered her his hand to step across the last. "Good morning, Elizabeth. I hope you slept well."

She arched her neck just so. "I dreamt of you last night."

With a start, he tugged her a little closer and took both of her hands in his. "You did? What did you see?" Why was her confession so alluring?

"Well, I saw two young men racing through the fields on horseback. The other gentleman was the victor and enjoyed his triumph greatly. He teased you before becoming serious. He mentioned another man, a Wickham I believe, who had caused you problems in school."

He winced. He had anticipated this meeting, and her mere mention of Wickham had dampened the lightness in his chest with little effort.

"George Wickham is the son of my father's steward. He is a reprobate and tormented me whenever he had the opportunity. I shall tell you everything, but pray, should you ever happen upon that man, do not let down your guard. He possesses no more than a talent, but he is cunning, and though your magic is considerably stronger, he does not fight fair. I have no doubt you could win, but I fear he would attempt some mischief and harm you before you could best him."

She scraped her teeth along her bottom lip. "I understand, but I do hope when we are afforded the opportunity, you will share with me what you have held back."

"Once we are wed, I shall tell you all. I swear it."

He bent down and claimed her lips. He would give all he had to keep Wickham far away from her as well as from Georgiana. That man would do all in his power to destroy anything and anyone who brought Fitzwilliam happiness.

Today, he had no desire to hold back. They were not before Longbourn, and Herne was nowhere in sight. Before he could be caught, his lips parted hers and he finally dipped his tongue in and caressed the softness within. She inhaled sharply but did not withdraw. Instead, one of her palms rested on his cheek while the other pressed against his side. His chest swelled. She was accepting his kisses without reservation.

When he drew away, he pressed his forehead to hers. "Do you know how you tempt me?"

Her thumb brushed along his jaw as she pulled away. "Would you tell me who the other gentleman was in the vision?"

He cleared his throat. "That was likely my cousin Richard Fitzwilliam. He is the second son of the Earl of Glen."

"From the feeling I had during the dream, the two of you are close."

"Yes, we are like brothers. He and I also share guardianship of my sister, Georgiana."

She linked her arm through his, and they started towards the stones. "He is in the Regulars?"

"Yes, if the vision is what I believe it to be, you saw a conversation we had not long after my father's death. Richard's father had purchased the commission a year prior. He was to be sent to the peninsula, so he had come to Pemberley to discuss our plans for my sister. She is twelve years my junior, and my father had intended for her to attend school, but we had decided to wait until her mourning was complete."

"Does she still attend school?"

"No, we removed her from school in April. She is currently at Pemberley with her companion, Mrs. Annesley."

Elizabeth stopped and spun to face him. "Mrs. Joseph Annesley?"

His chin hitched back a hair. She knew Mrs. Annesley? "Yes, her husband's name was Joseph."

A happy laugh bubbled from Elizabeth's throat. "Mrs. Annesley cared for me when I was a baby. She was in my father's employ until I was five when another magical family had need of her abilities."

He pulled his shoulders back and released them to alleviate some of the sudden tension within. "She first worked for the Darcy family when my mother died in childbirth. We required a nurse for Georgiana."

"And Mrs. Annesley is a nurturer," said Elizabeth almost to herself. "My father told me another family had desperate need of her, but I was so young. All I knew was that the only mother I had ever known had left me. Nurturers are rare, so pray, do know that I understand why she had to leave, although at the time, I was desolate."

It was no wonder. Nurturers had the ability to care for a child at any part of their lives, even if it meant being a wet nurse. Mrs. Annesley had been with them until Georgiana had left for school. After Ramsgate, Mrs. Annesley had returned at his request. She had served in another household, but the child was old enough that a maid would suffice. He had been fortunate indeed that Mrs. Annesley had been in a position to return.

"I can understand why your separation from Mrs. Annesley would be painful. By the time Georgiana was placed in school, you did not require Mrs. Annesley as much as when you were young, so your father would not have required her return."

She wrapped her arm through his as they continued walking. "No, and Papa could not spare the expense. Mama enjoys shopping, and the herbs for her tea are costly. He does not temper Mama with the dressmaker, so he must curtail his spending in other places."

When they reached the stones, the white stag rested at the border of the clearing in the last tuft of green grass. He snorted at their approach.

"I see our chaperon has anticipated us," she said with a smile.

"At least he allowed me to have you alone for the walk here." Any opportunity to steal a kiss was welcome!

She pivoted around near the altar. Her mouth firm, and her hands clasped in front of her. "I believe we should combine our powers on the stone again."

He wasted no time in shaking his head. "No, I recall how weak you were the last time we made that attempt. I shall not have you harmed."

"I was not harmed. Papa mixed the potion to remove the residual magic that leaked through. I also mixed some of the potion the duchess mentioned in her letter myself and have it with me." She removed two small bottles from her cloak pocket.

Should he give in? If he did, they could know more about what was to come, but they could also increase the risk of harm to Elizabeth. Too many unanswered questions existed! Who was this person? Did they know of Elizabeth? Anyone with enough magic to cast spells of that calibre should be capable of visions as well.

"I am not sure." He had just obtained her consent to marriage. He could not lose her now. His heart had been entwined with hers since his first vision of her. In the beginning, she was a beloved friend who visited him in his dreams, but as she matured and became a young lady, his feelings had gradually deepened until he could not pinpoint the moment when he had fallen in love with her.

She had been sheltered from their engagement, so she had not understood the connexion to him throughout her life, but now that she was aware of him and had come to know him, she had become more receptive to his attentions. Not that he had many opportunities with Herne always nearby.

He breathed in an effort to calm himself. If he was too emotional over Elizabeth, the altar would focus on their lives not only from before but also what would come after their marriage and not what they wished to know.

"Mr. Darcy?"

He spun around at the voice behind him, his arms outstretched to protect Elizabeth. When the lady dropped the hood of her cloak, his arms fell to his sides.

"Your Grace, you should not have left the protection of the cottage." He had only met the Duchess of Ormonde twice in his life, but he recognised her with ease.

"My guards told me they had seen you with Miss Elizabeth in the forest most mornings since our arrival." She glanced over her shoulder. Just behind the treeline stood two sizeable men who watched their surroundings with keen eyes.

"I need a message relayed to Henry Bennet, but I did not want to put it in writing in the event the letter was intercepted. I also could not venture out to call on Longbourn."

Elizabeth stepped beside him. "Now that we have seen your men, you can send them to Longbourn should you require one of us to attend you. I can find the cottage with ease."

Her Grace lifted her eyebrows. "I am certain you could."

He pressed a hand to his betrothed's back. The duchess was not a threat, was she?

"Miss Elizabeth," said Her Grace, "my husband visited me last night for Samhain."

Fitzwilliam's body gave a jolt, and Elizabeth's hands covered her mouth before she let them slide down and come together at her chest. That could only mean one thing.

"Your Grace, pray, accept my condolences," said Elizabeth.

The duchess gave a dip of her chin. "I felt his loss the evening he died, Miss Elizabeth, so his presence last night was not as shocking to me, I suppose. I had left my windows open to invite his visit. As you are aware, we must cater to the beliefs of the non-magical as well as those who still believe. While I knew of his death, if I had said as much to the constable or had a letter to your father been intercepted, I would have appeared a killer."

She was correct. No one without a knowledge of magic would understand the bonds binding those who were meant to be connected for life—or even an eternity.

Her Grace brushed a tear from her cheek while her other hand rested on the swell of her abdomen. "My husband was limited by the bindings of death, of course, but before he was forced to leave, he told me what he could. An individual with a dangerous talent has somehow learnt to harness their ability, and is capable robbing others of their power. My husband was the second heir to have their magic stolen."

Elizabeth grasped one of his hands in a tight grip. "What is their intention?"

"He never mentioned one," said Her Grace. "But I believe we must assume the worst. Your father is well known in our circles. Due to the connexion to Merlin and Niniane, the Bennets possess what is likely the most powerful magic in the world. Whoever this is will not overlook him. He is in grave danger—as are you."

The duchess took three steps closer, coming face to face with Elizabeth. "My husband saw visions of you several times over the past few years. He took his knowledge of your identity and the strength of your magic to the grave, I assure you, but your ability is also why you must take great care. You are in just as much danger as your father should your position as heir be revealed."

Fitzwilliam made to speak, but Her Grace lifted a hand. "Miss Elizabeth has the support of the Ormonde dukedom, and always will. I believe the time has come for a woman to be heir. Whether it is due to the Bennet ancestry, or some other happenstance is irrelevant. I shall be of aid to you, Miss Elizabeth, in any way possible."

His betrothed shook her head. "I would not have you or your child come to harm. We must return you to the protection of the cottage."

"I heard you mention combining your powers on the altar," said the duchess. "Allow me and my men to be present so you are protected while you probe the stone. You know as well as I that you will be vulnerable."

Elizabeth's lips pressed into a line. "I appreciate your willingness to help us, but I would be more at ease if you were safe."

"Thus far, my men have only seen you and Mr. Darcy in these woods. I am certain some from the village come to make offerings from time to time, but we have had yet to see anyone. We shall be well. Matthew has the ability of concealment. He can ensure we are not visible until you have completed your task."

He glanced at Elizabeth. Her Grace's plan had merit. "I believe the sooner we make our attempt, the sooner Her Grace will agree to return home."

The duchess clasped her hands in front of her. "Mr. Darcy is quite right. So, shall we begin?"

Elizabeth gave him a side-long look as they approached the giant stone. When she stood before it, she placed her palm upon the smooth surface and closed her eyes. The duchess had turned her back on them, so he pressed his chest to Elizabeth's back and set his palm over hers. Should she collapse or the magic take a turn, he would be aware sooner with such intimate contact.

When he closed his eyes and turned his magic into the stone, the black of his closed eyelids soon gave way to them at the altar just as it had the last time they had made this attempt. In the next moment, Elizabeth stood at the altar, beautiful with the crown of rosemary and sage upon her head. Mr. Bennet was every bit the proud father standing beside her. The scene before them soon blurred and was replaced with one of the parlour at Netherfield.

"Brother, Miss Bennet is quite pretty, but she would accept you for the sake of her family and your wealth. She does not love you. I do not know what Mr. Darcy is thinking of, connecting himself to such a family. The Bennets are hardly suitable. You will be laughed out of London with a match like Jane Bennet."

"Caroline, you know not what you speak. You have ignored magical matters your entire life, and now, you give precedence to those who do not deserve it. Jane Bennet is highly suitable. You would not understand the prominence of her family because you failed to listen at Samhain nor did you wish to spend the autumn equinox here; you insisted upon journeying to Stonehenge." He stood and shifted before his sister. "Now, since you cannot be pleasant, you will be sent to my aunt in Scarborough. Do you understand?"

Before Miss Bingley could answer, everything around him vanished and was replaced with a drawing room. Where were they?

The room was full of people. A party was happening. Mr. Philips stood near the doorway while he greeted guests. As Fitzwilliam glanced about the room, he paused at a figure in a red coat that appeared familiar. No, it could not be. Why would he be in Meryton?

When the figure turned, Fitzwilliam had to keep from charging forward to break the blackguard's nose—not that he could in a vision. How had Wickham purchased a commission?

The drawing room blurred, and suddenly, he was outside. The clash of magic drowned out the chirping of the birds, although any local fauna surely fled to avoid becoming hit in the crossfire. He approached the flashes of light that filtered through the hedgerow that was white with snow.

This was the garden at Longbourn! When he stepped through, Elizabeth stood to one side her hands raised as she spun to deflect a spell. She was magnificent. Her hair had become unbound in the fracas and flowed down her back in a cascade of curls while she moved her hands in a circle then threw them forward sending a blast straight at—

He was jolted back from the altar, and Elizabeth hit him in the chest. His arms came around her to keep her from falling.

"Are you well?" She had not been struck in what he had seen, but that was not to say the exertion of probing the stone had not caused some fatigue.

He brought her to a rock, which had been set as a step to reach the altar, and aided her to sit. That was when a crimson stain upon her shoulder caught his attention.

"How did you become injured?"

Elizabeth pressed her palm to her forehead. "Whoever it was threw a dagger at me before we duelled. I believe it was laced with something. The fatigue was overwhelming."

"In what I saw, you were fighting brilliantly." As he spoke, he pulled back the shoulder of Elizabeth's cloak and gown to reveal a slash. The wound was not dangerous, but it was deep. Her colour was what worried him most. She was too pale.

"Allow me to be of aid." The duchess lowered herself beside Elizabeth, placed her hand upon the wound, and began to sing the most haunting melody. Her Grace frowned while she sang, but when she stopped and removed her hand, the injury was gone.

Elizabeth's hand rubbed over the healed flesh, and she gasped. "You are a phoenix."

He stared at the duchess. The non-magical believed phoenixes to be birds who could conceal themselves as humans when in fact, they were the opposite. He had never met a phoenix before.

"I am," said the duchess. "My family has concealed our abilities for generations. The eldest son is always the heir like in all magical families, but the females are phoenixes. To keep our abilities hidden, we always claim talents that no one would care to see. Most people believe I am capable of no more than summoning insects. My husband understood the necessity to hide what I am, and if someone wished to witness my ability, he would have ensured my success by calling the bugs himself. He was an excellent man."

"We shall not reveal your identity to anyone," said Elizabeth. "I swear it."

Her Grace pushed herself to stand. "Your father knows, of course. The Bennets have had knowledge of my family's legacy for centuries. I am certain he would have told you when the time was appropriate. You must know the adversary you faced in your vision was attempting to drain your power. I could sense the residual when I healed you."

Elizabeth's gaze met his. Her colour had greatly improved. "That explains the fatigue when the visions end."

As Fitzwilliam helped Elizabeth to her feet, he placed his arm around her back in the event she required further support. "Your Grace, we are indebted to you for your help, but if you would allow us, we do need to return you to your home before we return to Longbourn to speak to Mr. Bennet."

She stepped to Elizabeth's side and looped her arm through his betrothed's. "I shall accept your kind offer. I thank you."

Elizabeth found the site of the house with ease and, with a quick charm, rendered it visible to them until the duchess entered with her guards and closed the door behind her. Once she was within, Elizabeth re-cast her charm that concealed the home and took his hand. "We need to speak to Papa."

Chapter 11

1ˢᵗ of November 1811 cont. . .

When they entered Papa's library, he looked up from the sizeable book on his desk and his forehead creased. "What has the two of you at sixes and sevens?"

Elizabeth hastened forward and placed her hands on the desk. "The Duchess of Ormonde found us at the stone circle. Her husband visited her last night with the most disturbing news."

Her betrothed came to her side and placed his hand upon her back while she relayed the information Her Grace had shared in the forest. He added his opinion here and there on certain facts, but he spoke for no more than to support her statements. His pride was not wounded by her place or that her magic was similar to that of a man's. Her father had selected the best possible match for her. Fitzwilliam would never attempt to claim her power for his own or attempt to suppress her. He was all that a gentleman should be.

Once she finished her recitation of all that had occurred, her father sat back in his chair and rubbed his beard. "I am wary of delving too far into the future using the altar. With the aid of Her Grace and the visions you have already seen, we have an idea of what is to come. If only we had a more definite knowledge of when."

"Sir," said Fitzwilliam. "As I mentioned before, the hedgerow I slipped through had a coating of snow."

Mr. Bennet tapped his fingers upon the desk. "Yes, so we have every reason to believe this will happen sometime this winter. I just wish we had more." He stared ahead as though seeing something not there for a moment. "As I said, I do not want you seeking more information in the altar. If you happen to have a vision, that cannot be avoided, but the draining of energy you experience from the sight of what will happen, is disturbing—particularly combined with the knowledge the duchess imparted this morning.

"I am not averse to the two of you continuing to practice, but I wish to spend as much time as we can poring over books in the hopes of discovering whatever magic this person is using to accomplish such a feat. I have never heard of it, and that disturbs me most."

"If I may, the duchess claimed it was an ability," said Fitzwilliam. "We may not find a reference to such a talent in any book. After all, unheard of talents and abilities are discovered all of the time. It is the diverse nature of our number that is what is so rich about our community." He stepped back and began to pace. "You must know that one of the visions I saw was of a man I have known for my entire life. It seems he is to come to Meryton as part of the militia quartering here over the winter. His name is George Wickham, and he is not to be trusted. Thankfully, this Wickham was not the heir. The elder son died as a babe, so Wickham has no more than a talent for persuasion. He swindles shopkeepers and gentleman, cheats at cards, and has no scruples about seducing women. I suggest we prepare the village in advance of his arrival."

She bit her cheek. The officer standing in Sir William's drawing room had been unfamiliar to her, but apparently, he was known to Fitzwilliam. With her two youngest and silliest sisters, this man could be dangerous.

"We need to find some way to shield Kitty and Lydia."

Her father groaned and leaned his head back against his chair. "We could hope Lydia uses her ability early, and he rejects any further advances from her."

"Papa! If they both enchant the other, she could be with child before he becomes immune to Lydia's charms."

"No peace will exist in this house if I restrict them to Longbourn." He sounded like a petulant child.

"Sir," said Fitzwilliam. "Wickham is not to be trusted with even the lowliest maid. Your daughters should be protected at all costs. I shall await Elizabeth in the mornings behind Longbourn so I may accompany her to the forest, but you should make preparations to protect your other daughters when they are not at Longbourn."

Papa rubbed his temples. He valued his peace above all else. He was her beloved father, yet he was not the most diligent. After all, he had come to the forest the first couple of days Elizabeth had practised with Fitzwilliam, then had left Herne to chaperon their meetings. Thank heavens Fitzwilliam could be trusted to behave with honour!—Well, mostly behave.

Her father stood and crossed to the window. "I understand your concern over this Wickham, but the duchess's news is much more dire. Someone is robbing heirs of their powers. Ormonde had substantial magic, and though we know little of this other heir, we must assume this rogue has acquired enough power to be dangerous. If this person is attempting to divert your magic to themselves in the vision, it also explains the residual effect you feel when it is over.

"No, first and foremost, we must discover who this individual is and put a stop to their treachery. Someone hoarding magic is dangerous. There is a reason the earth has a limit to the amount of power one person can wield."

Fitzwilliam took Elizabeth's hand in both of his own. "The Bennets' abilities have always surpassed most, but it is no wonder given the history of your family. You and your ancestors have preferred to live quietly without stirring unrest or striving for status, so you have never been perceived as a threat. Whoever this is, they must be hoping to elevate themselves above all. We must warn as many families as possible. They must guard themselves and their heirs so this thief cannot succeed in their plans."

He was correct. Steps had to be taken to protect not only the magical but the non-magic. If someone acquired enough power, they could enslave those they perceived as threats or lesser than them. The moment her status was revealed, they would, no doubt, seek her out. As a lady, they would assume she was weak. She would have to prove them otherwise.

They had to defeat this person. Whomever this was could not succeed, or the results would be dire!

2ⁿᵈ of November 1811

When Elizabeth entered Lucas Lodge for Sir William's party, she was tighter than she had ever been in her life. Would the Wickham Fitzwilliam had told them about be in attendance? The militia was to remain for the winter, so this may not be the correct circumstance or even setting—they had been in Uncle Philips's house in the vision—yet that knowledge did not relieve her discomfort at the prospect of meeting such a man.

"I see no one from the militia," said Fitzwilliam in hushed tones near her ear. "You can relax."

She took in everyone milling about the drawing room. "Why do you not believe me to be relaxed?"

"Because you are squeezing my arm so tight, I am losing feeling."

With a start, she released his forearm. "Forgive me. I had not realised I was hurting you."

He kissed the back of her hand. "I shall suffer no lasting harm. As for Wickham, only a few men have arrived in preparation for the remainder, but since your father has set forth his restrictions for now, your sisters will not argue as much later when Wickham is in town."

Papa had insisted Lydia and Kitty remain behind with Mama. All three objected strenuously to his edict, which was why her father stood in front of them to greet Sir William. In his eyes, a party was much better than suffering the complaints and flying objects at Longbourn, so he accompanied them. Mrs. Hill had provided Mama, Kitty, and Lydia her special calming tea. Hopefully, they would all soon retire for the evening.

"Bennet!" Sir William grinned widely as he and her father bowed to each other. "You have not attended one of our parties in some time. I am honoured you came." He looked behind to her and Fitzwilliam, then Jane and Mary behind them. "But where are Mrs. Bennet, Miss Lydia, and Miss Kitty?"

"My wife had a headache, and my youngest daughters remained behind to keep their mother company."

Sir William clasped his hands. "Well, that is a shame. Maria will be disappointed, but Charlotte will be pleased to have the opportunity to speak with Miss Elizabeth. She called to congratulate you on your engagement yesterday, but you were on one of your walks."

She withheld a wince. "Mrs. Hill mentioned Charlotte's call, and I was sorry I was not home. I shall make sure I speak with her this evening."

"Mr. Darcy," said Sir William with another bow. "I am pleased you could join us. Your friend Mr. Bingley arrived a moment ago with his sisters."

Papa shifted to allow Fitzwilliam to step closer to their host. When her betrothed approached Sir William, he returned the gentleman's welcome.

"Yes, Bingley said they would attend, but Mr. Bennet had offered for me to join their family tonight, so I accompanied Miss Elizabeth instead."

"And why would you not! What gentleman would decline an invitation to join his betrothed? How can you refuse when such beauty is before you?" Sir William's voice carried with the last part of his statement as Charlotte approached. Her nose crinkled at her father's statement.

Elizabeth's cheeks warmed. Sir William often praised the Bennet daughters' comeliness, which often offended Lady Lucas and Charlotte, who was sometimes called plain. Poor Charlotte deserved some recognition. She was a practical sort—a trait that deserved admiration. She was also intelligent. Her ability to sense someone's feelings or mood was also a useful talent. She deserved more notice than Sir William gave.

"Ah, here is my daughter," said Sir William. "I am sure you wish to share confidences, so I shall greet your sisters. I hope you enjoy the evening."

Elizabeth smiled at Sir William before approaching Charlotte and clasping her hands in her own. "How are you?"

"I am well, Lizzy. I am sorry I did not congratulate you on your engagement on Samhain, but you were surrounded by all and sundry who wanted a bit of the fire, and my mother wished to return to Lucas Lodge."

"You need not apologise. I had not considered there might be calls yesterday and held to my usual habits. I should have been home when you came."

Charlotte shook her head. "I understand it is difficult for you to be around your mother for long periods. I would not have you alter your day for me." She looked over Elizabeth's shoulder and curtseyed. "Mr. Darcy, it is agreeable to see you again. Congratulations on your engagement to my friend. She will make an admirable wife."

After dipping his chin, Fitzwilliam offered Elizabeth his arm. "She makes an admirable betrothed, so I have no concerns."

Her friend's eyebrows rose while she smiled. "Indeed." She turned to Elizabeth. "I hope you will play for us tonight."

Ugh! "Oh, no, Charlotte. I have had little time to practice of late. No one wishes for me to torture their ears with a performance." She had been spending all of her spare time with Fitzwilliam. Her playing the pianoforte also called her mother's attention to her presence in the house. She avoided that whenever possible.

"While I would love to hear Miss Elizabeth perform," said Fitzwilliam. "I can attest that she has spent little time preparing for others to hear her play. I have occupied as much of her attention as her father will allow, and she has been afforded few opportunities to sit down before an instrument."

Charlotte's shoulders fell. "I am disappointed, but I shall not press. Your father has always demanded much of your time to be spent helping him in his library. I am certain you have been quite busy."

Elizabeth nodded. "I have. I thank you for understanding."

Maria and Mary passed arm in arm. At least Maria seemed willing to spend the party with Mary, who usually spent gatherings alone. Jane was quickly intercepted by Mr. Bingley, who led her over to where some of the young ladies had set up a space to dance. Miss Goulding sat at the pianoforte ready to perform.

"Would you care to dance?" asked Fitzwilliam.

Before she could respond, Mrs. Goulding approached. "Congratulations, Miss Elizabeth, on your engagement."

Soon, Charlotte's aid had been required by her mother, and their neighbours continued to offer their well wishes. They had no reprieve until Mrs. Lucas announced dinner was served.

"Come." Fitzwilliam steered her into the dining room. Their seats were beside each other, and Elizabeth sank into her chair. She had never minded conversation, but they had not had time to draw breath since speaking to Charlotte. Perhaps after the meal,

Fitzwilliam would be amenable to sneaking outside for a moment of peace. He should not object since he was not fond of gatherings.

She had to admit he had been all that was agreeable this evening. He had not smiled much, but he had thanked every person who offered their congratulations and extolled on his good fortune—even sounding gracious and complimentary despite his economy of words. She could not complain.

"Miss Elizabeth, Mr. Darcy," said Sir William while everyone was beginning to eat. "Your father has told me you will be married before the solstice. Not a traditional time for a wedding, but a rather fitting beginning: starting your life together as the days become longer in preparation for the spring and rebirth."

Elizabeth set down her fork. "I have always loved the solstice traditions, so having our wedding accompanying it will make it even more special." The candles and greenery used to decorate for the solstice made Longbourn seem like an extension of the forest. Her family always decorated more than most, but with Christmas being shortly after, the boughs of evergreen and candles remained for the festivities to come.

She nearly jumped when a hand squeezed her leg, but she placed her palm over Fitzwilliam's and rubbed his knuckles with her thumb. He never failed to become more affectionate when their upcoming nuptials were mentioned. His attentions did not always involve touching, but at times, his gaze would soften or he would look upon her in such a way her breath would catch in her chest.

It was fortunate she had been ambidextrous, a trait she inherited from her father. All of the Bennet heirs had been able to use both hands. She had always hidden her abilities with her left side due to the superstitions around the use of that hand as well as to keep her identity as the heir secure. Tonight, everyone was so busy, they should not notice her using her left hand to eat.

The conversation flowed around them. A few extolled their congratulations over their upcoming wedding, but the discourse soon ventured to other topics concerning those of Meryton—the militia encampment as well as their neighbours' plans for the upcoming winter.

The whispers on the wind had indicated a cold winter. In case the ground froze, her father's tenants had already tilled hay into the fields as soon as their livestock had eaten down whatever remained of last year's wheat, barley, and oats in preparation of next year's planting. The winter wheat had already been sown. While they spoke, she said little. She loved nature. Regardless of their conversation consisting of farming matters, she absorbed every word. Any talk regarding the earth soothed her. Was it the same for all heirs?

As soon as the meal ended, Mr. Bingley and Jane met them by the door to the drawing room.

"Miss Elizabeth, congratulations on your engagement to my friend. He is certainly less taciturn in your presence. I believe you will be good for him."

She laughed and hugged Fitzwilliam's arm a little tighter. "He is not so taciturn. I have witnessed more than one smile in my time with him."

"That is because they are all meant for you," said Fitzwilliam. He spoke softly and near her ear, but Jane's eyes widened and Mr. Bingley grinned. They had heard.

"Such pretty words, Mr. Darcy."

"Do not tease, Lizzy," said Jane. "Many ladies would kill to have such devotion."

An odd heat to the side of her head made her turn. Miss Bingley was once again staring at her with the same glare she had used on Samhain. Instead of holding that lady's gaze, Elizabeth returned her attention to their party.

"Oh, look, Miss Bennet," said Mr. Bingley. "They are lining up for another dance. Would you do me the honour?"

Elizabeth's heart swelled. Mr. Bingley had danced with several of the young ladies in attendance, but he had now singled out Jane twice. If Mama had been here, she would crow with pleasure just like she had after the assembly.

"I would be honoured, Mr. Bingley."

As soon as they excused themselves, Fitzwilliam faced her. "Would you like to dance?"

She shook her head. "No, I would prefer something different."

He frowned but did not enquire further. As soon as the music began and most of the guests were watching the dancers and Maria Lucas's performance, Elizabeth tugged Fitzwilliam to the back of the group. When no one was looking, she opened one of the side doors and pulled Fitzwilliam into the garden.

"You will freeze," he said.

"Not when I have you to keep me warm." Yes, her response was provocative, but he had been affectionate yet reserved. What was he like when he was not so regulated?

"Elizabeth?"

She pulled him around the brick wall that separated the garden near the house from the orchard and walked backwards, beckoning him with her finger. It was darker here with nothing but a crescent moon and a modicum of candlelight from the house, but the lack of light was not disturbing. On the contrary, the dimness suited her purpose.

"What are you about?"

She stopped when her back hit the trunk of a tree. Fitzwilliam came to a halt a respectable distance away, but she hooked a finger into the "v" of his waistcoat and drew him to her.

"Kiss me, Fitzwilliam."

A smile stole across his face before he dipped down and claimed her lips. She almost burst into flame and was forced to grip his topcoat by the shoulders to remain standing.

His lips cupped hers softly, first the top then the bottom, before he teased her mouth open. He had done this once before, and she had not known at that time what he was about, but now, what was coming was not a mystery. She welcomed the sweet taste of his tongue as it caressed hers.

Her entire body was melting as he slid his hands around her to bring her closer. After a moment of becoming more accustomed to his kiss, she mimicked his attentions and allowed her tongue to reach forward and touch his.

The growl that erupted from his chest made her start, but she could not pull away as he pressed her as tightly to him as possible, his palms flat against her lower back while he devoured her.

Her head spun, and her breathing was erratic while she attempted to follow his lead. He was demanding more than just a kiss, yet she had no intention of stopping him. Her heart pounded against her chest while she slipped her fingers into his hair.

She whimpered when his lips abandoned hers and began a fiery trail down her neck. Her grip on his hair tightened as she held him to her. He must not stop! He nibbled her ear lobe and suckled gently on her neck. His hands grasped her buttocks and pulled her hips to his. Something hard pressed into her belly, and she squeezed her legs together at the ache that bloomed in response.

"Darcy, I trust you and my daughter are merely talking."

Fitzwilliam flew back from her as though stung. His chest was heaving, and he clenched and released his fists.

"Yes, sir."

"Come, Lizzy. We shall return together. Your betrothed will follow."

She did her best to inhale slowly. This heat needed to dissipate before she joined her father. He was not behind Fitzwilliam, so he must be on the opposite side of the wall.

When her weakened legs could support her, she pushed herself from the tree, but before she could pass Fitzwilliam, he took her hand and pressed one more kiss to her lips. "I shall not be long."

When she rounded the brick wall, her father stood with his arms crossed over his chest and his one eyebrow arched. "You are fortunate no one saw you depart but me. Of course, the charm I cast when you quit the room helped. Now, let us get back inside before someone notices."

She glanced over her shoulder. How long would Fitzwilliam remain? They were betrothed. If they both returned with her father, the situation would not be quite so scandalous.

"Darcy will follow. I am certain he requires a moment."

Elizabeth frowned and peered back one more time. What could her father mean?

Chapter 12

11th of November 1811

Elizabeth gasped as Darcy nibbled at her collarbone. She had to have no idea how her innocent responses drove him mad with want! Since that evening in the gardens at Lucas Lodge, she had allowed a few chaste kisses—as much as his kisses could be considered chaste—but her behaviour with him had become less guarded. She teased him more freely and arched that blasted eyebrow that made him want to whisk her to the nearest bedchamber and throw her down on the bed. As it was, she would drive him to Bedlam. He could not object to her methods, however. She now owned his heart—completely.

Even though employing his best dignified restraint, Darcy could not take it anymore. He needed her lips on his like he needed the air to breathe. She whimpered when he pulled her back against him and kissed her as though he was starved for her, which he was. Her hands slipped inside his great coat and clung to his sides, the press of her small hands wreaking havoc on his control. What was he thinking? Control was not possible when it came to Elizabeth Bennet. She not only owned his heart, but also his body. No one else could compare. And they had yet to be wed!

His palm slid over her breast, and he drew back just a little. He had to witness her response to his touch. She was intoxicating, yet he wanted her to be just as lost as he had become.

Her teeth dug into her bottom lip as he traced his thumb around the centre. "Fitzwilliam." Her voice was husky and held a quality that he longed to hear while he buried himself inside of her. A Herculean effort was required to wrench himself from her softness and step back.

"Forgive me."

She slumped against the tree behind her while she breathed heavily. "What have you done that requires forgiveness?"

He chuckled. "I cannot reason when we kiss like that. You have no idea how much I wish we were already married." Darcy propped his hands on his thighs and squeezed his eyes closed in an effort to make his erection subside. Of course, it was stubborn. He needed to forget that she was in front of him panting and somewhat dishevelled.

"My entire body is on fire."

When he opened his eyes, she ran her palm along her stomach while he focussed on his breathing to calm himself. As if that would ever work with her touching herself.

"Fitzwilliam, are you in pain?"

"A little, but the discomfort will soon pass."

She pushed away from the tree and hastened to his side. "If I am the cause, I should be the one begging *your* forgiveness."

He straightened and pulled her into his arms. "You have no need to beg forgiveness. I know what I am doing when we are together. The fault is entirely my own."

Her gaze lowered between them, and she tilted her head. "What is—?"

His hand grasped hers, and he laced their fingers together. "You will discover the answer to that question soon enough. In the meantime, I need to think of something else."

"Tell me of Pemberley," she said. Her gaze met his once more, her vivid green eyes holding his with ease.

"Well, the estate is old, though not as old as Longbourn. My family was gifted the land by William the Conqueror. My grandfather decided the original house was not grand enough, so he decided to add to it and remodel the older portion to match the new. The original structure is now the east wing of the house where the family rooms are located.

"The park is approximately ten miles around and includes the Nine Ladies stone circle as well as a large portion of the River Derwent. A tributary of that river feeds a sizeable lake on the property that is excellent for fishing. My father saw to it several follies were erected around the lake. I cannot wait to walk those pathways with you. You will adore the prospect from a good number of places.

"The house itself sits in a valley with a forest behind the gardens. We have an extensive herb garden for potions. Mrs. Reynolds, the housekeeper, is adept at potion making and keeps us all hale." Elizabeth admired nature so much. He could not imagine her disliking the Peak or Pemberley. What he wanted more than anything was for her to love the estate as he did. It would be their home after all.

She toyed with his cravat. She did that often when they were close as they were. The pin fascinated her, and she would circle it with her fingertip. Her rapt interest was likely because she had seen it more than once in her visions.

"If you recall, you have seen a room of Pemberley during the first probe of the altar. You also saw some of the grounds when you had the vision of me and Richard riding."

Her forehead furrowed, and he brushed his thumb along the creases. "What is wrong?"

"What is Nine Ladies like? Is it similar to our stone circle?"

He turned to lean against the tree and brought her between his legs so she could lean against him. Hen grazed nearby undisturbed by their activities.

"Nine Ladies is quite different. Your circle has the larger stones near the altar, which is flat upon the ground, while Nine Ladies is nine stones mostly buried in the earth. One is a bit flat on top, but it is nothing like your altar. The only similarity is the range of the stones. They are arranged at a similar diameter, not that their size determines their power. One could easily dismiss their significance by sight alone."

A slight curve graced her lips. "I look forward to seeing them and learning their special qualities."

All stone circles had their own signature, so to speak, depending upon the vein of magic that fed them. Stonehenge and Oakham were sourced from the same vein, so their magic was similar, though Oakham seemed to be a little more powerful. It was no wonder with the number of people who crowded to Stonehenge. He had witnessed those with less power touching certain stones and mumbling spells to increase their skills. People needed to cease believing those old wives' tales. All they ended up doing was wasting time and money on a fruitless endeavour.

She lifted onto her tiptoes and kissed his cheek. "I should go inside. Papa will become unsettled if I do not return soon." With whomever was acquiring power possibly nearby, her father's uneasiness would be understandable.

He traced a finger along her cheek. "I should be on my way to Netherfield. I am sure Bingley will be wondering why I have yet to return since he believes I have been riding all this time."

Her bubbling laugh made him smile. "Does he really?"

He shrugged one shoulder. "In all fairness, I depart before he awakens, and I do not usually see any servants on my way out of the house. One of my own men saddles my horse, and he does not share my activities with anyone."

She walked with him to fetch Hen. "As long as the weather is decent, we shall meet here tomorrow?"

"If it is raining, I shall come to Longbourn to help your father research whatever magic is being used to steal powers."

He kissed her forehead then mounted. "Now, you know I shall watch you until you are inside the house, so do not just stand there."

She scoffed. "As you are aware, I can protect myself."

He remained in his spot until she turned on her heel with a huff and marched back to Longbourn. Before opening the door to the kitchens, she glanced over her shoulder with a mischievous grin. As soon as she stepped inside, he turned Hen to make his to return to Netherfield.

As he rode, he could not remove the smile upon his countenance. He had not been so happy in years. Elizabeth's recalcitrance, while frustrating at times, was largely endearing. She was correct when she said he knew she could protect herself. Her skills would overwhelm most, but whoever she would eventually face would not be like most people. By robbing others of their abilities, this worrisome individual would be powerful. Even if the person who was the first victim was of a middling power, the duke's magic alone was formidable. Many magical families had died out or ceased to believe over the centuries, leaving about a quarter of the country as magic. If this creature continued, their pursuit of power could be devastating.

Upon his return, his groom took Hen, and he hastened his steps into the house, where the servants were hurrying about as though lost.

"What is happening?" he asked the housekeeper.

"Miss Bingley invited Miss Bennet for tea. She has insisted the entire house be cleaned from top to bottom and has threatened to dismiss the maids should their work not be satisfactory."

He took in the maids who were all wiping furniture or removing the draperies in the drawing room to be taken outside and shaken. "What is her reasoning? Miss Bennet would never expect such a fuss to be made over her."

Mrs. Nichols glanced about them, then leaned closer. "If you will pardon me, sir, I believe Miss Bingley thinks this will show her superiority over the Bennets."

An incredulous bark escaped before he could stop it. Miss Bingley was the most ignorant person he had ever met. It was not as if Bingley had neglected to explain so many different situations in life to her, yet instead of learning, she had refused to listen and repeatedly interrupted him with every attempt. Miss Bingley believed she was above his advice.

"I do not suppose she invited Miss Elizabeth too." If she had, then perhaps he could find another stolen moment with her.

The housekeeper shook her head. "Unfortunately, she did not. I believe Miss Bingley would prefer to chew off her own hand than pen an invite to your betrothed."

He made an indecorous noise with his nose at the housekeeper's quip. "I shall refresh myself and return to have tea with Mr. Bingley should he ask."

She gave a dip of her chin. "Of course, sir."

When Elizabeth entered Longbourn, her mother's strident tones carried down to the kitchen.

"What has Mama in a fit of nerves?"

Mrs. Hill looked up from kneading bread. "Miss Bennet received an invitation to tea with those Bingley sisters. Your sister wishes to go and requested the carriage from your father, but your mother insists she ride on horseback since it looks like rain."

She clenched her teeth to keep her jaw from dropping. "Mama is hoping Jane will need to spend the night." Of all the conniving, rude, and insufferable things to do, Mama had picked the worst.

"Precisely, miss."

Without another word, Elizabeth hurried through the house and entered the breakfast parlour where her mother was standing in front of her chair and yelling at Papa. A dish of toast flew from the table, barely missed her father's head, and slammed into the wall behind him.

Jane made to rise, but Papa shook his head. "And yet, I am unmoved. I shall have the carriage prepared for Jane. She will not impose herself upon the Bingleys any more than necessary." He nodded to Elizabeth. "Lizzy, you will accompany her."

"Lizzy! Accompany Jane!" screeched Mama. "Whatever for?" Elizabeth had the same question.

"I do not expect you to understand my concerns," said Papa.

Her mother threw up her hands and let them fall. "You have confined Lydia and Kitty to the house, and none of the girls can leave without someone attending them. Meanwhile, your favourite leaves every morning on her walks—"

"And she is accompanied on each and every one, Frances. A great deal has happened, and I wish to protect my daughters. You should wish for their safety as well."

A fork flew and Papa held up a hand, making it fall to the floor. He rarely intervened in her mother's fits unless her aim was true. This time, however, all of the plates and utensils vibrated upon the table. Mary stood and backed against the wall, as did Kitty and Lydia.

"I want to see our daughters married!" screeched Mama. Three plates flew and crashed against the wall behind her father.

Mrs. Hill bustled in with the tea set. "Forgive me, sir, but the water took a prodigious amount of time to boil this morning." She set the tray next to Mama. "Here is your tea, Mrs. Bennet."

"What do I want with tea when my husband will not help his daughters marry? Jane could have charmed Mr. Darcy, but no, you had to have the richer man for Lizzy." A serving spoon flew at Papa, but again, he lifted a hand making it fall onto the table with a clatter.

Instead of raising his voice, Papa stood and stepped around the table. He placed a hand upon Mama's arm. "Calm yourself, my dear. I am certain all of the girls will make fine matches. Just give them time. Now, drink your tea. It will make you feel better."

Mama dropped into her chair, but Papa did not release her. He allowed his palm to shift to her shoulder until her mother took her first drink of the tea. As soon as the calming effects showed, he returned to his own chair and took a sip of coffee as though nothing out of the ordinary had just occurred. The silver and china upon the table ceased their rattling, and her mother looked around herself.

"Why are you all standing about the room? Sit down and eat."

Jane glanced at Elizabeth before returning to her chair beside Mama. While her mother was speaking to Mrs. Hill about their own afternoon tea, Jane slipped what appeared to be a note from beside Mama, folded the paper with care, and put it in her pocket.

As soon as Elizabeth had eaten, she followed Jane from the breakfast room and stopped her in the hall. "What was that you took from Mama?"

"Mama snatched Miss Bingley's invitation from my fingers before I could read it. Since she was calm, I grabbed the note before she became agitated again. When we depart, we shall tell her we are going to Meryton to pick up books for Papa. She will not find anything unusual about that."

"What of Miss Bingley? She will not be pleased to find that I accompanied you."

Jane held up her hands, palms forward. "All we can do is tell her the truth. She is not as bad as you think, Lizzy. She has always been especially kind to me."

"Believe what you will, dearest, but Mr. Darcy has told me some of what that lady has said of you. I do not want to hurt you, but none of it is complimentary. She considers our family below hers."

A gasp came from Jane. "That cannot be true. Mr. Bingley has a talent, and she must have one as well. Surely, they have heard of Papa."

She took Jane's hand. "Mr. Bingley is not so ignorant, but Miss Bingley . . . I daresay she probably is."

"I just do not believe it."

Poor Jane. She always believed the best of everyone. One day, her perfect little world would be shocked to the core. Hopefully, Elizabeth would not be far. Someone would be needed to pick up the pieces.

Chapter 13

12th of November 1811

The morning after their tea at Netherfield, Elizabeth sat with her family around the breakfast table. Her father was, as usual, at the head of the table, reading his newspaper and drinking coffee, Jane sipped tea and nibbled on a muffin, and Mary chewed bacon while reading Fordyce's sermons. Meanwhile, Lydia whispered in Kitty's ear, which made them both dissolve into fits of giggles. "Red coat" was the only part of Lydia's secret that was discernible. At least the two of them had not been allowed to leave the house and gardens since Samhain.

"Jane," said Mama. "I want you to tell me everything that was said between you and Mr. Bingley's sisters yesterday. 'Tis a shame he was out dining with the officers, but I suppose it could not be helped."

When Mama had remembered about tea with Miss Bingley was a question no one could answer. They had told her the bookstore excuse upon their departure and upon their return, and had claimed they had taken tea with Charlotte and Maria at Lucas Lodge. She had seemed oblivious until this morning, when her memory seemed to miraculously right itself.

While Mama listened to Jane as she recounted the entire conversation, hoofbeats and the familiar sounds of a carriage made Elizabeth look up from her toast. Fitzwilliam had arrived. They expected no one else this morning, so the visitor had to be him.

Much as Mama had predicted, a steady rain had begun yesterday and the fields were far too muddy to walk this morning, so Fitzwilliam had sent a message saying he would come to Longbourn so they could help Papa with their research.

A few minutes later, Mrs. Hill opened the door. "Mr. Darcy, sir."

"Darcy!" said Papa. "If you have not had breakfast, you must join us. Once you have eaten, we shall adjourn to the library."

Her mother glanced here and there at Fitzwilliam, each time lifting one nostril just enough for those who knew her well to notice. Did she truly despise Fitzwilliam for choosing her instead of Jane? Elizabeth ducked her head and stared at her plate. For the most part, she managed to ignore her mother's insults and dislike, but at times, she could not avoid a certain amount of melancholy. Why did Mama's derision still hurt after all this time?

As she was sipping her tea, a hand covered hers and entwined their fingers. She peered up to find Fitzwilliam watching her with a steady gaze. How had he known exactly what she needed? Could he sense her disquiet?

They both finished their food in silence. Thankfully, Mama had not spoken since Fitzwilliam arrived. Whether her silence was due to Mrs. Hill's tea or the presence of Fitzwilliam, it mattered not.

The moment Fitzwilliam set his napkin beside his plate, he stood and helped Elizabeth with her chair. He did not wait for Papa before leading her to the library and taking her in his arms.

"She must have said something to you. Your smile was forced when I arrived."

She sank into the comfort of his embrace. "Mama has been difficult these past two days. When I arrived home yesterday, she was arguing with Papa about sending Jane to Netherfield on horseback."

"That would have been unfortunate," he said. "Jane would have been drenched by the time she reached Netherfield."

"Yes, that was Mama's scheme. She hoped Jane would be forced to spend the night."

He exhaled near her ear. "There must be more than that."

She drew back and rubbed her forehead. "She questioned Papa over why he did not betroth Jane to you instead of me. I know she has no idea, and God knows that she cannot be trusted with the truth, but—"

"Her lack of feeling still hurts."

"Forgive me. I am just tired. She was hurling dishes and utensils across the room at Papa yesterday. He had to intervene before she destroyed everything on the table. I am grateful he insisted Jane not intercede. In the end, he calmed her until Mrs. Hill brought Mama her tea."

His thumb rubbed tingling circles on the back of her hand. "I heard you came to Netherfield with your sister."

"Papa insisted. He does not want any of us alone outside of Longbourn." She gave a weak laugh. "You should have seen Miss Bingley's expression when I entered beside Jane. I offered to sit in the drawing room with a book and not interfere with their tea, but she insisted I join them, which I know was not because she wished for my company.

"Fitzwilliam, the conversation that ensued was the most insufferable method of seeking information I have ever endured. She asked of my uncle who lives in Cheapside and of Uncle Philips. Her treatment of poor Jane became increasingly disdainful the longer the visit endured." It had been miserable. Jane still believed Miss Bingley liked her and was her friend. Miss Bingley, however, was nothing more than a sharp-tongued adder bedecked in expensive lace.

"Miss Bingley does not like that her brother is infatuated with your sister. Mrs. Hurst attempted to change her mind after Mr. Hurst insisted she understand the significance of the Bennets in magical circles, but Miss Bingley refuses to listen to reason, even after attending Samhain. Do not let them bother you."

"I do not like how Miss Bingley treats Jane. My sister has never harmed anyone and does not deserve that lady's disdain."

He bent forward a little to catch her gaze. "I wager you did not let Miss Bingley's barbs go unanswered."

She could not help but let one side of her lips quirk upwards. "Of course not."

"Ah, you are recounting the happenings at yesterday's tea," said Papa as he entered. "You should not take such offense to Miss Bingley's dismissal of our family. We have been content to keep to ourselves. The anonymity outside of Meryton can be a blessing. People know of us, but they do not know us at a glance."

"I do not crave her acknowledgement, Papa, but her wilful ignorance is annoying as is her obvious belief that we should be the dirt under her slippers."

"And she wants Darcy, which does not set well with you either, I suppose."

Elizabeth stiffened. "What makes you say that?"

Her father chuckled. "I spoke to Mrs. Nichols at Samhain. She had little good to say of the lady and warned me of Miss Bingley's hopes towards Darcy. If I thought him less than trustworthy, I might have worried, but George Darcy's son would never betray his vow. I also have seen how he looks at you, my dear. His father bore the same besotted countenance when he gazed upon Lady Anne. He would never act in a way that would harm you—not intentionally anyway."

She gave a start while Fitzwilliam's face reddened to a deep shade. "Well, perhaps we should begin going through these books of yours, sir. Should we start in any particular location?"

"I have searched the ones in that first set of shelves, so we should begin on the next."

Elizabeth groaned. "This is going to be like searching for a needle in a haystack." A very tiny needle hidden in an exceedingly large haystack!

Her father sighed as he stared at the shelves surrounding them. "Moreso, really. You must understand this will not be something that is spelled out. If it was, someone else would have discovered it by now. No, this is obscure. You must be diligent in your search, or we shall never discover what we need to know."

Her betrothed took in a deep inhale. "Then we should get to it. We have a great many books to sort through before whoever this is finds us." This could take weeks or months of searching. What if they never found the details of this person's attempt at increasing their power? The first snowfall would be here sooner rather than later.

"Indeed," said Elizabeth.

16th of November 1811

Fitzwilliam dropped the book into his lap and rubbed his eyes. This search would never end. How had someone discovered they possessed such an ability or stumbled across such a magic? They had been reading over magical tomes all week and had found absolutely nothing. His eyes were scratchy as though they contained sand. How many more books would they need to search? Five more sections of shelving were behind Mr. Bennet's desk. If only they could ask Miss Mary to search the books for them, but that would necessitate telling her of the vision, which they could not do. Nevertheless, they had to find something soon, did they not?

"I am stiff," said Elizabeth. She stretched her arms forward and twisted them in an obvious effort to find relief.

They had spent far too much time in the library this week, having been relegated indoors more often than not due to rain or damp weather. Both were also fatigued from the gloomy skies and required time in the sun to fully regain their spirits. The shorter days this time of year did not help their predicament one bit.

Elizabeth stood, arched her back, and walked about the room. "If the wind was not so chilly, I would be tempted to take a ramble in the rain."

"Hen will be in high spirits when I finally take him out. Four days without exercise will make him a challenge to control when the ground is dry enough to ride. Miss Bingley hoped to persuade me to walk through the gravel paths of the garden yesterday while the sun was out." It had come out half an hour before sunset, then the rain had begun again during the night. The weather had been absolutely dreadful.

Mr. Bennet placed a bit of paper in the book he was reading and set it on the desk. "I confess that I hope the rain continues. My cousin is to arrive on Monday, and I do not anticipate this visit. If the weather continues to be poor, perhaps he will not travel."

Elizabeth set her hands on the back of her chair. "By the letter you showed me, the man has little sense. Rain or not, I am certain he will arrive and expect us to be grateful for his condescension."

With a growl, Mr. Bennet dropped his head back. "You are correct, of course. He will be an imbecile, and we shall have to endure his ridiculousness until he decides to leave. And if I do not keep your mother sedated until he departs, she will attempt to match your younger sisters to him and reveal her abilities when I do not capitulate to her demands. I do not want Jane to feel compelled to control her mother's capricious moods, yet I do not see how we shall manage without her. Her calming influence is less noticeable than my magic."

Fitzwilliam's teeth ground against each other. He did not trust Mrs. Bennet not to make some attempt to disrupt his nuptials to Elizabeth. "I shall come after our morning practice so I will be here when Mr. Collins arrives."

A dry chuckle came from Mr. Bennet. "You wish to stake your claim on Lizzy in the event Mrs. Bennet makes an attempt to promise her to my cousin? I do not blame you, son."

Elizabeth placed a palm on his shoulder. "Mr. Collins does not possess magic. If I must, I can charm him or make certain he does not claim an attachment on me or any of my sisters."

"Lizzy," said her father in a chiding tone.

"'Tis not like we cannot alter his memory if need be."

Fitzwilliam winced. "You mentioned yourself the risk that could come of that. The more you tinker with the man's mind, the more he may become damaged. Knowing my aunt, this man bows and scrapes and obeys her every command. She also holds the ability to use magic if she wishes. If she has used a submission potion and ordered him to take a wife from amongst your sisters, he will be persistent. He will do all he can to please her.

"You must also be aware that my aunt has suffered under the delusion that I shall marry my cousin Anne de Bourgh. She insists my mother and she planned the marriage while Anne and I were in our cradles. As you know, this is not true. My father disabused her of this notion many times, but she persists. I imagine Mr. Collins will mention that information at the most inopportune moment." He looked back to Elizabeth, whose eyes had widened. "I would not see you hurt and believing I deceived you."

"I would have known better," said Mr. Bennet. "Your father mentioned your aunt's hopes when we signed the agreement. You need not worry."

Elizabeth turned and leaned against her father's desk. "Why did you not mention this sooner?"

With a sigh, Fitzwilliam rubbed his temples. "Because I have dreaded this visit, and I did not want you to feel the same way. I am uncertain of my aunt's response to this, but at some point, I expected her journeying here to insist I wed her daughter. I have not written her of our engagement yet for that very reason."

"Well," said Mr. Bennet. "We shall do our best to prevent Mr. Collins from sending his patroness any correspondence until after the two of you are married and secluded away in the dower house. I only hope that by the solstice, he will be gone. I would prefer he not be here when you are announced before the altar in the stone circle for our neighbours to witness. The entire family walking to the stones would not go unnoticed. We would be forced to alter his memory or ensure he sleeps through the entirety of the evening."

Fitzwilliam stood and took his betrothed's hands in his. "We have spent all of our time together for the past fortnight or so. Have you had a gown made for the solstice? Since this will be, for all intents and purposes, your introduction, you should."

"No, I have always remade Jane's gowns for myself. Mama often replaces her clothing before it is necessary, and altering those made matters simpler. I have always avoided the dressmaker, so they do not see my birthmark."

He stared at their joined hands. "I had not considered your mark." He paused. Would it be possible? "What if I sent for Madame Gérard? She is circumspect and would never speak of the birthmark."

She bit her lip for a moment. "If you believe it to be necessary and that she would not speak of me being the heir, then I will not object."

Mr. Bennet looked at them over his spectacles. "You are certain of this woman, Darcy."

"As certain as I can be. I would not risk Elizabeth's life for such a triviality if I was not convinced."

"Then you may do as you wish," said Mr. Bennet.

"I thank you, sir."

Chapter 14

18th of November 1811

When the carriage came to a stop in front of Longbourn, Elizabeth's younger sisters all flew to the window to catch the first glimpse of Mr. Collins stepping down out of the vehicle while Miss Bennet remained beside her mother, poised to calm her mother's agitation should it be required. Mrs. Bennet had taken her tea a quarter hour before, but that did not mean the lady could not nor would not have an outburst. They had all borne witness to Mrs. Bennet's illness overpowering the calming effects of the potions on more than one occasion.

Meanwhile, Fitzwilliam's bearing was taut with the need to grab Elizabeth and keep her in his embrace. Each and every one of the discussions regarding today had not been in eager anticipation. On the contrary, the only person at Longbourn who had looked forward to Mr. Collins's visit had been Mrs. Bennet. She had been gleeful at breakfast when her husband had announced the vicar's visit as well as his purpose. If only Mr. Bennet had not mentioned Mr. Collins's search for a suitable wife! That was enough to set Mrs. Bennet on a hunt, and little did Mr. Collins know that he would be the fox in that scene. Mr. Bennet would need to be vigilant in the coming weeks. So would Fitzwilliam for that matter!

"Well, what do you see?" asked Mrs. Bennet.

Kitty peered over her shoulder. "He is definitely tall, but he has only stepped down and is now reaching inside for something."

A moment later, Lydia burst into a fit of giggles. "La, but he is almost as round as Sir William Lucas."

Mary returned to her chair, picked up her book, and began to read once more.

"Well, this should be enlightening," said Fitzwilliam in Elizabeth's ear.

Mr. Bennet entered and took a seat in the chair near him. "I hope you are prepared for the worst."

"Papa!" Jane shook her head while she placed her needlework on the side table.

At a knock on the front door, they all jumped. Who knew why? They expected the man after all. This was not a surprise visit by any means.

Mrs. Hill entered. "A Mr. Collins, sir."

The tall gentleman entered with a gliding step, his nose slightly higher than one would customarily carry it. He looked down at each of them as he came to a halt.

"I welcome you to Longbourn." Mr. Bennet bowed.

The clergyman returned the gesture with a sniff.

The elder gentleman was undeterred. "May I present my wife, my eldest daughter Jane, my second-born Elizabeth and her betrothed, Mr. Fitzwilliam Darcy of Pemberley, then we have Mary, Kitty, and Lydia."

Mrs. Bennet clasped her hands in front of her. "I hope you had a pleasant journey, Mr. Collins."

He glanced around. "The roads were rather muddy, but that is to be expected when the weather has been rainy." The gentleman's gaze latched onto Fitzwilliam. "Did I hear correctly? Are you truly Mr. Darcy of Pemberley?"

Fitzwilliam's spine became painfully rigid. "Yes, I am." Why else would Mr. Bennet have introduced him as such?

"Then I am happy to report that your aunt and betrothed, the lovely Miss Anne de Bourgh, were very well when I last saw them four days ago." The weaselly man glanced at Elizabeth and Mr. Bennet each while uttering his erroneous comments.

"I believe you have been misled, Mr. Collins," said Fitzwilliam. "I have never been engaged to my cousin, regardless of what my aunt tells you. My parents would have never arranged my marriage with Miss Elizabeth had they done as my aunt claims."

"B-but, Mr. Darcy, your aunt—"

He stepped forward so he was looking down at Mr. Collins. "I have told you the truth of the matter, so now I expect you to abide by my wishes and never refer to my cousin in such a way again, or I shall be quite displeased. Do you understand?" He kept his tone hard and did his utmost to ensure his countenance was implacable. The only hope of shutting this man's obsequious mouth was to be as stern as possible—to behave as his aunt would. Lord, but he despised his aunt's imperiousness!

Elizabeth took his arm, and his bearing relaxed a little. How had she managed to soothe him when he was so agitated? He had already been tight at the prospect of being in company with this man, yet she could alleviate at least some of his tension with an innocent touch.

The parson's eyes darted to Elizabeth's hand, so Fitzwilliam covered it with his own. He would protect Elizabeth as much as he could, even if it was no more than a subtle claim in company. "I suggest you enjoy your visit with your cousins as well as your rest from the rigours of your living. You will surely be overwhelmed with my aunt's instruction when you return."

Mr. Collins bowed before him, his hand waving in front of him in the most ridiculous fashion. "You are mistaken, sir. I am grateful for your aunt's unfettered condescension. She has been generous in bestowing this living to me, and I shall never deny her anything that is in my power to provide."

A gagging sound from behind Mr. Collins caused the man to lift from his scraping position and glance over his shoulder. Miss Kitty giggled into her hands while Miss Lydia examined her fingernails as though dying from the tediousness of it all.

Miss Bennet sat with a rigid deportment beside her mother while one hand rested on her mother's arm. Mrs. Bennet's mouth twitched here and there. A slight rattle from the mantel made Fitzwilliam reach back as though leaning against it, his hand pressing down on the base of the candlestick.

"I believe we require tea," said Elizabeth.

Her father rang the bell, and a maid scurried in with a tea tray for the family. "Mrs. Hill will be in shortly with the mistress's tea."

"Mr. Collins, would you care to sit?" asked Miss Bennet. Her hand reached around to her mother's back. "Mama, are you going to prepare the tea for our guest?"

Mrs. Bennet flinched a little. "Oh, yes, of course."

With a shaky hand, Mrs. Bennet prepared Mr. Collins's tea while Miss Bennet sat quietly. Her countenance appeared serene, but anyone who had been in company with her would take note of the set of her shoulders. She was concentrating with all she had to temper her mother's behaviour.

"Mr. Collins," said Miss Mary, "I have often wondered what most clergymen believe to be their first and most important duty to their parishioners. Are you more concerned with the sick or the overall spiritual well-being of your flock?" A heavy exhale came from beside him.

When he looked down, Elizabeth had squeezed her eyes closed. "I do not believe I have ever been so thankful for Mary's interest in theology until now." With Mr. Collins loudly expounding upon his dedication and attention to his patroness, Elizabeth's softly spoken words did not attract anyone's attention.

"Come, my love. Let us sit and take tea. Hopefully, Miss Mary can keep him talking so the rest of us need not converse with him." He had his head turned away from the group, but Mrs. Hill had entered with Mrs. Bennet's tea, so he and Elizabeth remained out of everyone's notice.

Elizabeth's mother served her guest and family without incident, then took her own cup from Mrs. Hill. With the tea in her mother's hand, Miss Bennet took her palm from her mother's back and sipped from her own cup. At least she would have a reprieve. During his previous calls on Elizabeth, Miss Bennet had exerted herself to calm her mother, yet on this occasion, she had shown obvious signs of fatigue from maintaining such a powerful connexion.

Before they made to join the rest of the family who were already seated, Elizabeth squeezed his arm and stepped over to her eldest sister. She placed her hand on Jane's shoulder as though using her for support while Elizabeth reached for a biscuit. The entire exchange would have been unremarkable to most, except Miss Bennet's cheeks, which had lost a bit of their colour, became rosier and the slight circles under her eyes disappeared. The effect was subtle. Thankfully, Mr. Collins was too busy enjoying the sound of his own voice to notice Elizabeth's efforts.

As soon as she returned, Fitzwilliam took her hand, squeezing it while he aided her to sit in the chair beside her father. Mr. Bennet gave his daughter a crooked smile. Had he noticed his daughter's use of magic in the room with Mr. Collins? At times, one could sense the use of power when nearby, but Elizabeth had directed the energy so precisely that no one should have taken note of the vibration.

A good half an hour was spent having tea with Mr. Collins before Mrs. Bennet offered for the man to see his chambers after his travels. Mrs. Hill responded to the bell and hurried Mr. Collins upstairs to the guest room.

No sooner had the door closed behind Mr. Collins, than the candlestick on the mantel began to rattle once again. When it flew across the room, everyone ducked except Mr. Bennet, who held up his hand to keep the heavy silver piece from hitting the wall. They would have required a clever excuse for the noise as well as the hole in the wall had Mr. Bennet not prevented it from making impact with the plaster.

"Jane," said Mr. Bennet. "You must be exhausted. The weather is fine today. You may take a walk in the garden or even a nap should you wish. I shall accompany your mother to her bedchamber to rest."

During Mr. Collins's visit, Mrs. Bennet would never be alone. It was too risky.

"And, Mary, I have never been so thankful for your interest in sermons before today. You distracted Mr. Collins admirably. I am proud of you."

Miss Mary gave a slight twitch. "I thank you, Papa. Mr. Collins's opinions are greatly flawed, but I do not mind continuing to ask him questions or to engage him in a debate if I can be of aid."

"You would be of great help," said Elizabeth.

The remaining biscuits shot from their plate and slapped Miss Mary in the face. "I do not require you to entertain our guest. I am perfectly capable—"

Mr. Bennet held out his arm. "Come, my dear, I believe you require some time to lie down."

She made to push him away, but Mr. Bennet's hand landed on top of hers. "Come, Mrs. Bennet."

Her protest ceased immediately, and the lady stood and followed her husband from the room without question.

"Well, I have no interest in just sitting here," said Miss Lydia. "I am going to go remake my bonnet. Not that I get to wear it anywhere." She gave Elizabeth a sneer as she walked by.

Miss Kitty flounced after her sister, but without the mean-spirited look at Elizabeth.

Miss Mary stood and made to follow. "I shall practice the pianoforte."

All of a sudden, he was alone with Elizabeth. She peered up at him with that alluring eyebrow arched just so.

"Well, Mr. Darcy, I suppose we should adjourn to Papa's library and continue reading through his books."

"Mr. Darcy? Why are you suddenly addressing me as such? You have called me Fitzwilliam for a couple of weeks now."

One of her shoulders lifted. "I felt like it."

He drew her into his arms. "I prefer Fitzwilliam."

She grinned and pressed her palm to his chest. "What will you do about it. . .*Mr.* Darcy?"

With a growl, he pulled her back to him and kissed her hard. He usually started a bit slow, but not this time. He deepened the kiss from almost the first moment their lips met. She had no idea what she stirred inside of him when she taunted him so. If they were married and not in her father's drawing room, he would tease and caress her until she cried his name—Fitzwilliam—over and over again.

He trailed his lips from hers down to her jaw and lower. After nipping at her collarbone, he lightly bit the top of her breast.

She gasped. "Fitzwilliam, what are you doing?"

He pressed a kiss to the swell of her other breast. "Making you say my name."

Her small hands pressed to his chest and shoved him back. "Hardly fair, *Mr.* Darcy." With a tempting curve of her mouth, she pivoted on her heel and left the room.

My God, she would be the death of him!

19th *of November 1811*

Elizabeth stood outside Longbourn with Jane beside her. This was ludicrous! Her mother had ordered her to walk to Meryton with her sisters and Mr. Collins, and her father had allowed it. Yes, he likely feared her mother's ire should he refuse, but she should be in the library sorting through books, not walking into town.

Kitty and Lydia burst through the door giggling and tittering while Mr. Collins followed, his lips pursed, and his nose lifted. He wore that same expression whenever Lydia and Kitty behaved as they were now. His disapproval was written upon his countenance, so why he desired this walk was a mystery.

"Cousin Elizabeth, shall we?" He held out his arm beside her.

"I thank you for your kind offer, but I am soon to be married, and I am certain Mr. Darcy would not appreciate me walking on the arm of another man." She looped her arm through Jane's and led her towards the road. Mr. Collins lacked a quick wit. She was thankful for that as well!

"Mama told him I was soon to be wed," said Jane softly. "She directed him at you. I tried to interject."

"Where was I when this happened?" She always seemed to miss these small matters that affected her more than anyone else.

"You were speaking to Papa. Mr. Collins had petitioned her to court me, but she would not have it."

Elizabeth looked to the sky. Patience! She could not let her temper get the best of her.

"I just need to avoid him for the next week and a half and all will be well."

Jane frowned. "What do you mean?"

After looking over her shoulder to be certain Mr. Collins was not right behind them, she hugged Jane's arm to draw her a bit closer.

"Papa intends for Fitzwilliam and me to wed on the full moon. Our marriage will then be announced to the neighbourhood at the stones on the winter solstice."

Jane's free hand flew to her chest. "How romantic! Full moon weddings are blessed by the moon and the earth. When were you to tell me this?" She could not tell Jane of the threat—of what they had witnessed in the altar or of the Duke of Ormonde's information. Poor Jane would be beside herself. It also violated Papa's warning over revealing visions. She trusted Jane with her life, but if someone overheard, everything could change.

High Street was busy when they entered the market town. People bustled here and there, visiting shops or making their way to their next destination. A few men in red coats could be seen amongst the villagers, conducting whatever business the militia had that day.

A loud squeal erupted from behind Elizabeth. Lydia and Kitty ran by to intercept a young man wearing a red coat. He walked beside another man who was not dressed in the militia uniform but who appeared a gentleman. After a sigh, Elizabeth steered Jane to join them. If they did not curb Lydia and Kitty's behaviour, the two would embarrass the family.

"Oh, Mr. Wickham, I daresay you will be exceedingly handsome in a red coat," said Lydia while batting her eyelashes. Good Lord, this was the man Fitzwilliam had warned them of—the man from the vision—and Lydia was attempting to charm him!

Elizabeth held her breath while Mr. Wickham smiled. "I am pleased you think so, Miss Lydia. I only hope everyone in the village is as welcoming as you have been."

"I cannot think of anyone who would be ungrateful for your willingness to serve our great king," said Mr. Collins with another deep bow.

Elizabeth gradually released her breath. Thank heavens for Mrs. Hill and her knowledge of herbs and potions! At the mention of the potential problem, their housekeeper had reminded Papa to burn asofoetida while chanting the name of the person they wished to leave them alone. Asofoetida was costly since it had to be imported, but her uncle sold the herb in his warehouse, so they had managed to procure some without much effort.

The only problem with the spell was asofoetida, also called "Devil's Dung," smelt horrible, which was why they burned it out of doors. The stench was blown away on the breeze, and no one would need to suffer through it.

Their astute housekeeper had also been slipping herbs with protective properties into their meals and tea. Her mother's tea, however, was unchanged since the mixture was specific for her agitation.

As an additional protection, Elizabeth had finally managed to hold Lydia's hand this morning and placed a binding spell on Lydia's ability, rendering it ineffective for the time being. Elizabeth had only managed a few seconds before Lydia batted her hand away, but it had been long enough. The last time Lydia and Kitty and gone to Meryton had been with Papa, so the charm had not been necessary. Her father could negate Lydia's talent with ease if need be.

Her cousin was still rambling on about Mr. Wickham's gallantry when Elizabeth looked up to find Fitzwilliam and Mr. Bingley approaching on horseback. Jane released her arm to greet Mr. Bingley while Elizabeth met Fitzwilliam as he stopped Hen and dismounted.

Elizabeth stroked the horse's striking white blaze. "I am pleased to see you this morning, Fitzwilliam."

He glanced behind her, his expression stormy. "So, he has arrived, I see."

She took her betrothed's offered arm. "Yes, and Lydia has already attempted to charm him."

Mr. Wickham's gaze met Fitzwilliam's, and the man who had been jovial until now, straightened and his countenance fell like a rock as they stepped closer.

"What are you doing in Meryton, Wickham?" Fitzwilliam's tone was not genial but held an edge that was easily discernible.

"I have joined the militia," said Wickham. "My friend Denny was just showing me the town. I was making some new acquaintances when you happened upon us."

"Yes, I see that." Fitzwilliam shifted so he was partially in front of her. "The inhabitants of the area have been warned about you Wickham, and they have taken precautions so they cannot be not swindled by you."

Mr. Wickham lifted his eyebrows. "Swindled? I mean no harm to the people of Meryton. You have likely frightened them for no reason whatsoever."

A dark laugh came from Fitzwilliam. "Keep to your duties and stay away from those in Meryton. I shall be watching you." Mr. Denny backed away. It seemed if there was to be violence, that man wanted no part in it.

Meanwhile, the wide eyes of Mr. Collins darted back and forth between them. "Oh, Mr. Darcy, I am certain Mr. Wickham would have no reason to cross someone as illustrious as yourself. Why, your aunt—the great Lady Catherine de Bourgh—would take great offense to so much as a slight towards her favourite nephew."

"Lydia, Kitty," said Jane. "We must return to Longbourn." She grabbed Lydia's arm, and whatever Lydia was to stay in protest died on her lips. Without her youngest sister's refusals, Kitty looked about her as though lost, then followed. Mr. Collins began a succession of profuse apologies for their abrupt departure.

Fitzwilliam turned his penetrating gaze upon Elizabeth. "I hope nothing untoward happened before I arrived." How did that gaze always turn her insides into a fluttering mess?

She shook her head. "No, I bound Lydia's ability before we departed Longbourn." Jane, Mr. Bingley, Kitty, and Lydia were a good distance ahead of them while Mr. Collins was just leaving Mr. Wickham and Mr. Denny. He could not hear her.

"I thought your father would cast that spell."

"No, he saw no need until we were to leave the house. Mama insisted I accompany Mr. Collins to Meryton with my sisters, so I bound her when I had my first opportunity. I am grateful she did not notice. Papa told Mary, Kitty, and Lydia my talent had no real value, so they have never asked to see it."

"Your mother is still pushing the match between you and your cousin?"

"So it seems. Do not worry. I refused his arm for the walk to Meryton, and Jane and Papa will help me avoid him as much as possible."

"They will not be the only ones," said Fitzwilliam in an almost growl.

She laughed and hugged his arm tighter. "You are rather adorable when you are jealous."

He gave her a dark look, but she only laughed harder.

Chapter 15

20th of November 1811

The party at the Philips's was not to Fitzwilliam's liking. He had never been one to play cards or games at events. His dislike of dancing was well-known, even though he had stood up with Elizabeth more than once now. He would never miss an opportunity to have Elizabeth on his arm. Dancing afforded him the opportunity to hold her hand and touch her in a gathering without censure. That made the diversion tolerable.

Tonight, he was thankful that he and Elizabeth had both managed to avoid playing whist or lottery tickets thus far and sat near the windows having their own private conversation. An ideal way to pass an evening.

"Mr. Wickham just entered," said Elizabeth.

"You know that is not what I hoped to hear you say." He spoke the words low before peering over his shoulder. His gaze collided with Wickham's and held for a moment before the man continued speaking to Mr. and Mrs. Philips. Once he finished greeting the hosts, he moved further into the room and engaged a freckled young lady in conversation.

"That young lady is Mary King. Lydia claims she has a fortune of ten-thousand pounds, but I have never heard anyone speak of it but my sister."

"She is just the kind of lady Wickham would single out. Do you know if her family has been warned?" Wickham would not require any sort of confirmation of such a rumour. He would bewitch the poor girl simply in the hopes that the gossip was truth. If this Miss King indeed had a fortune, he would then continue charming her until he could get his greedy hands on the funds. If she had nothing, he would abandon her, likely with child. He was a revolting individual!

"As you know, Papa attempted to spread word, but I am unaware if her uncle was told."

Fitzwilliam peered once more over his shoulder. Miss King smiled and appeared enamoured of Wickham. He would need to speak to the lady's uncle as soon as possible. Wickham's pursuit of Miss King would mean that the Bennet girls were probably safe for the moment, but he could not sacrifice another to protect the woman who owned his heart or her family.

"At least Lydia has not noticed him yet. I crept into her bedchamber early this morning while she slept and ensured her ability was still bound."

One of her hands rested upon the cushion in the window seat, and he covered it with his own. Someone would have to be standing directly before them to see their disregard for propriety. He would never willingly harm Elizabeth's reputation.

"The solstice will be here soon. Do not risk everything." He had bent forward so he held her gaze. She needed to know he was sincere. He had not shared his feelings with her yet, so he had to convey all he felt in some manner. His love for her would be revealed on their wedding night—on the full moon. How he prayed she held some depth of feeling for him. With the brevity of their acquaintance, he could not hold out hope for more.

Elizabeth turned over her hand to clasp his. "I understand, but if Papa will not check her, then someone must. Lydia sleeps like the dead, and since she was not awake, it is not as though I cannot ensure she sleeps through me touching her arm."

Her powers would indeed allow for her to creep into her sister's bedchamber undetected, yet it still did not mean he wanted her to risk herself so.

"Why, Mr. Darcy! I never expected you to attend such an inauspicious event."

At Caroline Bingley's cloying voice, his hand twitched, but he did not remove it. Let Miss Bingley see that he truly cared for Elizabeth—that he would marry her. No one would stop him.

"Why would I avoid such a gathering? My betrothed is here, as is her family. I have every reason to attend."

Miss Bingley sniffed. "I have met your cousin, Miss Elizabeth. Your mother has insisted you are to marry him and not Mr. Darcy." The lady tittered. "I do wish you joy."

His betrothed stiffened, so he stood to tower over his friend's sister. "Miss Bingley, though no one speaks of it because it is rude, everyone here knows Mrs. Bennet is ill. If you have not noticed, those around her do not argue because such an endeavour is fruitless. Instead, they pay her assertions little mind. Besides, she has no authority to marry off her daughters without her husband's consent. Have you heard Mr. Bennet speak of Miss Elizabeth marrying Mr. Collins? I know for a fact that you would never hear him utter such words."

"Mr. Darcy—" Miss Bingley reached out as if she would take his arm. He batted her hand away.

"Do not test my patience. Your brother has said he will send you to Scarborough should you continue to make a pest of yourself. I shall speak to him on the morrow." Thank heavens no one was close by to listen to their conversation.

Miss Bingley looked down at Elizabeth who had never risen but watched with a slight curve to her lips. "I shall not live with my aunt." She gritted the words out with a pinched expression.

"The decision is not mine to make," said Elizabeth. "I do not know why you are now directing your statement to me."

After a huff, Miss Bingley strode across the room to where Bingley chatted with Miss Bennet, allowing Fitzwilliam to sit once again.

"Despite my efforts to prove otherwise, Jane still believes Miss Bingley to be kind."

"My friend and your sister make quite the pair. He is too amiable by far, and your sister believes everyone to be good. I do hope they never meet someone of Wickham's ilk. They could lose everything."

He looked about the room. "Would you like a cup of punch? You have not had anything to drink since our arrival."

"Punch would be agreeable. Thank you."

Elizabeth watched her betrothed walk across the room to the refreshment table. Fitzwilliam was surely the most handsome man she had ever seen. He was tall and broad shouldered but trim. When he wore his buckskin breeches, which he was unfortunately not wearing this evening, his legs appeared muscled from his hours on horseback. Her stomach always fluttered when he turned those clear blue eyes at her, particularly when he was attempting to convey his sincerity. He would lean closer, his cedar scent tickling her nose, while he spoke in those low tones that rumbled through her. What could she say? She was enamoured of her future husband.

He never disparaged her magic because she was a lady, and he seemed to take pride in her accomplishments. How many gentlemen would have accepted her as she was? They had yet to discover how people would respond to her position as the heir. How unfortunate she could not inherit Longbourn to retain it with Bennet blood! They may have been magical communities, but they were subject to the laws of the crown. The monarchy had lost their belief and their magic after the last of the Tudor monarchs.

"You appear deep in thought, Miss Elizabeth."

Her attention jolted to Mr. Wickham who now sat beside her. When had he done so? She shifted as far to the edge of the window seat as possible. His mere proximity made the fine hairs on the back of her neck stand on end.

"I am merely waiting for Mr. Darcy to return with some punch. Are you enjoying my aunt's card party?"

He smiled and glanced back at Miss King. "I have been made to feel welcome."

"Then I am glad." She kept her hands clasped in her lap and made an effort to keep her expression neutral. She would reveal naught if she could help it!

"Are you?" he asked. "Then you do not believe Darcy's slander of me?"

"Slander?"

"Darcy has told lies of me since we were children. He could not bear that I was his father's favourite and has exacted his revenge well. I have lost friends and those I cared for like family. Does that seem fair to you?" As he began to speak, a bitter taste formed at the tip of her tongue and began to spread.

"Mr. Wickham, the Darcy and Bennet families have been friends for generations. I first made your acquaintance yesterday, so I can hardly say I know you. In fact, your approaching me as such and speaking of your personal matters is hardly proper, particularly when you are speaking of my betrothed."

"Why are you here, Wickham?"

At Fitzwilliam's voice, she stood and accepted a glass of punch with one hand while the other slipped into the crook of his arm. "I am certain Mr. Wickham was invited as a member of the militia and nothing more, is that not correct, sir?"

The man rose, his smile slipping back into place in a manner that sent a shudder up Elizabeth's spine and caused the bitter taste upon her tongue to become overpowering. He had been attempting to poison her opinion of Fitzwilliam, but he had not used his full ability until now. She had taken a draught that revealed a persuasive tongue before they departed for tonight's party. Her father had never attempted the mixture, but she could now attest the potion was successful. The foul taste in her mouth was evidence of its efficacy.

She swallowed down a gag. "Mr. Darcy, if you would accompany me outside for a moment; I am a bit ill all of a sudden."

Before she had finished the sentence, Fitzwilliam was hastening her towards the door. No sooner had they stepped outside than the cool air brought her some relief. One or two others milled about in the garden, likely seeking air as well.

She stepped over to an oak tree and leaned against the trunk in case she cast up her accounts.

Her betrothed took the cup of punch from her hand, but she snatched it back. "Wait! That may be of aid." She took a sip and let the sweet liquid coat her tongue.

"If you are nauseous, the spirits in the punch are the last thing you should be drinking."

She shook her head. "I am merely suffering from the effect of the revulsion potion I drank this evening. Mr. Wickham attempted to bewitch me while he spoke of you slandering him. I first noticed the foul taste in my mouth then. His smile when you confronted him was enough to make me heave."

"Did you not understand how the potion worked?"

"I read the grammar from cover to cover two days ago, and I re-read the portion on the potion before I brewed it yesterday. Nothing in the text speaks of the taste becoming stronger or even overwhelming as the person enchanting you continues."

The more of the punch she consumed and the longer she was away from Mr. Wickham, the more her nausea subsided. She had only taken a sip of the draught, and the results had exceeded her expectations. She was fortunate she had not taken more.

"Did the potion itself taste bad?" asked Fitzwilliam.

"No, it was actually rather tasteless."

He crossed his arms over his chest. "How much did you make?"

"A small cauldron-full, but I did not consume all of it." Why was he asking her so many questions?

"What did you do with the excess?"

She pulled open her reticule and held up a small bottle of green liquid. "I brought some in the event I needed to take more."

With a wide grin, he lifted her hand and placed a loud kiss on the back. "What if we pour it in the punch?"

Her chin hitched back a hair. "But no one will know why they are suddenly ill or have a rotten taste in their mouth."

"No, but the effect does render his charm ineffective, does it not?" He took the bottle.

She gave a start. "You are right. I was never swayed to believe his tale."

He grabbed her hand and brought her back inside. She slid her hand to his elbow, so they were more proper when they entered her aunt's small drawing room. The Gouldings' son was spooning punch into a cup, but as soon as he hurried back to Maria Lucas, Fitzwilliam stepped up to the bowl and uncorked the bottle.

At that moment, Lydia guffawed at something Mr. Denny said, and the entire room looked in that direction. When Elizabeth returned her attention to the bowl, Fitzwilliam had already poured half in the punch. The second half drained quickly, and he re-corked the bottle and slipped it into her hand.

While she returned the empty bottle to her reticule, he took the ladle and swirled the contents before pouring a fresh cup that he handed to her. His eyes shifted towards Lydia, and Elizabeth could not help but grin. Fitzwilliam could scheme when necessary!

She moved to stand behind her sister and bent forward to place the cup next to her. "Here, Lyddie. I thought you might be thirsty." Elizabeth held her breath. Had she gone too far using Lydia's childhood nickname?

"La! I am parched," said Lydia. She drank down the entirety and set the glass back on the table. It was all Elizabeth could do not to let her breath out in a rush. Lydia drank it! Now to see if Wickham would approach her or share his lies with others.

She and Fitzwilliam returned to the window seat while the remainder of guests continued to mill about or play cards. Mr. Wickham returned to Miss King for a time before fetching her a glass of punch. Fitzwilliam's breathing paused as the lady took a drink from the glass. She then sipped while she and Mr. Wickham spoke. After almost ten minutes, Miss King turned a violent shade of green, shoved the empty glass into his hands, and dashed for the door. Her uncle noted her abrupt departure and made to follow. Meanwhile, Mr. Wickham was left holding the glass with his forehead furrowed.

The shaking of Fitzwilliam's shoulders could be seen out of the corner of her eye, and she had to press her own lips together to keep from laughing at the picture before them. Mr. Wickham had no idea what had just happened.

As the night wore on, Mr. Wickham attempted to talk to others, and it was obvious whenever he attempted to use his ability. Anyone who he hoped to charm would first smack their lips then wrinkle their nose. Most seemed to excuse themselves to speak with someone else, but one or two made their way outside for a few moments before returning. They usually sought out someone new to converse with. Miss King never returned.

"It never occurred to me that he could vary the intensity of his enchantment," said Fitzwilliam softly.

She gave a light laugh. "I should feel some remorse for making poor Miss King sick, but I cannot."

"If she stays away from him because of our efforts, then the potion in the punch was worth it."

"But we do not know how long the potion remains effective. If he calls on her tomorrow, she may not have the same response." Each solution had a certain amount of time it worked at full potency. After, it might not produce the desired response or only have partial results depending upon how much time had passed since it was consumed.

"As much as we want to protect everyone, we cannot. Your brilliant efforts tonight helped ensure most of our friends could not listen to Wickham's lies. I am fortunate that I shall soon call you wife."

She had never before so wished to be alone with Fitzwilliam. If no one else was around, she would kiss him senseless. What other way could she show her appreciation for his sweet words?

Chapter 16

23rd of November 1811

The shrill tones of Miss Bingley carried through Netherfield, making Fitzwilliam wince. She always used harsh or ear-piercing tones when dealing with servants. They pained his ears, and he was not even in the same room. Why did she insist upon such behaviour? After all, people responded more favourably to being spoken to in a genial manner instead of her incivility, not to mention that Bingley had been forced to increase the wages for several of the maids as well as Mrs. Nichols out of his own coffers because of her cruelty. If matters continued as they were, Miss Bingley would have a detrimental impact on Bingley's savings as well as his household.

"I shall be forced to give them all more money if Caroline continues," Bingley said in a growl.

"Then why do you not put a stop to it?" By God, he would pay just to relieve himself of the cacophony!

His friend set down his pen with a firm hand. "What do I know of planning a ball? I know she must eventually go to Scarborough, but Louisa has said she and Hurst will depart with her. I would have no hostess."

Fitzwilliam thrummed his fingers against the arm of the chair. "I am certain Mrs. Nichols is capable enough to plan the event. We could also ask Mr. Bennet if his daughters could be of aid if necessary. Due to the relations between her and her mother, I believe Miss Elizabeth likely has little experience with planning balls, but I am certain Miss Bennet has been taught."

Bingley had been present for one of Mrs. Bennet's fits. Mr. Collins had gone upstairs to rest before dinner, and Miss Bennet had relinquished some control over her mother's mood. Their housekeeper had arrived soon with some of Mrs. Bennet's tea, but not soon enough to prevent Bingley from having witnessed Mrs. Bennet's favourite candlestick flying at her husband's head.

Without delay, Bingley sprang from his chair and rang the bell. His butler responded within moments and, at the behest of the master, hastened away to fetch the housekeeper, who entered through the servants' entrance a few moments later.

"I shall not mince words with you, Mrs. Nichols. The problems my sister's behaviour causes within the household has become intolerable, and I need to send her to Scarborough to live with my aunt. Should I do so, would you be able to complete the preparations for the ball or would you require someone to help you?" This was an enormous leap for Bingley. He rarely stood up to his sisters, but Miss Bingley's ire had only increased since Fitzwilliam's engagement. Why she believed she would ever marry him was a mystery. He had never said or done anything to give her hope.

The woman stepped forward. "I have planned many balls in this house, sir. If you send Miss Bingley away, I am capable of completing the planning, and if you will forgive my candour, I shall prepare an elegant event without some of the useless expense your sister has insisted upon."

"Then I wish for you to take charge and do as you have indicated," said Bingley, clasping his hands in front of him. "Now, if you will excuse me, I need to send my sister upstairs to pack." He made to turn and quit the room, but pivoted back at the last minute. "Oh, and she will not require any of the maids to assist her. She can help her abigail for once." The gleeful expression upon Bingley's face was comical. He was always happy, but he had obviously had enough of his sister's behaviour.

Darcy followed as Bingley strode to the ballroom where his sister stood, explaining her expectations as though she was queen of the castle. "Caroline, I have had enough."

Miss Bingley gave a slight lift of her chin. "I do not understand what you mean. These maids are incompetent, as is the housekeeper. I am simply ensuring they follow my directions."

Fitzwilliam had to bite his cheek to keep from laughing at the silent scoffs of the maids behind Miss Bingley.

"None of them are incompetent," said Bingley. "But you are treating them abhorrently, and I have been forced to increase the wages of most of them to compensate for the abuse you have inflicted upon them."

"Why that is ridiculous—"

"No, Caroline! Just so you are aware, their increased wages will come from your own funds. I have also spoken to Mrs. Nichols. She will be finishing the preparations for the ball without you."

"*I* am capable of planning—"

"That may be, but you will be returning to Scarborough. You depart at first light. I suggest you go to your bedchamber and begin packing."

"That is what the maids are for!"

Bingley leaned into his sister's face. "I do not care. For once, I shall spare them your vitriol. You will not screech at any more of the servants here, and you are confined to your bedchamber until your departure. Your meals will be brought to you. Your maid will also not be required to assist you in packing. And do not believe you will leave your belongings behind to buy new. Whatever you leave will be given to the poor, and I shall not purchase any fabric or pay any dressmaker to make you new gowns. My aunt can buy gowns off the ragman if you are in need of clothing, but the funds will be from your fortune—not mine."

Miss Bingley gasped with wide eyes. "You would not dare!"

"I desire peace in this house, and it has become obvious I shall not have it unless you are gone. I am also certain Darcy would prefer if you also ceased in your diatribe against his betrothed. She has done naught to you and does not deserve—"

"She is beneath us! She is beneath him! Mr. Darcy requires a lady of fashion! One with more of a fortune. Do you know that she has nothing?"

Bingley opened his mouth as though meaning to speak.

"Brother, Miss Bennet is quite pretty, but she would accept you for the sake of her family and your wealth. She does not love you. I do not know what Mr. Darcy is thinking of, connecting himself to such a family. The Bennets are hardly suitable. You will be laughed out of London with a match like Jane Bennet."

Bingley scoffed. "You know not what you speak. You have ignored magical matters your entire life, and now, you give precedence to those who do not deserve the honour. Jane Bennet is highly suitable. You would not understand the prominence of her family because you failed to listen at Samhain nor did you wish to spend the equinox here." He scowled and leaned into his sister's face. "Now, since you cannot be pleasant, you will be sent to my aunt in Scarborough. Do you understand?"

Miss Bingley opened her mouth to speak, but Fitzwilliam laughed. "Even in non-magical circles, the Bennet ladies are above you because their father is a gentleman. Whether he has five thousand a year or not is irrelevant. He has land, which your brother does not." How many times had he and Bingley ridiculed Miss Bingley's insults and spoken of this very fact?

"In magical circles—"

"Her family's lineage can be traced to Merlin and Niniane. The Bennet family has boasted of the purest magic in England for centuries. They are skilled mages but prefer to remain in the country and keep to themselves. They do not seek additional power or to be revered, but that does not make them less. If anything, those traits make them more honourable than most."

Miss Bingley's face had contorted while he spoke. As soon as he stopped, she clenched her hands into fists at her sides.

"She is nothing. Her ancestors mean nothing. She is but an ignorant country girl who is not worthy of being Mrs. Darcy."

"And that is why you will be departing at first light," said Bingley. "Just know, I shall be penning a letter to be sent ahead of you by express. Aunt will be told of your opinion, and I must warn you, she will not take kindly to your opinion of the Bennets."

Bingley's sister gave an odd cackle. "As if she knows of them!"

"Most people who are still part of the magical world know of the Bennets," said Bingley. "Only those who refuse to learn the history deem them unworthy of notice. In fact, Aunt wrote of her excitement at me courting Mr. Bennet's eldest daughter. She recognises what you refuse to acknowledge: that the Bennets are not the nobodies you believe them to be. Now, off to your bedchamber. I shall have a tray sent to your rooms. I shall not see you again until I send you off in the morning."

Miss Bingley stamped her foot with a shriek and marched from the room. No sooner had she gone, than one of the maids giggled then clapped a palm over her mouth.

"Forgive me."

"You need not beg forgiveness," said Bingley. "I can understand your relief and likely excitement at the prospect of my sister's leaving. For now, seek out Mrs. Nichols. She will be completing the preparations for the ball."

The maids both curtseyed. "Yes, sir." They did not tarry after but hurried from the room.

Bingley groaned and rubbed his neck. "Well, that is done. I should be relieved, but I am certain she will attempt to cause more trouble before she leaves."

Fitzwilliam could not argue. Miss Bingley would never go quietly. He would ensure his valet knew to take every precaution until that lady departed.

Before he could comment on what had occurred, the door opened, and Mrs. Hurst burst through. "Charles, Caroline just told me you have ordered her to go to Scarborough. If you insist upon this, you should know Hurst and I intend to accompany her."

"No," said Bingley in a stern tone. "Should you and Hurst wish to depart, you are welcome to take your carriage and go, but Caroline will journey north in my equipage and with my servants accompanying her. After all, should she travel with you, you will take her to London and allow her to continue overspending her pin money and making a fool of herself. No, she will return to Scarborough, and you will not intervene. Do I make myself clear?"

Mrs. Hurst crossed her arms over her chest. "This is unfair to her! She is your little sister. How could you treat her so?"

"Between overspending her allowance and the servants she has mistreated, she has cost me tens of thousands of pounds since my father died. I shall not continue to support her mean-spiritedness and shallow disregard for those she considers beneath her.

"Should you leave, I have made arrangements for the ball to continue as planned. Your departure will have little effect on my hopes or plans."

"You will continue to court Miss Bennet, even after learning of her connexions to trade." Mrs. Hurst had always been as ignorant as her sister.

Bingley gave an incredulous guffaw. "*We* are from trade! Your contempt for their uncle is laughable considering my father was a tradesman! I am so relieved he is not here to hear you and Caroline speak. He would be heartbroken. He saw you educated and married to a gentleman in an effort to make you more than him. He did so because he loved you. And this is how you repay him."

Mrs. Hurst opened her mouth, but Bingley held up a hand. "No, not another word. I do not care to have you here any longer. You will be leaving on the morrow as well. I care not where you go, but Caroline will be going to Scarborough. Should you defy me, I shall take the funds Caroline has overspent from her fortune, and you will be forced to support her until she weds, and you will never find her a husband who will take her for the sum that remains."

Fitzwilliam's eyebrows shot up. Miss Bingley was six and twenty and had come out at seventeen. Nine years of overspending would be a substantial amount.

Mrs. Hurst's lips twisted for a moment, and he stiffened. She stood there for a moment, then swivelled around on her heel and departed. What a relief! Bingley had never in his life stood up for himself as he just had. If pressed, would Fitzwilliam have relented? He would have likely done no more than allow Miss Bingley to accompany the Hursts, but the plans now were a much better solution.

Bingley crumpled into the nearest chair. "I always suspected standing up to them would be exhausting. I was right."

"Yes, but now that you have done so, they will not challenge you as much; but you cannot falter. You must remain steadfast if you are to regain control of Miss Bingley's spending and behaviour."

"My aunt has said she will take Caroline to some of the village events. Mayhap she will find a suitable husband."

After schooling his expression, Fitzwilliam cleared his throat. "Miss Bingley would never accept someone from the country, but her behaviour has ensured she will never marry for the wealth and connexions she desires. You may have to resign yourself to forcing her hand in the matter or being responsible for her for the remainder of her lifetime, or yours." He would not lie to Bingley. His friend deserved better.

Bingley grimaced. "You are not improving my mood."

"Then let us visit the ladies at Longbourn. I believe seeing Miss Bennet would improve your spirits."

His friend chuckled as he rose. "Do not make this about Miss Bennet. I know you want nothing more than to gaze at Miss Elizabeth like a mooncalf." A mooncalf! He was insulted!

"If only I could have an artist paint your countenance when you gaze upon Miss Bennet. Then, we would see who is the true mooncalf."

"She is an angel," said Bingley, his expression already that of a besotted pup.

"No, she is a lady—and a gentle one at that. You do have a propensity to fall in and out of love. All I ask in this circumstance is that you do not toy with Miss Bennet's feelings."

Bingley clapped a hand to Fitzwilliam's shoulder. "I assure you, Darcy, my intentions are honourable."

"Then I shall welcome you as my brother when the time comes."

Elizabeth lifted her head and let the book she was reading fall to her lap. A familiar creaking of the floor was coming from the hall. Her gaze met her father's, and he lifted his eyebrows.

As soon as the creaking disappeared, voices rose in the parlour for a moment and the noise in the house diminished. Only the louder effusions from Lydia and Mama carried through the hall.

Elizabeth placed the book on the desk and rose. After muttering a tostaich incantation, she opened the door to the library and crept to the long table along the wall. On the salver was a thick letter. Her cousin had written another. With careful fingers, she lifted the missive. The direction was to Lady Catherine de Bourgh of Rosings Park. She could not be surprised. This was not the first.

After a swift glance towards the parlour, she took the letter and hastened back into her father's sanctuary. As soon as she closed the door, she said the counter to the previous incantation and strode to the desk.

She handed it to her father. "Are you going to read it?"

Her father chuckled as he broke the seal. "Of course, I am." He glanced along the pages and sighed. "Although I doubt I need to read every word. Our cousin is as loquacious in his writing as he is in person. He has given a thorough detailing of every event we have attended and every conversation. Good Lord!"

Papa's brow remained creased while he continued to look over the missive. "Just like the previous letters, he has mentioned your disappearance in the mornings and his suspicion that you are meeting Darcy. You are shameless it seems." He chuckled, but then sat up with his expression dark. "It also appears as though your mother's plotting has played into his plans."

Her insides gave a sudden jump. "What do you mean?"

"Well, Lady Catherine apparently insisted you be the wife he brings to Hunsford. Your engagement to Darcy has him panicked. He begs for his patroness's aid with the matter as well as Miss de Bourgh's. 'I have attempted to put an end to the engagement between them, but naught has been successful. My attempt at ruining Miss Elizabeth last night was a failure. Her bedchamber door was impenetrable; not even Mrs. Bennet's key worked; it would not even slip into the keyhole.'"

A shudder ran up her spine. "Since his arrival, I have placed a dothreáite charm on my door and windows before retiring; even on the cupboard that connects my bedchamber to that of Jane's."

Papa placed the papers on the desk and steepled his hands in front of his mouth. "If she had received this, Lady Catherine might reason out why your door could not be breached. Mr. and Mrs. Hill know to separate out his post and bring it to me, but I do have concerns of him walking into town to send his letters should he come to suspect us. Lady Catherine may also wonder at the long absence of correspondence from her clergyman."

"Should we amend his words and let it go out?" It was the simplest solution.

He placed the letter flat on the desk. "I believe that is exactly what we should do." He traced his finger along certain passages while he made a humming sort of sound. Certain phrases disappeared, others rearranged, and some appeared in Mr. Collins handwriting until all traces of Fitzwilliam and their engagement disappeared from the page.

Her father's abilities were so effortless. She loved watching him perform those simple bits of magic that showed off his true skill. Would she ever display such ease with her power?

When he was finished, he took great care in folding the paper in the same way Mr. Collins had then fixed the seal.

"Ring the bell."

Mrs. Hill came promptly, and he handed her the adjusted missive. "I still want all of Mr. Collins correspondence brought to me, but ensure this one is sent. We do not want his patroness to become suspicious."

The housekeeper took the letter, curtseyed, and bustled back to the kitchen.

"We shall surely need to do that again before we can rid ourselves of him. I intend to put it about that you are in London visiting your aunt and uncle after you are wed. No one need know the truth until we are prepared for what is to come."

She crossed her arms over her chest and hugged them tight. Would they be ready? All glimpses of the person that was coming indicated they had substantial power. As much as she and Fitzwilliam practiced, was it enough?

At a knock on the door, she started. Mrs. Hill entered and stepped to the side. "Mr. Darcy and Mr. Bingley have arrived and are in the parlour with the ladies and Mr. Collins."

Papa rubbed his temples. "Come, Lizzy. We must join our guests. It would not do to leave Jane to control your mother for too long."

"Mama becomes agitated whenever Fitzwilliam is here." Her mother seemed to believe she deserved nothing good. Mama had always been that way, so why did it still hurt?

With a hand to her back, Papa guided her into the hall. "I believe you need your betrothed to lift your spirits. I know it is difficult, but do not take too much of your mother's behaviour to heart. Much of it is her illness."

As soon as the door opened and Fitzwilliam came into view, her heart lightened a bit. How was that possible from a mere glimpse of him?

Fitzwilliam came forward, kissed her hand, and led her to sit beside him on the sofa. As the conversation flowed around them, he leaned near her ear.

"I do not know if I can wait seven more days to marry you."

Her cheeks warmed and she could not keep from allowing a small smile. "Are you saying you are weak, Mr. Darcy?"

His low chuckle vibrated through her. "Only when it comes to you, Elizabeth. Only when it comes to you."

Chapter 17

26th of November 1811

A welcoming light glowed from the windows of Netherfield as the Bennet carriage approached the great house. Since Wickham was reported to still be with the militia, Papa had insisted Lydia and Kitty remain at Longbourn with Mama to prevent incident. A relief indeed!

If only Mr. Collins had stayed behind as well. The snivelling little man was currently seated across from her with Papa while Elizabeth sat with Jane. Thank heavens for observing propriety! Papa was not thrilled with the seating arrangement. To most, he had accepted the position with grace if one had not noted the sigh and slight grimace he wore at the prospect. Yet, he had no other choice.

When the equipage came to a stop, Fitzwilliam and Mr. Bingley bounded down from the portico and stood waiting for the door to be opened and the step to be placed. Papa climbed out, followed by Mr. Collins, then Mr. Bingley aided Jane. Mr. Collins lurched forward as Elizabeth stood to alight, and she hesitated. She did not want Mr. Collins touching her, even if she was wearing gloves.

More than once since they had intercepted the letter where he told of his unsuccessful attempt at gaining access to her bedchamber, she had awakened to his subsequent tries. He had not succeeded in his endeavour, but when they were in company together, the way he sometimes stared at her made her fight down a gag.

"I beg your pardon, Mr. Collins," said Fitzwilliam in a commanding tone. "But I shall assist my betrothed."

"But, sir—"

"Mr. Collins, you try my patience. If you continue to pursue Miss Elizabeth, I will be forced to call you out."

The weaselly man gasped and bowed, his hand over his heart. "Forgive me. I did not mean to insult such an illustrious man as yourself. I only meant to be of aid to the genteel and beautiful Miss de Bourgh, who I know has a prior claim to your hand."

Fitzwilliam grabbed Mr. Collins by the lapels and shoved him against the side of the carriage. "I have told you more than once to cease spreading your lies. If you mention my cousin or myself in regard to marriage again, I *will* take action against you. Do you understand?" Fitzwilliam dropped the insolent man like rubbish. While he extended his hand for Elizabeth, the small parson once again began bowing and scraping.

Her entire body released a huge exhale as she placed her hand in his palm. As soon as she was by his side, she hugged his arm to her. Since her betrothed had learnt of Mr. Collins's scheming, he had given his aunt's parson no quarter. Mr. Collins attempted at every encounter to separate them and ingratiate himself to his patroness's nephew, but Fitzwilliam put Mr. Collins in his place on each and every occasion. Thank heavens!

Yesterday, Mr. Collins had even requested the first set for tonight. How grateful she had been to inform him that particular set had been taken! But he had not stopped there. He had faltered for but a second before requesting the second. After she had kindly informed him that Mr. Bingley had requested that set, Mr. Collins had not asked for another. Would it be too much to hope she did not have to sit out tonight? If Mr. Collins caught one hint of her being in need of a partner, he would swoop in and claim her without delay. That could not happen.

When they stepped inside the great hall, servants emerged to take their coats. Her betrothed stepped in front of a maid who had approached, and he helped her with her cloak, handing the garment to the girl before offering Elizabeth his arm once more.

Her heart beat quickly as they entered the grand ballroom. Everything was so beautiful! The chandeliers were lit and the crystals sparkled with the light of the candles, the freshly polished silver gleamed, and the entire neighbourhood was bedecked in their best gowns and suits while they milled about the room.

After greeting their host, Fitzwilliam drew her away from their party. "My cousin is here. I should like to introduce you now, if you are willing."

"Of course."

After returning to where he was beside her father, Fitzwilliam set a hand upon Papa's shoulder. "I should like to introduce Elizabeth to my cousin, Richard."

Papa's countenance brightened. "Colonel Fitzwilliam is here. Do send him my way when you are done. I have not spoken to him since he was a gangly boy at Eton."

Her betrothed chuckled. "I am certain he will be flattered by the remembrance, sir. I am also sure he will seek you out at his first opportunity."

As he led her through the ballroom, those she had known all of her life nodded and smiled. She had received a number of calls since Samhain, congratulating her on her engagement. Fitzwilliam, while not overtly talkative or friendly, had impressed the neighbourhood with his quiet affection for her. They all noticed how he remained by her side, spoke to her with an endearing expression, and fetched her punch. What he displayed in public was only a pebble in the ocean when compared to what she had come to know of this gentleman beside her. He was free with his affection and treated her with a respect she could not have imagined receiving from a husband. Despite her earlier reservations, she was fortunate her father made this match for her.

She had been reluctant and somewhat scared when Papa first mentioned their union. How she have ever imagined the reality of her situation now?

Before she was ready, she stood before a gentleman in a red coat. He was not handsome but carried himself as every bit the gentleman. He wore a smile that hinted at the mischievous streak Fitzwilliam had mentioned on more than one occasion.

"Miss Elizabeth Bennet, may I present Colonel Richard Fitzwilliam?"

She curtseyed while the colonel smiled and bowed. "Sir, I am pleased to make your acquaintance. Fitzwilliam speaks of you often."

Colonel Fitzwilliam's smile grew, and he laughed. "He does, does he? I would hope he could think of something better to speak of, but perhaps Darcy is dumbfounded due to your beauty."

"You did not mention your cousin was such a charmer." In most cases, a gentleman's blatant compliment would unnerve her, but the colonel's was done in a manner that spoke of his good humour. She was not put off by it.

"No, I seem to have forgotten," said Fitzwilliam, his tone flat. "I apologise for not mentioning my cousin's way with the ladies sooner."

The colonel stepped a little closer. "So, I must know. What does my cousin say about me when I am not around?"

She arched her eyebrow. "You have little to fear, sir. He speaks quite well of you. You share guardianship of Mr. Darcy's younger sister, do you not?" Fitzwilliam had mentioned that more than once if she remembered correctly.

"Yes, we do. Speaking of Georgiana, am I to bring her for the solstice? I am certain she would wish to witness the announcement of your marriage."

"Wickham is here," said Fitzwilliam in a low, hard tone. "He joined the militia."

The colonel chuckled and rubbed his hands together. "Pray, tell me you speak the truth. Nothing would please me more than to teach that reprobate a lesson."

"The local merchants have been warned, and Elizabeth ensured no one fell for his lies at the last gathering."

"And how did she do that?" asked the colonel.

Fitzwilliam leaned forward and whispered near the colonel's ear. The gentleman spluttered and coughed. "I applaud you, Miss Elizabeth. He was likely bewildered at why no one would listen to his false tale of woe."

"False tale of woe?" She had heard naught of this.

Her betrothed sighed. "He tells all and sundry the same story: that I refused him the living my father meant for him. In truth, he would make a terrible vicar, and he refused the placement. He desired three thousand pounds in lieu of the living, so I gave him the funds and hoped to never see him again."

Colonel Fitzwilliam looked between them. "Let us not worry about Wickham this evening. I understand my aunt's parson has expressed his intention to marry you, Miss Elizabeth."

She groaned and shook her head. "He is relentless. I can only hope I have enough dance partners that I will not be forced to stand up with him." If only she could use magic! Then she could hide herself in a corner and no one would notice she was without a partner.

The colonel straightened. "Then let me be of aid in the endeavour. What set do you have available?"

"My first and second are taken, but the remaining are thus far free."

Fitzwilliam covered her hand with his. "Do not forget that I am taking the supper set and the last."

His cousin guffawed. "Three sets? You will be considered rude, Darcy."

"If my rudeness keeps her from being plagued by that imbecile, then so be it." Fitzwilliam's growling tone along with his protective stance made butterflies take flight inside her belly. For some reason, when he strove to protect her as he was, she had begun to have flutters. An oddity, to be sure!

Elizabeth squeezed his arm. "I believe most here would see him as besotted."

Colonel Fitzwilliam held her gaze with a grin. "Well, then, I would be pleased if you would do me the honour of dancing the third with me. We shall do our best to ensure Mr. Collins does not have his opportunity to pester you. Oh, look. The guests are lining up for the first dance."

"Shall we?" asked Fitzwilliam.

After nodding to her betrothed, she nodded to his cousin. "I look forward to our dance, Colonel."

They stepped into the centre of the ballroom with the others and stood across from each other. When the music began, they honoured their partners before beginning the first steps of the quadrille. The dance was lively, and by the time they bowed and curtseyed at the end, she was grinning.

"Miss Elizabeth, I believe the second set is mine," said Mr. Bingley as he offered his arm.

Fitzwilliam kissed the back of her hand before offering his own to Jane, who he had asked to stand up with him for the second.

After they began the dance, Bingley glanced over to Jane and Fitzwilliam. "Do you know; I have never seen Darcy dance the quadrille before. Who knew he could be so light on his feet?"

"He danced at the assembly. Did you not notice his skill then?" Fitzwilliam had proved to be an agreeable partner. He had not trod on her toes once.

"I do not argue at his ability, only his willingness to dance when it is you, Miss Elizabeth. He appears amenable to the most disagreeable diversions—his opinion of course—in order to spend time with you."

She glanced over her shoulder. Fitzwilliam was executing the motions of the dance perfectly, but his countenance was not as open as it was with her. He cared for her deeply. He had to. Why else would he be so relaxed in her company?

"Mr. Darcy is a dear man."

Mr. Bingley smiled, but before he could speak, they were separated by the dance. When he returned, he bent a little closer. "I would say it shows the depth of his love for you."

Love? They had been spending a prodigious amount of time together. He sought her out and showed her affection. He had confessed that he cared deeply for her, but did he truly love her? She bit her lip as she watched her betrothed for a moment. She stumbled, and an arm kept her from falling.

"Are you well, Miss Elizabeth?" Mr. Bingley looked at her with a frown.

"Forgive me. I was distracted."

His jovial countenance returned. "I believe I understand." He glanced at Jane, and her heart leapt. She had the vision of Jane's happiness due to Mr. Bingley's proposal when she had first touched the altar with Fitzwilliam. It seemed this was all how it was meant to be.

"I am happy to hear it, Mr. Bingley."

As soon as the set ended, Fitzwilliam claimed her. "Come."

"But what of your cousin? I agreed to dance the next with him."

"He will understand."

They approached the side of the room near a door and stood for a moment.

"Fitzwilliam—"

All of a sudden, a surge of power flowed through her just before she was pulled into a dimly lit room. Fitzwilliam's arms wrapped around her, and she was pulled close. "I noticed you almost fell during the set. Are you well? Did Bingley say something to upset you?"

She shook her head. "Not at all. He was very kind. But what if someone saw us leave?"

"No one saw us. I hid us from sight before I pulled you from the room." He trailed his fingers down her cheek. "What has upset you? You stumbled during the dance and kept turning to watch me. What did Bingley say to you?"

Her hands trembled as she joined them so Fitzwilliam would not notice. He would not relent until she told him what had discomposed her, but would he think her silly?

"Mr. Bingley commented on your willingness to dance with me. H-he implied . . ."

"He implied what?"

"Well, I suppose he did not imply it, but he said it was proof of your love for me." She inhaled a great breath. "Since you have not said those words to me, I simply wondered if what he said was true. That is all." The last rushed out on one long exhale. She braced herself. He would not be upset, would he?

Fitzwilliam took her forearm and tugged her until she was in his embrace. "Bingley speaks before thinking."

She looked up at him with a frown. What could he mean?

With a chuckle, he took one of her hands and placed her palm on his chest. "I had hoped to tell you on our wedding night, but it seems that with only three days or so to go, Bingley has stolen that from me."

Her chin hitched back. "I do not understand."

He leaned down and claimed her lips in a sweet kiss that she clung to when he drew back. "What I am saying is that I love you. I believe I have cared for you since the first vision I had of you, but I did not love you as a betrothed or a husband should until I first met you in Oakham Forest. Since that day, the depth of attachment I have felt has only grown. I admire your adept use of your power as well as your mind, and I anticipate the life we will have together. I know I shall never be distracted."

She rested her forehead against his chest and breathed in the familiar notes of his cologne. "How could you steal my heart with so little effort?"

His finger tipped her chin up. He was smiling. "I thought you would change your mind in the beginning. I do not know how I convinced you to let me court you, but I shall be forever grateful that you were somehow persuaded." His thumb caressed her cheeks. "Now, you have said I stole your heart, but I should like to hear the words if you are inclined to say them."

She cradled his dear face in her hands. "Despite what I said, I do not know if I am in love with you. I have never fallen in love before, but I can no longer imagine my future without you in it. In truth, I believe I am falling in love with you, and I hope you can understand that I want to be certain of my feelings before I say those words. I never thought I would be happy to have an arranged match, but you and my father have proved me wrong."

"I find that I can accept such an answer without reserve. You have given me hope that I shall not have long to wait for your heart to be mine." His expression was joyful as once again, he pulled her to him and kissed her deeply. As he held her close, his hands stroked along her back, pressing against the small.

A knock made them separate, and Elizabeth moved over beside the fire while Fitzwilliam answered the door.

"I am uncertain how Mr. Bennet knew you had sneaked away from the ball, but he was indeed correct," said the colonel as he entered. "He sent me to request your return. He said Miss Elizabeth should make her way first."

She set off for the door, but Fitzwilliam stopped her with a hand to her arm. "Go this way." He opened a door to the side of the room. "This will take you into the hall, and it will not be so obvious that we were together when Richard and I go through the other door."

"And do save that dance for me, Miss Elizabeth. I believe your cousin is searching you out in the hopes of claiming you for himself."

"If only he would understand that I will never marry him."

Fitzwilliam squeezed her arm. "In a few more days, all will be settled. In the meantime, I shall return to your side in a trice. I promise."

After nodding, she exited the room to a corridor that led to the great hall. When she entered the ballroom, she approached her father's side.

"You will be wed soon. No one seemed to notice Darcy's charm which caused you both to disappear so abruptly, but I did. You should not keep sneaking off when others could notice you are missing."

"We had a matter to settle. Nothing more."

Her father tilted his head with a questioning expression. "And?"

"Nothing is amiss, Papa. We shall be married and be the happiest couple in the world."

He offered her his arm and patted her hand when she rested it in the crook. "I could not be more pleased to hear that."

Chapter 18

26th of November 1811 cont. . .

Fitzwilliam clasped his hands behind his back while Elizabeth departed. "Bingley upset her. I just wanted to ensure she was well."

His cousin laughed. "You need not worry about me, cousin. Her father noticed your departure and requested I relay his message. What did Bingley do? He is hardly one to cause mischief."

After a sigh, Fitzwilliam ran his fingers through his hair. "No, he was not causing mischief. He simply explained my reticence at events and that my willingness to dance with her showed my affection for her. I had hoped to confess my feelings after our marriage, but—"

"Bingley's perpetual happiness and need to see others so ruined your plans," said Richard. "Speaking of ruining plans, where are Miss Bingley and Mrs. Hurst? They can ruin anyone's best laid plans in a matter of moments." Richard had never liked Bingley's sisters. Miss Bingley had insulted Richard's mother once. A grave mistake. The countess saw to it that few but those who thrived on gossip now associated with Miss Bingley. Her brother was better off with her secluded in the country.

"Believe it or not, Bingley sent Miss Bingley to Scarborough to live with their aunt, and Mr. and Mrs. Hurst left the same morning for London. They had hoped to take Miss Bingley with them, but Bingley insisted he would withhold Miss Bingley's fortune should they do so." It had been far past time for Bingley to take control of his family!

Richard lifted his eyebrow. "I never thought Bingley would stand up to them so. I must say I am impressed. I have also not experienced one surge of joy while in the ballroom. You seem to have taught him to control his ability."

"He sometimes allows a little of his happiness to leak out."

"By the way, Father sent me to Rosings last week. Lady Catherine has insisted you come to marry Anne soon, and my father wanted to see if Anne was healthy enough to bear you an heir."

Fitzwilliam pinched the bridge of his nose. "You told him I am already engaged, did you not?"

"I did, and he also knows it is to Mr. Bennet's daughter. As far as my father is concerned, your betrothed is much more suited to you than Anne, but he insists upon being informed as to what Lady Catherine is doing. He does not trust her."

"So, what did you discover?"

His cousin leaned on the back of the sofa and crossed his arms over his chest. "Anne has grown weaker since the last time I saw her four months ago. She smiles and insists she is well, but she is often aided to walk about by Mrs. Jenkinson. On one occasion, her companion even fetched a footman to help Anne upstairs to retire. As father and I both suspected, she is in no condition to be your wife, so my father sent a letter indicating he would not interfere in the marriage your father arranged."

"Did he mention Elizabeth or her family?"

"No, he feared Lady Catherine would journey here and let her sentiments on the marriage be known. During the dinner after my arrival, she spoke of several magical families, and she belittled them all. You should know how she is. No family is as great as the de Bourghs and the Fitzwilliams."

An almost growl came from him. "She suffers from delusions."

Richard shrugged. "I cannot understand why she is insistent Anne is much improved when she is clearly declining. The apothecary came to examine her and does not know what afflicts her. He left several tonics, but Lady Catherine tossed them into the fire. She is fortunate none of them exploded. You know how volatile some potions can be."

Yes, he did. Wickham had once tossed a potion into the fire, and it had exploded. The blackguard had a small scar over his eyebrow as a result.

"You should also know," said Richard, "that I spoke to Colonel Forster upon his arrival. Wickham does not leave the camp since Miss King's uncle threatened to call him out if he showed his face in the village. None of the merchants will give him credit, and the ladies all turn green when he attempts to speak to him, including Colonel Forster's wife."

Fitzwilliam guffawed. "Mr. Bennet sent out word that the tobathrú potion Elizabeth brewed was effective and kept those who imbibed it from falling for Wickham's charm."

"Your Elizabeth makes potions?"

He whispered a charm and drew closer to his cousin. "My Elizabeth is the heir to the Bennet magic." He trusted Richard. No reason existed for him to hide what everyone would soon come to know.

His cousin's eyes widened. "Surely you jest! No woman has ever—"

"Even though we are alone, I have made our conversation unable to be overheard, but still, do not speak so loudly. The secret has been well-guarded since her birth. My parents knew, which is why we are betrothed. Even though she is capable of great feats of power, she—"

"She will require someone strong and trustworthy to be her partner. Too many will doubt her and any who seek to do evil may come after her if she was without such protection." He shook his head. "She bears the mark?"

"My father and mother saw it. I have also seen it in a vision. For obvious reasons, she keeps her birthmark covered." She had worn naught but sleeves that touched her elbows or wrists since the weather was cool. More than likely, she wore those sleeve lengths year around for fear of discovery. He whispered the reversal for the silencing charm. "We should also return. If you do not appear soon, Lady Catherine's parson will claim Elizabeth for that set."

As they started for the door, Richard frowned. "Why is he so insistent on marrying your betrothed? From what you have told me, there are five Bennet daughters. He could choose another and not risk rejection or being called out."

"We do not know why he is so adamant on Elizabeth, but Mr. Bennet will never accept his application for *any* of his daughters. A non-magical clergyman could be dangerous if he came to understand his wife's talents." No, Mr. Collins needed to find a wife somewhere else.

"You make an excellent point."

When they returned to the ballroom, Elizabeth stood holding her father's arm while she watched the dancers. As he continued to look about the room, he found Mr. Collins dancing with Charlotte Lucas. From what Elizabeth had told him, Miss Lucas had a middling magical talent. She could do no more than sense the feelings of others, yet what she could sense was really little more than what anyone could tell in speaking to someone. Few believed her talent to be a true ability, so none of the magical families considered her marriageable. Could Mr. Collins be the answer as a husband for her?

They approached Mr. Bennet, who peered at Fitzwilliam over his glasses. "You did not have enough time with my daughter, Darcy?"

He grinned as he caught Elizabeth's sparkling gaze. "No, sir. Not nearly enough."

Mr. Bennet chuckled and shook his head. "You will be wed soon."

"Papa, I promised Colonel Fitzwilliam the next."

Her father patted her hand before relinquishing her to Richard who took her to the edge of the dancers to await the start of the music.

Fitzwilliam shifted beside Mr. Bennet and once again whispered an incantation that would allow him to speak but not be heard by those around them. "I had a thought to solve our problem with Mr. Collins."

Mr. Bennet turned slightly to face him. "I thought I heard you muttering a spell. What is it you want to do with Collins?"

"Well, what if we bewitch him to believe himself in love with Charlotte Lucas?"

He startled and looked to the couple amongst the dancers. "Miss Lucas is a practical sort, but I almost feel sorry for her if this is your solution."

"She is unmarriageable amongst those in her neighbourhood. Perhaps she will not care if he is an imbecile."

"And if she does?" asked Mr. Bennet.

"Then we can reverse the spell. We are not harming anyone."

Mr. Bennet turned while muttering and caught Sir William before he could pass them by. "Lucas, if Mr. Collins singled out your daughter, do you know if she would accept his suit?"

Sir William stroked his beard while he watched his daughter dancing with Mr. Collins. "She has given up any hope of marriage, but should the opportunity present itself, I believe she would accept. He has spoken little of anyone besides his patroness and Miss Elizabeth. Do you think his affections would shift so easily?"

"Lizzy is to be wed, and soon. My cousin has said Lady Catherine told him not to return without a wife. I thought Charlotte might have some interest in having her own home, but I wished to enquire before I suggest her as a possibility."

Fitzwilliam held his features as firm as possible so he would not give away his position on the matter. Scheming and using magic against others in a harmful way could cause the person casting the spell their own grief. In asking Sir William of his opinion, Mr. Bennet was protecting himself, Elizabeth, and Fitzwilliam. His forethought did him credit.

"Charlotte is a sensible lady," said Mr. Bennet. "She would make an excellent parson's wife."

Sir William glanced at his daughter with Mr. Collins. "I agree. I thank you for thinking of the match."

After a clap to the shoulder, Sir William wound his way through the guests to the opposite side of the ballroom. The set ended, and Mr. Collins bumbled his way to stand beside Mr. Bennet.

"My dear cousin, I do not suppose you know whether Miss Elizabeth has a free set. I had hoped to dance with her next, but I see she has been claimed by one of the officers."

"Colonel Fitzwilliam," said Fitzwilliam. "He is my cousin and Lady Catherine's nephew." Mr. Collins's knowledge of Richard's family would help if the little man approached his cousin. Collins would not insist on anything for fear of offending one of Lady Catherine's nephews.

"I had no idea! Of course, I would never interrupt an officer from such a prestigious noble line."

Before Mr. Collins could continue, Mr. Bennet placed his hand on his shoulder. "You seemed to enjoy your dance with Miss Lucas. Her sensible nature would lend well to being the wife of a parson such as yourself. Mayhap you should dance with her again."

Mr. Collins's eyes widened for but a moment before he nodded. "Yes, she is quite sensible. Perhaps I should request the honour of another dance." He shook his head. "But Lady Catherine—"

Mr. Bennet's fingers squeezed just a bit. "Would be pleased with such a lady nearby; I am certain."

"Yes, my aunt would appreciate Miss Lucas's reasonable nature. Such a match would be a prodigious one for you."

The parson frowned, then nodded again. "I shall seek her out right now."

As soon as he departed, Mr. Bennet laughed. "I hope I am not overstepping. If she shows any hint of not desiring such a marriage, I shall reverse the spell without delay."

Mr. Collins approached Miss Lucas, who stood with Miss Mary and Miss Maria. He gave a simpering smile and bowed as he spoke while Miss Mary and Miss Maria glanced back and forth between them. When Miss Lucas nodded, Fitzwilliam let out a long exhale.

"So far, she appears amenable. She is agreeing to a second dance."

The supper dance came, and Fitzwilliam's heartbeat accelerated as he led Elizabeth in the last set before the meal. He would not be separated from her until they returned to the ballroom.

Their set was pleasant. Elizabeth was quiet, but their gazes held as they made every turn required by the dances. When they finally sat beside each other at the supper table, he relished her form beside him, and even took her hand under the table when they had finished eating and while they held a quiet conversation.

Upon their return to the ballroom, Elizabeth rose on her tiptoes to reach his ear. "Mr. Collins has not approached me at all and has stood up with Charlotte for two sets. Do you know what is happening?"

"I may have suggested charming him to pursue Miss Lucas."

Elizabeth grimaced. "She could not be willing to accept such a man, could she?"

"Your father and I watched for any hint of unwillingness, but we did not notice any. She accepted Mr. Collins's offer of a second set with a smile."

His beloved shuddered. "If she complains—"

"We shall reverse the magic. I promise."

"Very well," she said. "Since I need not fear another application from my cousin, perhaps we could join my sister and Mr. Bingley for a time."

Fitzwilliam relished every second of having Elizabeth on his arm as they strode through the crowd to talk to Bingley and Miss Bennet. They enjoyed a lively discourse until the final dance was announced.

"I believe this set belongs to me," he said to Elizabeth.

"I suppose I must." She showed every bit of her good humour with her response, and he did not hesitate to lead her to the middle of the room.

When the set was over, Mr. Bennet and all of his daughters were invited to sit with Bingley, Fitzwilliam, and Richard in the drawing room until their carriage was brought around while Mr. Collins insisted upon seeing Miss Lucas to her family's equipage.

"I beg your pardon, Mr. Bingley," said Mrs. Nichols. "The Bennets' carriage is in front of the house."

Fitzwilliam kissed Elizabeth's hand as they walked to the hall. "I wish you did not have to go."

"Soon. We shall be wed soon, then we shall never be forced to part again."

"That day cannot come soon enough."

Bingley was the first to hand in Miss Bennet, Mr. Bennet handed in Miss Mary, and when Fitzwilliam stepped forward to hand in Elizabeth, she rose onto her toes and kissed his cheek. Bingley coughed and turned as did Richard.

"Good night, Fitzwilliam," she whispered.

Chapter 19

30th of November 1811

The full moon gave an ethereal glow to the trees as Elizabeth walked with her father and Jane to the stone circle. As was his wont, Herne met them at the edge of Oakham Forest and accompanied them to the clearing where he laid down and nestled into that one verdant patch of grass he favoured. If her guess was correct, he would be her chaperon until it was no longer required. Even then, would he still follow her all over the forest? Her heart hurt at the thought of him no longer roaming through the trees and grazing in the clearing with the pheasants.

Mr. Lawson, the vicar from Meryton, entered the clearing five minutes later. "Ah, you have arrived. I saw Mr. Darcy approaching from Netherfield when I entered the wood. He should not be far behind."

"Excellent," said Papa.

They had been fortunate when Mr. Lawson had applied for the position four years ago. Since he was magic himself, he understood the complexities of marriages and the traditions of their world. He placed the registry upon the altar and opened the large tome to the page she and Fitzwilliam would sign after they were wed. He also removed a bottle of ink and a pen that was wrapped in oiled wool to protect his clothing.

Elizabeth took in a deep breath and released it. Her entire body trembled, and butterflies seemed to be flying circles in her stomach. Yet, she was not as nervous as her body would have her believe. After the visions from the altar as well as the connexion she had experienced with her betrothed through visions all these years, she and Fitzwilliam were surely meant to be together. Every interaction she had with him only confirmed what the magic that flowed through them whispered to both of them—they were more than a charmed contract. The power that flowed through the earth meant for them to be together for whatever reason, even if they never understood why. Their marriage could have repercussions during their lifetimes or even repercussions meant to happen centuries into the future. The consequences of their marriage was impossible to know.

When Fitzwilliam stepped into the clearing, he pulled the hood of his cloak from his head as his cousin emerged from the trees behind him. Her betrothed was so handsome. He took her breath away when he turned those vivid blue eyes on her. Even when he was uncomfortable, his gaze would convey his love for her. And what she felt for him—well, the attachment had formed so swiftly that she always seemed lightheaded when he was near.

He joined their party beside the altar, and Mr. Lawson glanced between them. "I must say, Miss Elizabeth, when your father explained your position and why you needed to marry in the circle, I was astounded. I can still hardly believe it."

Her father nodded at her arm, so she slipped the cape off her shoulder and pulled her elbow-length sleeve up to reveal her birthmark.

The rector gasped and shook his head. "I assure you, I shall not breathe a word, but this is an exciting development indeed." He clapped his hands in front of him. "If all parties are ready, then let us proceed. Thankfully, the weather cooperated with your plans, and the moon is out to bless your union with good fortune. This is truly an auspicious occasion."

As Mr. Lawson began the ceremony, her father stood beside him while her sister and the colonel flanked her and Fitzwilliam. At the moment they joined their hands, the moon seemed to bathe them alone in its celestial light. Their hands also shone while they exchanged their vows, and the gold ring that was slipped upon her finger glinted in the moonlight. Mr. Lawson again gasped at the sight.

"I have never seen the like."

"We have never seen two heirs married before either," said Papa drolly.

Her gaze, however, never strayed from Fitzwilliam's other than to glance down when they joined hands and when he placed his ring upon her finger. Her entire body hummed and trembled, but she now recognised what was happening. The power from the earth as well as the moon were blessing their union.

As soon as Mr. Lawson declared them husband and wife, he uncorked the ink so they could sign the register. She wrote her name, then passed the pen to Fitzwilliam, so he could sign his own. When her now husband had completed his signature and barely lifted his pen from the paper, both their names appeared to light into flame, and when the glow dissipated, their signatures were dry.

Papa chuckled. "'Tis a shame your father was not here to see this, Darcy. He was always fascinated with the vagaries of the earth's magic. The earth and the moon have seemed to align to bless your marriage—a singular occurrence indeed."

Mr. Lawson brushed his fingers over their names in the registry. "Fascinating." He murmured as though speaking any louder would disturb those around them. Jane grasped her hand. Her sister's eyes were wide.

"My father will be upset at missing this," said the colonel. "Like Darcy's father once did, he studies rare magic."

The vicar shut the registry book and corked the ink. "Forgive me for rushing off, but my wife will wonder why I have been gone for so long. I told her I was visiting a parishioner. When she learns I have married you, Mrs. Darcy, and that she missed it, she will give me no quarter, particularly when she learns you are the heir. At least I shall have a few weeks' respite before she discovers what I have done."

Once Mr. Lawson disappeared into the trees, Papa crossed his arms over his chest. "Colonel Fitzwilliam, perhaps you could bring a letter to your father for me when you depart on the morrow? I had forgotten about his knowledge of rare magic, and we have been searching for answers to a vision for some time now and have found none."

"Of course, sir. I would be honoured to be of aid."

"The information is of a sensitive nature and cannot fall into the wrong hands," said Fitzwilliam. "Pray, have your father take care with who delivers the return correspondence. At least one person has died already, and the person responsible will continue to kill if we do not stop them."

She squeezed his arm. He phrased their situation as well as he could without giving away the contents of their vision. Thus far, they had only told Papa. They could only hope nothing changed as a result of telling him. With his knowledge of magic, they prayed it would help for her to succeed in defeating whoever was coming for her—or Papa. If they were draining magic, the evildoer would have to be a fool not to come for Papa. She shuddered. What if the vision had taken place after that person had already stolen her father's magic? Between the duke's and her father's power, they would be formidable, if not indestructible.

Fitzwilliam wrapped an arm around her and pulled her closer. "Are you cold?"

"I am well." She attempted to smile up at him as though undisturbed. How could she not be ill at ease? They had found nothing to be of aid. In the visions, Fitzwilliam had noted snow on the ground. With December fast approaching, the colder days would bring the weather he had witnessed. It was imperative they find the information they required before whoever the voice was sought them out. Hers and her father's life depended upon it.

Fitzwilliam pulled her a little further into his side. He was surely thinking the same thing. His frustration at the end of fruitlessly searching day after day was obvious. When they had indulged in an embrace, he had begun to hold her closer and tighter. He surely feared what was to come.

"We should go," said Papa as he waved Jane to him. "If we do not return to Longbourn soon, we shall be missed." They had given Mama a sleeping draught before they had departed. Mrs. Hill and Mary could manage Lydia and Kitty without aid, and as long as Mama slept the entire time they were gone, all would be well.

The colonel accompanied them to the edge of the forest, where his horse awaited him. "I shall be departing first thing on the morrow, Mr. Bennet."

Papa gave a dip of his chin. "I shall pen the letter as soon as I arrive home, and I shall expect you near dawn."

As soon as Colonel Fitzwilliam rode away, Papa gestured towards Longbourn. "Come. The dower house is not far from Longbourn. I have ensured it remains hidden in the event it is required for some secret purpose—as it is now."

Her husband kept her close to his side as they walked. Her husband! Her heart was so full at this moment. How was she to keep it all from overflowing?

She had been to the dower cottage many times since she was a little girl. When her father began teaching her spells, he would bring her there to practice. No one happened upon them when it was just the two of them. His propensity of keeping matters to himself was prudent. No one knew precisely what resources Papa had available to him.

When they reached the cluster of trees that bordered the cottage, Papa held up his hand. "Oscailt súl." The dower house became visible, and he muttered another couple of words which removed the remaining protections.

"Once you are inside, I shall place the enchantments back upon the cottage to keep you from harm. I shall return on afternoon of the solstice to retrieve you.

Elizabeth hugged Jane and her father before her husband took her hand and led her inside the stone cottage. She had always loved this place. The house was only a little smaller than Longbourn, with furniture that was outdated but in excellent condition. None should show wear since the house was hardly ever used. Her father had ensured the kitchen was stocked with some food and any necessities they would require. He had taken her trunk yesterday and had sent it in preparation for this evening.

As soon as Fitzwilliam closed the door behind them, his arms slipped around her body. "I thought we would never be alone."

She laughed. "We have spent most mornings alone since we met."

His nose nuzzled along her neck. "We were in the forest with your protector. We were not without a chaperon."

"You mean Herne?"

He helped her remove her cloak and hung it on the hook by the door. "Yes, that great white beast who snorts and paws the ground if I dare to touch you. I never thought I would be chaperoned by a stag, but what else could he be?"

"He is my friend." She began to take off her gloves while he saw to his own cloak. "So, Charlotte called on me this morning."

"I hope Miss Lucas is well."

She set her gloves on the table and backed further into the hall. "After four days of courting, Mr. Collins has declared his love for her and proposed." Elizabeth could hardly credit it. Yes, Charlotte would likely never receive another offer of marriage, but Mr.

Collins was all that was ridiculous. How would she bear a lifetime with him?

Fitzwilliam paused and gaped. "He did?"

"Yes, and she accepted. She declared all she desires is a home of her own and not to be a burden upon her family. I do not understand her decision, but your instincts were correct in this instance, although Papa did catch Mr. Collins wandering Longbourn two nights ago. Your aunt's insistence he marry me was certainly done in a forceful manner, and he must have been struggling with Papa's charm."

He stared off for a moment while biting his lip. "She has always been one to consult seers. I wonder if one saw and told her of your identity. My father always told her I was betrothed, but he would never divulge your name. My aunt can be a harridan, and he did not want your family bothered. He also never trusted her. Richard and I look into her daughter Anne's condition on a regular basis, but we have little contact with Lady Catherine if we can help it. If Mr. Collins has been compelled so strongly, I would suspect she used a potion on him. She has no gift for potion making, so she, no doubt, purchased the tincture from someone who does."

"Yes, Papa thought the same. He suggested to Charlotte that they do not hesitate to wed. He has concerns that if Mr. Collins returns to Hunsford and tells Lady Catherine that he is betrothed, she will compel him to end that engagement and once again pursue me."

Fitzwilliam frowned. "But we are married. He would have no hope of success."

"I believe Papa is more concerned with her using some other means to get what she wants. If she has someone who is making potions for her, then Mr. Collins could wreak havoc without knowing what he was truly doing."

After he set his gloves beside hers, he shook his head. "I do not wish to speak of my aunt or Collins or even Miss Lucas at this moment."

His intense gaze made her flesh prickle with heat. "What would you care to speak of then?"

He began to stalk towards her with a grin she had never seen before.

She took a step back. "What are you about?"

With a chuckle, he lunged forward and pulled her back into his arms. "We are finally alone—completely alone—and you want to talk about my aunt and Mr. Collins when we have much more agreeable matters to discuss?"

"Once again, what do you believe we should speak of?"

He claimed her lips, tugging at both before deepening the kiss. Her chest and stomach filled with a fluttering that made her breathless as he drew her tight against him. His fingers dug into her sides while he groaned into her mouth.

When he trailed tiny nibbles along her jaw, she curled her own fingers into his hair. "I do not hear any talking, Fitzwilliam."

Chapter 20

30th of November 1811 cont...

"I do not hear any talking, Fitzwilliam?" Her voice sounded so tremulous and low, so different than what she was accustomed to.

With small steps, he steered her into the parlour. She stumbled when he turned her away from him, but his strong arms kept her from falling into a heap on the floor. Her entire body could have melted into a puddle when he continued his assault on her neck, his fingers trailing along her sides then up her stomach, but she stiffened her legs. She needed to withstand the assault on her equanimity. His palms cupped her breasts and gently squeezed while he gently scraped his teeth along her shoulder. Her knees faltered, but his hold saved her once again.

"Fitzwilliam," she breathed. They were going to do this. . .here?

In a second, he had pulled back, whirled her around, and was fumbling with the fastenings of her gown. "I cannot wait and struggle through senseless conversation while I can think of nothing but holding you close. I do not want to keep my hands to myself. I want you—now." While he had spoken, he made quick work of removing her gown and her petticoats before she spun back around and grabbed his hands. "Then I believe I deserve to see you in a similar state before you are allowed to continue." In the end, did it matter where they consummated their marriage? At the moment, she simply longed for nothing more than to be as close to him as possible.

He wore a wicked grin as he unbuttoned his topcoat. While he pushed it down his arms, she started on his waistcoat. He removed his cravat while she caressed the muscular planes of his chest through his shirtsleeves. He was so strong and solid. Was it wrong that she wished to touch all of him?

Fitzwilliam was blessed by his looks. Even though she had yet to see what was beneath his final layer of clothing, by the muscle evident under the expensive linen of his shirt, he was surely as beautiful unclothed. Her palm covered his heart, which thrummed beneath his flesh with vigour. The rhythm beat against her palm in a strong and steady cadence.

"You are so quiet all of a sudden."

She shrugged and stepped back from him as she untied and loosened the front of her stays. His chest rose and fell in great breaths while his eyes never wavered from hers. Without hesitation, he unbuttoned the fall of his breeches and pulled out the long ends of his shirt tails before removing them completely.

He drew her chemise over her head. "I have dreamt of this, Elizabeth. I can hardly believe you are finally mine."

She traced the tips of her fingers over his bare stomach. At the first touch of her lips to his chest, he gasped, and all movement ceased. He did not protest. Had he liked it that much? Emboldened, she trailed her lips to his collarbone and kissed him again while her palms explored along his waist.

"I am trying my damnedest to go slow, but you are shattering my resolve with every touch," he said as he lifted her chin so he could kiss her once more.

She was frozen in place while he took her back into his embrace. Her mother had always said her body would never attract a man—her breasts were too small, and her hips were not as wide as Jane's. Would he change his mind now that she stood here unclothed?

"Elizabeth, relax. You were so bold a moment ago. Where has my fearless wife gone?"

She forced her gaze to meet his. He was smiling at her with so much love. She inhaled a shuddering breath and hugged him tight.

"You have no need to be shy with me."

"I feared you would be disappointed."

He cupped her cheeks in his palms and forced her to meet his gaze. "I assure you that I could never be disappointed. You take my breath away with your beauty. I am the most fortunate man in the world, because I am the only man who is allowed to see you thus. I love you so much."

She rose onto her tiptoes and kissed him until her mind muddled. Before tonight, she had not considered that she would be naked in front of him. Mrs. Hill had explained marital relations the day before, but she had been quite vague. The description had never prepared Elizabeth for her husband removing all of her clothing, and in the parlour no less.

He turned them so his back was to the chaise, then sat before he struggled to remove his boots. As soon as those and his breeches were tossed to the side, she could only gape at the sight before her. His stunning body was on full display, his erection pointing in her direction.

"Come." He tugged her so she straddled his legs, his rigid length resting against her belly.

"Ignore that for now," he said as his hands stroked her thighs.

What did he mean by that? Before she could ask, he pressed her tightly against him and began to kiss her once more. She tried to pretend that the hard part of him between them did not exist, but how was she to ignore it when it poked at her so?

His hands stroked her until she was dizzy. A powerful ache had bloomed between her legs. The throbbing was so intense that when his fingers began to stroke between her folds, she could have wept. Before now, she would have found the act shocking, but in that moment, she had not one complaint. In fact, she would have certainly protested if he ceased those attentions.

Every touch and caress sent pleasurable waves through her that only became more intense as he continued. His lips left hers and began nibbling along her jaw then her shoulders. All she could do was cling to him and allow him every liberty he wished. He would never hurt her. She was sure of it.

She gave a sharp inhale when he pressed a finger inside of her and began to move it in and out with his caresses. The initial act relieved that unbearable ache, but within moments, that need became more intense.

She was lost. She was being consumed from the inside out by the fire he was stoking inside of her. Her arms tightened around him so as not to lose herself, but her efforts were futile. The intensity had increased and increased until she tipped from a high peak with a loud cry. Her fingernails dug into his shoulders while he doubled his efforts making her soar until she could do no more than slump against him in an attempt to keep from disappearing into the dark night sky.

His arm wrapped around her waist, and he lifted her some.

"Elizabeth," he said, tipping up her chin with his finger. "You have to tell me if it becomes too much."

Too much? She opened her mouth to ask what he meant, but when his length prodded at her entrance, she gasped just before he began to press her down upon it.

The intrusion stung a bit and stretched in a way that was not necessarily painful—though it was not exactly comfortable either. Just before the pressure became too much, he lifted her some and started again. He did so three times before she was fully seated. Her breathing was as though she had been running. Would that always happen?

"Is that it?" Her forehead rested against his shoulder. Her eyes closed.

"No," he said in a tense voice. "I had hoped for you to be accustomed to this first."

She pressed her cheek against his. "Fitzwilliam, show me what is next."

The arm wrapped around her lifted her and brought her back down. He thrust into her a couple more times before she began to use his shoulders as leverage to assist in the movement. She drew back and met his gaze while he pulled the pins from her hair, allowing it to tumble about her shoulders. He tightened his grip upon her, so she was pressed against him while they rocked together.

With a groan, he dropped his head onto the back of the chaise. "You are so perfect. I love you."

She had to work to keep her eyes open as that fire within her that had burned so brightly earlier rekindled. She could not think or breathe. A current travelled through her from every point where they touched. It was all she could do not to give herself over to the pleasure.

She turned her face so it was buried into his neck while she moved faster and faster. She faltered once or twice, but his strong arms ensured their efforts were not in vain. Then, when she could not take much more, bright lights erupted beneath her eyelids before the dark consumed her. Why could she not move? She was frozen and at his mercy while he continued his efforts to make her senseless. A moment later, he let out a great bellow and struggled to move.

When he finally stilled, the only sound in the room was that of their laboured breaths. So, that was marital relations. That was certainly not what she had expected!

Fitzwilliam stared at the ceiling of the parlour with Elizabeth draped over the side of his body, one of his arms holding her close.

After they had consummated their vows, he had covered them while they laid together on the chaise. Little was said before she dozed off with her head on his chest.

His fingers trailed along the soft skin of her back while she slept. He had confessed his love for her, but she had yet to say those precious words in return. She obviously cared for him, but they had only known each other a few short months. Was it too soon to expect more? Or was she more guarded with her heart than he was?

Her childhood could not have been easy. Her mother resented her, and her mother's illness made it impossible for the woman to hold her tongue. She received his assurances of his feelings with a shyness he could not have predicted. Was she uncertain of him? Had her mother's derogatory statements about Elizabeth made her wary of sharing what was in her heart?

He pressed a kiss to her crown. "I hope you learn to trust me."

"I do trust you." She lifted her head and propped it on the back of her hand resting upon his chest. "I would trust you with my life."

His fingers brushed her curls from her forehead. "I thought you were asleep."

She lifted from him some. "So, are you to always speak to me of your feelings while I am sleeping?"

"No," he said shaking his head. "Forgive me. While I do not wish to rush your feelings, I am an impatient man. I was considering your relationship with your mother and that perhaps you do not trust easily."

"I do not put my faith in most people at a first acquaintance, but we have been connected for my entire life. We have experienced each other's most profound emotions and had visions of each other's happenings and futures. Since I had only dreams of you before you came to Hertfordshire, in which I had no knowledge of your identity, I have been forced to face what has occurred between us all these years. Whenever I believe I have come to terms with it all, I have a new vision of you or come to understand an old vision or connexion I had not recognised in the past."

He cradled her cheek in his palm. If he had been in her position, would he feel the same? "I had not considered how overwhelming this has all been for you. I—"

She pressed a finger to his lips. "Do not apologise. You have been all that is patient and kind, and I am fortunate to call you husband. I do care for you, but I require some time to regain my equanimity and to understand what is in my heart."

He kissed her finger then opened his mouth and lightly bit the tip, making her gasp. "You will not require me to keep my hands to myself or sleep in a separate bedchamber, will you?" Now that they had been intimate, she could not expect him to return to the almost chaste kisses and behaviour, could she?

"No," she said before nibbling at his collarbone. "We need to be united to face whatever evil is coming. Our marriage was blessed by the moon and the earth, and I do not know if you have felt it, but we have gained power through our union. We would dishonour the gift if we held back from each other."

"I noticed the surge when we said our vows. Another burst of power ran through me when I placed the ring upon your finger and when I signed the register; however, I was not sure if the effect would last."

"Perhaps we should practice on the morrow. The back garden is hidden by the enchantment. We can cast spells without alerting anyone to what we are about."

His hands stroked down her back until he grasped her buttocks and pressed her against him. "What shall we do in the meantime?"

"Why, I do not know. What do you suggest?" She grinned while her tone was that of feigned innocence. Why did that heat his blood further?

She squealed when he rolled her under him. They had a great deal of time until morning, and he intended to make the most of it.

Chapter 21

1ˢᵗ of December 1811

Fitzwilliam propped a piece of wood atop the wall of the garden and hastened to her side. "Should I place the target on the ground instead? I do not believe your father would be very charitable if the wall is damaged."

She stood on the path of the cottage gardens. She had never been in such dishabille out of doors, but here she was in a gown with no stays or petticoats, just her chemise underneath; her hair was in a long braid over her shoulder, and she wore slippers on her feet.

Fitzwilliam had argued that no one would see them, so he was not dressed properly either. His shirttails were tucked into his breeches; he was barefoot and wore no waistcoat or topcoat. His hair was also a sight! Curls stuck up in places and the back of his hair was flat from sleeping on it. His cheeks also possessed a shadow of a beard since his valet was not with them, and she did not mind the alteration one bit. He was just as handsome when he was not so meticulously attired.

When he reached her side, he leaned in and gave her a loud kiss on the lips. "What do you think?"

"If you are concerned, we can move the wood; however, I would prefer it on the wall to the ground. I would rather not send dirt flying if I can help it."

With a step backwards, he lifted his eyebrows. "Well, let us see if what occurred at our wedding made any difference to your power."

She rubbed her palm with her thumb. Would their marriage have truly led to such consequences? Her hands shook a little as she raised them.

"Bris!"

A bolt of yellow shot out and hit the log in the centre, shattering it into fragments that sprayed through the air. She drew her hands back and gaped down at her palms. Magic had never been difficult, but it had never flowed so seamlessly through her. How had doing nothing more than marrying Fitzwilliam increased her power?

"Elizabeth?"

"I do not understand this." She pointed to the chopped wood they had found in the garden. "You try. I want to see if yours has altered as well."

Without argument, he took another of the larger chunks of wood and set it where the last had been. At his return, she shifted so he could stand where she had cast the spell. He set his feet and lifted his arms.

"Bris!"

Once again, yellow light shot forward and splintered the wood into tiny pieces. He clenched his hands into fists, then released them.

"I confess that I have envied the ease you demonstrate with charms and spells. I have always felt the need to force the power through me. My father taught me that way, so I know he had to do the same. But just now, before I could brace for that push, the magic just happened."

He looked at her. "That is what it feels like for you? You need not push to make the spell happen?"

"I have never required force, but even now, the swiftness in which the power flows through me is easier. I cannot explain it." She rolled her hand. "Teine." A small plume of fire burned brightly over her palm. Conjuring fire from nothing or altering matter took enough energy that it could be almost depleting. Most mages would need some time to recuperate, yet she was holding proof of how substantially her power had increased. She could not credit it.

Fitzwilliam rolled his hand and said the incantation. He gasped when a flame appeared in his hand as well. "I cannot explain how this is possible. I can cast a great many spells, but this one was. . ."

"I successfully cast it once, but I found difficulty in summoning the simplest of spells for a day afterwards. Papa can do so, but he also requires time for his magic to replenish. I believe when he taught me, he spent almost a day before he could use his magic again. The charm drains the user of what is within them at that moment. I should not be able to hold the flame this long either."

They looked back down to their hands, both still holding a golden plume of fire. She gave a flick of her wrist, and the flame extinguished. Fitzwilliam followed suit.

"No one could know what it would mean when we married, but we shall keep this quiet. 'Tis better that the evil coming has no knowledge of our current abilities. If they believe us both to be similar to our fathers, we stand more of a chance of taking them by surprise."

"I agree." Why did she always seem to be protecting some secret? Would she never be free to speak as she wished? Before Fitzwilliam, the only time she shared confidences was with Herne. After all, he could not speak. That made him the best guardian of her most closely guarded secrets.

She glanced up at the cloud covered sky. The sun had hidden itself away, and the weather did not appear favourable for the rest of the day. What if it snowed? She was not ready to face whoever was coming. She wanted more time. If only the snow would not come until winter was almost over. When she was little, snow had fallen on none other than the first day of spring. She could stand for that to happen again.

Fitzwilliam took her into his arms. "All will be well. You will see. How can this all end any other way? We have seen what is to come—we saw it in the altar. Remember? I have also seen other bits of our future."

"You have?" How had he known where her mind had wandered?

"I have, but I shall not tell you more since I want those visions to be reality." He wore a crooked smile before he kissed her forehead. "Fretting will do us naught. Tomorrow, perhaps the sun will be out and the day will be warmer, and we can practice more. With the concealment charm, our activities will not be visible to anyone who happens by."

She nodded. He was correct of course, and even though they were spending a good amount of time together alone after their marriage, they could spare some of it to practice. As far as becoming rattled by what was to come, she had to be prepared to calm herself. Who knew how much power this person had acquired thus far? Her father had not heard of any other significant disappearances, but even acquiring certain talents could significantly add to a magical person's abilities.

"I wish we had no reason to practice or to worry about what is to come. I just want to live in peace."

He drew her into his arms. "I understand. I would prefer if we had no need of this either. If that was the case, I could take you to Pemberley after the solstice, and we could take long rambling walks up to Nine Ladies and through the forest behind the house. I am not fond of London, yet I have a house there for when going to town is necessary."

She pressed her cheek to his chest. "I have only ever gone to London to visit my aunt and uncle. I should like to see them if we have reason to go, but my aunt was raised in Lambton. I am certain she would be pleased to come to Derbyshire."

"They would be welcome at Pemberley."

She gave him a warm gaze. "Thank you. Now, I believe Papa sent a stack of books for us to search. They are in the parlour."

He brushed some curls away from her face that had come loose in the breeze. "I was certain they had not been there before. Since we have had food magicked into the cottage, I suppose he charmed those here too."

A happy laugh bubbled from her throat. "He loves making things disappear and reappear. Those are his favourite spells. If you watch him during events, small items will vanish when no one is looking. He once moved Sir William's cravat pin. Sir William believed it to have fallen out during the assembly only to find it perfectly stuck through one of the draperies."

"Sir William had to have known who was responsible when he found it?"

"Oh, he was well aware. He and Papa have been friends for so long, he laughed and clapped my father on the shoulder. Sir William appreciates a good bit of magic."

"Come. I am certain breakfast has appeared in the kitchen. We can take our food and the books to the breakfast room. Then we shall have more time for other activities later."

Other activities? What could he mean? She lifted her eyebrow.

He nuzzled his nose near her ear sending a frisson through her. "I want nothing more than to spend all day in bed with you."

Her cheeks heated as she turned to walk backwards. "I am shocked, Mr. Darcy! Whatever could we do in bed all day?"

When he lunged for her, she squealed and hastened inside. As he had predicted, a tray with coffee, tea, muffins, and marmalade were in the kitchen. Another tray with bacon and toast was beside it. She took the lighter of the trays and started towards the breakfast room. Fitzwilliam followed with the remaining. While she prepared the tea and set out their meal, he fetched the books from the parlour.

"I sometimes believe this is a futile endeavour," said Fitzwilliam as he set down the stack. "Since we have found naught of it, this sort of magic cannot have been seen before."

"I have to agree with you, but if we overlook any information due to an assumption, then we may bring about our own demise."

Elizabeth sat, and he took the seat beside her. She would likely appear like Mary as she studied her book. Her younger sister always had a book with her at the breakfast table. The only time she did not was for dinner. Papa had set that rule a long time ago. Dinner was the one meal where they would behave like a family and talk.

Her husband handed her the book on the top. "I suppose we should begin."

That evening, Fitzwilliam leaned back against the headboard of the bed, a book on Elizabeth's back while he read. His wife was on her stomach across his lap while she perused her own book, her elbow on the mattress and her jaw resting in her palm while she read.

She was a distraction to be sure. In naught but her short chemise, her creamy shoulders and the smooth expanse of her legs beckoned. She was a siren—at least to him she was—and he was lost. They had already loved each other, but he did not want to read the book in his lap. He wanted her again!

After all, they had found naught to be of aid thus far. How many books had they read in the past few weeks? He could not say the endeavour was completely fruitless. He had learnt a few facts he had been unaware of before, but most of the words passed right through his mind and were not retained. Elizabeth surely had the same experience. Why should they not abandon this pursuit? After all, this mouse hunt was getting them nowhere.

Elizabeth gave a sharp inhale and lifted her upper body. He was forced to grab his book to keep it from falling off. "I have found something."

"You have?" Finally! But was whatever she had discovered worth the days and hours spent toiling over page after page of all these books?

"'Tis not much. It is actually more of a warning. 'Beware to the magician who seeks more magic than the earth is willing to provide. A high price is to be paid by those who covet the power of others.'"

He scratched the stubble on his cheek. "Yet the person in the vision seemed strong. What price could they face? They have already taken the power of the duke and whatever person they robbed previously—the one His Grace mentioned in his letter."

"Yes, but neither of us could see this man. We only have a perception from what we assume was the spell cast in my direction. I admit that this warning is vague, but if we can determine what this price is, then we may stand a better chance of defeating him."

"There is always the letter your father sent to my uncle. If anyone would know, it would be him." He took the book from her and set it on the side table. "We have a couple of weeks, at least, until we must face this person. I would much prefer to concentrate on you rather than these books."

She laughed and picked up the volume he had been failing to read. "And how much have you read on your own? I would wager by the way your fingers were tickling the backs of my thighs, little indeed."

He feigned a gasp and tugged her to him. "I cannot help it if you have consumed my mind. I also cannot read what is on the page because I cannot stop staring at you."

Her palm pressed against his chest. "I am a mess. You behave as though I am dressed for a ball."

He tipped her chin up so their gazes met. "You need not be attired for an event to capture me. I find you much more alluring as you are. Your chemise does little to hide what is beneath, and as we were, your legs and rear begged to be stroked."

"My rear? You must be joking."

While he ran his fingers up the softness of her thigh, his breathing deepened at the knowledge of what he would soon touch. "I would never joke about such matters." He drew the garment over her head, and his hand covered her breast, his thumb teasing the peak. "As much as I am tempted by you clothed, you bewitch me in this state. You are so beautiful." Most of Meryton thought Miss Bennet the beauty of the Bennet girls, but he only saw Elizabeth. She had been all he had seen since that first night in Oakham Forest. Her vivid eyes drew him into her soul. He would never have admitted it then, but he had been lost in an instant. As it was, he would never be recovered.

Elizabeth cradled his cheek in her palm. "You are blind, sir."

He shook his head. "No, I see all of you, Elizabeth. I am certain I have noticed more than anyone, which is why I know your worth and your beauty. I wish you could see yourself through my eyes. If you could, you would never doubt yourself again."

Chapter 22

*12*th *of December 1811*

Elizabeth strode with purpose to the wall at the edge of the garden, then pivoted and walked to the wall on the opposite side, turned and repeated the action. The morning air was heavy with dew, and a thick fog hung heavy outside the wall, preventing her from clearly seeing the branches of the orchard behind the cottage.

They had been secluded in the cottage for a fortnight, and her legs itched to walk. A long, brisk ramble through Oakham Forest and a visit to Herne and the stones would do much to relieve the restlessness within. How had her father thought she could ever be cooped up for three weeks and survive with her equanimity intact?

She and Fitzwilliam had spent all of their time together whether in bed or finding ways to pass the time they had before the solstice. Her father had ensured the cottage was filled with diversions. They had played chess and backgammon several times by now, they had read the books Papa had sent, and of course, they had loved each other.

The last made her cheeks burn. That diversion was, without a doubt, Fitzwilliam's favourite. He did not shy away from expressing his desire or love for her and had done so often since they were wed. By this time, he had surely touched every part of her. She stopped and covered her face with her hands. If only she could stop blushing!

However, she could not claim she despised relations between them. On the contrary, he had been determined she would find each encounter pleasurable. He was also determined to make her be as unladylike as possible. The more he discomposed her, the happier he seemed to be. His smug countenance greeted her on several occasions when she opened her eyes after her peak.

She scrubbed her face and continued to pace. When she made to turn once again, strong arms wrapped around her from behind and prevented any further movement.

"What is amiss?"

"I am restless. I have never been so long without walking in the forest. What if Herne's protection spells have faltered?"

He turned her in his embrace. "You know those charms last until someone removes them. Who would do so? Your father would not, and how many in the area know of the existence of a white stag? I have been the sole person who could see him, and I have questioned more than once if he is magical and allowed me to do so. I have no other explanation for why he is visible to me despite your protections."

"I had not considered. . ."

He shrugged. "I considered that perhaps the long-standing bond between us was why, but then why would Miss Bennet not be able to see him? No, something greater is at work here. Do you not think?"

"I suppose after I first realised you could see him, I questioned the novelty of it, but I thought nothing more of it as time passed. We had other, more pressing, considerations." They had their first vision of the thief who would attempt to steal their magic not long after they met. Their attention had been diverted to other matters.

He brushed some curls away from her face. She had done no more than comb and plait her hair this morning. Those shorter curls in the front were not long enough to join the plait, and she had not been inclined to pin them back.

"I had not considered that you would feel restricted. We have managed to pass our time without much tedium. We have practised duelling since we discovered the increase in our powers. We have not been idle. Are you truly so unhappy?"

She grasped his dear face in her hands. "No! I am *not* unhappy. I believe we needed this time to know each other better. I also confess that you have been all that is considerate. The fortnight we have been together has been dear to me, but I cannot help the urge to stretch my legs. Do you not miss riding Hen at a break-neck gallop through the fields?" She was not exaggerating. She had seen him more than once giving the stallion his head. The sight had made her turn away. She could not watch if he took a fall.

He sighed. "I do, but I would not sacrifice this time with you for anything."

She lifted up onto her tiptoes and kissed his lips. One thing she had never anticipated was how much she would love kissing Fitzwilliam. His lips were soft and brushed against hers in such a way that her entire body melted. When he nibbled and caressed other places with them, she found it pleasurable, but when he kissed her lips was by far the most enjoyable. He could render her senseless with those two soft bits of flesh.

After sufficiently discomposing her with that activity, he drew back. "Should we practise this morning?"

"I do believe it helps with the restlessness. I cannot imagine how I would feel without it—and you—to distract me from the inability to ramble as far and wide as I desire."

After one last kiss to her forehead, he backed to the opposite side of the garden. "Shall I begin?"

She nodded and shifted one foot back to brace herself for a blow. They never used dangerous magic, but that did not mean that if one of their spells hit, nothing happened. Of late, they had practised casting charms in a hurry without speaking them aloud. The concentration required to do so had never been easy, but of late, they had both become more adept at the practice. Silent casting was a better method to gaining the upper hand.

Fitzwilliam stood silent for a moment and his head tilted a bit. He was deciding what magic to throw at her. After all, she had witnessed this behaviour more than once now.

His hands shoved forward with a great deal of might, and a shot of violet light hurdled towards her. She threw up her arms. *Ceilt!* His spell was absorbed by the shield charm just before she threw her hands forward. *Dúr!*

Before he could protect himself, the binding spell hit him square in the chest, and he fell stiff to the ground. She gaped for a second before hastening forward.

"Bogadh," she said pointing at him on the ground.

He groaned and sat up. "You threw that quickly. It hit me before I could stop it."

"Are you well?" She squatted beside him and plucked a dead leaf from his hair.

"It hurt, but I shall suffer no lasting damage. Shall we go again?"

They had both improved greatly since they had started their meetings a few months ago. Without those mornings spent in Oakham Forest as well as here, they would not be so proficient. They had not needed to be so quick before the knowledge of a threat, yet she should have been more diligent in her practice. She was familiar with the spells, but the ones she had not used often did not flow from her with as much ease as those she used every day—like the shield charm.

As soon as they resumed their original places, Fitzwilliam nodded. They swapped back and forth who would attack first, so now was her turn. She shook out her hands and rocked back on her heels. When she pressed her hands forward, she moved her weight to her front foot. *Mearbhall!*

A white light erupted from her palms and shot towards Fitzwilliam. He threw up his arms and the spell was absorbed by the shield charm he cast. He threw a charm at her, and she spun away from the blast of yellow light, hurling another binding spell in his direction. This time, he ducked, and it hit the brick wall behind him, an odd creak coming from the stone as the charm took effect. The magic would fortify the wall and make it nearly impenetrable.

A hard blow hit her directly in the chest. Her body became weighted as though she had heavy objects tied to her limbs, and she fell backwards just before darkness consumed her.

Elizabeth dodged the spell with ease, so he slashed his arm in front of him. *Stiúdú!* A blast of indigo light shot forward and hit Elizabeth in the middle of the chest.

"No!" Before he could reach her, she blinked with a wince and crumpled to the ground. She was so quick. She was supposed to whirl in the other direction and dodge the stunning spell with ease. Why had she not moved?

When he reached her side, he dropped to the stone pathway and pulled her into his arms, cradling her against him.

"Múscail," he whispered.

Her eyelids fluttered then she heaved in a large breath. She groaned and lifted her hand to her head.

"I am so very sorry. You were dodging my spells so well. I had not expected you to be hit."

"What was that?"

"I stunned you." The effects of some spells were obvious. This one could have been a couple of charms, but why was she asking?

"I shall have to remember that one."

"Blast." He scooped her up into his arms and carried her inside to the parlour, but instead of lying her down on the sofa, he sat her in a chair near the fire, knelt before her, and brushed her hair back from her face. "Forgive me."

She grasped his fidgeting hands and held them firm in her lap. "Fitzwilliam, we are practicing duelling. I am not irreparably harmed. I am developing a devil of a headache, but I shall be fine. I also learnt an important lesson."

"What is that?"

She leaned her head against the back of the chair. "To never become distracted. When your binding spell hit the brick wall, the creaking of the magic knitting the masonry together caught my attention, and I was not attending you. The fault was mine, not yours, and I take responsibility for what happened as a result."

He shook his head. "I should not have cast two spells in succession."

She grasped his face in her hands. "And why not? Any foe who is as evil as to steal the powers of others will use underhanded means to defeat me or you. A real duel would not be fairly passing spells back and forth as though we were trading ribbons. You did exactly what you were supposed to do, and I made a mistake. As I said before, I learnt a valuable lesson. I shall need to ignore what is happening around me in favour of my opponent. This man I am to face will not stop at a stunning spell. Such a mistake during a duel could cost me my life."

Her explanation made perfect sense, but he still was not satisfied. He had hurt the lady he loved. Even if the harm was inadvertent and necessary, his insides roiled. Now, he must aid her in recovering from the spell. Stunning would cause headaches and body aches. A potion would be beneficial, but he had not seen one hint of potion-making supplies in the cottage. How was that possible? Their cottage was part of a magical holding after all.

"I need to make a potion."

"Papa does not keep any supplies here. Since someone using this place is rare, he does not want to have to maintain two stores. If certain herbs go bad, it can be costly."

Some ingredients were quite expensive, so Bennet's reasoning did make sense. "I saw a pen and paper in the escritoire. I shall return in a moment."

He strode to the small desk and tore a smaller piece of paper from one of the sheets. The ink was not dried up, so he dipped the pen into the bottle.

> *"I require a rejuvenation potion for Elizabeth.*
> *While practising, she was hit with a stunning*
> *spell."—F.D.*

As soon as the pen was returned to the holder, he waved the paper to help dry the ink, then set it flat on the desk. He hovered his hand over it, closed his eyes, and pictured Mr. Bennet's desk.

"Seol."

When he opened his eyes, the paper was gone. He and his father would send notes to each other within Pemberley, but even in magical families, one used the post for most of their correspondence. If you accidentally misdirected your letter, anyone could get their hands on it.

He returned to the chair and lifted Elizabeth so he could once again have her in his lap. "How is your head?"

"Not any better."

She rested her forehead upon his shoulder, and his thumb traced circles on her temple. "Breakfast will help. It should be sent to the kitchen soon."

"Mmm," was all she said. Soon after, her breathing evened. Sleep would help as well as allow her to escape the headache for a time.

He rubbed her head as he almost seemed to float in and out of sleep. At some point, he startled and looked about them. What was different?

With care, he lifted Elizabeth and laid her on the sofa, then crept around the room. Naught had changed in here, so what had caused him to wake so abruptly?

He made his way to the kitchen, and on the board were the usual trays of breakfast. Beside the coffee pot was a familiar vial with a glowing liquid inside—the potion he had requested. He brought the first tray into the parlour and set it on the low table near the sofa.

"Elizabeth, your father sent the potion. Wake up."

She frowned. "My head."

"I know." He sat her up. "But if you take this, it will be of aid."

Her hand pressed to her forehead while he uncorked the vial and brought it to her lips. She swallowed without hesitation, and he held his breath while he waited.

A minute later, she straightened. "You were correct. That was of great aid. Now that the blinding headache is gone, I am hungry. What did Mrs. Hill send us?"

"She sent sausage, eggs, and toast today, as well as a couple of muffins and a pot of jam with the coffee. What would you like? I shall serve you."

"Fitzwilliam, that is not necessary."

Despite her assurances that stunning her had not been his fault, he could not dispel the heaviness in his chest. He had hurt her. He could never tolerate causing her harm if he could help it.

"I wish to do it." He handed her a cup of coffee. "Sip on this while I retrieve the other tray. I shall return in a moment."

When he returned, he fixed a plate but did not hand it to her. Instead, he forked some eggs and held the food in front of her.

"Really, I am well. You need not feed me."

He shrugged one shoulder. "It is of no concern. Allow me to care for you. I need to do so after what happened."

She sighed. "Very well. But do remember this should I ever hover over you when you are ill."

He allowed a hint of a smile. "I believe having you tend to me would not be objectionable in the least." How could he take issue with Elizabeth mopping his brow? If she was in her nightgown or clad in her dressing gown, he would never reject her ministrations.

"Just remember this when I make you a tonic or a tisane. Some of the most effective taste rather foul."

He stroked her leg. "But with you administering them to me . . ."

"Rein in your enthusiasm for me, husband. I should prefer to eat before whatever is running through that mind of yours."

He laughed and held up another forkful of food. "As you wish, my dear."

Chapter 23

22ⁿᵈ of December 1811

Elizabeth stood in front of the long mirror in the dressing room of the cottage. Her palm smoothed down the gown Fitzwilliam had arranged for Madame Girard to make for her. The famous dressmaker had come to Longbourn before the full moon and taken her measurements then returned to London until the gown was completed. It had been delivered to Longbourn at some time while they were secluded in the cottage, and this morning, her father had magicked the dress to the table in the parlour where he had sent the books during their stay.

They had found nothing else to help them with their quest for information about the magic thief, which was disappointing, but they had duelled every morning unless rain had interfered. She had not been struck by a spell since the last instance, whether from her own skill in avoiding them or from Fitzwilliam's reticence to hurt her again, she was not certain. He had thrown multiple spells at her in a row since, but she had deflected each. She preferred to believe she had not been distracted again. Hopefully, that was the case.

She bit her lip while she took in the new gown. She had never worn short sleeves before—even when she was a small child. Mrs. Annesley had arranged for all her clothing to hide her birthmark when she was a babe, and now, she simply adjusted Jane's old gowns for herself. Jane was taller, so a few inches of fabric was always removed from the hem. If one was creative, the material could be added to the sleeves in an artistic design and would hide the mark with ease.

Her entire being was unsettled. Everyone would be able to see the four point star. How would they respond?

"Your neighbours all love you, Elizabeth. They will not be unkind." Fitzwilliam stood behind her. When had he come to be there? How could he know her feelings better than she did herself?

"You chose white and silver?"

"Madame Girard suggested the colours, and her reasoning made sense. While you said nothing of the mark or what it meant, she recognised the star for what it was. You must understand that her ability is to sense the nature of an individual. She confided before she departed that she had detected your power and the good in you. She requested to make you a gown that fit who you are.

"Neither your father nor I revealed the date we would marry, but I had requested short sleeve lengths so you could display your mark without difficulty."

The gown itself was white, which in magical circles meant truth and harmony. Madame Girard, however, had added silver spangles to the bodice as well as silver embroidery around the hem. A silver ribbon wrapped around her waist. A silver cord also wound through her curls, which were piled atop her head in a design comprised of narrow plaits and curls. Silver stood for lunar energy or influence. How could Madame Girard have understood that they would have the blessing of the moon before they had even known it themselves?

"You look beautiful, Elizabeth. You are every bit what the heir should be. Do not let what anyone may say make you doubt your gifts."

"I am nervous. I have never told anyone other than Jane and Mrs. Hill, who have always known. How am I supposed to stand before everyone and proclaim what I am?"

"You do know your father will announce you, do you not?" His hands rested upon her shoulders. The warmth did very little to settle her.

A knock came from downstairs. Papa had arrived. She took in a breath and let it out on a shuddering exhale. "I suppose that means we are to go." How odd. As much as she had wished to escape and ramble in the forest for the past fortnight, now that she could do so, she would prefer to remain. These past few weeks had been idyllic—except for her whinging about being confined. Poor Fitzwilliam! He deserved better.

She made to turn, but his solid arm wrapped around her waist and pulled her to him. "Cease whatever absurd thoughts are running through your head."

She started. "What do you mean?"

He touched his forehead to hers. "I love you. You are the perfect wife for me, and I could not want for better."

Her eyes squeezed closed. She could not look at him. "I am a coward."

A warm hand cupped her cheek as he drew her face back. "Elizabeth, look at me."

When she opened her eyes, he gazed down at her with an expression that made her insides flutter mercilessly.

"You are not a coward."

"I cannot speak of my feelings. Why can I not? Should I not be able to by now? Whenever I even consider it. . ."

He smiled and laced their fingers together. "Do you believe that I was not scared when I told you I love you? I was petrified. Even so, I do not begrudge you for wanting to be certain of your own feelings before you say those words to me. I knew of you and of what our connexion meant before you did. It is only natural that I would recognise my attachment before you."

"I have been a bother during the past fortnight."

A laugh burst from him. "What? Because you are not accustomed to being confined? You know very well that I would have loved to take Hen out for a good gallop, but being alone as we have been will not be a common occurrence. I wished to savour our time together."

"And I complained about it."

"And I understood. I shall say it again, then no more. You are the perfect wife for me. Now, we must join your father before he seeks us out."

She nodded and released him. As she picked up her cloak, Fitzwilliam held out her gloves.

"You will need these."

"Thank you."

As they descended the stairs, her father stood at the bottom. "When you did not answer right away, I let myself in. I do hope the last few weeks have been enjoyable. I cannot tell you how often I have wished to seclude myself away here with my library and shut out the world."

She could only shake her head. How like her father to desire such a situation!

"Are you ready, my dear?" asked Papa.

"No, but I do not have much choice. 'Tis odd. I have desired nothing more than to be free to cast spells and charms at will. Now that I shall have that opportunity, I believe I should prefer the concealment."

Papa chuckled. "I believe that is understandable. We have spoken of this day and what it would mean for years. Your reticence when the prospect is before you is to be expected. This day is likely of anticipation as well as dread."

"We have never been hidden as you have," said Fitzwilliam. "Even though the measure was necessary, you are not accustomed to everyone seeing you for who you truly are."

Perhaps that was why she was uncomfortable about tonight. It was akin to the idea of removing her clothing at a party. She pressed her hand to the churning of her gut.

Fitzwilliam wrapped an arm around her and pulled her into his side, kissing her temple. "You will be well."

"I know, but your reassurance does not make this any less disconcerting."

"Come." Papa waved them forward. "We must go."

When they closed the door behind them, the colonel and a young lady stood before them.

"Georgiana!" Fitzwilliam rushed forward as the girl lunged towards him and hugged him. "I am pleased you could be here, even if I did tell Richard that you should remain at Pemberley." He drew back. "I should like you to meet your new sister, Elizabeth. Dearest, this is my sister, Georgiana."

The young lady curtseyed. "I am pleased to meet you."

Elizabeth took Miss Darcy's hand in hers and squeezed. "I have heard much of you in the past few months. I am happy to finally put a face to the stories I have been told."

The younger lady groaned. "Fitzwilliam, what did you tell her?"

"Nothing bad. Now, we must go or we shall be late."

Elizabeth held up both hands. "I shall not object."

"Come." Her husband grasped her hand and tugged her after her father. "We shall get this done, then you will see that all will be well."

"Are you excited, Mrs. Darcy?" asked the colonel. "I hope you do not mind, but Darcy told me of what is to be revealed, and I told Georgie. She was insistent to come for that reason."

Miss Darcy's smile could be seen, even in the dark. "A female heir is a wonderful happening. I could not miss such an auspicious event. I hope you do not mind, but I made this for you." Miss Darcy lifted something from her side, and Elizabeth barely held in her gasp. The crown of rosemary and sage from their vision was in her new sister's hand.

"If you do not like it—"

"No! I appreciate the thought and the meaning behind your gift. I will be proud to wear your crown."

Fitzwilliam took the crown from his sister and stared at it for a moment before lifting it to Elizabeth's head. "This is a truly thoughtful gesture, Georgiana." His gaze met hers while he situated it just so. The significance of this moment was not lost upon him—it could not be.

Her father lifted his eyebrows before waving them to follow. "If only the solstice was not so late this year," said Papa in a grumble.

With a tilt of her head, Elizabeth shrugged. "Ten at night is not so bad. What if it was at two in the morning or even four?"

As they reached the field, the remainder of her family awaited them. Mrs. Hill stood on one side of Mama while Jane stood on the other with Mr. Bingley at her side. They appeared prepared for any eventuality should her mother act out.

The walk to the forest was not long after that, and when they reached the edge, Herne's subtle glow near the entrance could not be missed.

"He has come to greet you," said Fitzwilliam near her ear.

"And I am glad to see him. I know it is nonsensical, but I did fear for his safety without being here to ensure he was well."

The others in their party behaved as though the stag was not nearby even though he followed alongside them until they reached the stone circle, which reinforced the belief that the creature could control who saw him. When they reached the stone circle, Herne did not continue into the clearing where many of their neighbours already awaited them.

Papa opened his watch and tilted it towards the torch carried by the colonel. "We have five minutes."

Her nerves had emerged without mercy since they had entered the clearing. She swallowed hard to quell the lump that had risen and now plagued her. She could do this!

"Bennet!" Sir William Lucas approached. "The night is clear and the moon, although not full, is bright in the sky. I declare this to be the perfect evening for a solstice celebration. I am certain my Charlotte will be sorry to have missed it."

"I am sorry, Sir William, but why would she miss it?"

Sir William placed his hands on the sides of his round belly. "Why, because she married your cousin a week ago. Did your father not mention their wedding upon your return from London?"

"I believe we had some pressing concerns to discuss," said Fitzwilliam, "and the joyful news was delayed as a result."

"Lizzy?"

Elizabeth straightened and stifled a gasp. When she turned, her aunt Gardiner stood a few feet away. Her aunt and uncle coming for the solstice was not unusual, nor out of place since the neighbourhood believed them to have returned her to Longbourn today.

Her husband placed a hand to her back and nodded. Despite not saying the words aloud, he was giving her permission to join her aunt and talk without Sir William hearing all. She looped her arm through Aunt Marianne's, and they stepped to the edge of the trees.

Elizabeth squeezed her aunt's hands. "I am so happy you are here."

"You seem nervous. What has you at sixes and sevens?"

She shook her head. "You will discover soon enough. Forgive me for not being able to tell you sooner."

Aunt Marianne gave her a side-long glance, then grasped Elizabeth's wrist and turned her arm. When her aunt made to look at the inside of her arm, Elizabeth unthinkingly made to flip it back.

"Do you think I have never noticed what is right before me?"

She surely gaped at her aunt. Had she known all along?

"What do you mean?"

"Your father was so ridiculous about only Mrs. Annesley caring for you when you were little, and when you were old enough to dress yourself, he was adamant you could do so. Your uncle and I realised he was hiding something about you. Then, during our visit to Longbourn last year, there was that storm. Do you remember?"

She nodded and squeezed her eyes closed then reopened them. "I remember."

"We were in the gardens looking for little Joseph, and the wind and rain were horrible. Lightning hit that oak at the edge of the field where Joseph was hiding. What occurred after happened with such swiftness, that I could not understand in the moment. Joseph had run out from the limbs before the lightning hit, then he flew forward and out of the way of the huge tree as it fell. You saved him. That night, when I had more time to reflect upon all that had occurred, you had waved your arm in a manner I had only seen your father and my brother do."

The entire time she told the story, her aunt had kept her voice low. She had not attracted the attention of anyone around them—although they were bound to know soon.

"If Papa would have allowed it, I would have told you."

Aunt Marianne placed her hands on Elizabeth's shoulders. "I know you would have, but I understand why you did not. Now that you are married—and to Mr. Darcy no less!—it is much safer for the world to know of your existence."

Before she could respond, her uncle joined them. "This appears to be a very serious conversation."

"I assume all is to be announced this evening," said her aunt. "Otherwise, your father would not have insisted we remain." She once again turned Elizabeth's arm and flicked her eyes towards the four-point star.

Her uncle allowed a slight curve of the lips. "You were right." He stepped forward and hugged her. "Thank you for saving Joseph last year. I should have known to trust Marianne, but I could not believe her suspicion until I saw the proof with my own eyes."

Fitzwilliam stepped beside her. "Your father is ready to begin."

She nodded, the swirling in her stomach returning to the fore. She had a reprieve of sorts while speaking to her aunt and uncle, and now she would have to face what was destined to occur. Eventually, she had to reveal her identity, and now was as good a time as any. But would the neighbours still accept her once they knew the truth?

Chapter 24

22ⁿᵈ December 1811 cont...

Her husband led her to the altar to stand beside Papa while he took his place at her side.

"Good evening to all!" her father said loudly so everyone in attendance could hear. "Before we begin our celebration of fire and light, I should like to share several pieces of news with you all.

"Firstly, at our Samhain celebration, I mentioned the marriage of my daughter to Mr. Fitzwilliam Darcy of Pemberley. I am happy to announce they were wed here in the stone circle on the last full moon. Forgive me for excluding you from the ceremony, but we had good reason to hold their nuptials in private, which brings me to my next announcement.

"It has been assumed for many years that the Bennet family lacks an heir to our magical line. I am here to tell you that this is not true. Much to our own shock and surprise, upon her birth, our daughter Elizabeth bore the mark of the heir."

Papa gestured to her, so she removed her arm from the cloak and held it so those around them could see the birthmark. Many in the crowd leaned closer to the person beside them while a murmur rose from the group. To the front stood her mother and Jane, the latter with two hands holding Mama's forearm while Mama's lips quivered. Poor Jane was exerting all she had to keep Mama calm, but her mother's agitation was obviously too strong. How long before Jane would become fatigued?

Elizabeth flicked a finger at Mama. "Tost," she said in the softest of tones.

Her mother's mouth opened, but whatever she was trying to say made no sound whatsoever. Mama's eyes widened then narrowed in Elizabeth's direction. She snapped her mouth shut and crossed her arms over her chest. Jane lost her grip on one of Mama's arms but placed her hand on her mother's shoulder to continue to exert her calming influence upon her.

Papa raised his hands for quiet. "For Elizabeth's safety, we have kept her identity hidden, but she has trained as diligently as any boy, and I believe her abilities will soon surpass my own. She has great talent—"

An almost collective gasp rippled through those around them. "No lady could be more powerful than a man!"

Whoever spoke was not visible. He hid behind the crowd, yet everyone parted so Mr. Wickham was easily discernible.

"Yet she out-smarted you," said Fitzwilliam. "She is the one who concocted the potion that repulsed those you attempted to charm with your seductive tongue. Mr. Bennet and I did no more than spread word of your past deeds, but Elizbeth discovered the potion and brewed it. She tested the tonic on herself, and when it was found to work, we mixed it into the punch at the Philips's as well as at the Netherfield Ball. Her actions helped anyone who neglected to take such a threat seriously."

Wickham had stepped closer while her husband defended her. By the man's sneer, he did not believe a word of it. Meanwhile, the colonel stood beside an exceedingly pale Miss Darcy. During their time in the cottage, Fitzwilliam had spoken of what had occurred with Georgiana in Ramsgate and of Wickham's attempt to persuade the poor girl into an elopement. She had already been through enough. They could only hope Wickham did not see her standing nearby.

Meanwhile, many around him were whispering behind their hands and shaking their heads. This was not enough to convince those who held doubt of her magic.

She stepped up to the altar. "Now that my father has made the announcements, we are here to celebrate the solstice. Our bonfire is laid, and the children have brought their lanterns. Making the lanterns was always my favourite part of this day. So, now let us celebrate." She held her hand over the altar, palm down. "As we have been plunged into this day of darkness, we anticipate the coming of the light!" She rotated her hand, which now held a plume of fire nestled in the centre of her palm.

Those around them gave a collective inhale.

Elizabeth rolled her hand forward and pushed sending the plume into the stacked logs. Within seconds, the bonfire was engulfed in flames. Then with a flick of her finger, the lanterns held by the children in the crowd all lit at once.

"Now, let us continue with the games!" She threw up her arm and sent sparks flying into the night sky. Her father had never gone to such lengths due to the draining nature of the fire spells, but with her newfound increase in power, she was not fatigued in the slightest. Fitzwilliam's hand on her back also served to replenish some of the magic she had expended.

Fitzwilliam leaned close. "I shall return in a moment."

As he disappeared into the crowd, the children all hung their lanterns from the lower branches of the trees, then disappeared into the forest. She had always loved playing hide and seek on the solstice. Jane was too good and ended up being the child who sought out the rest every year, while Lydia adamantly refused to ever be the seeker. She threw a tantrum the few times Papa had insisted she take her turn.

When her father turned to face her, Elizabeth held out her hands. "Forgive me, Papa. I know you always introduce the celebration, but lighting the bonfire seemed the swiftest way to convince everyone I was indeed heir."

"You have no reason to apologise, my dear. While I had not yet shared my intentions for tonight with you, I have meant for you to do just what you did. Everyone here needed to see your powers with their own eyes to believe them."

"Wickham!"

Elizabeth followed the direction of the yell just as Wickham came charging in her direction. Without thought, she held up her hand towards Wickham. "Dúr!"

Before the man could take another step, his legs snapped together, and his arms were suddenly pinned to his side. Within a moment, he was face first on the ground since he was unable to break the fall. The colonel strode up behind him and laughed. "Mrs. Darcy, I cannot tell you enough how happy I am to have witnessed that."

Two officers from the militia encampment stepped up behind the colonel. "We shall return him to camp, sir."

"Colonel Fitzwilliam," said Papa. "Why are there unknown officers at the circle?" If they were not magical, they could cause trouble for the village.

"Mr. Bennet, if you will pardon me for answering," said one of the men. "Colonel Forster is from a magical family and sent us to find Wickham since we are from magical families as well. He is not unaware of the history of Meryton or you, for that matter. If we had not been required to fetch Wickham tonight, we would have worn labourer's clothes and come to celebrate with you."

Papa's shoulders relaxed. "I am relieved. Thank you and pray, thank Colonel Forster as well. His discretion in this matter is greatly appreciated." It was indeed!

Both men bowed before they grabbed Wickham by the arms. One of the men looked at her with a grin. "By the way, miss, I cannot wait to tell my mam of you. She has said for years there needs to be a lady heir—that they would be better than a man. After all, you bound Wickham so effortlessly, and he fell as though he had a boulder tied to his body." The young man chuckled.

She moved a few steps closer. "Will you need someone to release the spell before you reach camp?"

"No, miss. I am an heir. I have never been able to manage fire and sparks as you just did, but I can unbind him." An heir—in the militia?

Before she could enquire further, the young officer and his friend hauled Wickham's stiff body off.

"Who is he?" she asked the colonel.

"From what Forster has said, he is an orphan. Likely born out of wedlock. Whoever the father is, he likely has no idea he already sired his heir."

Fitzwilliam placed a hand on her back. "I should think few would doubt you now. Not only did you handle fire, but you bound Wickham for all to see."

"I had not intended to do either."

"You were nervous on our walk here, but when you saw the need to prove yourself, I would wager you forgot why you had been frightened in the first place."

"Mrs. Darcy!" Sir William joined them and clapped his hands together in front of him. "How exciting that you are the heir to the Bennet magic! I do wonder what will happen when you and Mr. Darcy, who is heir to his own legacy, have children. With two such powerful families, this child will be blessed indeed."

Children? She and Fitzwilliam were barely married! "I believe we have some time before that happens, Sir William."

"Maybe not that long," said Fitzwilliam in her ear.

She elbowed him in the ribs. Yes, the altar had shown her great with child, but they had no way of knowing when that was. Neither of them appeared much older in the vision, but what they saw could still be five years into the future.

"Has Charlotte written since arriving in Hunsford?"

Sir William nodded in an effusive manner. "Oh, yes, the first evening she spent in the rectory. She says the house is well-kept and she looks forward to making it her own. I know she has many plans for sewing draperies and making tablecloths."

"I am pleased Charlotte is happy."

"She did ask me to wish you joy today. When her husband informed her they were to depart and return to Hunsford, she asked if they could remain for your wedding, but he refused. His patroness was eager for his return."

"I can only imagine," said Fitzwilliam.

She elbowed him in the ribs once again.

He cleared his throat. "My aunt will appreciate having such a practical sort nearby. I am certain Mrs. Collins will be an excellent help to the neighbourhood."

Considering Mr. Collins had been magically coerced into proposing to Elizabeth, Lady Catherine's acceptance was doubtful, but whether the lady would make her displeasure known to Charlotte was another matter. Her husband believed Lady Catherine would conceal any ire she felt at Mr. Collins marrying another.

"I am only disappointed I cannot share the news of you being the heir until she visits next or when I take Maria to Hunsford for Easter. Charlotte hoped to have her stay with them for a month."

"I am certain Maria is very excited."

"Oh, she is. She is!" At a call from behind him, Sir William glanced over his shoulder. "Forgive me, but my wife is calling."

As soon as he bustled away, Fitzwilliam took her hand and entwined their fingers. "Is it horrible that I want to return to the cottage and have you all to myself?"

"You had me all to yourself for three weeks. Am I not allowed to be seen by others?"

"Mrs. Darcy!" Mr. Bingley strode forward with a wide grin. "I am astounded by what I have learnt this evening. Not only did you go and marry my friend in secret, but you are also the heir. You will have those men who were not the heirs of their family jealous—not that I would be one of them. I had no wish to be heir, but here I am with all of the responsibility, yet no magic; however, I believe you have the best situation."

Her chin hitched back a little. "How is my situation better than most?"

"Because you have all the power without the responsibility of the estate and what goes with it." He turned somewhat pink. "Not that you would not want to inherit Longbourn if you could. . .blast it. Forgive me. I did not think before I spoke."

She rested a hand on Mr. Bingley's forearm. "Do not worry yourself over it. I believe I understand what you mean. You were thrust into your role without learning what you would need to know. I am certain it was difficult."

"You are too charitable, Mrs. Darcy."

Fitzwilliam squeezed her hand. "Speaking of Mr. Collins, I do not wish to harm the prospects of Mrs. Collins, but I do wonder if I could persuade Mr. Collins to bar the entail. Perhaps enough money would make him sign away his claim."

"Papa would not object."

"Brother," said Miss Darcy who bounded up to him and hugged him. "It was all so exciting. Is that why our parents arranged your marriage to Mrs. Darcy?"

"Pray, call me Elizabeth or Lizzy as my sisters do. And yes, our parents signed and sealed a magical contract just after my birth."

Miss Darcy bounced on her toes. "Then you must call me Georgiana."

Fitzwilliam placed a hand on his sister's shoulder. "Were you not disturbed by Wickham's appearance?"

"Oh, of course I was, but Richard was beside me, so I knew he would protect me should Mr. Wickham attempt to harm me. Thankfully, he did not seem to notice I was nearby."

Fitzwilliam nodded. "I had not expected Richard to bring you for the solstice due to the presence of Wickham, so I am relieved nothing came of the man's challenge of Elizabeth. Of course, she managed the situation brilliantly."

The colonel held up a hand. "After my conversation with Forster when I was last in Hertfordshire, I was assured Wickham would be managed and watched. Yet, I could not have anticipated tonight's escape from the encampment."

"I am not angry," said Fitzwilliam. "Yet we know danger is coming, so I am unsure of Georgiana's remaining at Netherfield."

Georgiana inhaled sharply. "But I want to stay and get to know Lizzy. Pray, say yes. I shall hide if the situation warrants it. I promise."

After placing her palm upon Fitzwilliam's chest, Elizabeth caught his gaze. "Should evil arrive, we have you, me, and my father to fend off   an attack. We also know they are more likely to seek us out than someone with a talent."

"She could be used to lure us away from each other."

He made a valid point. "So, we agree here and now that none of us will venture off on our own to confront this person."

Fitzwilliam's lips pressed together tightly. He did not like being questioned, but it was unlikely Georgiana would be put in danger.

"Very well," he said. "She can stay."

Chapter 25

31ˢᵗ of December 1811

The Bennets were gathered in the drawing room while they awaited midnight and the new year. Mrs. Bennet had planned a grand feast for their dinner before they had gathered to play games and cards to pass the time until midnight.

Even though Miss Bennet kept her mother's mood from boiling over during the solstice celebrations, Mr. Bennet and Mrs. Hill had ensured the matriarch had remained calm in the days following. She was given plenty of her tea and potion, and Mr. Bennet had exerted himself on a couple of occasions when the lady had attempted a tirade. He still preferred Elizabeth to avoid interceding unless absolutely necessary, and Fitzwilliam could not agree more. Elizabeth's intervention would only harm her tenuous relationship with her mother.

He and Elizabeth had stayed at Netherfield, yet each morning, after breakfast and spending some time in Oakham Forest, they would pass the better part of the afternoon at Longbourn, poring over books with Mr. Bennet.

His uncle's missive shed no light on the magic possessed by whoever was coming, and they had found nothing other than the warning Elizabeth had read while they were sequestered after their wedding.

They had spoken of journeying to Pemberley, but they could not leave Mr. Bennet to fight off the danger by himself. Yes, he was one of the most powerful mages in the world, but they had no way of knowing how much power this individual had absorbed. What if all three of them were needed to defeat this person? No, they would not and could not leave a single mage to face the threat alone.

Elizabeth rested her head on his shoulder with a sigh.

"Are you well?"

"Yes, just tired. I know the tradition is to wait up for midnight, but I am ready to retire."

"Could you be with child?" She had been more fatigued of late.

"Are babies all you can think of?" She gave a light laugh. "You seem so eager for me to become fat."

He shrugged and kissed the top of her head. "I do not know about eager, but we know you should be with child soon. We saw it at the altar."

"That could have happened years into the future. Besides, since we wed, you have kept me from sleeping more often than not. Perhaps this is your fault."

He wrapped an arm around her shoulders. "We shall see then. But you should know that I would not mind if a child came now or in three years. They will come when they come."

"That is good then." Her voice had softened further just before her breathing evened out. He should have known she would fall asleep by the sound of her voice.

"Is Lizzy well?" asked Georgiana, who sat nearby with Miss Catherine.

"I believe so. Are you tired as well?"

"Not yet. Kitty and I are drawing the figurine on the mantel. I have never been accomplished at sketching, but Kitty has taught me some useful tips. I am eager to return to Pemberley and draw the grounds or the house. Maybe I shall become a better artist than I originally thought."

"Why is Elizabeth asleep?" asked Mrs. Bennet. Her screech made all conversation in the room come to a pause, and Elizabeth startle awake.

Mr. Bennet sat beside his wife and took her hand. "She and Darcy have only been married a month. I seem to recall you being rather fatigued when we were first wed."

Mrs. Bennet's cheeks turned pink, and she hit her husband on the arm with her fan. "You should not speak of such things in front of the girls, Mr. Bennet." With a sniff, she pursed her lips and turned her attention back to her needlework.

The problem with this constant supervision was that Mrs. Bennet's frustration over Elizabeth being the heir was building and building because she could not let go of the fury. How long before she exploded and vented all her venom at Elizabeth? The furor had to come at some time. If only they could erase Elizabeth from the woman's mind completely. She would have no more frustration over the situation, and they would not need to exert such an effort to keep the lady calm.

As much as Fitzwilliam had expected some word from Lady Catherine, a letter had yet to come. Since he had made no pains to announce his marriage himself, she would soon discover his wedding had long passed, so it was only a matter of time before she sent him some missive ordering him to rid himself of his wife. How many times had she threatened him with that eventuality should he follow the contract?

Richard, meanwhile, had departed and returned to London and his duties. They were fortunate the journey was not long, and his cousin could make a swift return should they require him.

"Brother, is Mrs. Bennet well?" Georgiana had shifted closer and spoke in low tones. "She keeps staring at Elizabeth with a frightening countenance."

Mrs. Bennet's formerly blushing face was now more fearsome than he had ever witnessed before. Her narrowed eyes bore into Elizabeth while the lady's hands fisted in her lap. Bingley, who sat beside Miss Bennet, seemed to see nothing, but Miss Bennet's fingers had tightened around her mother's wrist.

A familiar rattling made all eyes dart to the mantel where both candlesticks now shook. His wife lifted her head from his shoulder, then looked to her mother.

"Mama, calm yourself."

When the first candlestick flew at Elizabeth, Fitzwilliam lifted a hand to shield his wife from the blow. Meanwhile, Elizabeth stood and approached her mother, who was struggling to move.

"Release me," screeched Mrs. Bennet.

"Mrs. Hill will likely be here soon with your tea and tonic. You will temper your urges in the meantime."

"You should have been a boy! I hate you even more now that you are the *heir*! This family did not need more magic. We needed someone to inherit the estate, and you could never do so."

Elizabeth rubbed her forehead. "I can stop your mouth as well should it be required." Her voice was not loud or agitated, but the slight trembling of her fingers could be discerned if one looked hard enough.

"Lizzy," said Mr. Bennet. "You know she cannot control her outbursts."

"Maybe not all, but she does not even try—especially with me."

While this was happening, Miss Lydia continued to trim a bonnet she was redoing while Miss Catherine continued to draw. Georgiana still sketched, but with wary glances at Mrs. Bennet here and there. Miss Mary was absorbed in her book and appeared to have ignored the entire scene. Bingley, meanwhile, stared agape at the sight in front of him. Of course, he would be shocked. He had witnessed Mrs. Bennet's outbursts on more than one occasion. Why was he surprised?

"Ah! It is almost midnight. Come, let us go to our small hall."

Mr. Bennet hopped from his seat and strode into the front of the house with everyone following. Elizabeth watched her mother like a hawk while she released the spell that kept her bound. As soon as the lady was freed, she stood with a huff and stalked after her husband.

With a sigh, Elizabeth visibly relaxed every bit of tension in her shoulders. "I should not have subdued her."

"She was about to burst. If you had not, the other candlestick would have flown."

"Yes, but you, me, or Papa could have stopped it. I should have let her vent her anger."

He wrapped her in his arms and kissed her crown. "You have taken her anger for years. I cannot find fault in you stepping up to defend yourself for once. If she makes an attempt to rein in her ire some, then your interceding will have been worth it."

She took his hand and tugged him towards the front door. "Come. The sooner we usher in the new year, the sooner we can return to Netherfield."

"I wish we knew what was coming so we could plan our return to Pemberley." When they entered the hall, they joined the circle of the family. At the chime of the clock for midnight, Mr. Bennet opened the front door to usher out the old and welcome in the new. As soon as the chimes ended, Mr. Bennet closed the door, and they all returned to the drawing room.

"Mr. Bennet," said Bingley as they entered. "I have thoroughly enjoyed this evening, but I believe the time has come for me to return to Netherfield." They had shared a carriage, so that meant his and Elizabeth's departure as well.

"Of course." Mr. Bennet kissed Elizabeth's cheek and shook Fitzwilliam's hand. "I should see you on the morrow."

"Yes, we shall be here."

Before they could return to the front hall, a banging ensued on the door. With a frown upon his countenance, Mr. Bennet hurried out and opened the door while Mrs. Bennet began wailing about them all being murdered.

"Happy New Year, sirs. I have letters for Mr. Henry Bennet and Mr. Fitzwilliam Darcy." When the man held out the missives, his foot crossed the threshold. They gave the man some money for his delivery.

"I beg your pardon," said Mr. Bennet, "but since you have entered the house."

"You wish me to depart out the back?"

"Yes, precisely."

The housekeeper appeared and led the man through the servants' passages while Fitzwilliam flipped his letter over so he could see the direction. "'Tis from Lady Catherine."

A chuckle came from Mr. Bennet. "Her messenger being our first footer does not bode well for the coming year. Do you know, I did not even look to see if he had light or dark hair under his cloak. I would assume light since he brought us these."

The first footer was an omen for the rest of the year and being light haired was bad luck. Fitzwilliam could not argue that their first visitor bringing news from Lady Catherine was not a good sign. He glanced over his shoulder. Was the man, in fact, light haired?

The messenger had already disappeared through the servants' door, so Fitzwilliam returned his attention to the missive. After sucking in a deep inhale, he broke the seal and opened the paper.

28 December 1811
Rosings Park

Dear Nephew,
I am dismayed and disappointed by some news that
reached me today. I have been told that you were
joined in matrimony to a young lady without status

or fortune. Of course, being your closest relation, I am writing to inform you of my opinion on the matter. Even though I am assured she is from our circles, she is not what the wife of a Darcy should be.

Your dear mother would be heartbroken. We discussed your marriage many times, and as you surely know, you have been destined to marry Anne since you both were in your cradles. My daughter is the only lady from our world who is fit to be Mrs. Darcy. You must know that in your heart as well as your mind. This lady you have impulsively married will never hold any consequence, so I must insist that you end this farce and finally come wed Anne. I am certain your uncle can be of aid whether it be with an annulment or a divorce. I care not which as long as you come to marry Anne as soon as you are rid of the interloper.

I shall be most displeased should you choose to defy me on this matter.

Your aunt,

Lady Catherine de Bourgh

He had no sooner read the last line than he handed his aunt's ridiculous opinions and commands to Mr. Bennet. The older man arched an eyebrow while he read then shook his head while he handed back the letter.

"Will you respond?"

With a nod, he took the letter and handed it to Elizabeth. She should know not only what was being said but also what was possibly coming.

"Yes, I shall pen a response in the morning. I have no patience for it tonight, and I am too angry at the moment to state my thoughts in a rational manner."

His wife rubbed his arm. "I should be pleased to be of aid in the endeavour. I can read what you have written and offer my opinion. Or, perhaps I should mend your pen if it is required. What do you think?"

He kissed her forehead. "I believe your presence will be of great aid to my state of mind. I shall welcome you unreservedly. Now, let us return to Netherfield. 'Tis late."

Once they had wished the Bennets well, they climbed into the carriage waiting for them. As soon as Bingley sat across from them and the door was closed, Fitzwilliam rapped his walking stick on the ceiling of the equipage.

"Do you think Lady Catherine will ever accept your marriage?" asked Bingley.

Fitzwilliam shrugged. "Whether or not she does, I do not care. She will never have a say in whom I marry. I have attempted to tell her so over the years, but she has doggedly refused to listen. Her demands will always fall on deaf ears."

After all, he had never given in to her wishes before, so why would he concede now?

Chapter 26

12th of January 1812

Elizabeth opened her eyes and blinked at Fitzwilliam, who was lying beside her, his head propped on his hand while he watched her. One of the fingers on his spare hand twirled one of her curls around and around. He wore a lazy sort of smile that spoke of contentment. He was so very dear.

She rolled to face him and reached to caress his cheek, which was covered in a day's worth of stubble. He was so handsome when he was unkempt, his hair mussed and his beard visible against his skin. She was the only one to see him thus. These moments were her favourites.

"Good morning," he said in a hoarse voice. His voice always held that rough tone when he first awakened. He could not have been staring at her for long.

"Are you enjoying yourself?"

He grinned. "You make the most adorable expressions while you sleep. I was just enjoying them before you opened your eyes. My favourite was when you crinkled your nose. You looked like a rabbit." He tapped the tip of her nose as he spoke.

"A rabbit? I doubt that, but I am certain you finding humour in my countenance while I sleep is uncharitable. I shall need to seek some form of retribution, so you should be warned." She sat up, holding the sheet to her chest. Fitzwilliam had removed her nightgown last night when they were intimate, but she still was not particularly comfortable with leaving herself bare whenever they were alone in their chambers. On the other hand, he had no qualms striding about the room sans clothing. He was beautiful, so she would never insist he don a dressing gown. She simply could not fathom how to behave in those situations.

At the familiar sounds of a carriage approaching the house, her husband threw off the coverlet and strode to the window as naked as the day he was born. Since the new year, they had been holding their breath, waiting for Lady Catherine to appear on their doorstep. Could this finally be the day she arrived? If it was, Fitzwilliam would want to know as soon as possible.

"Who is it?"

He shook his head. "I do not recognise the carriage, but I can say with certainty it is not my aunt. She spared no expense putting the de Bourgh crest on the door in gold leaf as well as outfitting her men with expensive livery. Whoever this is has not wasted their funds in such a way."

She slipped on her robe and hastened to his side. When the door of the equipage opened, a lady emerged with a gentleman stepping down behind her. Elizabeth inhaled sharply.

"Miss Bingley—but how?"

"Well, she must have found someone to bring her here. Now we only need discover what nefarious scheme she is about before she is sent back." Fitzwilliam's countenance appeared stormy.

"You believe Mr. Bingley will return her to Scarborough? From what you told me, he was not one to stand up to her until just before she departed. What if he allows her to remain?"

Her husband let the drapery fall back into place, set his hands upon her shoulders, and kissed her forehead. "I shall dress and make my way downstairs. I hope Bingley will hold fast to his resolve in order to keeping Miss Bingley in check, but your concerns are not without merit. I have seen him waver on her behaviour before."

After he departed to his dressing room, Elizabeth bit her lip and shifted the drapery as a gentleman stepped down from the portico to the drive and re-entered the carriage. When the vehicle drove away, she exhaled and departed to her own dressing room. She had to know what was happening!

Her maid's efficient work had her dressed in a morning gown and on her way downstairs without delay. As she descended the stairs, the shrieking tones of Miss Bingley echoed through the hall.

"I shall not return! My aunt is all that is ridiculous. She says I am unladylike. Me! I learnt decorum at one of the finest schools in England. What does my aunt know? Nothing!"

"Caroline, I made myself quite clear when I sent you north. I shall not have you ruining my chances with Jane Bennet, and you will not make yourself a nuisance to Mr. and Mrs. Darcy."

"Mrs. Darcy!" screamed Miss Bingley. "She is not worthy to be Mrs. Darcy. Miss Elizabeth Bennet with her country fashions and her country manners. She is a disgrace to the Darcy name!"

"You should not speak when you know naught of what you are saying," said Fitzwilliam's deep voice.

"Darcy is correct. You should not speak so."

As the hall came into Elizabeth's view, Miss Bingley drew herself up. "I actually know a great deal, Charles. It is you who refuses to listen. That lady will be laughed out of the drawing rooms of London. The entire neighbourhood has spoken of the fact that she has never shown any sign of an ability. She has no talent. How does that happen in a magical family?"

"And I have told you, Miss Bingley," said Fitzwilliam who stood near Mr. Bingley but somewhat behind him. "My wife is immensely talented but has never flaunted her magic before everyone. As for drawing rooms, neither of us has any intention of taking part in the diversions of London. At our first opportunity, we shall journey to Derbyshire and spend our days in the country—at Pemberley."

Miss Bingley threw up her hands. "Someone will need to guide dear Georgiana when it is time for her to come out. You cannot expect such a simpleton to do so. Otherwise, how will she marry well?"

When Elizabeth stepped down from the last step, Miss Bingley turned to face her. "You should not be Mrs. Darcy! You know nothing!" The lady began rushing towards her, her countenance hard and her gaze murderous. "Mr. Darcy was meant for me! You had no right—"

As Miss Bingley's fist made to swing, her brother hastened to grab it, but Elizabeth's arm flew up, palm out. "Plab."

Before Miss Bingley's hand could connect with Elizabeth's body, the woman flew back until she slammed against the door. Elizabeth's hand remained lifted as she pinned Miss Bingley, keeping the woman from lifting any part of herself from the door. She could not get down nor could she retaliate.

Miss Bingley's eyes widened, and her mouth opened and closed several times. "How is this possible?"

Elizabeth continued to hold Miss Bingley aloft while she rotated her arm so Miss Bingley could see the birthmark. "Because I am not merely a Bennet daughter. I am also the heir."

"Ladies are not heirs!" The lady's chest heaved in order for her to yell as she had. She had been compelled to heave out the words one at a time due to the force of the spell pinning her.

"This one is," said Fitzwilliam. He gazed at Elizabeth in such a way that everything in her longed to kiss him. She was not yet ready, however, to relinquish her hold on Miss Bingley.

"I tried to warn you about this, Caroline." Bingley stepped closer to his sister but made no move to remove her from where she was still pressed flat against the door. "Darcy's parents would not have betrothed them to each other as they did without good reason. He has said as much many times, but I did not know the truth of the matter until Mrs. Darcy's abilities were announced on the solstice.

"I warned you of the prominence of the Bennet family in magical circles. Have you not noticed how those in the neighbourhood defer to them? Mr. Bennet led the ceremony at

Samhain, and Mrs. Darcy lit the bonfire for the solstice. When word of her existence spreads, she will be accepted by the highest of magical circles. You have erred greatly, sister."

Elizabeth winced. She doubted she would be accepted by the highest circles, but she had no worry for whether she was or not. Just as always, Mr. Bingley saw things in the best light. He would never believe anyone would discount her magic because she was a lady.

"Put me down!" screeched Miss Bingley.

Elizabeth tilted her head. "Will you calm yourself? I can stun you if I must."

Fitzwilliam shifted closer to her side. "I can assure you, Miss Bingley, her stunning spells are unpleasant to say the least. The last time we practised, she hit me with one that gave me the worst megrim. Even with a potion to be of aid, two days passed before the entirety of the pain dissipated."

Miss Bingley gave a shriek. "Very well! I shall be calm."

After a quick glance at the gentlemen, Elizabeth narrowed her eyes. Should she believe Miss Bingley? The lady had shown she was little to be trusted during their brief acquaintance. "Very well. But I shall provide you no leniency if you attempt to hurt me, my husband, or even your brother."

"I thank you for your protection, Mrs. Darcy," said Mr. Bingley.

As Elizabeth lowered her hand, Miss Bingley gradually dropped until her feet were once again on the floor. At the release of the remaining spell, she heaved in a great breath.

"I shall not return to Scarborough."

Mr. Bingley gave a dark chuckle and shook his head. "You have no choice. You do not have enough funds remaining to establish yourself in town as you would wish. I still cannot believe you convinced Mr. Grantley to convey you and your maid here on their family's way to London for the Season. My aunt surely wrote of your escape, yet I have yet to receive her letter. Knowing her, she refused to send the missive express due to the expense.

"Nevertheless, you will be returned without delay. I shall notify the inns this afternoon, and you will depart in the morning."

"Charles," said Miss Bingley weakly. "Pray, do not do this to me."

"If you had shown even an ounce of respect for others, regardless of their position, you would not be in this predicament now. Due to your behaviour, your lady's maid is overpaid—likely more than any servant in the country. The more you mistreated her, the more I had to pay to hire a new maid or to retain that one. That said, I shall not pay her wages anymore. When you return, you will care for yourself. Maybe that will give you an appreciation for all that a maid does. In the meantime, you will save me a fortune. With the new chores you will be forced to take on, you will also not have enough time to plan another escape."

The lady's complexion turned ashen. "You cannot be serious." She was shocked, but how? According to Fitzwilliam, Miss Bingley had been given numerous warnings over the years. Her brother had to take a stand eventually.

"Mrs. Nicholls, pray, see my sister to her former chambers. She will have no need to unpack, but if you would be so kind as to teach her how to air her travelling gown so she can wear it again on the morrow, I would be appreciative. And Caroline, I shall not hesitate to have Mrs. Darcy stun or bind you for the return trip, so I suggest you do as I ask."

The housekeeper gestured to two footmen, who came to stand behind Miss Bingley. "If you would follow me."

"Charles," said Miss Bingley. Her voice was pleading, yet her brother turned his head away as she was led from the room. He was truly done with her.

"Forgive that scene if you would." Mr. Bingley scrubbed his face with his hands. "Mrs. Darcy, I cannot apologise enough for my sister's behaviour towards you."

Elizabeth placed her hand on his forearm. "Do not think on it a moment more. I believe we all have relations whose behaviour is not what we would always wish. In those situations, a good memory is unpardonable."

Both Mr. Bingley and her husband chuckled.

"I am thankful for your view on the matter. You make an excellent wife for my friend. I do hope he deserves you."

"What do you mean by that?" asked Fitzwilliam wearing a feigned frown.

"I am speaking in jest, of course. You have been a good friend. I would not have made a success of learning to run an estate without your aid. You also helped me with my ability for which I am grateful."

While Mr. Bingley spoke, Fitzwilliam pulled her to his side, his muscular arm wrapped around her to keep her there. "I was happy to do so, but that does not mean you may flirt with my wife."

Mr. Bingley gave a jovial laugh. "That was not flirting. If I had decided to charm your wife, I would have said something more clever than that. Besides, I am interested in none but Miss Bennet."

"I am pleased to hear it," Elizabeth said. She could not help but grin at Mr. Bingley's pronouncement. While she and Fitzwilliam had seen what they both believed to be the day of Mr. Bingley's and Jane's engagement, they could not be certain of anything in a vision until the event took place. Yet, in regard to the visions coming from the altar, those seemed to be more reliable than most. Her father believed them to be accurate as well.

With a happy shrug, Mr. Bingley waved them in the direction of the breakfast room. "Come. I would prefer to have some tea and a hearty breakfast and speak of more pleasant matters. I cannot dwell on what has become of Caroline. It is too difficult."

Fitzwilliam gave him a clap on the back as they made their way to breakfast. As much as what had just occurred would hang over Mr. Bingley for the rest of the day, perhaps they could distract him from it for a time. A good friend could do no less!

Chapter 27

13th of January 1812

As Hen galloped over the dusting of snow that had fallen during the night, Fitzwilliam's teeth ground together. He had been about to give up on waiting out the vision and return to Pemberley with his wife, but when he awoke early this morning to ensure Miss Bingley had departed, the sight of the fields covered in a slight white hue was an unwelcome discovery.

The person who would attempt to take everything from them would be here soon. Was he prepared? Moreover, was Elizabeth? After all, the vision indicated she would be the one fighting this person. He had seen nothing that indicated he would be forced to face them, yet he would if it meant saving Elizabeth—if it meant sparing her life, he would do so without a second thought. Even now, their child could be growing in her womb. He would sacrifice himself for the two of them if need be. He could do no less for the one he loved so greatly.

After handing Hen off to the groom, he hastened into the house and upstairs. As he entered their bedchamber, he paused for but a moment before tossing his great coat and hat on the nearby chair. He had been too quick for the butler and footmen to take them downstairs.

Elizabeth lay on her side, her hands nestled up by her face. She was so peaceful. He had no wish to disturb her equanimity, but they must be ready.

He trailed his fingers down her cheek, making her nose crinkle. She brushed her hand across her face before settling back. He bit his lip to keep from laughing.

"Elizabeth," he said softly in a sing-song tone.

"Just a few more minutes."

He nuzzled his nose near her ear, and she gasped. "Fitzwilliam Albert Darcy, your nose is freezing."

"But you are awake."

"That was uncharitable. What if I did the same to you?"

This time, he did laugh. "That would require you to wake before me, which has yet to happen, so I doubt you will ever have the opportunity."

She gave a playful growl and rolled on top of him, straddling him in her nightgown. With her hair trailing down her back, she was beautiful. "I could wake early if I wished."

"If you say so, my dear."

He did not argue as she unbuttoned his topcoat then his waistcoat, but when she reached around his side, he grabbed her by the wrist. "What are you about?"

"Do you not know?" She pressed her lips to his and began to kiss him in a way that he had no power to resist her. That is, until a sharp pinch to his side shocked him from those pleasant activities.

"And you call *me* uncharitable." Her mischievous grin warmed his heart.

"I am merely seeking my revenge."

He rolled them so he was on top and began to tickle her sides. "Revenge? What need you of revenge?"

Her laughter filled the room. "Stop! Pray, I beg you!"

He drew away his hand but held it so his fingers were poised and ready to continue their assault. "What do you have to say to me?"

"If I decided to use magic, I could win."

"Not what I was looking for!" He continued tickling her until she was gasping, then gave her a reprieve. "How about now?"

She scraped her teeth over her bottom lip in a way that stirred his blood. "I shall never concede that this is fair, but I shall forgive you since I cannot remain angry with you for too long. I love you too much to do so."

He paused and lifted himself from her, sitting back on his heels. "What did you say?"

"I said, 'I love you, Fitzwilliam Darcy.'"

His hand lifted to her cheek and caressed down the velvety softness of her flesh to her chin. "I have waited so long to hear you say those words."

"Since you knew of me before I knew of you, your feelings formed without impediment, even before we met. I am certain waiting for me to love you in return has seemed interminable." She combed her fingers through his curls. The slight scratch of her fingernails against his scalp soothed him in a way nothing else did. "In hindsight, I likely loved you for some time, but with such a new emotion, how was I to be certain what I felt was love? This morning, when you awakened me with your cold nose and childish antics, you made my heart overflow." Her words made his own heart overflow!

He shook his head. "The hardest part was seeing the love in your eyes and not rushing you to say those precious words. At least I hope I did not make you believe you had to say them. I wanted nothing more than to hear it, but I hoped you would soon understand what was in your heart first."

A tear landed upon her cheek and trailed down into her hair. "You were perfect, Fitzwilliam. You never let any impatience or hurt be known to me; I assure you."

Her words were all he needed to peel himself out of his topcoat and waistcoat and throw them away. Where they landed, he knew not since he settled himself back upon his wife and began to kiss her with all the passion in his heart. They loved each other, and he wished for no other occupation than to show her.

He kissed and caressed her until he had to touch her everywhere and removed her nightgown. When he sat back on his heels once more, he gazed, enraptured by her loveliness while he had removed all but his breeches. He had to feel her pressed against him. Even his breeches were too much, but he could not peel himself away from all her glorious skin to remove them just yet.

As it was, he never did fully remove his breeches. At the moment that he finally cried his release, he collapsed atop her with a loud groan. When he regained his wits, he chuckled.

"What amuses you so?"

"We must appear everything that is ridiculous." He lifted his head and propped his chin on his hand.

She glanced down and frowned.

"Here you are without one stitch of clothing and on top of the coverlet while my breeches are still wrapped around my thighs. I am still wearing my boots as well."

Her small feet lifted, and she pulled down on his breeches with her toes.

"You will never remove them that way." He could not help but grin at the silly expression she wore while her feet slid along his legs pushing his trousers down a little at a time.

"I can try."

"My boots will never come off. They are too difficult to remove as it is." He pulled himself from her, his heart cracking with the separation. "Give me one moment."

While he made for his dressing room, he pulled his breeches up. Thankfully, his valet was pressing some freshly laundered shirts when he entered.

"Sir?"

"I require the removal of my boots."

Hastings had his feet free in a trice. "I thank you."

"Are you ready to dress for breakfast, sir?"

"Not just yet." Without another word, he hastened back to his wife's bedchamber. At the edge of the bed, he came to a sudden halt. She was on her side, with her dark curls spilling behind her, and on full display. The morning sun peeking in from the windows gave a tantalising glimpse of his beloved's curves.

"You are still wearing your breeches."

He lifted his eyebrows, grabbed the waist, and shoved them down to the floor. As soon as they were completely removed, he dove onto the bed while she laughed and rolled out of the way.

"You will crush me like that."

With one arm, he pulled her back to him. "I would never harm you."

She kissed his bare shoulder. "I know that."

He sighed. As much as he despised the idea of ruining their light-hearted mood, he had no choice. "There is a dusting of snow on the ground this morning."

Her eyes widened. "So much for our return to Pemberley."

He pressed his forehead to hers. "If I thought that would prevent this confrontation, I would remove us without delay, but I believe the inevitable will come no matter what, and I would not have your father lose his life to have another month or two with you." How could she forgive him if that happened? How would he forgive himself?

She dropped onto her back, so he nestled his head into her chest. How he loved spending time with her thus! The softness of her breasts under his cheek would never grow tiresome.

"I suppose we need to keep to our usual routine."

"I believe so. Even if we change our habits, this may still come, but I do think we should continue as we have been."

His head lifted as she took in a large breath. "We should begin our day then."

He turned and caressed his lips against the side of her breast. "Not just yet."

She gasped when he took her nipple in his mouth and sucked hard before releasing it again. "At the moment, I am not ready to leave this room." Before she could respond, he continued his assault, which meant they arrived to breakfast after Bingley had already departed to spend the day with Miss Bennet at Longbourn. Neither of them was particularly upset about their late arrival. Instead, they ate their meal while they chatted in soft tones.

But before they could depart for Oakham Forest, the arrival of a carriage made them hesitate. Who could be calling? The hour was still early. It was not even noon yet.

He hastened them into the drawing room, which had a view of the drive. When he peeked out the window, his heart dropped like a rock. Lady Catherine had finally arrived.

A response had been sent to her letter on the winter solstice. He had explained his betrothal to Elizabeth occurred not long after her birth, and how he would never dishonour his parents by betraying their wishes for his future. Because his aunt had no belief in love other than the affection she held for her daughter, he had never mentioned any of those tender feelings he held so dear. She would not be moved by their love match. Instead, she would consider this a weakness and all the more reason for him to remove Elizabeth from his life. She was a heartless woman indeed!

Within moments, the familiar creaking of the door meant his aunt was being welcomed into the house, so he hastened to Elizabeth's side. He would not leave her to face Lady Catherine alone. He would be with her throughout whatever was to come.

"Where is my nephew?" echoed through the house.

The door opened, and before Mrs. Nichols could announce the visitor, his aunt shoved the housekeeper out of the way and entered. She had not removed her coat or her hat, which boasted of a couple of peacock feathers that wrapped around the brim and trailed behind her. It was the most ridiculous thing he had ever seen.

"You must know why I have come. Your heart must have told you I would not ignore this farce and leave you to your idiocy. I am here to ensure you do what I say.

"I have instructed my servants to gather your trunk and your belongings. We are to journey to London to meet with your uncle. He will aid me in ending this travesty you have insisted upon."

His chin hitched a little. They had not even bowed or curtseyed. His aunt had ignored every propriety, which should not surprise him, but it did.

"No, I shall not." He stood tall and straight. His bearing could show no signs of weakness.

She sniffed. "You have no choice in the matter." With a flick of her fingers, two burly men entered behind her. "Grab him."

"Stiúdú!" Elizabeth stepped in front of him with her arm raised. Indigo light flew from her hand and hit the first of the men directly in the chest. His partner gaped as the man cried out and crumpled to the floor.

"That is impossible." The remaining man stared wide-eyed at Elizabeth as she turned her hand on him. He shifted on his feet as though considering his options, but rather than hasten from the room, he made to lunge.

"Pairilis," said Elizabeth with a turn of her hand. Instead of the shocked eyes and cry, this man seemed to trip on his own feet and fell on his face.

His aunt's jowls quivered. "What is this? Women do not have magic."

He pulled Elizabeth back against his chest. "The Lady of the Lake did. Why could her descendent not have power as well?"

"Niniane was a water fairy. This. . .woman has had her blood polluted by too many inferior humans to carry Niniane's powers."

"Yet, she bears the mark of the heir." He turned Elizabeth's arm and slid up her sleeve. "You would do best to abandon your pursuit. You would have to subdue me as well as my wife and the servants, who are willing to defend their guests. Your scheme will not work."

"Do you believe these two imbeciles are the only help I have arranged?"

He did not waver at the hoofbeats coming from outside. How many more men had she brought?

Elizabeth stepped to his side. "Then bring them in, Lady Catherine. Between the two of us, we can subdue them."

Lady Catherine cackled. "You cannot move quickly enough."

He gritted his teeth. They would never manage whatever men his aunt had brought with her by merely standing there.

"Forgive me, aunt." He lifted his hand. "Stiúdú."

She had made to speak but the spell hit her before the sound could come, and she joined the other two men on the ground.

He grabbed Elizabeth's hand. "We have to get out of this room. We are trapped if we remain."

When they entered the hall, several more men had entered. The first one charged at him.

"Táthaigh!" Elizabeth sent the spell at the man whose arms and legs snapped together, making him fall forward like a statue. Before Fitzwilliam could lift his hand, she spun on her feet and swung both of her arms forward.

"Pairilis!" This time, both of the men at the door dropped. One, who had landed upon his back, glanced all around the room, his eyes darting here and there even though his body did not move otherwise.

"Come!" She grabbed his hand and dragged him through the servant's door. The maids and cooks in the kitchen all gasped when they ran through, but Elizabeth did not stop until she had pulled him out the back of the house and into the kitchen gardens.

Here, they were no longer hemmed into the house but could defend themselves more readily.

"You could allow me to defend myself here and there. It would not do for all and sundry to believe I require your protection."

She scoffed. "You and I both know you do not require my aid. In this circumstance, it was easier for me to use my magic while you provided the distraction. Because they are after you, they are assuming I am no threat. Their stupidity makes it much easier to take them unawares."

His wife made a brilliant point. Lady Catherine had paid these men to capture him. They had no use for Elizabeth, so they discounted her.

"I also have had no wish to damage the house. How would poor Mr. Bingley explain that to the owners?"

He chuckled. "You make valid points, my dear. Now, what are we to do about the remaining men, and how do we rid ourselves of my aunt?"

"Well, I have an idea." He took a step back at the mischievous expression upon his wife's countenance. What could she possibly be about?

Chapter 28

13th of January cont . . .

"Each of us will go around to the front of the house. I will take the east side and you the west—"

"No." He shook his head. "I will not leave you to fend for yourself. We are stronger together than we are apart."

Elizabeth grumbled out an exhale. Why was he so adamantly opposed to her plan? He had not even heard the whole of it before refusing. Stubborn man!

"I do not disagree, but we will be working together when we begin to take these men out from each side of the house."

He crossed his arms over his chest while he tapped his foot in a furious rhythm. "I understand what you wish to do, and I agree the scheme has merit, yet we do not know how many men my aunt brought with her."

"Well, there were the two in the drawing room." She held up two fingers as she mentioned them. "Then three that we incapacitated in the hall."

"The stunning spell on my aunt will not last forever."

That was the only drawback to the stunning spell. The worst of the effect would wear off, unless the individual was more susceptible to that spell than most. No one knew why some were slower to rouse than others, but it happened from time to time; however, they would never be so fortunate that Lady Catherine was one of those more susceptible people. Still, she would have a devil of a headache when she awakened.

"Sir!"

They both turned with a start at Fitzwilliam's valet, who was on his way out the door to the kitchens.

"The servants have subdued three men inside in addition to the five the mistress bound with her magic. Lady Catherine has not

269

roused as yet, and the servants have tied all of the men captured thus far. Two more await Lady Catherine's instruction in front of the house."

Elizabeth allowed one side of her lip to lift. "She brought ten men to capture you, but only brought two into the drawing room with her?"

"I would not say my aunt is an expert at strategy."

"I should say not. If she had brought all ten in and had you been alone, perhaps she could have seen some success, but she underestimated you, to say the least."

"We should not complain. She is now aware she requires more. We also do not know much about the men she left outside. What if one of them has magic? We cannot be too careful."

He was correct. They needed to ensure the men in the front of the house were captured so they all could be turned over to the constable. His aunt would be put back on the road to Kent. This was unlikely to be the end of her schemes. They had spoken of her tenacity often enough. But, at least, the end of this campaign would not be difficult.

His hand took hers. "Come."

He charmed their feet so they moved without sound. They kept close to the side of the house as they tiptoed to the front near the portico, where they stopped and peered around the edge. Two men stood in front of the steps as though a barrier to anyone attempting to enter.

Fitzwilliam pointed up, and she glanced up before frowning at him.

She sucked in a breath as he lifted her to the edge of the portico where she could fit a foot along the edge. With a firm grip, she held the stone railing and hoisted her leg over then the other until she was standing on the portico. The two men still stood facing the fields in front of the great house.

"Good morning, gentlemen," she said in her cheeriest tone. "Is there something I can do to be of aid?"

The men whirled around to face her. She had definitely startled them, which had been her intention. As they turned, Fitzwilliam ran out from his hiding place and extended both arms.

"Ò mò táthaigh!" The blast of light that accompanied his spell splintered into three beams.

She crossed her arms. "Caisg."

The part of the spell that shot towards her bounced off her shield and dissipated. She had never multiplied a spell. Doing so was risky since the charm split into however many people were nearby. You could inadvertently strike anyone who happened to be around, which was why she had to shield herself. In the drawing room, casting such a charm could have hit Mrs. Nichols or one of the servants. In this case, however, she could defend herself from the effects while the remaining men collapsed to the ground.

When she opened the front door, the butler and housekeeper were just inside with several footmen. "Pray, bind them so we can hand the lot over to the constable. They were hired to kidnap Mr. Darcy, so that should carry a fitting punishment."

"What of Lady Catherine?" asked Mrs. Nichols.

Fitzwilliam stepped up beside Elizabeth. "Bind my aunt's wrists and put her in her carriage. I shall speak with the driver and instruct him to return her to Rosings Park without delay. She will likely return, but let us hope not until after we have departed for Pemberley."

"You do not believe she will follow us to Derbyshire?" Elizabeth attempted her most doubtful countenance. Lady Catherine was not known for her docile nature.

"Not until the weather is warmer. This was but a day's travel. She likely travelled to London and stayed for the night before rising early and finishing the trip this morning. My aunt prefers comfort, and a cold carriage for a three-day journey north would not appeal to her, no matter how much she objects to our marriage."

While one of the grooms departed to fetch the constable, those remaining joined the footmen in binding up the men and putting them in the back of a cart. Once the constable had the testimony of the servants, he removed Lady Catherine's lackeys.

Meanwhile, Fitzwilliam spoke to Lady Catherine's servants and paid them handsomely to return his aunt to her home. His aunt's maid appeared horrified when she saw her mistress bound and carried to the equipage, but she said naught.

As soon as the carriage pulled away, Elizabeth set her hand on Fitzwilliam's arm. "You know her maid will untie her before they reach Meryton."

He shrugged one shoulder. "I stunned my aunt again before I carried her out. I believe the likelihood she will rouse before London is low. She may have them stop for the night, but I do not foresee her returning to Hertfordshire today or even tomorrow. Without the appropriate potions, her headache will linger for at least a week. She would also have to find new men to hire before making another attempt."

She chuckled. "I suppose we have practised for today."

Fitzwilliam shook his head. "We should call at Longbourn and inform your father of what has happened."

They returned to the house to gather their warm coats and hats and await the curricle he requested. Fitzwilliam sought out Georgiana, whose maid had ensured the girl had remained in her rooms. Once he had apprised her of what had occurred, he returned downstairs at the same time as the vehicle arrived in front of the house. He assisted her atop before climbing up himself, then cued the horses forward.

The cold air stung her cheeks some as they travelled, but she wrapped her arm through Fitzwilliam's while she took in the beauty around her. The light dusting of snow glittered with the sunlight beaming down upon it. Despite what it meant as to the vision at the altar, the fields and trees were lovely with their bare branches coated in white.

"I hope you do not mind the curricle. Since my aunt's attempt earlier, I preferred an open carriage."

"No, I am enjoying the crisp air and the unfettered views of the fields and trees. The snow may not be heavy, but the view it affords still has its charms."

He nodded. "It does indeed."

When they arrived at Longbourn, a groom rushed out to take the equipage, and Mrs. Hill hurried them inside the hall where Mrs. Bennet stood with her ear pressed to the parlour door.

Elizabeth lifted her eyebrows. "What is happening?"

With a light laugh, Mrs. Hill glanced at her mistress. "Mr. Bingley requested a private audience with Miss Bennet. Your mother shooed everyone from the room before they could say a word and has been standing thus ever since."

Fitzwilliam gave her a glance, his lips turned up just a little. "Your mother may never forgive you for marrying better than Miss Bennet, but I daresay she will be crowing for the remainder of the day as soon as Bingley and your sister emerge from that room."

"We should speak to your father." Her husband took her hand and led her to the library.

Papa peered up at them over his spectacles as they entered before placing a ribbon inside his book to mark the page and setting it down. "I heard rumour of a disturbance at Netherfield."

She paused before taking her usual seat. "How did you hear word of that so quickly?" Her father always seemed to know what had occurred in the village. Had he learnt some magic she had not?

Her father laughed. "Hill had a message sent to Mrs. Nichols, who was to send a note in return. The messenger heard the beginnings of the row inside the house. As soon as you incapacitated the men in front of the house, he departed for Longbourn. I assume the matter has been handled by the constable?"

"He took the men," said Fitzwilliam. "I stunned my aunt a second time and bound her before loading her in the carriage to return to Rosings.

"We expect her to try again."

Papa laughed and tapped his finger on the desk. "She will not come back so readily. Lady Catherine is not circumspect and will speak of her misfortune in the encounter. I am certain she will not find men cheaply nor will she find them so ready to serve when her last attempt failed in such a miserable manner." He was correct. Not many men would agree when the last were carted away to gaol.

"I had not considered," said Fitzwilliam. "I do wonder what my uncle will say to her if she tells him."

Another chuckle came from Papa. "I wager she will be more guarded with him. She knows who Elizabeth is and that she is my daughter. Your uncle and I have been long-time correspondents and friends. He will take our part. I am certain of it."

At a knock on the door, they all looked in that direction as it opened, and Mr. Bingley entered wearing an enormous grin. A surge of joy coursed through her as Fitzwilliam's hand tightened around hers. The gregarious gentleman was so delighted, he could not control his talent. Since he had been shuttered away with Jane when they arrived, that only meant one thing. Jane had said yes to Mr. Bingley's proposal.

"I also wager you are here to request permission to marry my Jane."

Another gust of cheer filled the room as Elizabeth stood. "I believe I shall wish my sister joy." As she approached Mr. Bingley, she held out her hands, which he took readily. "I wish you joy."

Mr. Bingley gave a slight dip over their joined hands. "I thank you, Mrs. Darcy."

"If you would prefer privacy," said Fitzwilliam, "I shall join my wife in wishing my sister well."

The gentleman shook his head. "No, I would be pleased to have you remain. I do not know the first thing about negotiating a marriage contract."

Fitzwilliam grinned. "And I do? Do remember my parents wrote mine when I was no more than eight years of age."

Elizabeth glanced over her shoulder and blew her husband a kiss. He blushed a bit, which was well worth the gesture. He always turned a little red when she flirted with him like this.

The men were already in quiet conversation as she closed the door behind her, but the house around her was far from silent. Lydia's raucous laughter could be heard from upstairs. Kitty's joined in a moment later, and from the parlour, Mama's excited chatter filled the hall.

She sighed. At least Mama would be pleased with the marriage of one of her daughters. The notion stung, but instead of dwelling upon what would upset her, Elizabeth straightened and entered the room as Mama bustled towards the kitchens muttering about punch for the servants.

As soon as Elizabeth entered, Jane held out her hands. Her dearest sister wore a smile brighter than she had ever seen, and her eyes were slightly red. Jane had been crying joyful tears it seemed.

"I am so pleased for you, Jane. He is the kindest of men."

"I am so happy," said Jane while she dabbed at her eyes with a handkerchief. "Is everyone this happy when they become engaged?"

Elizabeth laughed and shrugged. "I would not know. I was but a new babe when I was betrothed."

Jane's expression faltered. "But you are not displeased with your situation, are you?"

"I am exceedingly satisfied with Fitzwilliam. I must admit that I have come to love him most dearly. He is the perfect man for me, even if I was uncertain of him in the beginning."

"Then I can be content," said Jane. "I could not be so if you were miserable."

"Forgive me. I should not have made jest of how our engagement came to be. I would never want you to be disappointed or sad when you should be the opposite."

"There is naught to forgive. Charles has spoken of how you and Mr. Darcy behave with each other. I was certain you had feelings for him, but I am relieved to hear from you that I am not mistaken."

She held up her hands, palms out. "Now, enough about me. Let us speak of what just happened. What did he say?"

While Jane recounted Mr. Bingley's apparently bumbling speech, she could not stop smiling. Neither could Elizabeth for that matter!

Even so, another of the visions from the altar had just occurred. Since she was not with child, that vision would not be so soon, but what of the duel? Snow was on the ground and Jane was engaged. How much longer did they have before this unknown mage would arrive?

Chapter 29

15th of January 1812

The clearing was still this morning while Elizabeth wove her way through the stones. Herne sat on his usual tuft of verdant green grass that winter had never seemed to touch. Even though the rest of the clearing boasted of a coating of fresh, pristine snow, that patch was unblemished.

Herne appeared to care less why his favourite bed was green and not affected by the season while he nibbled on the grass that grew around him—another curiosity. He often ate from that very spot, yet the offerings were always abundant. Given the location near the stones, the presence of magic in some form or fashion should be expected, but that it lent itself to maintain Herne's existence was a rather astonishing circumstance in itself.

As she neared the altar, she brushed her fingers over the top, something she had done many times. She and Fitzwilliam had been awaiting any hint of this person coming, and thus far, except for the snow, the stones' rumblings had not increased. But the altar was humming stronger today. This had been the entire reason for her visit. With the fresh dusting of snow, she had been drawn to the stones.

She steeled herself and closed her eyes for a moment while she continued to stroke the altar. When her hand reached the middle, a jolt of power surged through her, making her fall onto the large stone.

"When I learnt of your existence, I sought to prevent you from claiming your full potential, but you thwarted me. But that has come to naught, and you are now nothing to me. Bow before me, descendant of Merlin!"

Her hands pressed against the altar as she attempted to push herself off, but the energy coursing through her would not allow her to escape. What was this? Why was it keeping her tied to the stone?

Fitzwilliam had gone riding this morning, but he would come at any moment. They were to meet here then call on Longbourn.

She squeezed her eyes shut and attempted to heave herself free. Behind her eyelids, colours swirled until they coalesced into an image of the gardens at Longbourn. Fitzwilliam stood before her, a cloudy spiral stretching from his chest to a small hand. He was limp while a cackle filled the air.

"He should not have tried to protect you. Now, his power will join the others."

With a cry, she forced herself from the stone, landing on all fours upon the hard ground. Her breath rushed in and out in gasps while she shook herself.

"No!" She inhaled in a great heave in an effort not to sob. Fitzwilliam would not sacrifice his life—his power—for her.

She prised herself from the ground and stumbled down the well-worn path towards Longbourn. She had to speak to Papa. Something had to be done! Fitzwilliam could not die!

Small branches slapped her cheeks as she ran without heed through the forest. When she reached the field, she did not look back but continued forward as fast as her legs could carry her to the hedgerow that separated the fields from the gardens. Longbourn!

No sooner had she slipped through the gap in the hedges than a bright light flashed from the side of the house.

"Papa!" Her father was powerful, but whoever this was had to be stronger. Why else would she have experienced residual effects from mere visions of their battle?

When she rounded the side of the house, her father stood tall and strong, his arm outstretched while he attempted to push back the cloud inching towards him.

The spell he had been fighting dissipated, but he continued to stare at his opponent. Elizabeth let her eyes stray from him to where a frail young lady stood near the brick wall that separated that part of the gardens from the orchard behind it.

"Ah, the lady I came all this way to see. When I called at Netherfield, they said you were here. Your father refused to tell me where you might be, so I thought to persuade him to reveal you. Now that you are here, I have no need of *him* anymore."

Instead of balking, Elizabeth strode forward so she was at a better angle to engage the woman before her. "Who are you?"

The lady was exceedingly pale and wore dark circles under her eyes. She was not well, yet she had some sort of power. Had she become a full mage when she stole the duke's powers as well as those of her first victim?

"You do not know of me? Has Fitzwilliam never mentioned my name?"

Elizabeth's body gave a slight start. "You know Fitzwilliam?"

"Since we were children. My mother and his planned our union while we were in our cradles until an upstart like you captured his attention."

A chill overtook her. "You are Miss Anne de Bourgh."

The lady's lips curved ever so slightly. "I am. And you stole what was rightfully mine, so I have come to take that and more from you."

"I do not understand. I was born an heir, but you have powers too. Were you born an heir as well?"

Anne cackled, which caused gooseflesh to crawl up Elizabeth's spine. "No, I was born with a talent, like most women. However, my ability is the power to strip another human of their magic."

"The Duke of Norfolk," said Papa. "*You* were the one. . ."

"Yes; that was most unfortunate. He was a great friend of my father's. Did you know that? The duke always suspected more existed to my father's death than my mother claimed, and he never ceased investigating what occurred that night. He had come close to discovering the truth, and I could not allow that to happen."

Papa took a step closer. "What is the truth?"

After shrugging, Anne glanced down at her fingernails. "That when I was five, I drained him. He was the first person I stripped of their magic. Of course, I did not know what I was doing at the time. My father was not a good man and was about to hit my mother. I did what had to be done.

"After, my mother panicked and claimed he had an apoplexy. I was too young to argue and was overwrought. Yet, now that I am older, I understand what I did had been necessary. My father had to die.

"From that point on, my mother and I have sought to keep my ability from becoming common knowledge. Can you imagine what fear that would cause?"

"A woman who can steal the magic of others and possibly wield it," said Papa. "You could be imprisoned if not killed for what you have done. Those who have used their magic for evil have been sent to Bedlam for less."

Anne tossed her head back with her next cackle. "If they can subdue me. You cast your spells against me. They did little, did they not?"

Papa clenched and released his jaw at Anne's words. Elizabeth had done no more than glance at her father and caught his response; indeed, what she had witnessed upon her arrival verified Anne's magic was difficult for Papa to fight. But Papa's magic had little effect against her? How was that possible?

"You need not answer," said Anne. "Your response tells me all I need to know. That is all well and good. Once I have drained your daughter of her magic, I shall take yours. Fitzwilliam will have little choice but to take me as his wife once I hold so much power."

"No man is meant to wield so much of the earth's magic." Papa's tone held a warning.

A chilling grin overtook Anne's wan face. "I am no man, Mr. Bennet. And I have been waiting and biding my time for this very moment. My mother attempted to stop me, but how was she to do so? She wields no true power. After all, she required a potion to convince Mr. Collins to assist us in our plan; not that he did as he was told."

"What plan do you speak of?" Other than removing her as Fitzwilliam's betrothed, was some other scheme afoot?

"We intended for you to come to Rosings. At some point, you would come to the house for tea, and we would then take your magic." Her grin widened into almost a terrifying skeletal visage. "It would be such a shame. Poor Mrs. Collins, the lady who ate some strawberries and choked to death. Your fool of a husband would be none the wiser, and I would possess the power of Merlin's heir."

"But I could not marry my cousin since I was already promised to yours."

"Yes, and now I must remedy that. I do not mind, though. This way, I shall take the magic of two Bennets." Anne threw both arms forward as a white cloud burst from where her thumbs touched.

Ceilt! Elizabeth threw up hers to shield herself with the charm and at the same time, spun.

The white haze ricocheted off her crossed arms and hit a holly tree. The dark green foliage withered in front of her and browned, the spell draining its life under their appalled gazes.

"Take care, Lizzy. She is powerful, but she continually throws whatever ability she has. I do not believe she has any other magic."

"Shut your mouth, old man!" Anne flung her arms in his direction, but he shielded himself as well. This time, the spell rebounded to the ground, leaving a spot bare of grass in its wake.

Dúr! Elizabeth twirled to the side as soon as she cast the charm in Anne's direction in case the lady turned her ability back on her. The binding spell hit Anne square in the chest and seemed to work, but Anne closed her eyes and held her breath before she burst free.

"Is that all you possess? You are pathetic." Anne crowed and stepped closer. "When I learnt of your existence, I sought to prevent you from claiming your full potential, but you thwarted me. All that has come to naught since you are now nothing to me. Bow before me, descendant of Merlin!" Anne threw up her arms. This was it! This was what Elizabeth had seen in the altar!

"*Stiúdú!*" Elizabeth made to shift to the side in an attempt to avoid Anne's spell, but when she stood facing the woman once more, a knife was embedded into her shoulder. Her head spun. *Dur!* She tried to spin around and out of the way of another spell coming her way, but she stumbled. Her vision blurred. *Pairilis!* A sudden searing pain radiated through her. She gritted her teeth.

"No!"

The shout was Papa's. Light bounced around before her, but she could make out little and she could not move. Countercurses! She needed a countercurse! *Bogadh!* That released a binding spell, but she still could not move. It had not worked! How could you counter a curse with no known incantation?

Her surroundings became more visible, but she could do naught. She was trapped in a sparkling white web while pain shot from her shoulder and through her body in waves. The dagger in her shoulder surely had some sort of potion meant to weaken her. Meanwhile, the spell squeezed mercilessly while she struggled to draw air. How was she to defend herself against this?

Múscail!

That released a stunning spell but also did not work in this instance.

Beware to the magician who seeks more magic than the earth is willing to provide. A high price is to be paid by those who covet the power of others.

She had read that passage what seemed like years ago at this moment. During the remainder of their time in the cottage, she and Fitzwilliam had pored over how many books in an attempt to find more—to discover precisely what that meant. But how could it help her? Now, here she was, no closer to discovering what she needed than before.

Ròiseal! From deep within her, the magic began to build. She had never attempted this charm before as it took a vast amount of power to cast. Her father had even warned her that attempting this particular spell would deplete her of magic and require a lengthy recovery after, but at this time and place, she had nothing to lose. She would die if she did not do something! But would the charm even work now while she was being drained of magic? The force inside her grew and grew. Since she had never used this magic, she had only a hint of an idea of what would occur in theory. Pain was unavoidable, but Anne's spells had become unbearable. She had to try!

When the wave of magic that had been building finally burst from her flesh, she screamed at the moment the blast radiated out from her.

"Elizabeth!"

Fitzwilliam's cry was barely audible over the boom of the surge spell she had cast.

His cousin's hold on her wavered enough for Elizabeth to regain her footing—Anne had been forced back a few steps. But instead of knocking her over as had happened with her father and Fitzwilliam, Anne jumped back and threw her arms forward.

"You bitch!"

The cloudy tendrils shot out with more force and encircled Elizabeth, forcing the air from her lungs. Searing pain coursed through her as the energy ebbed from deep within her. Light flashed before her, but from where it originated, she could not tell. She was too weak to make the attempt at even turning her head.

The pain of the vision had been real, yet only a modicum of the excruciating agony she now experienced. Her flesh burned and stung while her insides twisted and pushed at her as though they were attempting to free themselves. This was it. She was going to die. They had done all they could to prepare for this eventuality, but all their plans had come to naught. The beautiful vision of Fitzwilliam rubbing her belly swollen with their child would never happen. Would he be forced to marry his cousin?

Silver burst in all directions, but she could no longer hold her eyes open. They fluttered closed and she succumbed into nothing.

Chapter 30

13ᵗʰ of January cont . . .

The chill of the morning air whipped across Fitzwilliam's face as he galloped Hen through the field towards Oakham Forest. He had awakened restless and in need of a good ride, but even allowing Hen his head to race across Netherfield lands had not calmed his insides.

He should not have left Elizabeth to walk on her own. That realisation had come to him while riding, and he had turned Hen in the direction of the forest in the hopes of catching her before she made her way to Longbourn. He had to find her.

Upon reaching the forest, a sight he never would have imagined greeted him. Herne stood facing Longbourn. He threw his head once or twice, and he pranced in place. Why was the beast so agitated?

Fitzwilliam turned his head, and his entire body stiffened. Flashes of light were easily discernible above the trees at Longbourn. Oh, God! He had come. Whoever they had seen in the altar was here!

He urged Hen forward, once again giving the stallion enough rein to gallop without restraint. He had to join the fight. Was Mr. Bennet with them? Had they managed any spells successfully against this unknown enemy?

At the edge of the hedgerow, he pulled Hen to a stop and jumped down to enter the gardens. He followed the gravel path of the kitchen garden to the side of the house where he almost fainted. Anne? How was Anne the powerful individual they had been anticipating? She had been a common enough child but at some point, had become weaker and sickly. How could someone without a strong constitution wield so much power?

"No!"

Anne gave him a glance, her smile widening, yet the oddest thing was happening. The more the webbing from Elizabeth pulsed, the paler Anne became. She seemed to be thinner than she was a moment ago, and the dark circles under her eyes had become more pronounced.

He threw several spells at her, but they all seemed to be absorbed into her. What was this magic?

After one last binding spell, he threw out his arms due to a strange vibration from the earth. What was that? An odd rumbling began, and his head darted up to Elizabeth. No. No, no, no! She was not surging her power, was she? Anne would absorb it and lick her lips like a satisfied cat after drinking the richest of cream.

He raced towards his wife, but before he could reach her, a blast threw him back against the ground. His ears rang and his body smarted with the force of the blow, yet when he rolled to his side to get to his feet, Anne had been disoriented for no more than a few seconds. She lifted her arms again, the white web resuming its deathly task.

Something had to be done, but what? He had thrown some of the most common spells to subdue someone at Anne, but none had been successful. As he lifted his arms to try anything, Herne came racing into the garden. He did not slow or stop but ran straight at Anne. About five feet from Anne, the great stag lowered his head and accelerated so his impressive antlers speared Anne across the chest.

Her mouth gaped open and her eyes bulged in a horrifying skeletal sight he would never unsee. The white web that surrounded Elizabeth released its hold, and Anne screamed before she seemed to turn in on herself, and an explosion of silvery white filled the garden, raining what almost looked like cotton fluff down upon them.

When the explosion cleared, Anne and Herne were gone.

He scrambled over to Elizabeth and dropped to his knees. "Wake up, Elizabeth."

Mr. Bennet stumbled to her side. "Lizzy!"

With a careful touch, Fitzwilliam brushed her hair back from her face. She was pale, and her lips held a bluish tinge.

He pressed his palm to her cheek. "She is cold."

"Between the surge and your cousin's ability, she is depleted. Too much of her power is gone to help her heal. I do not know how she can recover from this."

An unbearable pain ripped through his chest. Elizabeth had to survive. She had to make it through! He could not live his life without her. In the short time they had been married, she had become essential. Her wit was one of the few things that could make him laugh, and how was he to sleep without her light snoring?

He had awakened this morning in the most idyllic manner: Elizabeth curled into his side without a stitch of clothing and pressed against him as though she required every bit of his warmth.

He needed her bubbling laughter to ease his less than agreeable moods. She found humour in what most people detested. Yes, he could be a taciturn and a disagreeable sort, but she had changed that aspect of his character. He could not remain in such a dark mood when he had her lightness to lift him from the doldrums.

"No, she is *not* dying."

Mr. Bennet opened his mouth to speak, but Fitzwilliam lifted Elizabeth into his arms and strode from the garden.

"Darcy! Wait! You cannot just take her!"

He ignored the calls as he hastened through the gap in the hedgerow. "Hen!"

The horse nickered and stepped forward.

"We are going to the forest." Whether his horse understood a word of it was unknown, but Hen held his place while Fitzwilliam situated Elizabeth onto his shoulder, mounted, then shifted her to a more comfortable position for them both.

"We must hurry."

With Elizabeth held tightly to him, he cued Hen to a gallop. Holding Elizabeth to him was a trial, but he maintained a firm grip on the saddle with his thighs so he could remain atop his horse's back. As he approached the forest, he slowed his mount but pressed him forward.

The path split just to the other side of the brook, and he steered Hen to the right. The left would take him to the altar, and he had no need to go there at the moment. Elizabeth needed something entirely different.

Soon, he reached a familiar place. Was this it?

"Help! Pray, help me!"

Birds chirped and the branches of the trees swayed in the breeze, but nothing. This had to be it.

He shoved his hand up towards the sky. "Aithris!"

A shower of colourful sparks shot high into the air and rained down upon them. "Your Grace, I need your help!"

He dismounted and pulled Elizabeth to him. "Your Grace!"

His legs collapsed, and he rocked Elizabeth in his arms. "Help!"

He pressed his head to Elizabeth's. She was so cold. How much longer could she survive without aid? He could not lose her now.

He ground his teeth and sat up. No, he would not lose her. They had just barely begun their life together. She would not die!

"Oscailt súl!" The words were guttural when they pierced the still air of the forest. As he watched the empty place in the clearing, a fog-like whiteness appeared in the air then dissipated to reveal a small cottage.

He left Elizabeth on the forest floor. As much as he despised abandoning her on the cold snow, he could not know if Mr. Bennet had other spells on the cottage. He would not have his beloved harmed further in the hopes of helping her.

As he took each stride forward, he braced himself for another shield or barrier of some sort. When he reached the door, he lifted his fist and struck the door with every bit of force he had in him. At the touch of his flesh to the wood, he flew back and landed upon the snowy ground not far from Elizabeth.

A repulsion charm. He should have known. He dragged himself up to a seated position then pulled himself over to Elizabeth. It was all he could do to keep from sobbing while he drew her back into his embrace.

A sudden creaking had him glance over his shoulder where the duchess was now standing in the doorway of the cottage.

"What has happened?"

"The person who stole your husband's life came to Longbourn. Elizabeth tried, but she was too strong."

"She?" Her Grace hastened over to them.

"The magical thief was my cousin, Anne de Bourgh."

The duchess shook her head. "Lay your wife on the ground. Let me look at her."

As much as every part of him protested Elizabeth leaving his arms again, he did as Her Grace requested. If Elizabeth was to be well again, the duchess was his only hope.

The lady ran her hands over Elizabeth and tutted. "She has used too much of her power. At the moment, she is hovering in that place between life and death."

"Can you not heal her?"

Her Grace bit her lip. "I can, but not here. We need to hurry to the altar before it is too late. We shall require the energy coming from the stones for my ability to be of any help. You must go ahead. After I fetch my son, I shall follow."

He scooped Elizabeth back into his arms but had to temper his pace, so he did not leave the duchess behind.

When he neared the clearing, the duchess appeared at his side, a babe tied to her chest with what appeared to be a long piece of fabric while she held him securely as she moved with haste. "Place her atop the altar."

He rushed forward and brushed off the snow before placing Elizbeth gently on the frigid surface. His wife appeared so small spread out on the large stone.

His hands brushed the surface, and he recoiled. What was happening with the altar? The stone was more than vibrating or giving a slight hum. A shake rumbled through it that was so fierce, it shook the ground.

Her Grace nodded as she approached. "Just as I suspected. The altar is pulling magic from the vein in the earth.

She placed her hands on Elizabeth's chest and closed her eyes. "Her heartbeat is weak and quite slow."

As a glow emitted from the duchess's hands, she bent over the stone with a sob. Tears began pouring from her eyes and falling upon Elizabeth while she began to sing the same haunting melody as the last time she healed his wife. Her Grace shifted from Elizabeth's chest to her head while the tiny droplets continued to rain down on her. Soon the glow not only came from Her Grace's hands but also each of the tiny tears that peppered over Elizabeth's chest and face, but the duchess did not stop. Instead, she moved lower to Elizabeth's stomach and allowed her tears to continue to fall upon his wife.

Soon after, Her Grace stepped back from Elizabeth but held out her hands, which continued to give off a soft white glow.

"You were smart to bring Lizzy to Her Grace."

He startled and turned to where Mr. Bennet stood several yards away.

"I saw your show of sparks come from the forest and followed. I assumed you had brought my daughter to the altar, but you somehow found the cottage."

"I recognised the clearing then yelled and begged in the hopes the duchess would open the door. When that did not happen, I removed one of the protections upon the cottage, but I missed the repulsion charm. The duchess emerged from the house not long after I was thrown away from it."

"The charm that threw you would have caused a loud boom inside. Even though you did not succeed in getting inside, your being thrown brought her attention to you."

He nodded. "I had considered that. If she had not come out, I would have reversed the repulsion spell."

Mr. Bennet clapped him on the back. "I had other protections in place, but you would have been able to knock after removing the repulsion charm. However, if you had not sought out Her Grace, I would have brought her to you. If anyone can save Elizabeth. . ."The older man then set his palm upon Fitzwilliam's shoulder. "You know the duchess is doing all she can. Her tears have healing properties and setting Elizabeth upon the altar will help replenish some of the power she has lost. The remainder will have to return with time."

"What if the duchess cannot save her?" His voice cracked. A solid lead weight rested upon his chest. The only way to remove it was to have Elizabeth well and in his arms once more.

"A chance exists that Lizzy will never be the same. You must prepare yourself for that."

"What do you mean?" His heart had already been beating quickly, but now it raced. How could it continue at such a rate?

"Between your cousin draining her magic and Lizzy employing the surge spell, she may never be as powerful as she was. That said, Lizzy had little choice. With her bound as she was, the surge was the only way to release herself, even if all she gained was a few mere seconds. Between Sir Lewis de Bourgh's power and that of the duke's, Anne had too much strength. Since she could not wield their power for herself, the magic became a shield, which is why our attacks upon her were for naught."

"Sir Lewis?"

Mr. Bennet sighed. "Yes, it seems Sir Lewis did not die of apoplexy after all. Instead, your cousin drained him of his power and his life. Anne was five at the time. When did your cousin become sickly?"

Fitzwilliam's breath left him in a rush. "She became sick right after her father's death. Richard also told me that Anne had become weaker of late."

"Also a result of draining the life and power of another. Do you remember what Lizzy found in that book?"

"Beware to the magician who seeks more magic than the earth is willing to provide. A high price is to be paid by those who covet the power of others."

"Precisely. Your cousin was weakening further while she drained Lizzy. She had said she would take my magic after, but I am unsure if her body would have allowed it. I had not considered the possibility before, but there are limits to the amount of magic one can wield, and your cousin seemed to be quickly approaching that barrier. I believe Herne caught Anne at the precise moment required to kill her. As I said, the magic within her was providing protection, even if she knew not how to use it. The large amount of power she had stolen was rendering her impermeable to spells and charms, but it had degraded her body to the point the magic was surely seeping through the cracks. Perhaps Herne's magic also was of aid."

"When he pierced Anne, the power was released in full."

"Yes, and the magic returned to the earth. Whatever had fallen to the ground was absorbed not long after you took Elizabeth away."

A loud raspy inhale came from Elizabeth as her entire body sucked in a heaving breath.

The duchess continued to watch Elizabeth. She now held his wife's hands while she remained hovering over her. An occasional tear fell, but they were not as frequent. "She is healing, though it is slow. The draining of her magic alone has damaged her. Your child survived, though."

His stomach tightened into a brick and fell into the bottom of his abdomen. "Child? She is with child?" They had known a babe would come, but was that why the altar had shown them the image? To let them know the child would have been conceived before Anne's challenge?

Her Grace placed her palm upon Elizabeth's flat stomach. "The babe is too young for her to feel the quickening, but I can sense the child within her. Her body and power shielded the new life within while she was being attacked. It is why her magic surely seemed to ebb so quickly; a certain amount belongs to the child."

Elizabeth began to tremble violently upon the altar. He rushed forward while removing his great coat and placing it over her.

"She is freezing. When can I return her to Longbourn? I need to get her warm." He could have taken her to Netherfield, but something in him screamed that she needed to be at the seat of her family's power. Longbourn had housed centuries of Bennets—since Arthur had hidden Merlin's son in the heart of Hertfordshire.

"Do you still feel the rumble of the earth? When that has ceased, the altar will have completed its part." The duchess helped to tuck the coat around Elizabeth.

His wife's teeth chattered, although some of her colour had returned. Despite the chill of the stone and the air around them, her forehead was warmer than at the cottage. She was improved.

Mr. Bennet joined their vigil and added his coat to protect Elizabeth. The duchess placed her hand over the layers and on top of Elizabeth's abdomen. Did that have something to do with his child?

"She is out of danger," said Her Grace.

He closed his eyes and lowered his head to kiss Elizabeth's lips. "Fight, my love. I need you to open your eyes."

"She is unlikely to awaken for a day or two. Her body needs rest more than anything."

They stood there for what seemed to be hours before the ground stopped its restless movement. Her Grace stepped back from Elizabeth. "The earth has done all it can."

"Your Grace, we should move you closer to Longbourn now that the threat is gone. We need not keep you so secluded. I shall send a cart to the edge of the forest for you, your lady's maid, and your guards at three."

She nodded. "We shall be there."

Fitzwilliam required no further invitation to take his wife. He scooped her into his arms, and began to turn, but at the last moment, faced the duchess.

"I cannot thank you enough for your aid."

Her Grace smiled and placed her hand upon Elizabeth's crown. "The Bennets have been friends to my family for centuries. Your wife is not only important to carry on the legacy of magic within the Bennet family, but also to the balance of magic within our world. I could do no less."

With Elizabeth held tightly to him, he made his way to where Hen still stood near the turn to the cottage. He led the stallion out of the forest. Mr. Bennet emerged from the trees soon after and took Hen's reins.

"I shall take your horse to the stable. When you reach Longbourn, you and Mrs. Hill can settle Elizabeth into her old bedchamber."

He lifted her higher, so her face rested upon his shoulder. In that position, her warm breath fanned upon his cheek. He needed that—he needed that reassurance that she was still alive, that she would not go anywhere. She was his, and she would be his forever.

Chapter 31

For a time, there had been nothing—it had been as though she had been asleep. Then, all of a sudden, snippets of sounds flooded in here and there. Fitzwilliam's frantic voice pierced the fog in her mind, but she could not pull herself from wherever she was. Was she dead? Had Anne drained her completely, and she was waiting in some sort of purgatory?

The cold was painful, as though a million needles poked her flesh over and over again. The frigidness enveloping her was also interminable. At first, she just had to bear it, but after a time, she trembled and convulsed in an attempt to generate some sort of warmth. Slowly but surely, the voices became more frequent, and the chill began to give way.

As her body warmed, more voices reached her. Fitzwilliam saying he loved her and could not live without her. Her father told her he was proud of her—that they would be waiting for her to open her eyes.

A lady's voice was there from time to time. Was it the duchess? She spoke of matters that did not make sense: a body protecting a child. Whose child? No child had been present when Anne had come for her and her father.

Soon, a familiar scent enveloped her. She had lived since her birth at Longbourn, so that smell would be recognisable anywhere, yet how was she cocooned in that comforting essence of her family—of her home for twenty years?

She was no longer cold. Wherever she was had become warm, and Fitzwilliam had never left her—at least she believed he was with her, but how? She was nowhere, suspended within a black void from which she could not escape.

"Elizabeth, I know you need your rest, but pray, open your eyes. I should trust that you will come to me when you are ready, but I miss you. A part of me is terrified you will never open your eyes again. I am certain my fear is nonsensical when the duchess says you will return when your body is able, but I have never been a patient man. I want my wife."

If only she could reach for him, but how? Every last part of her mind worked to move her hand. If Fitzwilliam was speaking so, she had to be alive. She had to be with him. Her hand just had to squeeze, if for no other reason than for Fitzwilliam to notice.

"Elizabeth?" His voice was pleading. "Did you squeeze my hand?"

"Fitzwilliam?" Jane! That was Jane! Her sister had never addressed Fitzwilliam so informally before, but under the circumstances and if they were staying at Longbourn, likely any remaining hesitation had disappeared.

"Jane, I am certain she squeezed my hand. Elizabeth, your sister is here too. Georgiana has been waiting downstairs for word of you as well. Will you not open your eyes?"

If she could squeeze his hand, perhaps she could open her eyes if she really tried. She focussed all of her energy towards her eyes. First was a small sliver of light, but that small bit of brightness expanded into a blurry mess. The intensity caused a sharp pain through her head, and she squeezed her eyes closed.

"Hurts."

"Jane, would you close the bedcurtains on the other side?"

A warmth cupped her cheek. "Elizabeth, the sunlight from the windows is blocked now. Will you not try again?"

She pushed her mind, concentrating on lifting her eyelids just enough to see Fitzwilliam's beloved face. She had been in this darkness for so long. She had a desperate need to see him as much as he surely needed to see her.

The room was dimmer when it came into view, and although her vision was not clear, Fitzwilliam was more discernible in the low light.

"There you are, my love."

"So tired." Her jaw was heavy, and her tongue was made of lead. Why was everything so difficult?

"Just sleep." His warm hand rested upon her crown. "I feel infinitely better now that I have seen your eyes."

"Wait, Lizzy," said Jane. "Fitzwilliam, will you help me lift her a little?"

Her entire body protested as she was raised to a seated position and a bottle was brought to her lips.

"This will be of aid. Papa made a rejuvenation potion. Since it worked for the residual from your vision, he thought it may be of some aid now. The duchess agreed."

The potion burned as the effect travelled through her, but she could not take much. Swallowing was too difficult.

"No more."

"You can take more next time you awaken." Jane kissed her forehead. "Just rest for now."

Fitzwilliam's low voice soothed her before she drifted off once more.

His hushed tones surrounded her again. The weight of her eyelids had lessened, and she was able to open them without the extreme effort that was required earlier.

"Fitz. . ."

The bed shifted as Fitzwilliam's distinctive shadow loomed over her. "You are awake."

"It is dark."

His warm chuckle soothed her. "Well, it is nighttime. Your family have all retired, but I had not fallen asleep. I cannot rest while you are still so weak."

"Papa is here to protect us." The words were raspy and required almost too much effort, but somehow, she managed.

He rose to shift the bed curtain, allowing more light into their warm haven. "Jane insisted you drink more of the potion when you awakened."

The room became a little brighter. He must have lit a candle.

"Now, let us see if your father's potion is of aid." He lifted her and placed a small bottle to her lips. A trickle of liquid was tipped into her mouth. She swallowed before he allowed more to fill her mouth. Soon, he removed the bottle.

"Good. In the past, the effect was more pronounced, but you had not been subjected to Anne's full ability, just traces."

"What happened?"

He sighed. "I tried to stop her, but any spell I cast seemed to be absorbed by her. Your father believes the magic within her shielded her even though she did not know how to wield it. At some point, he thinks the power became too much for her since at the moment when she had begun to falter, Herne charged into the garden and ran her through."

She inhaled sharply. "Is he. . . ?"

"Elizabeth, let us do this when you are well."

"No," she managed with a difficult shake of her head. "I want to know now."

With a growl, he pulled her into his arms. "He was consumed by the explosion of magic. White fluff, similar to newly sheared wool after it is washed, fell to the ground and was absorbed."

"The magic returning to the earth." The words were easier to say this time.

"Yes, your father has indicated as much," said Fitzwilliam while propping her up on pillows against the headboard.

He released her long enough to step over and pull the bell. "You need to eat something while you are awake."

"How long have I been asleep?"

"Two days have passed. You first opened your eyes this morning, and Jane gave you that first sip of the potion, which I believe is helping. You seem to be speaking easier than before."

"I am."

"After Anne was gone, I took you to the duchess. She is now staying in the dower house and has come every day to ensure you are healing as you should."

"She is kind to do so."

At a knock on the door, he bade them enter.

Mrs. Hill bustled in with a tray and placed it on the table beside the bed. "Since you rang so late, I made the assumption Mrs. Darcy is awake. I am pleased to see that I am right. The fare is light since you are recovering. I have some broth and toast as well as tea. Will you require help to eat?"

"I believe we shall manage, Mrs. Hill. Thank you," said Fitzwilliam with a slight lift of his lips.

"I thought you would, but I needed to ask." The housekeeper departed with a light laugh.

Fitzwilliam sat facing her. "You have no idea how relieved I am now that you are so improved. I love you so much." His hand engulfed hers and squeezed. She returned the gesture as best she could.

"Now, let us get you fed. I am certain you will tire yourself soon, and you require nourishment."

20th of January 1812

The entire Bennet family sat in the parlour. A merry fire burned in the grate while Lydia and Kitty trimmed bonnets and Jane sat with Mr. Bingley in the corner where they spoke quietly. Mama concentrated on her needlework, which seemed to be progressing well. She had just drank Mrs. Hill's special tea, but for the most part, Mama's behaviour was improved of late.

Mary had confessed that when Elizabeth first appeared after the duel with Anne, that Mama had been in hysterics over the possibility of Papa dying, but at the news that Elizabeth had intervened and almost been killed in Papa's place, her mother had not been venomous towards her. Mrs. Hill also let it slip that Fitzwilliam had spoken to Mama, but he would not reveal the contents of his conversation. He did not deny it occurred. Nevertheless, she was in the dark.

Her husband, however, sat by her side, his arm protectively around her shoulders. He, no doubt, had estate business that had come from Derbyshire, yet he refused to leave her side. Last night, she had awakened to find him hunched over the small desk in her room writing by candlelight. She had attempted to push him into Papa's study for such matters, but he refused. He was so stubborn!

At the familiar sound of hoofbeats on the drive, they all paused in their activity—not that she had much of one. A book rested in her lap, but she had read little with Fitzwilliam rubbing mind-numbing circles on her upper arm.

The knock at the front door rattled through the house, and everyone seemed to hold their breath at the voices in the hall. When Mrs. Hill opened the door, they all stood. Fitzwilliam helped her so she would not be rude to whatever guest was joining them.

"Lady Catherine de Bourgh."

Fitzwilliam's breath rushed out, and his entire body tensed like a statue, yet when his aunt entered, she was altered.

"And Lord Glen."

The earl, Fitzwilliam's uncle, entered beside his sister with a stern visage. "Forgive us for calling without notice, but after a letter from Bennet, I sought out Lady Catherine to offer her apologies to you for not only her behaviour, but also Anne's.

"Fitzwilliam!" said Papa from behind the earl. When Lord Glen stepped aside, her father stood with Mary, whom he had been tutoring in his library.

"Ah, there you are. I must thank you for making me aware of the situation with Catherine and my niece Anne. I never suspected anything afoul with Sir Lewis's death, but now that I am aware of how he died as well as Anne's and Catherine's involvement, I wanted to assure you the matter will be managed within the family. My sister will cause no further mischief."

The imperious lady sniffed. "I wish to see where my daughter died."

Elizabeth stepped forward. "I should like to do so if that suits you, Lady Catherine."

"Elizabeth, no."

She grasped her husband's forearm. "I have been cloistered inside this house for almost a week. My legs are stiff from disuse. It is nothing more than a short walk into the gardens, and you will accompany me, I am sure. Nothing bad can happen."

According to her husband and Jane, some of her colour had returned, but she was still pale. The duchess had mentioned the child within her, so she could not help but understand Fitzwilliam's concern, but he could not hover over her all day every day.

With a growl, he nodded to Mrs. Hill, who hurried off to fetch their coats. At least he understood the point was not worth arguing over.

"Darcy," said Lord Glen. "Would you introduce me to whom I presume is your wife?"

After the introduction and their bows and curtseys, the earl joined his hands in front of him. "I thank you for your forbearance. My sister will not trouble you after today, I assure you."

"It is no trouble, sir."

When they departed the house, Fitzwilliam kept an arm around her as though steadying her, not that she had required steadying for a couple of days. Lady Catherine followed behind with two guards the earl had insisted join them.

At the place where Anne stood when Herne struck her, a patch of snowdrops had sprouted and were now blooming. The flowers had never grown there in the past, so it was assumed they had been seeded by the magic that had been released in that place.

"Your daughter stood here," she said gesturing to the spot.

"The stag that struck her. Did he die as well?"

"He did," said Fitzwilliam.

Lady Catherine set her shoulders as she exhaled shakily. "A lore exists of a stag who appears to protect one of significant magic and importance. They are white and can show themselves at will to whomever they wish. If the stag dies to save its mage, snowdrops will grow upon the site of its sacrifice."

Elizabeth turned her face into Fitzwilliam's chest. Her eyes burned and she squeezed her eyelids closed to keep tears at bay. Herne had been her constant companion since she was a little girl. As much as he had done for her, she had not wanted him to die in her place—she would never have anyone die in her place.

She sucked in a breath and, once composed, turned back to Lady Catherine. "I do not know why I would be so important."

The woman lifted her eyebrows. "Do you not? You are the first lady to carry on Niniane's legacy. You are the lady chosen to carry on the Bennet magic."

"I would never scheme as Niniane did."

"Whether you are like Niniane is irrelevant. You seem to be her chosen successor. No other lady has wielded such power. Anne's was not her own, and as much as we attempted for her to learn spells, she could do no more than hold the power within her and let it whither her body away. I did not understand the implications of her ability until she had drained her father. Taking in another's power created this need within her to absorb more. I kept her away from most people because of the thirst she had acquired. When she came after you, she had escaped."

"You wanted me to marry her to help hide her ability and likely insanity." Fitzwilliam's tone was matter of fact.

"I did. I knew you were promised to another, but I could not let Anne go to Bedlam because that is where she would have been sent when I died."

Fitzwilliam shook his head. "You intended to leave me without a decent wife and still in need of an heir to suit your own purpose. Whatever Uncle has planned for you, I doubt it is punishment enough for what you have done. Two good men are dead, and my wife is still recovering from your daughter's ill-deeds."

He scooped Elizabeth into his arms. "We shall take no leave of you."

Once inside the house, he took her to her father's library and kicked the door closed behind him.

"Fitzwilliam, put me down." She cupped his cheeks in her palms. He was so pained by his aunt's actions, and who could blame him? Lady Catherine had acted in no one's best interests but her own.

"I love you so much. I do not know what I would have done if you had not survived."

"But I am here, and I am not going anywhere. The altar showed us proof of me great with our child at Pemberley. Do you not remember?"

He buried his face into her neck with a shuddering breath.

"When Papa told me he had promised me in marriage—without my consent—I was not best pleased, but now that we are here as we are, I cannot be anything but thankful for that contract your parents and my father signed all those years ago."

She drew his face from her neck.

"Fate conspired to provide me with precisely who I needed for now and forever. Now, if only you would cease your infernal hovering and take me home to Pemberley."

He grinned and pressed his forehead against hers. "As for my hovering, I shall do so until I am assured you are completely well. As for the other demand, your wish is my command, my love."

Epilogue

10 years later

Elizabeth stepped out of the house into the warm summer sunshine. The gardens of Pemberley were so beautiful this time of year. She could never resist the lure of walking the paths when the weather was fair, like today, even though she was heavy with child and her ankles were swollen to the size of gammons.

The bees buzzed over the lavender, and in the distance, the Peak had a pinkish hue from the heather growing in abundance over the hills. A butterfly flitted by, and she paused to follow its flight as it wound through the roses to join the bees feasting upon the lavender nectar.

"Ceilt," said a voice as she neared the walled garden.

"Do you believe it will hold this time?"

"I do." Her eldest son's tone was not as certain as his words. "Stiúdú."

She peered around the stone wall as Fitzwilliam's spell made contact with the pail they had placed on a garden bench. The form of the pail held as the charm ricocheted off the shield Bennet had conjured.

"You created a full shield this time, and the charm worked just as it should."

He turned to their eight-year-old daughter Rhea. "What of you? Can you remove your brother's shield?" When Bennet was born, he had borne the mark of the Darcy heir, a flame, on the inside of his arm; however, when Rhea was born, to their surprise, she possessed the four-point star of the Bennet heir on hers. Naught was known of what would occur in a marriage between two heirs, but in their case, it seemed as though they had an heir for each family. Only time would tell if the Bennet heir would always be a lady from now on.

"Oscailt," said Rhea, her tone more confident than Bennet's. Fitzwilliam had always said Elizabeth's magic seemed to come easier to her than his, and Bennet was every bit Fitzwilliam's son. They shared similar looks as well as a similar staid manner.

"Now, you cast your shield charm."

"Ceilt."

Fitzwilliam cast a crooked smile down at his daughter. "Stiúdú."

The pail remained intact, and Fitzwilliam grinned. "You have both improved prodigiously in the past few months. I am proud of both of you." Her heart swelled in her chest when her husband tousled Bennet's hair. He resembled Fitzwilliam so much that when their portraits were placed side by side in the portrait gallery, some of the guests believed they were likenesses of the same person.

While Fitzwilliam began discussing the next spell with the children, she leaned against the edge of the wall, her hand rubbing the bottom of her swollen belly. When she was not so heavy with child, she worked with the children some as well, but since she had become so unwieldy, keeping up with the house as well as Bennet's and Rhea's education had become more difficult.

At some point during his conversation with their children, Fitzwilliam lifted his gaze and paused when their eyes met. "You should greet your mother," he said with a slight smile. "It seems she has come to join us."

Bennet whirled around and ran towards her, only stopping when he wrapped his arms around her belly. "Will you teach me with Papa? You explain the spells better than he does." Since the battle with Anne all those years ago, her magic had returned to the power and strength she boasted of before the encounter, but her recovery took quite some time. At first, spells were difficult to cast, and her magic did not seem to cooperate at all. Now, she could wield an incantation with the same ease as when she first married

Fitzwilliam. Yet, her son did not quite understand the significance of her power thus far, but for him, his sister being an heir as well rendered his mother's ability commonplace. He saw nothing unusual in it.

She bit her cheek to keep from laughing. "You can always ask me if you do not understand, but from what I saw, your shield charm was exceptional." She combed her son's hair from his face with her fingers. "Your shield charm was brilliant as well, Rhea."

Both children beamed.

"Papa said I could ride or roam the forest if I wished as a reward," said Bennet. "Will you come with me?"

She had taken Bennet on rambles since he was small, but she did not have the energy for a long walk through the woods at the moment. "Not today."

"Did Papa tell you about the stag?"

A pang ripped through her chest as her gaze collided with her husband's. "What stag?"

"He is my friend," said Rhea, her arms crossing over her chest. "He would never harm me. You just want him for yourself!"

Her husband placed his hand on their daughter's shoulder. "From what I understand, Rhea has made a friend in the forest. She is greeted by a great white stag upon her entrance to the wood, and they explore together."

Rhea lunged forward and took her hand. "I was afraid at first, but he is gentle and follows me all over. Today, when Bennet told Papa about him, Papa said you were friends with a stag in Oakham Forest."

She nodded as her gaze met with Fitzwilliam's before she turned her attention back to her daughter. "I was indeed. I called him Herne, and I put a protection and shield charm on him so no one would see him but me, even though I now know he had a certain amount of magic and could control who could see him despite my spells."

Rhea was quiet for a moment with her forehead crinkled. "Do you think I could call my stag Herne too?"

"If you like, my love."

She threw her arms around Elizabeth. "I am going to go see him now!" Before she could stop her headstrong daughter, Rhea took off through the pathways in the direction of the forest through the back of the gardens.

"Wait for me!" Bennet tore after his sister without delay.

"Perhaps we should stop them," said Fitzwilliam.

"No, they both cast the charm well. Let them have some time to be no more than children. Nothing came of me roaming through the forest as a child."

"Is Thomas napping?" Their four-year-old son still slept for an hour after his luncheon. He was in the nursery with a maid.

"He is."

"Come. Let us have some tea in my study. You should not be walking this far so close to your confinement."

"I am not one to be idle." She leaned against the wall for support. Truth be told, she was exhausted. When she was this round with child, she did not sleep well.

Rhea was near the edge of the forest when a flash of white in the opening of the trees made Elizabeth gasp. "Fitzwilliam!"

He looked over his shoulder, then slowly turned until he faced the wood. "He looks just like your Herne, does he not? From what Bennet has said, the beast's allegiance is to Rhea. He never leaves her side."

As soon as Rhea disappeared behind an enormous oak, the young stag lowered his head to the ground before he lifted it once more and bounded back into the trees.

Fitzwilliam pivoted back around. "I suppose we cannot think Herne to be a coincidence anymore. If he was, then we would not have this stag protecting Rhea. He also seemed to bow before he followed her. Did you see?"

"Yes, I did." She still stared at the place where the beast had vanished.

They had spoken many times of Herne, and his presence in Oakham Forest. Neither believed him to be a coincidence, but why and how he existed was still a puzzle they could not solve. He simply was. Yet, he had saved her life, so Fitzwilliam would never question why an identical creature now wandered the forest with their daughter.

"Since meeting this stag, Rhea has walked without Bennet. She has slipped away and rambled on her own. I admit to scolding them both: Rhea for hiding from her brother and Bennet for not keeping better watch over his sister. Apparently, they oft times wander to Nine Ladies."

"Much like I used to do." When she was not so unwieldy, she would walk to Nine Ladies. The stone circle here indeed held slightly different properties than the one in Oakham Forest, which she was still discovering. She had lived near Oakham for twenty years. Would twenty be required to learn all the secrets of Nine Ladies? This stone circle here had more people who visited the site. They had to always be on their guard for the non-magical who sometimes happened upon the place. Since it was on Pemberley lands, however, that was a rarity.

Her husband nodded. "Yes, just as you used to do. But I am still tempted to send a footman out to keep an eye on them."

She tilted her head, and after a glance towards the forest, she shook her head. "They will be well." She could not explain how she knew, but she did. The stag was there for a reason, and while his duty appeared to protect Rhea, he would surely not let Bennet come to harm. After all, harming Bennet would injure Rhea, even if not physically.

She gasped and rubbed at her lower back.

"We should get you inside. If you walk much more, your ankles will not forgive you with ease."

"I am well, Fitzwilliam."

"I do not believe you. You must remember how you deceived me when Rhea was born."

"You insisted I take to my bed the moment my pains began with Bennet, and I laboured for three days before he was born. You will have to forgive me if I refuse to do so again."

"And you almost had Rhea at Nine Ladies."

"'Tis not my fault she decided to be born on the winter solstice."

With a growl, Fitzwilliam scooped her into his arms and began to stride back in the direction of the great house. "Yet, you did not tell me you had been having pains all day. If you had, you would have remained at Pemberley while I led the celebration. You will simply have to forgive me for wanting to keep you hale. I would not survive if anything happened to you."

"We have both seen visions—"

"And I intend to ensure they all come to pass, Mrs. Darcy. We shall have a very long and very happy life together. Do you hear me?"

She smiled and rested her head on his shoulder. "Who am I to argue with you?"

He shook his head with a laugh. "My wife who argues with me almost every day."

"If I did not, you would not love me as you do. You would never desire a wife who does naught but agrees with everything you say and do."

"I would if she was you."

"No, you would not."

He set her upon her feet and pressed his forehead to hers. "Do not tease me. I could not bear it if something happened to you. I almost lost you once—"

"You will not lose me. I intend to argue with you forever."

His breathing shuddered. "Do you promise?"

Her fingers curled into the hair at his nape. "Yes, Fitzwilliam, I promise. You own my heart. I love you. I would never leave you."

"And you will remain impertinent?"

"I have been impertinent for thirty years. I have no plans to change now."

"Thank God," he said before he swept her back into his arms and carried her into the house.

The End

Acknowledgements

I hope you enjoyed The Unexpected Heir. The scene with Elizabeth walking into Oakham Forest has been in my head for a little while, so when I began playing with the idea of writing this, I started looking up Arthurian legends. I also decided to take the time while waiting for the swimmers to warm up to talk about magic with the head coach of our swim team, who is a big Dungeons and Dragons fan. We discussed several theories on magic, including ley lines, and he gave me some inspiration for how magic exists in Elizabeth's world. So, I have a huge thank you to Ed for letting me pick his brain!

Next, a huge thanks to my friend and editor Carol S. Bowes for her help with the manuscript. I usually go through my stories more than once before she receives them, but I know that even if I didn't, she would mark them up so they were the best they could be. I'd also like to thank Marie for reading through the finished product and giving me any corrections she finds.

This book will release on my wedding anniversary, which I think is appropriate. I wrote my first book on a dare of sorts, but once it was written, my husband was the person who first pushed me to publish. He had more confidence in me than I had in myself. I wouldn't be where I am today (in so many ways) as well as the person I am today without him and our children. I love you!

Also, all my love to my friends and family, who help me out when I need it. I cannot thank you enough for your love and support!

About the Author

L.L. Diamond is more commonly known as Leslie to her friends, Mom to her three kids, and servant to her three cats. A native of Louisiana, she has been a wanderer for the past 20 years, living in Mississippi, California, Texas, New Mexico, Nebraska, England, and Missouri before settling in Maryland.

One day, Leslie may decide what she wants to do when she grows up, but for now, she enjoys writing the stories that live in her head and coaching age group swimming. She has degrees in biology and studio art, certifications to coach swimming in the United States and Britain, and numerous fitness certifications. Leslie is also a member of the Jane Austen Society of North America. Her accomplishments include drawing, watercolor, and playing flute and piano, but much like *Pride and Prejudice's* Elizabeth Bennet, she is always in need of practice!

Author's works:

Regency Works:

Rain and Retribution
An Unwavering Trust
The Earl's Conquest
Particular Intentions
Particular Attachments
Undoing
Agony and Hope
His Perfect Gift
The Montford Cousins:
Book 1: An Endeavour to be Worthy
Book 2: A Gentleman of Worth
Book 3: A Worthy Woman
Book 4: Worthy of her Love
Book 5: Worthy in Every Way

Contemporary Romance

A Matter of Chance
Unwrapping Mr. Darcy
Confined with Mr. Darcy
That Perfect Someone
Catching Lizzy
A Novel Holiday
The Wedding Planners Series:
Book 1: It's Always Been You
Book 2: It's Always Been Us
Book 3: It's Always Been You and Me

Book 4: He's Always Been the One

Science Fiction/Fantasy Romance
The Peculiarity of Mr. Darcy's Mirror
The Unexpected Heir

www.ingramcontent.com/pod-product-compliance
Lightning Source LLC
Chambersburg PA
CBHW060402260626
47160CB00006B/2403